THERESA CHRISTINE

In a Desert Daze

a novel

Other Books from Theresa Christine

The Half of It: A Spicy Small-Town Ireland Romance
A slow-burn romance with sibling's best friend tension, found family, a road trip through the Irish countryside complete with only one bed. Available now.

Match Made in the Maldives: A Brother's Best Friend Vacation Novella
A spicy tropical romance with forced proximity, a brother's best friend, a kiss from years ago that neither of them forgot, and found-family vibes. Available now.

Content Warnings

In a Desert Daze is a spicy contemporary romance intended for an 18+ audience. The book also tackles some emotional topics before ending in a Happy Ever After. Listed below is the content that may be triggering for some readers. Some of this content may be minor spoilers for what's ahead, so proceed at your own discretion.

Mentioned but not shown on page: death of a parent, alcohol consumption by a minor, use of psychedelics by a minor, pregnancy (this is not a surprise pregnancy book; pregnancy is merely mentioned)

Shown on page: marijuana use

For Little Bit.
Thank you for being mine.

Chapter One

Daisy, Now

Sweat slides down my temple, and I tug the wrench a final time, exactly like the online tutorial instructed. "I'll hop in my truck right away," I say into the phone wedged between my ear and shoulder, turning up my ultra-sweet customer service voice. "We'll get you taken care of and have you and your wife checked in to enjoy your weekend, Mr. Hollis."

I hang up and do a lightning-quick check of my handiwork in the terra-cotta bathroom. A couple of years ago, these fixes would have had me frantic and calling a handyman. Now, I understand why Mom insisted on doing these repairs on her own—that shit's not cheap. I have no clue how those soulless homeshares keep popping up, charging half of what we do per night.

I close my eyes and grant myself the briefest respite. As I exit the tutorial on my phone, my brain stutters over an incoming call.

Max Weber. My Max, not that he was ever mine.

That familiar freight train of mixed emotions pummels me in the chest, and the temptation to pick up has my thumb hovering over the green icon. But I don't have time to answer, and that's not what we do. He'll leave a voicemail. He always does.

"Six is all set." Stacey appears in the doorway, holding a pile of folded towels.

"Great." Startled, I tuck my phone into my back pocket. "Gotta run. Alma strikes again."

She rolls her eyes in exasperation, and I can relate. I send multiple emails to remind guests to follow my directions and not their GPS, which will lead them down an uneven, dangerous dirt road called Camino del Alma. But I can't show up to help the Hollises with an attitude. A happy guest is a returning guest, and we could use lots of those. Besides, it's not like I've never made mistakes in my life.

"Remember," I say, "serenity, warmth, and—"

"Wonder," Stacey mumbles, following me on the dirt path to the lobby. Even when she's grumbly, I adore her. "These people make me *wonder* if they know how to read. You could teach them a lesson. Let them sit out there and bake in the Mojave Desert for a bit."

"Stace."

"It's only the end of April. Not that hot yet." Her eyes gleam with mischief, like little sparks in the soft lines of her face, and I shake my head with a laugh.

"You're terrible."

"I'm here for housekeeping, not all the being-nice-at-the-front stuff."

We swing into the open-air lobby of The Mirage, and the jagged mountains on the horizon fill me with wonder. Nineteen years, and I still never tire of this view. It's not just the landscape that I love, but also the prickly cacti, the jackrabbits and the field mice scurrying over dry ground, and the treasure trove of stars glittering in the night sky. This place is as close to magic as it gets. I understand why Mom hauled me and Dad to Harlow when I was seven, trading the chaos of Chicago for a Southern California town of only five thousand.

That hollow ache returns at the thought of her, and I fight the tightness in my throat.

When I push the housekeeping cart against the wall, Freddie, my mom's blind, geriatric tuxedo cat, stirs in the fluffy bed by the monitor. My hustle has disturbed his dozing, so I apologize by running my hand along his back. A flurry of purrs begins, and I am forgiven.

"I'll refill amenities," Stacey says.

"Already did 'em." I grasp for my keys underneath the counter, ignoring her admonishing look.

"Daisy Johnson, I swear on my left tit." She drops her basket in a huff, knocking into a display shelf with some art and decor. A purple rock—amethyst, I think my best friend Gwen told me when she placed it there for optimal energy cleansing—goes off-kilter. I don't buy into the woo-woo stuff, but I move the gemstone to its optimally energetic place. Some extra help for The Mirage can't hurt.

"Doc says I'm one hundred percent cleared for all the heavy lifting I want," Stacey continues.

"She told me seventy-five."

"Tomato, tomato."

"I think you're supposed to pronounce those differently."

"If you're gonna take over my work, then you mind tellin' me why I'm here?"

"Because I need you."

Stacey has worked here from the beginning, and although she's in her early sixties, I can't picture running this place without her. On days when operating The Mirage runs me ragged, she brings levity into my life. I'll look into having interns or other employees again soon. Right now, though, I just want to get by until the end of the summer with the loan I took out. Once we manage through our slow season, I can continue tackling my never-ending to-do list.

I give Stacey a quick peck on the cheek, then turn to leave to save our guests from a blazing-hot afternoon. "Water," I say to myself, turning on my heel to fetch two bottles from the mini fridge.

"You can't do it all on your own, Daisygirl."

I search every corner of my brain for a task that won't earn me dirty looks from her chiropractor. "How 'bout turndown service in Two? I saw them leave early to catch the sunrise and explore the park. Said they won't be back until late."

"You still not sleepin'?" Stacey frowns. "You should try that batch I gave you. Potent stuff."

"You know how I am with weed." I wish a remedy like that were enough to clear all the worry from my mind. "Makes me antsy."

"Such a square."

Stacey has regaled me with tales of how she walked across the United States in the '80s, dropped acid with Elton John, and communicated with the ghost that haunted her first apartment. She's also been growing her own marijuana for ages, long before California legalized it.

"Oh, I'd love a bottle of prosecco in there." I sling the tool bag over my shoulder and scan the room to make sure I'm not forgetting anything for a backroads rescue. "It's their anniversary." I pat Freddie goodbye, planting a kiss on his furry head. He curls into a tighter ball.

Stacey trails me to my well-loved pickup. "Hey, hon, you alright?"

"I'll be better when the Hollises are here." I play dumb. Unless...is she talking about something else? Did she see the caller ID from earlier? My whole body heats, ashamed at how desperately I want to listen to his message.

Her voice goes softer, and I brace myself. "It's that time of year."

Something pinches in my chest, like a tiny serrated knife sawing my insides. Yesterday marked two years since the accident, so the wound has reopened yet again.

"You could take a day off," she whispers.

I settle into the driver's side and pat her shoulder through the open window, touched by her concern. "Be back soon."

The Mirage fades in my rearview mirror as I follow a dirt path I've driven and walked thousands of times before. Camino del Alma leads straight to Harlow's main highway, and I have no trouble managing its bumps in my pickup. But I have a lot of memories on this road, so I tend to drive the smoother, roundabout route, even if it takes longer.

Cresting the small hill, I spot a boxy vehicle in the distance traveling in my direction. My nerves loosen because maybe this means they've worked their way out of the rut. Then the neon-orange sports car at the bottom of the gully steals my focus. The vehicle has an inch of ground clearance, and it perches precariously between two washboard ruts. That must be the Hollises.

Once I pull up and introduce myself to them, I make sure they're okay and hand them refreshments. Mr. Hollis needs some convincing, but he allows me to inspect his car.

"Just...be careful," he grunts, shooting me an incredulous look that tells me the warning doesn't stem from concerns over my safety.

Serenity, warmth, and wonder, I remind myself. Mom was born to host and knew how to run a business, and I try my best to do it with half of her grit and grace.

As I bend down to inspect the damage, a gentle breeze reminds me this was a bad time to wear jean cut-off shorts. I position my ass away from the Hollises to preserve some modesty, giving the person from the other vehicle a show. Their car pulls up, the door slams shut, and footsteps crunch toward me on the gravelly earth.

"If you're a tow truck," I say without looking back, "I might have to kiss you."

They make a throat-clearing sound. "Need some help, Daze?"

My breath hitches, and I drop my flashlight. I'd know that voice anywhere. That voice plays through my phone every other week. I could be in the deepest, wine-assisted sleep of my life, and that voice would be my alarm.

But it couldn't be him without any advance warning—unless he mentioned it in the mystery voicemail I got ten minutes ago. I swallow a pang of disappointment at not being worth more notice, but I know what I let our friendship dissolve into, so I shouldn't be surprised.

"Max?" I shield my eyes from the sun, and although all I see is a silhouette, it's unmistakably, distinctly his.

"Hey."

Scrambling to my feet, I wipe the dirt from my knees and tug my shorts down. He's taller than I recall, and I have to tip my face upward to get a good look at him. How can he be the same but so different? Same intense gaze, same dark brown eyes, and same goofy grin that stirs up a weird sensation like homesickness. He's still lean, but his shoulders are wider, and he has more muscle. Max has really grown into his own—he used to be a boy, and now he's a man.

And he's back.

Chapter Two

Max, 7 Years Old

"What are you drawing?"

A pair of pastel pink cowgirl boots with yellow stars appeared in the corner of my eye. Someone must have sent her over on a dare. I kept my head down and continued to scribble, gripping my sketch pad tighter in case she tried to steal it.

"Nothing," I replied.

"Looks like something." The girl leaned close and surveyed the page. "It's cool."

"Okay."

"Can I sit?"

I glanced up, wary and prepared for a prank. I hadn't seen this girl before. She wore her red hair in two braids, and she had freckles like dark dewdrops across the bridge of her nose.

I narrowed my eyes at her. "Who sent you?"

"Nobody."

"It was Steven, wasn't it?" He always picked on me.

"I don't know Steven. It's my first day."

"Where's your shadow?"

Every new student got a shadow—someone in their grade to follow them and help them adjust. Since I grew up in Harlow, I never had one.

"She left early 'cause her stomach hurt. So can I sit?"

This girl seemed harmless, and she wouldn't stick around, anyway. New kids spent their first few recesses with me until they found other second graders they liked better. Kids who were cooler or more popular.

I shrugged and went back to my sketch. After a moment of silence, she asked, "What's your favorite thing to draw?"

"Dragons."

"Why?"

"'Cause."

"Mmm. So you can only draw dragons."

"That is *not* true." I glowered at the girl, and her eyes sparkled in the sunlight. To prove her wrong, I flipped through my sketchbook, the papers swishing with each turn. "See?" I pointed to the drawings, one after the other, to make my case. Horses. Airplanes. Made-up house pets with six legs and three tails.

"You're good."

Her compliment took me off guard. "Th-thanks."

"Would you draw me?"

Most of the people drawings I did happened when the subjects didn't know I was drawing them. I begged Mom and Dad to sit so I could try, but they always got distracted by work or something on their phones. My nanny let me do it once, but then the dryer finished, and she had to put away clothes.

"Here." The girl reached out a hand, fingers extended. "I'll draw you, you draw me."

I tore a page from my sketchbook, slid it across the table, and placed my pencil bag between us. Someone in homeroom would probably say something nasty about us sharing, I was sure—like the girl gave me cooties. Our hands bumped against each other once while rummaging around for the right shades of green and pink, but hers didn't feel sticky or gross. Cooties were unlikely.

While we drew, I met her dark brown eyes multiple times, but they didn't make me wiggle in my seat with discomfort. I relaxed under her gaze while the sounds of the playground faded into the background: shrieks from a game of tag, squeaks of rusty swing sets, thuds of basketballs against the pavement. And then the bell.

She held up her paper. A stick figure stared back at me.

"That's me?" I asked.

"Never said I was any good."

She was funny. I turned my sketch pad around, and a loud laugh burst out of her. Once she caught her breath, she looked at the drawing of her with wings and a tail and then crumpled over with laughter again.

"I knew you could only draw dragons!"

Teachers called out for stragglers, so we walked to the spot where the other kids were lining up.

"What's your name?" she asked, using her hand to block the sun.

"I'm Max."

"Daisy," she said, handing me her drawing and pointing to where she'd signed it. She dotted her *i* with a flower. "See you 'round."

Chapter Three

Max, Now

We haven't seen each other for eight years, but my mind and my heart tell me no time has passed. I don't know if hugging is the right move here, though—it *feels* right, considering our history. But her brown eyes darken to the hue of coffee, and a crease forms in her brow.

"What are you doing here?" she blurts out. I think I know her well enough to recognize the snap in her voice and the angry flush flooding her cheeks.

I'd imagined us meeting over lunch or drinks, catching up like friends—because I still consider us friends—if people who didn't talk for six years and then played voicemail tag for two more could be called that. After everything that happened in Dublin, I could really use a familiar face.

"Nice to see you, too." Maybe I misinterpreted the ease in our messages, but she's talking like I didn't grow up here. "In case you forgot, my parents have a house right over the hill."

She doesn't crack a smile like I'd hoped. "Is this why you called?"

"Sort of."

I've called her countless times before, but she must mean the most recent one.

Her face falls. "Is your family okay?"

"Yeah."

"I thought...I don't know, maybe there was an emergency or something."

"Oh, no. Judy and Bill are fine."

"Ava?"

"She's good."

Daisy rests a hand on her chest, eyes closed in silent relief, and my stomach drops. I didn't want to put her in panic mode. She must have endured a living nightmare when her mom died.

"'Scuse me." The manbro owner of the toy car wipes his sweat-soaked forehead. "It's really fuckin' hot out here. Any chance you can have your reunion later?"

"Yes, absolutely," Daisy says, her demeanor flipping to something more upbeat. "It looks like you punctured the transmission pretty good. I can call a tow, and in the meantime, I'll bring you over to the hotel and get you checked in."

He gestures to his Tic Tac with wheels. "I've got a guy in LA, and he's the only person allowed to touch this baby."

"Of course." Daisy rubs the remaining dust from her hands onto her lean, sun-kissed thighs, and her face stretches into a smile. She remains the epitome of grace. "I'll drive you to The Mirage, you can call your guy, and I'm sure by the time he's done working on it, this will all be a minor inconvenience."

"You should let people know not to take this road," he says, crossing his arms.

"I usually send an email at booking with all the details, and a follow-up seven days before the reservation...but those can be easy to miss."

"And it's on the website," I chime in.

Daisy's attention flickers to me, and I shrink. Nothing screams *Yeah, I check in on my best friend and former crush from high school by reading the sporadic posts she makes to her business's blog* quite like that.

But I smell the entitlement on this guy. I've worked with artists who let fame and money launch their egos into another solar system. This man wants a vacation to one of the most inhospitable environments to go as smoothly as a resort stay in Cabo.

"Look," he says, tipping his sunglasses halfway down his nose, "if you're not—bare minimum—handling our rental car, then cancel the reservation. This is ridiculous."

"Babe, no!" The woman interrupts her selfie with a cactus to join us. "We wanted remote, and this place is *perfect*."

"There's a billion other listings online, and cheaper, too."

Daisy opens her mouth, but this guy must know what she's going to say because he barrels over her.

"And whatever your cancellation policy is, I'll call my credit card company and dispute the charge. I have an Amex."

I bite the inside of my cheek until I taste iron to keep from saying something I might regret to him.

"Please, Mr. and Mrs. Hollis." Daisy picks at the cuticle around her thumb. "I'd love to host you at The Mirage."

A stranger wouldn't notice the strain behind her words, but I can—and it whips me to attention, like a Pavlovian dog craving a treat. Daisy needs help, and I want to be the one to help her. Less than twenty-four hours in my middle-of-nowhere hometown, and I'm back to my old habits.

"That's why I'm here." I step forward and put on a winning smile. Daisy's eyes bulge as if she wants to ask me the same thing I'm asking myself. *What are you doing?*

"Who're you?"

"Max Weber, private driver for The Mirage of Harlow." Being the wiry art kid who everyone either ignored or bullied meant I learned how to win people over and pretend I belonged.

"Ohmygosh, I can't believe it." The woman slinks an elaborately manicured hand around the man's biceps and squeezes. "That's perfect."

"That's—Max." Daisy looks at me. "That's not necessary. I'll take you two back to The Mirage myself, and we'll get everything sorted out there. Privately."

We all eye her beat-up Ford truck that she's had since high school. She'd have to pay someone to steal it.

"Or," I say, "you could be the first to experience the, uh, *our* exclusive private driver service, free of cost. Clean, comfortable, and it puts Harlow at your fingertips." I channel complete confidence, my hand sweeping to the new off-road vehicle my parents bought for all the weekend trips they never take. "We soft-launched today, and it would be an honor to drive you two lovebirds around."

"Remember what our therapist says." The woman tucks her phone into her hoodie pocket and grabs her husband's hands. "I cannot control what happens to me. I can—*C'mon*." She stomps her foot, and he halfheartedly joins in on some kind of mantra, mumbling under his breath.

I don't want or need to witness this bizarre, private moment between them, so I look at Daisy. She's putting her fiery hair up, leaving a few curling tendrils that frame her face and some stray bits in the back. One of her arms is tan and bare, but the other has a full sleeve of tattoos, like a colorful scrapbook, including a postage stamp with a desert landscape and a vintage-style woman holding a cat. Daisy's more than I remember—more tattooed, more freckled, more poised.

"Okay, we'd love to take you up on your offer." Mrs. Hollis squeals and claps her hands, breaking me out of the spell.

"Brilliant," I say, not missing a beat. "Let's get you two settled in the vehicle, and Daisy and I will load your luggage into the trunk."

Once our delightful guests are out of earshot, Daisy turns to me. "What the hell are you doing?" She doesn't wait for an answer, just goes for the small duffel crammed in the back.

"How about 'Hey Max, thanks for helping me out'?"

"I don't need help."

"I…" Although I had good intentions, I shouldn't have butted in. "Okay. I'll let them know I rescind the offer."

"You can't take it back now."

"Daze, someone like that will settle for nothing less than the gold-standard experience."

"And I couldn't do that on my own?" she scoffs.

"I didn't mean it that way."

"The Mirage isn't fancy, but I'm the owner, and I am perfectly capable. I would have figured something out."

Her stubbornness checks out, but it's jarring to hear her say she runs the place.

"That guy's an impossible prick who—"

"He is a *guest*," she hisses, looking at my parents' car as if the couple might hear. "And they're staying all weekend." She watches as I pull out a heavy rolling suitcase, her gaze trailing from the luggage up to my face. "Don't you have anything better to do than play chauffeur?"

"I don't mind." Actually, I like the excuse to get out of the house—to *stay* out of the house.

"What are you doing here, anyway?"

"Needed a break."

Her eyes narrow, and for a moment, I fear she'll press further. "I'm surprised you got time off from work."

"Managed it."

I don't want to tell her how my job went spectacularly up in flames. My visa would have granted me a few more months, but I'd burn through my savings looking for curator jobs no one would hire me for. Although I couldn't stand the smug look on my parents' faces when I showed up at their doorstep, I had to distance myself—literally—from my old job and make a plan to get my life back on track.

I always wanted to leave a legacy, but this wasn't it.

"You staying with your folks?" she asks.

"For now."

"Is that...okay?"

"Yeah," I say, shrugging off her concern. She spent too much of her childhood worried about how my parents treated me. "Hey, at least they've given me access to one of their fancy cars." I load in the luggage, luxuriating for a few moments in the blast of AC. I'm not built for this kind of sweltering heat anymore. "What room should I bring these to, boss?"

"Four. And don't call me that. We're not colleagues. This was your idea, so just make them feel super special for their anniversary."

"Daisy." I rest a palm on her shoulder, and the contact zips through me. I pull my hand back since the gesture was too close, too familiar. "They'll get star treatment, and I promise to make The Mirage proud."

"Thanks." She stares at me and opens her mouth to say something else, but stops herself with a shake of the head.

"What?"

"Nothing. When do you go back?"

"Soon." I don't have an honest answer for that, but I'll spare her the details. "Didn't buy a return flight yet."

Rapid tapping sounds on the car window.

"Well, let me know before you leave. Uh, you can take them to the hotel for now," Daisy instructs. She said she's not my boss, but she sounds like one. Formal and matter-of-fact. "I should call the insurance company before you go anywhere else with them."

I had thought—hoped, maybe—that our messages would mean we could fall back into our old friendship in person. Our relationship isn't what we had in high school, and that's a good thing, I guess. That would only make my eventual departure tougher. All the more reason for me to figure out my life and get the hell out of Harlow as quickly as I can.

Chapter Four

Daisy, Now

My best friend holds out her phone, smiling at the Instagram photo of her crystal shop. This one has hundreds of likes and comments, putting anything I've ever shared to The Mirage's account to shame.

"*Of quartz we hope to see you this weekend,*" I read out loud. "Cute. So I should write short and snappy captions?"

"Sometimes." Gwen leans over the lobby counter, scrolling through her posts. "Longer, honest ones can work well, too. I vary it based on my mood."

I'd love buzz for The Mirage, but posting online is the first task I ignore when other to-dos pile up, which is always. Thankfully, Gwen offered to share some tips and tricks she learned from her social media manager. My budget is tight, so I can't hire my own—not until I take care of the termite damage in the barn and finally tackle the HVAC maintenance I've been putting off. Maybe this is a last-ditch effort for a moment of virality, but I'll do anything to keep The Mirage going. Between Gwen's generosity and Max swooping in to play taximan, I've reached my limit of accepting favors, though.

Thank god the Hollises kept him busy, so he wasn't on the property distracting me all weekend. He never mentioned how long he'd be in town, and after he took the guests back to LA last night, I haven't heard from him. Maybe he's getting in quality time with his sister; maybe he's halfway around the world, setting up another museum. Although it stings to think he wouldn't say goodbye, I need to let him return to his life so we can both get back to the more comfortable, candid voicemail game that we play.

"You okay?" My friend rests a hand over mine as she searches my face. "You seem—"

"I'm fine," I say, not wanting to tip her off. "You're just way better at this than I am."

"You're doing great, really. The Facebook page has holiday wishes every year, and you update followers about inclement weather, like flash floods. But something my social media gal always says is to crowdsource from others to make posting easier."

"Like stock photos?"

"No, actual visitors. Think of all the guests who've stayed here, or the professional photographers who have shot weddings at The Mirage."

The money from hosting weddings in the barn is a nice boost since the newlyweds have to do a full buyout. I've secretly enjoyed not having them as I figure out renovations, though, because they're stressful as hell. I wish we didn't have to rely on them for income. Handling someone's most important day of their life involves way more than turndown service and wake-up calls.

"Or..." Gwen taps on her phone a few times, pulling up some stunning photos of the property that I've never seen before. Mr. Hollis has his arms wrapped around Mrs. Hollis like they're about to go to prom, the sun setting behind them in a radiant display of oranges and pinks.

"Did they send these?"

"They tagged you. See?"

With my bb in Harlow <3 Had a rocky start to the weekend (literally lol) but u know how it is, always an adventure w/ this

1! Big love to The Mirage for hooking us up with a driver and for being the most aesthetic ever. Perf for a romantic getaway. Xx

"These are gorge." Gwen's mouth hangs agape. "Oh my goddess, I'm falling in love with this town all over again, seeing these pics."

She swipes to a selfie with three people. Max stands tall, sandwiched between the Hollises as they grin wide at the camera. He can make friends with a wood cabinet, so it's not shocking they enjoyed the weekend with him. Max loves people, and people love Max.

Most people, at least. My pulse sprints, and if I could burn all of Instagram so Gwen never saw that photo, I would.

"Babes." She sets the phone down and places both palms on her chest. "I knew your vibes were off."

"My vibes are fine." I sigh because my ever-attentive, emotionally in-tune friend wants to overanalyze this.

"What was he doing with your *clients*?"

"He sort of appeared on Friday and saved me in a pinch."

"Like an apparition?"

"Kind of."

"And you didn't mention this to me because..." She draws out the last word, giving me the chance to fill in the blank.

"I didn't want to upset you. And it wasn't important." I adjust one of the small succulents on the counter, wishing she'd let this go. "I couldn't care less."

"Let me guess, he left a message after the beep?"

I shoot her a look. Mom and Gwen knew what happened in Dublin, but my best friend is the only person who knows about the voicemails. She never said so, but I got the sense that she didn't like me talking to him again. I don't know *why* it feels so good to share what's going on in my life with Max, but somehow, the distance and time made our back-and-forth messages a safe space for me.

"So...how are you feeling?" she asks.

"Fine."

She assesses me. "I only knew him for a few years in high school, but you knew him your whole childhood. What's he doing here?"

"Hanging out with his family, I think." I recall his short voicemail from the other day. His messages have always been calm and relaxed—like he found some time and curled up on the couch to update me on his life. His last voicemail seemed different, though. Strained.

"He'll head home soon," I go on. "Back to Ireland. And then things will be normal again."

"I'm worried about you. You were a mess when you got back."

My heart jumps into my throat at the memory. Breaking off communication with him was like letting all the oxygen leave the room. But I made the right choice.

"Please don't worry about that." I deflect her attention away from Max. "What you should worry about is my social media accounts."

"They're not that bad."

I let out a hopeless huff of air, wishing I didn't have to chase online success in order to keep Mom's hotel open.

"Hey. What's goin' on in that brain of yours?" she asks. Gwen wraps her arms around me in the same pose Mr. and Mrs. Hollis had in that picture.

"I want to believe that a photo could solve all my problems." The quiet confession tumbles out of me. "But what if that doesn't happen?"

"My manager says that consistency matters more. Show up, that's all."

"And reduce the hotel to a snapshot and a punny caption? It's bigger than that. Doesn't feel right."

Gwen's head bobs on my shoulder. "But it totally makes sense for my shop."

"No." I laugh, pinching her lightly on the arm so she releases me. "You make it look genuine."

"You could too."

"Maybe. My mom created The Mirage to be a literal oasis in the desert. Not a Best Western, not some trendy hotel with no substance. She wanted to have a hidden gem."

"*Hidden* makes earning a steady profit kinda hard, don't you think?"

"I wish…" The corners of my eyes prickle, so I look to the ceiling to chase the sensation away. "I want to do a good job here."

Gwen has been privy to many of these conversations. My first major meltdown happened when I discovered Mom had misreported a room renovation, which led to a minor tax headache the year I took over. When I switched to an entirely new booking software because the old one was clunky and outdated, I almost lost my damn mind. Even though Gwen's gem shop is thriving, she has her own business-owner breakdowns, and I love being the person she can talk to. We know what to say to each other, how to bolster each other up.

But rather than bounce back with a reassuring reply, like "You are doing a great job," or offer me an overflowing glass of wine, she clicks her tongue and says, "And I thought you didn't believe in ghosts."

I follow her line of sight to the overgrown parking lot at the far end of the property, where Max exits his vehicle. My stomach twists into knots.

"The apparition is back," she mutters, and her gaze snags on me. "I can get rid of him."

"Are you going to raid my spice cabinet and leave salt circles around The Mirage to cleanse it again?"

"I figured I'd just ask nicely, but I like how you think."

Smiling, I pat her shoulder. "I'll handle it."

Max catches my eye and tips his chin up in a casual greeting, a carefree smile painted on his face. And for the second time in three days, Max Weber walks back into my life.

Rather than subject Max to a sage cleansing from Gwen, I greet him in the lot and tell him to meet me at one of our old favorites. It's that or welcome him into the casita, which I'm not mentally prepared for. He waits by the entrance to Sal's Saloon until I arrive, and when he opens the door for me, the pungent smell of stale beer hits me first. Dusty, western-style decor covers the walls, from rusty license plates to splintered wagon wheels that have been there as long as I can remember. Music from the jukebox blares, and conversations rattle in all directions. For strong drinks and greasy eats, Sal's is the place to be.

"Wow." Max halts at the entrance as if the sticky beer on the floor has glued him there. "It's like stepping into a time machine."

"Would you rather go somewhere else?"

"Are you kidding?" He gapes at the bar with wonder, and warmth trickles into my limbs seeing him excited to be back here. "This is great."

A boisterous voice roars from across the bar. "There ain't no way." Sal throws a stained towel over his shoulder and speed-walks to greet us, his tiny white apron like a child's costume wrapped around his rotund belly. "My Daisy Duke and Maxster, together again?" He rests a hand on each of our shoulders, squeezing us so our sides meld. Max could be made of steel, he's so firm against me. The heat from his body surges into my arm, while a citrus scent overtakes the stale lager. Something sharp and fresh like lemongrass.

"We've missed you in here." He points his finger at Max, then me. "Both of you."

In high school, we weren't old enough for alcohol and stuck to sodas and lemonades, so Sal fusses over Max and serves him his first official beer at the Saloon. He even throws in complimentary tater tots to commemorate the occasion.

We claim an open booth by the papier-mâché antlers. I blend into the scene with my Levi's, vintage T-shirt, and much-loved boots, but in a crisp, plain tee and slacks, Max gives off out-of-towner vibes, although he's technically not. It's not only his clothes—his presence commands quiet attention. Either he doesn't notice, or he chooses to ignore the folks gawking at him, yearning for some small-town drama.

My heart races as we slide onto the still-warm leather seats because the man across the table is a stranger in so many ways—yet we know so much about each other. For the past couple of years, I found comfort in his voice and in knowing that, although we couldn't really be friends, I didn't have to lose him completely.

"They still have karaoke Friday nights?" Max's question snaps my mind back to the here and now.

"Definitely."

"You continue to devastate everyone with your rendition of 'Dreams'?"

"It's been a while," I say with a laugh as a mild melancholy hits my heart. Since taking over The Mirage, free time has become nonexistent for me. Most Fridays, if I'm lucky, I'm at the hotel doing check-ins. And even if no one's staying the night, there's always something to do. The girl who could pop in here all nonchalant and ready to belt out Fleetwood Mac isn't me anymore.

Max holds his beer out to me. "Cheers."

I tap my beverage against his and bring the cool glass to my lips.

"Whoa," Max exclaims, gripping my forearm so I spill some of the foam onto my fingers. His hand is powerful yet gentle, and the touch zings like a static shock. "Eye contact."

I pull a face at him.

"It's a thing. Eye contact when you toast and take your first drink."

"Says who?"

"Lots of European countries do it."

"Oh," I say, raising my eyebrows at him. "Sophisticated."

"It's considered bad luck if you don't—or some people think it means seven years of bad sex."

"Well." A flush creeps up my neck. "We can't have that."

We lock eyes in a surreal sort of déjà vu, familiar and foreign. How many nights did we spend here, grease dripping down our chins and high on sugar, carbs, and conversation? But now that he's back in this spot, I don't know how to act.

His unwavering attention as he takes that first sip—dark brown eyes burning into mine—makes me want to look away, but I don't. His Adam's apple bobs as he swallows, and my mouth goes dry despite the drink.

"So," Max says. "Kinda different hanging out in person instead of leaving voicemails for each other."

If I could crawl under a rock, I would. The voicemail situation wasn't something we discussed; it happened organically. He left one for me, and I was brave enough to call him back...when I knew he'd be sleeping because of the time difference. I've thought of picking up when his name flashed on the phone, but I never dared.

"I'm sorry," I say. "Things with The Mirage get so busy sometimes, it's easier—"

"Don't worry." He shrugs. "I understand. We could take turns sneaking off to the bathroom to leave a message after the beep, if you'd like."

"Well, since you suggested it..."

The corner of his mouth twitches, and a dimple appears. "Or, you know, we could always schedule a time to chat. I'd pick up."

I know.

"Maybe," I say.

"You look good." He eyes me, and I take the moment to admire the clean cut of his jaw. "And The Mirage...from what I saw, you're doing a great job."

"It's a helluva lot of work," I say, pulling a cocktail napkin onto my lap and shredding tiny tears along one edge. The compliments make my skin prickle. "But I enjoy it."

"Yeah?"

"Of course. Might seem silly to you, but I do."

"What you do is not silly." A crease forms between his eyebrows. "I would never think that."

"I always..." I shake my head, not wanting to live in the past. "Never mind."

"What?"

"Nothing."

"Tell me. I'll close my eyes, and it'll be like I'm listening to a message from you."

This makes me laugh. Our back-and-forth voicemails are a weird habit, but he talks about them like they're totally normal. And maybe it's because we're here in a booth at Sal's, where we've sat hundreds of times before, or maybe I sense some pleading behind his eyes, but something tugs at my insides—makes me *want* to talk about the hotel and my life and everything in person.

"Hotel management wasn't my goal." I rub my lips between my teeth, contemplating the right way to explain my feelings. "The Mirage was unexpected. You know, I'd always thought I might grow up to be a ranger or maybe a wildlife biologist and work in the park nearby. Taking over The Mirage...it just happened."

It happened because the alternative was unthinkable.

"You're happy?" he asks, his head tilted to the side like he's reading between the lines.

"Knowing her dream is alive in the world makes me happy." Some days I want to pull my hair out, but I don't manage the hotel for me. "People can go to this beautiful place she created and experience the love she had for Harlow...that makes it worth it."

Max pauses. "She was a legend."

"She was," I say, holding my glass up.

"I know you told me not to come to the funeral, but I...I feel terrible about missing it. For you."

"Don't. It was an overwhelming time." I swallow. "I appreciate you respecting my wishes."

Although my mom slots into the conversation easily with Max, I'd love to keep things light between us. That rules out benign "How're the folks?" questions—he's always been at odds with his parents, and I've already told him through our voicemails about adjusting to my dad's not-so-new girlfriend.

"How's work?" I ask to change the subject.

He makes a clicking sound with his tongue. "I'm, uh, actually between jobs right now."

"Like a different...they're called pop-ups, right?"

"Yeah."

"What's the new one?"

"No, I, um..." He rolls his sleeves up, exposing forearms etched with lean muscle. "I'm not working for that company anymore."

"So a new job?"

"Not quite. My work kind of blew up, and I'm...figuring some things out. Long story," he says, waving his hands like he wants to wipe any mention of this from my memory. "Just don't Google me, okay?"

"Well, when you put it like that, Googling you is all I want to do." I make a show of pulling out my phone.

"Daze." My nickname on his tongue makes me shudder. "I'm serious. I'll tell you later, but for now, let's just...have a nice time."

As much as I wish he'd stop being secretive and just explain what happened, I don't want to badger him. "Fine." I hold up my pointer finger, and he tracks my movement as I make an X over my heart. "So how long are you in town?"

"Not sure."

Our eyes meet, and I wonder if he can hear the questions bouncing around in my skull. What does *not sure* mean? A few days? A few weeks?

"Art curator openings aren't exactly overflowing on LinkedIn," he goes on, "but I'm looking for jobs."

"Some place'll wanna snatch you up." I nod, a wave of relief and pain surging through me. "Who knows, maybe you'll be even farther away than Ireland this time. You'll figure it out. I know you will."

Max was the opposite of me growing up. While I struggled in school and never found my calling, he was bound for something great. Straight A's, talented, charismatic. Too big for Harlow. Whatever he's dealing with, he'll overcome it.

"Anyway." He thumbs the condensation on his glass. "I always have a backup career as the private driver for The Mirage."

"The Hollises mentioned you by name in their Yelp review. First and last."

"They invited me to their kid's birthday party two weeks from now."

"Of course."

"What's that mean?" He launches a tater tot into his mouth and chews through a smirk.

"Classic you. Friends with everyone. I'm surprised they didn't invite you into their bed."

"Oh, they did."

I almost do a spit take. "Seriously?"

"I'm joking. Sort of. They implied the offer more than any-thing."

The confession pulls an unexpected laugh out of me, and for a millisecond, I am transported back to our high school days. "You always were everyone's favorite."

"What are you talking about?"

"There wasn't a single person when we were growing up who didn't like you."

"The dorky kid scribbling on notepads who everyone ridiculed?"

"Aw." I soften at the memory of adorable little Max drawing at a picnic table. "When you were older, you were Mr. Popular."

"No, I was Mr. I'm Going to Be Goofy and Outgoing So It Seems Like I Belong. You were the popular one. People either wanted to be you or date you."

"What?" My mouth hangs open at our vastly different mem-ories of our teen years.

"Guys would sprint down the hallways to find you when they heard about your latest breakup. You dated nonstop."

"I dated an average amount for a teenage girl and—"

"There was Everett, Billy, Marquez, Jack—"

"Ugh, *Jack*." I grimace, which elicits a chuckle from Max. He's teasing me, and the satisfaction of it fizzles in my belly. "I've forgotten all of those guys. If there were *so many boyfriends*, how do you even remember their names?"

"Dunno." He pauses, then looks right at me, expressionless. "I just do."

Relationships don't come up in our voicemails—and for good reason, based on how tense the air has become. It's thick enough to chew.

"Another round?" Sal asks at the end of the booth.

Max hunches over his beer, staring at the bottom of the emp-ty glass, and something about it breaks my heart. He's so out of place in a spot that used to be ours.

"No, thanks," he says to Sal with a toothless smile. "Just the check."

Chapter Five

Daisy, 11 Years Old

The black-and-white animal butted its warm head against my chin as we sat on the casita's front porch swing.

"She's cute." Max reached out with a cautious hand to pet the tiny creature, and it mewed. "Hi, kitty."

"How old do you think she is?" I asked to distract myself from the conversation inside the house.

"I don't know. Still a kitten." He inspected the feline's rear end. "Also, *she* might be *he*."

The cat climbed me like its personal jungle gym, with one of its claws needling into the threads of my shirt. Its fur radiated heat from the cloudless day. I knew people sometimes dumped animals on the side of the street. The bumpy back road by the house didn't get much traffic, so thank goodness Max heard the meows on his way over to ask if I wanted to play.

"A pet is a huge responsibility." My dad's voice carried outside, and Max and I stilled so we could eavesdrop. "At the end of the day, the work will fall on us."

"I'm fine with that," Mom said, irritation making her pitch rise.

"Of course you're fine with it, Amy, you'll be running around the hotel while I'm taking care of—"

"We're talking about a cat, Richard. We play with it, we feed it, we scoop its shit. It's not that complicated."

"I don't want a cat right now."

"What about what I want? Or what our Daisygirl wants?"

They hadn't had a blowup like this since Dad moved back in a few weeks ago. I couldn't bear for them to split again over this.

"Maybe..." I handed the wriggling animal to Max, not wanting to get too attached. "Would your parents let you keep him if mine say no?"

"You said your mom and dad had talked about getting a pet."

"Yeah, like a fish or a gerbil." My shoulders slumped. "Maybe Dad's right that a cat is too much trouble."

Max's face turned sour. He held the cat inches from my nose, crowding my personal space, as the feline reached out to paw me. "You owe kitty an apology."

"Stop," I said through a halfhearted laugh.

I wished Max didn't have to overhear Mom and Dad fighting, but I was so glad he was here to brighten my mood. He had a knack for that. I put on as much of a smile as I could while the cat made circles in my lap and laid down into a croissant shape. Peaceful, content. The little thing purred, safe perhaps for the first time in its life and comfortable like it had always belonged there.

Chapter Six

Max, Now

My mentor, Eleanor, picks up her wine, swirling the sample in front of her nose. After a sip, she nods to the server. "That's good."

I took workshops with Eleanor when she was a visiting scholar at my university. She works at the Los Angeles County Museum of Art, one of the most esteemed museums in the US, and we're having lunch at a high-end restaurant downtown. I've had countless business meetings in establishments like this, although this spot has an especially stuffy vibe to it. The whole place looks like a brightly lit, neutral-toned French chateau, complete with luxurious velvet curtains and a sparkling chandelier. Basically, the opposite of grabbing beer last week at Sal's with Daisy.

"I knew you were from the US," Eleanor says, "but SoCal?"

"Born and raised. My parents wanted more space and less of the LA crazy influence on their kids."

"Good for them. Los Angeles is a lot, and I love this city as much as I hate it. Plus, Harlow's adorable, really quaint."

"My friend owns a hotel out there," I say with a glint of pride. "The Mirage."

"I think I know that one. My wife and I don't get out there as often as we'd like, but when we do, even for the weekend, we release this breath we didn't know we were holding. And there's quite a burgeoning art scene."

I purse my lips, unsure I heard her correctly.

"I'm serious," she says, lifting her glass for a sip.

"Who's it burgeoning for? People who want to drop acid and paint sunsets for souvenir shops?"

"The town's a hot spot for creatives now. There's been a lot of fresh blood moving there in the past five years. Harlow's officially on the map."

"Are we..." I scratch the back of my neck. "Are we talking about the same Harlow?"

"Don't be so skeptical. I actually have a friend out there who wants to start an art school for teens. She's looking for instructors if you're interested."

"I never pictured myself teaching."

"It would just be the summer semester. You might end up loving it."

"Maybe." I give a noncommittal shrug.

"I've also heard rumblings of a position that you'd be perfect for."

"At LACMA?" I freeze, holding a chunk of bread halfway to my mouth. Anything that well-known opens up infinite opportunities.

"Tate," Eleanor says.

"Tate Modern?"

She nods, and the disaster with my last job becomes a pinpoint on the horizon behind me.

"Don't get too excited yet, and this"—she points back and forth between us—"stays here. They won't hire until October, maybe November, and I have no clue what the salary will be. But an old colleague who works there explained it as a new initiative curating traveling exhibits."

After a few weeks of endless awful things, this news fills me with hope.

"It would be advisable to, you know..." She bobs her head left and right. "Get something else on the resume."

"And you think that should be teaching?"

"The pay's abysmal. It's practically volunteer work. I'm happy to write you a glowing recommendation for Tate, and they'll like your real-world experience, but having Impressions as your last workplace might spook them regardless. But a teaching position? That'll look good."

"How long does the contract last?"

"My friend said she desperately needs someone for the summer classes, which gives you some breathing room. Job openings in your line of work don't come around every day."

I sink into the chair in defeat. "That's a long time for me to sleep on a leaking air mattress in my parents' home gym."

I'm already a disappointment for going into art, and being back only proves their point. But if I go elsewhere and stay with friends, I won't have a firm end date, and my savings won't last forever. No hiring manager in their right mind would want me, not with Impressions as the most recent thing on my resume. This teaching position is the only lead I have.

"I'll give you her contact info," Eleanor says, smearing a glob of thick cultured butter on a roll. "She'll love you."

"Thanks." I offer Eleanor as much of a smile as I can muster.

"Many talented artists teach," she says. "*I* teach."

"Teaching doesn't bother me. It's just not what I envisioned for my life."

"The air mattress or the job situation?"

"Both."

"Well, what did you picture?"

"What I was doing."

After graduation, I lucked out snagging a position at Impressions—the sort of place that called itself an art-up. They brought innovative exhibits to unexpected places. While we originally intended to do small-scale projects throughout Western Europe and the United Kingdom, we went worldwide as an almost overnight success.

"I'm sure all curators feel this way sometimes," I say, "but I really wanted to change the world with art. Give people experiences they wouldn't forget. I felt like we were doing that."

"You can't tell me that a pop-up museum dedicated to mushrooms was anything other than an Instagram trap."

"*The Fungus Among Us* was a hit."

That was my most recent pop-up and my least favorite by far. Since Impressions grew over the years, my latest work involved a constant battle with event coordinators, marketing specialists, and content writers. The team had become more concerned with engaging influencers and posting clever hashtags than producing something meaningful beyond viral images. People loved it, but they wouldn't remember it.

"Okay, I didn't exactly reach the pinnacle of my career there," I admit, staring at my utensils. "Not yet. If I'd had more time, I could have done it."

"Done what?"

"Created something that lasts. A legacy."

"I love the ambition, but legacies can easily come from something negative, too. I am sorry about that, by the way. What assholes." She shakes her head in disgust. "And now you and all the other employees there have to deal with the damage from their decisions."

"I'm avoiding the headlines, but..." My jaw clenches. "Last I read, some people think I must have known."

"Did you?"

"No, fuck, absolutely not."

I should have, though, and plenty of investigative journalists out there have claimed the same. That's why I asked Daisy not to look anything up, because I didn't know what she'd find. What began with environmental concerns over Impressions's massive set designs being quietly dumped into landfills, quickly escalated into sexual harassment claims against the CEO, who I worked closely with as the curator.

If I wanted a legacy, I got one.

"Not many people in the art world missed that headline," Eleanor says. "I can reason with Tate, but the teaching thing could be the perfect CV palate cleanser."

I rest my elbows on the table, my forehead in my palms. The server arrives with our food: elegant nests of pasta and a dazzlingly fresh caprese salad. Everything looks delicious, but I've got no appetite.

"Who knows?" Eleanor ferries some vibrant tomatoes and mozzarella to her plate. "Next month, some museum will have protesters gluing themselves to a Monet for world peace, and this will be old news. You're getting unfairly dragged, but people will eventually come around. You should consider doing something of your own, too."

"Like a self-imposed project?" Sparks of creativity are already crackling inside me at the suggestion.

"Mhmm. You can't go wrong with the teaching gig—it's respectable. But a little extra initiative can't hurt. If it doesn't go anywhere, you'll still have the teaching job on your resume. But if it's a success, you'd no doubt shed the shadow of Impressions and stand on your own."

That makes my ears perk up. If I'm serious about Tate, I need to do everything I can to become a top candidate—not just teaching, but also something of my own. If I want to create something extraordinary, though, I'll need a small team. After what happened at my last job, I'm pretty sure I will only ever go into business with someone I already know and trust, which makes things tricky. Not to mention the budget—although I've curated shows of all sizes around the world, the financial side has always eluded me. Other than selecting and working with artists, I'm inexperienced in managing a project on my own.

I chew the inside of my lip, considering the possibilities, the responsibilities, and the nonzero chance of fucking things up further.

"Don't look so worried," Eleanor says, resting a hand on my shoulder and plucking me out of my spiraling thoughts. "People have emerged from worse situations than this. And when people want to figure out their shit, they often go somewhere remote. Somewhere...desert-y."

Rubbing my temples, I wish with all my might she were wrong.

"I'm just saying," she says, raising her hands in a defensive gesture. "Whether you drop acid or not, that's up to you. But there are worse places to land."

My little sister, Ava, walks with me down a concrete hall glowing with fluorescent lights. Save for Sal, she's the only person who seems happy I'm back.

And maybe Daisy, although the verdict's still out.

When I open the sliding door to the storage unit, I immediately wish I hadn't gone full teenager mode and angrily promised my parents I'd clean this whole thing out tonight.

"How's this even gonna fit in the car?" she asks.

"We can do more than one trip." My reassurance is as much for me as for her. With the number of boxes and the amount of furniture in here, we'll be making trips all night.

When I went to college, I didn't make a plan for my bed, dressers, desk, clothes, art projects, or anything else in my room. I moved to Dublin with two checked bags and a dream, and I left the rest here. It's my "mess," as my dad called it when I got back from lunch with Eleanor—my memories, my childhood—and he and my mom want it gone. Not to save money, because they probably get a deal on the multiple units they rent, but because they want to teach me a lesson. Nothing highlights my failure more than emptying this room and having nowhere to put my stuff.

Since renting a unit as an unemployed transient doesn't make sense, I'll have to avoid sentimentality and donate a lot, leaving me with only the most important items.

"Any of your friends have a truck?" I ask. My car—my *parent's* car, which only adds insult to injury—can only hold so much.

Ava taps her chin, and her eyes light up. Seeing her so grown-up underscores how much can change in less than a decade. My first few years away, we didn't stay in touch too well—she was only eight when I left. But once she turned thirteen and had her own phone, I ventured into Snapchat territory, and we've become close. I'm selfishly relieved that she wants to follow my parents' footsteps into law so I don't have to worry about her struggling with them the way I always have.

"Actually, yeah, I do know someone." Ava pulls out her cell, and her thumbs fly over the screen. That's another bit of good news since my talk with Eleanor today. Depending on the size of the truck, we could do this in one go.

"Tell them I'll buy them pizza or something."

"Cool. Daze'll be right over."

"Daisy?"

"Yeah." My sister stares at me like she's never seen me before. "What?"

"You have her number?"

"We keep in touch. She's cool."

I scrub a hand down my face. I'd rather Daisy didn't witness this low point. "Daze is an adult with a job and things to do, and I'm sure she has a boyfriend and a busy social life and friends, so—"

"You still have a crush on her."

"I don't have a crush on Daisy."

"I was eight, but I wasn't stupid." She crosses her arms and cocks an eyebrow at me. "I'd seen enough Disney movies by that point to know how you looked at her. That was some Kristoff and Anna shit right there."

Unwilling to entertain this any further, I survey the dust-covered items by the wall. "I'll start with this pile of stuff."

"Did you write secret poetry about her?"

"Would you help me?"

"You can't hold it against Daisy for not realizing you were obsessed with her and for dating other people."

"I don't. And I dated other people too. Maybe not much in high school, but college and after."

"Sure, and you're good friends with all of them."

"Some people would consider that a positive thing. Most people, actually."

"Not when you stop being friends with the one person you want, all because you don't think you deserve her."

"That's not what happened."

Even if Daisy hadn't sent that text the first semester of college, I never felt unworthy of her.

Did I?

"You had a big-time crush on her."

"Okay, *fine*," I say, irritation getting the best of me. "I liked Daisy. So what? It was a crush, and it's done."

"She's single."

I shouldn't care about that. "Focus."

My sister grants me a few minutes of quiet, working side by side until she speaks up again. "Daze has been single for a while, actually. She and that guy broke up a few months ago."

I inspect a vase from my high school pottery class, wholly uninterested in Daisy's relationship status.

"He's a chef. He's *so* sexy."

"I would love to not hear how sexually attracted you are to grown men. Can you go through the bin over there?" I point to the other side of the room where there's a Rubbermaid tote with art supplies.

A chef. Daisy didn't mention him when we were at Sal's, not that we ordinarily talk about who we're dating. I stew on this information, and when I'm about to ask how serious they were, Daisy appears in the doorway, all tanned face and freckles and sunlight.

"Hey, you two."

"Hi!" Ava runs over and gives her a hug. "Max didn't want to call you, but I knew you'd help."

"Oh?" Daisy meets my gaze with curious eyes.

"I figured you were busy."

She shrugs. "I don't mind helping."

Daisy doesn't press for information. Within minutes, she organizes us and creates three separate spots for items we'll toss, donate, or keep. She plays some classic rock from her phone to lighten the mental load, and we tear through half the room in less than an hour.

"Oh my *god*," Daisy says, pulling a piece of fabric off of something in the corner. "This chair. Max, do you remember this chair?"

I peer around a small mountain of boxes and see Daisy plop onto my burnt orange barstool. She was with me when I thrifted it—a strange squiggly-shaped seat that looked like a padded curlicue. Despite the heinous design, it was comfortable.

"Sit in this." Daisy gets up and makes room for Ava, who *ooohs* the second her butt hits the chair.

"Want it?" I ask my sister.

"Seriously?"

"Consider it yours."

"Ohmygosh yes!" She runs and almost knocks me over with a bear hug. My attention flashes to Daisy, whose gaze is on us as the sides of her mouth tilt upward.

"So," my sister continues, "what other stuff of yours can I have?"

Ava and I sort out which furniture we'll donate and which we'll take to her room. I love that some of this is going right back to my parents, but more importantly, Ava seems excited to redesign.

"You're not keeping much," Daisy says, pointing to the small pile of items deemed both worthy and easy enough to hang onto.

"Not flush with extra space at the moment."

"Store it at The Mirage. The barn has lots of room."

"That's..." The barn would make life easier, even if the solution is merely a Band-Aid. My reunion with Daisy wasn't as joyous as I'd imagined it would be, though, so her offer gives me pause. "You don't have to do that."

"I'm happy to." She gives me a soft smile that makes my pulse jolt. "You helped me with the Hollises."

"And then you bought me beer and tater tots as a thank you."

"The tots were from Sal."

"What about these bins?" Ava asks me.

"Looks like it's all clothes, so donate."

"Oh," Daisy says with a gasp and beelines to Ava, who is pulling items from the box like a magician producing scarves from their ear. "You *cannot* donate this hat." Daisy throws on an old newsboy cap I wore in high school, and there's a comfort in seeing her wear something I used to love so much. "You tried so hard to make this a thing."

"Excuse me," I say, feigning offense. "It was one hundred percent a thing."

"Were these seriously your jeans?" Ava holds up some denim. "These are *so small*."

Self-consciousness clutches my insides. While I appreciate the help from Ava and Daisy, I want to blindfold them so they don't see the remnants of a dorky eighteen-year-old Max.

"Your brother was a Doberman puppy," Daisy says, fondness in her voice. "Paws too big for its body. All limbs."

"Aw, well, at least puppies are cute, right Daze?" Ava asks.

Daisy glances my way but says nothing. Instead, she gives a barely audible *mhmm* as a response and reaches into another bin.

Once we've organized everything, we swing by the thrift store first. When we stop by my parents' house with the items Ava will keep, she immediately starts moving furniture around in her room. Daisy and I haul the rest of my things to The Mirage alone.

"That's it," I announce, setting the heavy box of canvases down as carefully as I can. "Wow, this..." Examining the barn, I nod.

Large windows open the space up and allow the desert inside, and rustic wrought-iron chandeliers dangle from the ceiling. The exposed beams have all been treated with the same honey-hued lacquer, although some of them could use a fresh coat.

"This looks really good," I say.

"Don't lie."

"I'm not. It's way nicer than my last storage unit."

She laughs a full-on star beam of a laugh, and I forget where I am. Planet Earth, somewhere. California. Harlow. That's right.

"Is everything okay at your parents' house?" Daisy asks, picking at one of her nails.

"Yeah. You know how they are. They just want to prove a point."

"This is pretty low, even for them."

"They love exceeding expectations."

Having Daisy on my side lifts me up, but questions fly through my mind. *What happened between us? What haven't you told me after the beep? How can I get past these barriers you have—the ones that seem to be built for me alone?* There's only one question I feel comfortable asking out loud, though.

"Why are you helping me?"

"Because." She walks toward me, focusing her energy on the box of paintings. Daisy thumbs through them, the inky lines of the sun tattoo on her hand dancing, and I have the urge to grab one of the blank canvases and paint her as I see her now—unguarded, with a slight smile blooming on her face. "Your parents are giving you a hard time, and if I can ease that for you, I will. I enjoy looking out for people here. And for now, you're here." She keeps her eyes trained on the art in front of her. "Thanks for the sketch you sent."

"Of course." When Amy died, I did what I could from afar to support Daze. Scouring old photos and picking up my pencil was soothing for me too, especially because I didn't go to the funeral. The drawing of her mom was small enough to fit into a sympathy card, but I thought she might like it.

"I'm, uh, hoping to start back up with booking weddings in the fall, so do you think your stuff'll be gone by then?"

"I—" I can't tell if she's simply curious or pressuring me to give her an end date. "Sure, I can do that."

"I'd like to finish renovations by then. Or the ones I can manage, at least." The corners of her eyes crinkle as she inspects a perspective drawing of downtown Harlow, and she lowers her voice, almost like she's talking to herself. "You were always so talented."

Her russet-colored eyes lock onto mine, and I become hyper-aware of how close we are. I could reach out and slip an arm around her waist and pull her to me. I could recount all the freckles on her nose. I could kiss her.

As if she's reading my mind, her focus lowers to my lips, almost like she *wants* me to close the distance between us. Like she's curious and wants a taste. I've only seen her look at me like this once before—but I'd never forget it.

"Um," she says, brushing her bangs off of her forehead. She backs up, and the connection we have has broken, if it even existed in the first place. "So, temporary."

"Right." I take a step back, craving some space from the botanical perfume or shampoo or whatever Daisy's wearing. "End of summer, and this'll all be gone."

Chapter Seven

Max, 14 Years Old

After twenty minutes of scouring the thrift store shelves, the best thing I found was a motion-activated singing fish. My little sister would find it hilarious, but more importantly, my parents would despise it. I examined the rubbery texture of the fake fish's scales. The price tag listed $4.99, and it would be cheaper with my employee discount.

Daisy slotted into the space next to me, and our arms touched. The sensation made the hairs on the back of my neck stand up.

"I'm sorry they won't be there," she said.

I shrugged. Despite giving my mom and dad advance notice, they had a "very important work dinner" next Thursday. Of all the days, they had to pick that Thursday.

"I thought high school might be different," I said, placing the fish back on the shelf. "This is dumb."

"It's not dumb. I just think if you wanna piss them off, you're going to have to do better than a fish that sings 'Stayin' Alive' every time someone walks by your bedroom door. You need to be intentional but subtle."

"What says 'here's a big middle finger for missing my first showcase'?" I looked around the store to find something else, but my frustration boiled over. "God, I can't wait until I can move out and become famous and go to exhibits, and my parents will never be on the guest list, and if they ever show up I'll make sure they get turned away. They can't even pretend to care about what I'm interested in."

Daisy's mouth curved downward. She couldn't understand. Her parents had issues, but at least they were supportive. They watched her horseback riding lessons every week, her dad took her camping on the weekends, and her mom didn't pressure her for the best grades. *C's get degrees*, she'd say whenever Daisy brought home her report card.

"Will I be on the list?" Daisy asked quietly.

"Always." No hesitation. Of course I'd want her there. I always wanted Daisy around.

She smiled and trailed her hand across a clothing rack. One of the overhead lights flickered, casting a yellowish glow on the three other shoppers sifting through piles of potential treasures.

"What about a weird outfit?" She held up a pair of chaps.

"I could never pull off the cowboy look."

"Some home decor?" Daisy perused a shelf full of sheep figurines. "I love picking out that kind of stuff."

"Don't waste your talents on this."

We meandered toward the furniture section, testing out some sofas and a desk. Daisy gasped.

"Max! It's perfect."

She pointed to a stool tucked behind a filing cabinet. The base had a twisting, tornado-like shape, and the entire thing was the color of a neon-orange construction vest.

"That's definitely something," I said, giving the chair a dubious look.

"Exactly."

"And the wrong height for my desk."

"Impractical. Heinous. Bizarre."

"It's probably uncomfortable."

Daisy looked at me. "Only one way to find out." She grabbed my hand and led me to the barstool with the dangling price tag.

Chapter Eight

Daisy, Now

"Begin moving your fingers and toes." The soft-spoken instructor coaxes me out of *savasana*. Rather than finding a zen state after having my ass kicked on the mat, all I can think about is Max. Whatever his parents said to him must have really hurt. I'm happy to help him and be the counterbalance to what he's going through with them, if only for a short while.

Besides, helping him means he'll get back on his feet and out of Harlow as fast as possible, which is what he wants. It's what someone as intelligent and accomplished as Max deserves.

"The light in me sees and honors the light in you."

When I open my eyes, everyone in the class has already switched to a seated position. I shoot up to join them, tossing prayer hands up to my forehead with a rushed *namaste*.

While Gwen thanks folks at the exit, I move tables back to their original spots. My friend looks radiant as she tells the yoga instructor that they might want to do this twice a week instead of once. After everyone has left, Gwen flips the *Open* sign on the front door, sinks into a chair, and lets out an exhausted exhale.

"I had nightmares you'd be the only person." Gwen had begged me to attend the first-ever wellness class in her shop, offering to pay my admission if I'd help prep the space for guests.

"Would me struggling in downward dog alone for an hour have been that terrible?"

"You have a cute tush. And respectable form."

"I'm glad you noticed. Although I usually do yoga at home and at a much more forgiving pace. I don't think I'll be able to move tomorrow."

She chortles and then turns to me with sparkling eyes. "Thank you for being here."

"Always." I sit on the curved arm of the chair, my limbs loose from all the pretzel shapes I pushed myself into in the past hour. I'm lucky to have a successful businesswoman best friend, but I wish The Mirage had half of the runaway success she experiences with the shop. At least one of us won't be struggling this slow season. She must get tired of me yapping about money and dwindling reservations.

"You know," she says, "you could run events like this at The Mirage for your guests."

I tilt my head to the side, considering the suggestion. "Why can't I be hit with inspiration like you?"

"Because then you wouldn't need me, and I'd just be a sad, lonely witch with too many rocks."

"Unfortunately, barn repairs come first." I fiddle with the piping on the chair. "It's been damn near impossible to book weddings with the state it's in." Vector images only go so far. Engaged couples want to walk into the vision, not merely imagine it.

"Ugh, I *hate* those termites. I could punch every single one of them."

"Be my guest."

"What if I loaned you some money?"

My eyes flash to her. "No."

"Just a loan. For the summer, a little extra for the termite damage. You'll get some weddings, pay me back, and it'll be like it never happened."

"Thank you, but..." Money stuff with The Mirage sometimes sparked arguments between my parents. They fought over way more than the financial aspect of the hotel, but I won't taint my relationship with Gwen by getting cash involved. "I want to handle this on my own."

"Think about it. That's all I'm asking."

All signs point to me being a crummy hotelier, but she's still willing to put herself on the line financially for me. Without a word, she stands, situates herself in front of me, and drapes her arms over my body in a protective hug.

"I wish I had a guidebook," I say with a sigh. "I want someone to tell me what to do."

"You could—"

"Other than accept money from my best friend."

"Fine."

"I don't need you to always give me solutions." My words get muffled in her hair. "Sometimes I just want to vent."

"I know." She pulls me tighter into an embrace. The doorbell sings an ethereal chime, but neither of us moves because there's only one person who would enter at this time of night. Moments later, another pair of arms wraps around us.

"Hey, Bob," I say.

"Hello, my darling." Gwen greets her life partner.

"Is this a sad hug?" he asks. "Because it feels like a sad hug."

"Not sad," I say at the same time Gwen says, "Kind of."

"It's not," I insist and wriggle out of their clutches. "I'm simply overwhelmed from an amazing yoga class that was completely packed."

Bob's mouth flies open. "No way! I'm so proud of you, baby." He stresses the last few words with kisses. "So. Freaking. Proud."

Gwen and Bob are such a strange match to me. I didn't like him at first—my vibrant, incredible best friend is a complete hippie, while he's a total nerd for numbers. His idea of a wild Friday night is repairing old watches found at the flea market.

But seeing my best friend deeply in love with such a great guy heals something in me every time we're together.

"So." Bob turns to me and keeps an arm draped over Gwen. "Is that the only exciting thing you two talked about?" His gaze turns to Gwen, who gives him the purest smile in response.

"You told him?" I ask Gwen, deflated that she would share everything I told her about Max with her partner. It comes with the territory of knowing someone who's also found their soulmate, but I sometimes feel like I have to share my best friend.

"Wait, told me what?" Bob says, his brows forming a V.

"About Max."

"I did but only—"

"Who's Max?"

"Max, my love," Gwen says, reaching for Bob's hand. "Remember? Childhood friend, came back to town a couple weeks back."

"Oh, *Max*."

"I saw him a couple days ago, too." I adjust the pile of pamphlets advertising The Mirage, pretending not to count them. "His sister texted because they were busy clearing out his storage unit from high school. His stuff's in the barn until further notice."

I leave out the part where Max and I almost kissed. After watching his arm muscles flex while moving stuff around and then having the heat of his body so close, I got caught up in the moment. At least any time that's happened, I've stopped myself from taking things too far.

"For how long?" my friend asks, although I know what she's really asking—will *he* be here for long?

"A few months, at the most."

"As in moon-waxing-and-waning-fully months?"

"The barn is a temporary solution. When we got drinks, he said—"

"Wait, you got *drinks*?" Bob's eyes go wide.

"Sweetie, I told you this. Remember?"

"I'm sorry. My mind's...it's been elsewhere."

Honestly, I'm relieved Bob hasn't absorbed every humiliating detail about my personal life. "We went to Sal's, and I felt kind of bad for him. Sounds like the rug's been pulled out from under him at his last job, so he's in shock."

"Jeez. Well..." Gwen pouts. "You need to be careful."

"I am."

"I know you think you are, but using the barn for his things? Going to old haunts together for pitchers of beer?"

"We each had one beer." My defensive shackles rise. "Singular."

"Doesn't matter. You have been more than gracious in helping him out, but that does not mean you have to put yourself out there anymore. You're busy, you have your own life, and—"

"Okay, babe," Bob says, resting his hands on her forearms. "You shouldn't get worked up. You know..."

"You're right." Gwen bites her lower lip, and a girlish laugh escapes her. "You should say it."

"No, you."

"Say what?" I ask, confused by how my friend went from protective mama bear to giggling schoolgirl in three seconds flat.

"Um, well, I..." She loops a hand in Bob's and rests her head on his shoulder. "We're having a baby."

"A baby?" I look between the two of them to make sure I heard her correctly. "You're pregnant?"

"Mhmm. You're gonna be an auntie."

I go in for another group hug because the surprise has sucked the words out of me. Gwen talked about wanting to have kids one day, and I envisioned us in our thirties, pregnant together and raising our babies. That left me with years before the pressure to settle down. I didn't know she and Bob wanted a kid *now*.

And gracious friend that she is, she let me ramble on about Max and the hotel while she had news like this.

Gwen tells me she's feeling extra everything lately. Extra tired, extra hungry, and extra irritable. As she goes into details about how Bob plans to build a wall in the bonus room to make the nursery, and all the wisdom her doula has already imparted, my heart swells with joy.

And maybe, just maybe, a bit of fear. I don't have a sliver of a doubt that she's hired an amazing birthing team. My fears are unspeakable. Selfish. Because as Gwen gushes about the journey she's about to embark on, I can't help but wonder if I'm being left behind.

"Psst. Daze." Ava waves at me and gestures to the empty seat to her left. I already know Gwen won't be here—she's so nauseous that Bob had to fill in at the shop—so I snag the spot. Settling in, and still sore from that yoga class, I do a double take when I see who's sitting on her right.

Max nods a silent greeting to me, smiling in a bewildered *oh-you-go-here?* kind of way. He must clock my confusion because he says, "Driver," under his breath and points to his chest.

Ava attends meetings for the Harlow Sustainability and Desert Preservation Committee with regularity, as any over-achieving high school kid would. She only has a learner's permit, so one of her parents ordinarily accompanies her. They typically wait in the car, though.

Harlow's community center has a neutral look—sand-colored walls and laminate flooring—and attendees fill more than half of the metal folding chairs facing the podium. Ms. Willow, a stylish sixty-something who moved here for retirement, stands at the front of the room. Her waist-length braid sways as she guides discussions on fundraisers for trail maintenance and proposals for increasing the minimum wage for park workers.

I divide my interest: 99 percent to the people speaking and 1 percent to Max—2 percent tops. He doodles on the paper in his lap, the long veins in his hand flexing with the movement, but he keeps his attention on whoever is speaking. He doesn't squirm around like he did in high school, and he's not swimming in his clothes anymore, either. Grown-up Max is focused and self-assured, and even in simple tailored jeans and a Henley, he's more stylish and put-together than anyone here. None of this meeting involves him, but he nods along as residents beg for better bike lanes and request more legible signage on trails. When two folks kick off a heated argument over a hundred-year-old cactus and whose property it rests on, Max catches my eye. He slips me a quiet smile that sends songbirds soaring in my stomach.

I whip my head to the front. The last thing I need to do is rouse forgotten feelings for someone who will be leaving soon. I forgot those feelings for a reason. Secret smiles across a room, or worse, almost kisses—none of that.

"Finally, we have..." Ms. Willow refers to her papers. "The November town hall. We intend to petition the lawmakers for revised zoning laws, restrictions commensurate with hotels, and limits on nonresident investments for short-term rentals. This will be our last chance this year to appeal for rules to preserve long-term housing and reduce environmental strain. I think we can all agree that we want to maintain the character and livability of our community. A lot of you might travel this summer, but I'd love to get a couple folks working on this."

I sit up straighter and ignore how Max's attention skips in my direction. Homeshares evade the taxes that hotels pay, so they can naturally charge less. Not to mention, they make prices for locals skyrocket. When Ms. Willow says she wants some volunteers to draft the petition before fall's town hall, I see an opportunity to help The Mirage. She concludes the meeting, and I practically leap over to her.

"First person up here." She chuckles while writing my name down on her legal pad. "Color me surprised."

"It's not just about The Mirage." I pause as someone pats her on the shoulder and waves goodbye. "I'm concerned for Harlow. Sure, there's new business, but is there infrastructure for that business? And these listings have no character, no consideration for sustainability, especially with recent developments, so—"

"My dear, save the impassioned speech for the proposal." She trills a little laugh. "Just like your mom."

I stand taller at the comparison. Eco-friendliness has been integral to The Mirage's business model, and since taking over, I've invested in better insulation for guest rooms and LED lighting in common areas, and I switched us to bulk toiletries. I've also made sure to show up to these monthly meetings, just how my mom did, without fail. Ms. Willow's right—if Mom were here, she'd give those councilors a piece of her mind.

"I'd like to help." Dawn Liu sidles next to me, fresh-faced and eager, and I almost fall over. She documented her move from Portland to Harlow on her blog and YouTube channel. Dawn's now a go-to resource for events in town and local businesses, including hotels. She stayed at The Mirage once, and that didn't go well.

"Oh!" Ms. Willow scribbles Dawn's name down—with more enthusiasm than she did mine, I note. "A celebrity could really help."

She can't be serious.

"I can cover this on my site and all my socials."

"You two'll work wonderfully together." Ms. Willow rests a reassuring hand on my forearm. "I know you're not so big on public speaking."

I'm about to tell her it's fine—that I don't mind presenting in front of crowds if I have to, but Dawn talks over me. "Oh, yeah, no problem for me." She points to herself. "Theater kid."

"But you..." I pause when they both look at me, unsure how to encourage Ms. Willow to reconsider Dawn's participation. "I didn't know you were so passionate about the homeshares here."

"I'm looking at buying a new home. I won't bore you with the details," she says with a roll of her eyes, "but I'm totally priced out after only two years of being here, even after a profit on my old property. Plus, sustainability in tourism is a big thing these days, and travel is my beat."

My jaw tightens. All she wants is more views.

Ms. Willow jots down some notes and looks expectantly over my shoulder. "Will you be helping, too?"

"Oh, I'm the chaperone for that one." Max steps forward, pointing to Ava across the room and then to me. "And I came to support Daze here."

He gives Ms. Willow a dimpled smile. She extends her hand, which he shakes with a kind of suaveness I never saw in him growing up. I swear, her cheeks turn pink.

When Ms. Willow dashes over to say goodbye to someone, Dawn retrieves her cell phone from her cross-body shoulder bag. "We should probably exchange info, huh? Daisy or Daze?"

"Daisy."

"The..." She snaps her fingers a few times. "The Mirage, right?"

I inhale to the count of four, but the sting from her barely remembering the hotel remains. Dawn buries her nose in her phone, entering my contact information. Max nudges me, luring me out of my negative thoughts. He mouths, *You okay?* to which I loosen up and nod.

"We should go big here," Dawn says. "Interview business owners, and I can edit video footage. We'll blow their minds so they really see what regulations we're fighting for."

Interviews? Footage? The suggestions make me lightheaded. I propose something else. "We could email them instead."

"Unscripted is better. Best way to tug at heartstrings. Trust me. And a visual element would help." She turns to Max. "Don't you think?"

"Uh." His eyes widen, and he looks back and forth between us. "Visual is good."

"Exactly. Okay, gotta run. Let's meet for a brainstorm sesh soon!"

She prances toward the exit. Once Dawn is out of earshot, I give Max a playful smack on his upper arm. His muscles are startlingly firm. "Visual is good?"

"I'm an art curator. I'm a sucker for visuals." Max examines me with his head cocked to one side. "What's wrong?"

"Nothing. She—a while back, she left a mediocre review for The Mirage." I get closer to him, enjoying a whiff of that citrusy scent of his—is that cologne or something else?

"How mediocre?"

"Three stars," I hiss.

"The Mirage is a five-star experience, no questions asked."

"I *know.*"

The corner of Max's mouth quirks up, and he must think I'm such a country bumpkin.

"Sorry," I go on, grabbing my keys as I head toward the door. Max follows like he intends to walk me to my truck. "Small-town drama. How was your first-ever desert preservation meeting?"

"Exciting stuff."

"You don't need to tease me."

"I seriously thought there was going to be a fistfight at one point. Everyone's clearly very passionate about Harlow. You're volunteering and talking to lawmakers about changing your town for the better. It's cool to see people care and invest their time and energy into someplace they love."

As he talks, there's an earnestness about him. He's not being flippant or giving me a hard time—it's like he genuinely sees all the reasons I go to these meetings.

"These rentals really are awful," I say when we reach my truck. "People swoop in, buy property, and then rent it out without stepping foot here again. They skirt rules and regulations, and they outsource everything to the cheapest companies they can find. All they see out here is dollar signs."

"They can't compete with what you have."

"It's more than the hotel." I lean against the driver door. Max stands close enough that I have to crane my neck to look at him. "I want to protect this town, and these rentals suck the life out of it. No one will give a shit about this place if all that's here is a bunch of identical buildings for tourists."

"You think new legislation will turn things around?"

"I do."

I could fix the barn, run promotions, upgrade the mattresses, and put a fresh coat of paint on The Mirage. I could pull through this season. But we'll get a slow, painful kiss of death if Harlow collapses under the weight of these homeshares. So it doesn't matter whether I think new legislation will work—it has to.

Chapter Nine

Max, Now

I'm slammed by memories of sitting in this very room the second I step inside. The desks are newer and in a different configuration than the rows I remember. Paintings and sketches I don't recognize clutter the walls. And yet, entering this classroom, I feel the same as when I stepped foot in The Mirage last week. This place was a sanctuary. Here, I was me.

Some students notice me, and they scoot their chairs across the squeaky linoleum to face the front while gathering their art supplies. Others continue their shared conversations and laughter like I'm invisible. Summer school means a mix of overachievers on the path to graduate early, kids who flunked a class but want to graduate on time, and students looking for an arts credit to boost their college resume. No way will I let these teenagers eat me alive for the next three months. I am Max Weber, out-of-work curator of art. Hear me roar.

I straighten my posture and plaster on a smile with the express goal of winning every single one of them over before our hour and a half is up—regardless of why they're here, how much they enjoy art, or how talented they think they are.

"Hi everyone," I announce, which gets more of them to turn to the front. "I'm Max. Not Mr. Weber. Never Mr. Weber. Call me Max."

"You're the instructor?" a blonde girl in the front asks. Mercifully, the kids are required to wear name tags on the first day, and I squint at her rectangular sticker: Zoë.

"I am."

"What happened to Leslie?" she asks while adjusting her wire-frame glasses.

"Maternity leave," a boy named Xander in the middle of the room chimes in, his eyes on me but his hand bouncing over the page as he doodles.

"Man," someone in the back says. "Ms. Fairchild was the best."

Ignoring the mumbles of disappointment from some students, I snag a marker and write "Art as Self-Expression and Self-Exploration" on the whiteboard. "Here is the syllabus." I send a stack of papers down the rows for them to take one and pass along. "As you'll see, the first week—"

"Where are you from?"

"What sign are you? Also your moon and rising—"

"Can we eat in here?"

"Are you married?"

"Do you give extra credit? Ms. Fairchild always—"

"How old are you?"

The rapid-fire questions explode from all corners, and the moment I open my mouth to answer someone, three more people ask something else.

"Okay, whoa," I say over them. "Look, you don't have to do the thing where you raise your hand to talk, but what if we start with the syllabus, and then you can ask questions after?" The paper in my hands vibrates like a flag in a hurricane, so I set it down on the teacher's desk. There is no reason to be nervous. These are *kids*, and it's an easy gig. "And to answer your questions: Harlow, Pisces, but no clue about the other ones, no, no, maybe, and twenty-six."

A semi-content murmur passes through the group of fifteen students. Tough crowd.

"I'm a curator. Until recently, I worked in Dublin." All of their eyes are on me, and I clear my throat. "I've organized exhibitions around the world. My career focus is contemporary art on a global scale."

"Why would you leave Europe for this place?" Xander asks with a snort.

This kid is me twelve years ago. I want to say, *I know, right?* but I surprise myself by coming to Harlow's defense.

"There's actually a lot of art happening here." I echo what Eleanor told me at lunch the other week. Not that I buy it, but I have to make these kids believe that anything's possible. That's what my teachers did for me. "You know, when people want to get away from their lives and create something, they often come out here."

"Are you an artist too?" someone named Avery asks.

"My art is just for me." I sit on the desk, confident I've earned everyone's attention. "I curate."

"Why?" another person in the back asks.

"I like creating an experience. A story."

Sophomore year, I helped select pieces for on-campus shows at my university, and I not only liked it, but I was good at it too. All those years of training to be the most affable guy in the room gave me people skills, and all the geeking out on art meant I understood craft.

"Show us something you've done." Avery crosses their arms and leans back in the chair.

"Are you any good?" someone else asks.

"You're going to have to trust that the school hired me for a reason."

"Make something!" another kid taunts.

"Yeah!"

Conversations pop up again—agreement and giggles and gossip. As annoying as they are, I respect the tenacity. I'd probably be a little disappointed to have a group of students who didn't believe in questioning everything.

I lift my messenger bag of supplies from the chair onto the desk with a thud. These were backups for kids who might need them, but I guess I'm using them to prove something. "Medium?" I glance up to see fifteen faces who definitely didn't think I'd take them up on this challenge. "Don't be shy. You want to know what I can do, so let me show you. Medium?"

"Charcoal," Zoë blurts out.

"Great. What am I drawing?"

"Landscape," Avery says. "No, wait. Portrait."

I retrieve a pad of drawing paper and sit at the desk, some sticks of charcoal at the ready. "Someone set a timer for two minutes."

"That's it?"

"Believe it or not, I'm here to teach a class. So yeah, two minutes."

Someone says, "Aaand go," and a thrill courses through me like an electric shock. I don't have a subject or pose or anything in mind, which terrifies me—especially with a captive audience of teenagers—but the moment the willow charcoal hits the page, I tune the world out. My muscles work on their own, and every stroke lights up another part of my brain. Everything looks clearer, like I've replaced a light bulb in a room where I didn't know it had burned out. Drawing is meditation—heightened senses but inner calm. I reach a point of total relaxation, even though my hand continues to move as my fingers deftly smooth and blend.

The timer buzzes, snapping me back to my body and the space. Every student has gathered around my desk—some of them recording on their phones, others simply staring with slack jaws.

"Whoa," Xander whispers.

"You're, like, *really* good!"

Satisfied, I rub my hands together to get rid of some of the gritty crumbs and charcoal dust.

"Who is that?"

On the paper, a familiar face stares back. Freckles, long, wavy hair, and a coy gleam in her eyes.

"A friend of mine."

"She's pretty," Zoë says.

"Will you teach us how to do that?" Xander asks.

"Maybe." I admire the half-circle of them, each kid so energetic and eager. "If we can get the syllabus out of the way first."

We go through the lessons, and I detail my plans from Van Gogh to Frida Kahlo, plus a sprinkling of some of the most notable art movements. "On the final page," I say, "you'll find the grade breakdown. Your end-of-summer project is a portfolio, so as long as you keep up, you'll be well on your way to passing, and you'll have exactly what you need to apply to schools and art programs, or to get your work into an exhibit."

"Tons of those happening around here," Xander mutters under his breath.

"You have to have a portfolio if you want to submit your stuff anywhere," Zoë says, snapping at him.

"Don't you, uh…" I flip through the papers Eleanor gave me this morning. "Isn't there some kind of showcase?"

"They stopped doing those in the summer like two years ago. Now it's only for the fall and spring semesters."

"Okay. Well, then you'll have that locked down once the next semester starts."

Some shrugs, some nods. I get where they're coming from—the showcases are a big deal. Having to wait a few extra months until the fall semester one takes place must feel like an eternity for a sixteen-year-old. While most of the enthusiasm comes from supportive friends and parents, the event holds weight for students since art exhibits aren't a regular occurrence in Harlow.

And then something clicks.

If I want to guarantee I'm first in line for the job at Tate, then I know exactly what I need to do—and who I need to talk to.

When Daisy opens the door to her casita, her eyes have a glossy, pinkish haze that makes every muscle in my body stiffen. The eight years apart vanish, and on instinct, I step forward to wrap my arms around her and examine the sorrow in her face.

"What's wrong?"

"I'm fine," she says with a sniffle. "What's up?"

"You're not fine."

"What did you wanna ask me?"

"Hey." I can't think about anything, including what I came here to ask her, until she's okay. Seeing her upset guts me. "Talk to me. What happened?"

She folds into my embrace, and my lips brush her forehead, firing a shot of warmth through me.

"I'm a very good listener."

"I know."

After a beat, she slips out of my hold, and I fight the urge to wrench her back into me. Daisy welcomes me into the home I haven't stepped foot in since high school. She's updated some furniture, but much remains the same. I half expect her mom to poke her head out from the kitchen, and my throat tightens.

Daze has added knickknacks and framed photos scattered among colorful gemstones, and a golden glow from twinkle lights and vintage lamps illuminates the room. And the smell...it's something flowery but mysterious.

Without me asking, she hands me a mug of water. The cup has a drawing of Harlow on it and says *I'll never desert you.* Daisy gestures for me to sit on the couch and takes the mauve velvet lounger across the coffee table, crossing her long legs.

"What's going on?" I ask her.

"It's about Freddie."

As if she summoned him, her chunky cat—technically her mom's—stirs from his sleep and gnaws on his front paw.

"Hey. Remember me?" I run my hand down his back, which sets off a motor of purrs.

Daisy holds out a hand to Fred, which he ignores for attention from me instead. "Guess I'm back to second favorite."

"As long as you keep feeding him, you'll always be number one in his eyes." He nuzzles into my hand again. "He seems okay to me."

"The vet heard some irregular heartbeats. She couldn't tell me much more, but she referred me to a cardiologist. It could be bad."

"Your cat has a cardiologist?"

"I know." She rubs her temples. "He has his own team of specialists now."

"Maybe these are all precautionary measures."

"He's fifteen. Ten is senior for cats." Over the mandala design inked on her knee, she twirls a mug, which features a plump cactus and the words *FREE HUGS*. "My mom loved him so much. I'll lose something she cared for, if he—when he—" She sucks in a breath, gripping the bottom of her T-shirt to dab her eyes.

Freddie appears in countless memories at Daisy's house. He was always around, dozing on the windowsill or curled up on the couch. Just like how walking into this home without Daisy's mom feels off, I also can't picture it without him. I can only imagine what Daisy's going through.

"Hey." I circle the table and kneel next to her. Seeing her so broken up reminds me of how useless I was to Daisy since I left, especially these past couple years. Sporadic voicemails didn't give us this kind of closeness. I could kick myself for not listening to my gut when I got the news about her mom.

That scent hits my senses again, hard—floral masked by a sultry musk. She smells good, enticing. When I rest my hand on her shin, her skin is pure silk.

"How stupid." She sniffles into a tissue. "I'm upset over a cat."

"Freddie boy is not simply *a cat*. He's your guy. He's been there with you, through thick and thin."

"Sorry for the breakdown."

"Don't be."

"I doubt you texted me so you could watch me wipe snot into my shirt."

"That's actually exactly why I texted you."

"Stop," she says with a ghost of a smile. "None of that."

"What?"

"The Max Weber Charm."

"*Max Weber Charm*?" I say the words like I'm trying to taste them.

"Where you're all smiley and jokey and everybody likes you because you're this easygoing guy."

Daisy and I have different views on *charm*, evidently. I played the chameleon as a defense mechanism. Better to be liked by everyone than loved by only a few.

A knock sounds at the door, and I go to open it. Daisy probably wouldn't want to answer in her state; besides, I already know who's here.

I thank the delivery driver and present Daisy with a plastic bag of Thai food that bursts at the seams.

"Hidden Moon." She leaps out of the chair and peers into one of the take-out boxes, inhaling the steam. "Oh my god. Okay. You can stay. The Max Weber Charm can stay."

She goes to the kitchen sink and grabs two plates from the cupboard above. Daisy's lithe body moves like a dancer's, but she has enough muscle definition in her legs and shoulders that she could also kick your butt. She balances on one foot like a flamingo while refilling our mugs, and I envision my hand dragging up her shin, skating over the ink on her thighs, and landing on her peach-shaped ass.

"Dining room or coffee table?" she asks, snapping me back to reality. If I'm going to propose this grand plan, I can't feed into the tension that's built at the crotch of my pants.

"F-floor. Old times' sake."

Daisy rips the lid off the coconut soup and whispers a sweet thank you to me. "Not for the food. For being here." She pours the steaming liquid into her bowl. "Gwen's pregnant, so I feel silly going to her about this, considering she has so much other stuff happening. Stacey listens to me nonstop about everything related to The Mirage, so I don't want to bog her down with my personal life, too."

"You can talk to me anytime."

"What about you?" She bites into a spring roll and talks around it. "What did you want to discuss?"

She's deflecting, but I might have some news to put her in a better mood. Setting my plate down, I turn to her and rest an elbow on the seat of the couch. "What are you doing with the barn?"

"Storing your shit."

"Other than that. You mentioned renovations?"

Her chewing slows, and she peers at me. "Yeah."

"Expensive ones?"

"What are you getting at?"

"What if we did something this summer that paid for all of the repairs?"

"I'm not doing porn."

That's not what I had in mind, but it is now.

"I'm joking, Max," she says, nudging me. "You're turning red."

"I-I think we should go into business together."

"Again, not doing porn."

Great. Now I've got a semi. "Daze, seriously."

"Since when have you been interested in hospitality?"

"Not hospitality. You bring the hospitality, I bring the art. We combine our skills and plan something that people have never seen before here."

"An art show? Those happen here."

"Not an art show. Not even a gallery. I mean a whole *museum*."

"I can't turn my hotel into a museum."

"I'm not explaining this well." I take a breath and comb my hand through my hair. What seemed like a brilliant idea when I texted her now seems idiotic. Do I actually believe I can pull this off?

But if I want Tate to give me a second glance, this will do way more than the teaching gig.

"At my old job, I would create pop-up museums, and your barn is the perfect spot for one. Imagine this." I hold my hands up, palms open, painting a picture for her. "Renovations? Paid for. Reservations? Booked, back-to-back. You've got a space for art, and people from around the country—no, the world—drive—"

"The world?"

"That might be ambitious. But we're talking about lots of people coming here to Harlow. To The Mirage."

"What do renovations have to do with this?"

"We'd get investors. The money upfront could pay for renovations. We'd earn it back through the museum—not to mention all the reservations from having a must-see attraction on your property."

"That's cool." She sets her fork on her plate, and her lips pucker like she's chewing the idea over. "But these renovations are...they're not small things." Using her fingers, she counts off every change that she wants to finish before busy season picks back up in the fall. The bathroom stands out as the biggest project...until she mentions the termites.

At Impressions, I didn't deal with finances—I handled the artists, artwork, and the space. The renovations Daisy has on her list will rack up into the thousands, maybe even tens of thousands. But if there's one thing I know, it's that art lovers have deep pockets. And while doing this could capture the attention of someone at Tate, it absolutely will help Daisy, and that means more to me.

"What do you get out of this?" Her questioning eyes bore into me like needles. "Is this about your old job?"

"I need something new on my resume. There...there was some messy shit with my boss," I say more quietly. If I'm proposing a business endeavor, she deserves to know. My stomach clenches as I explain the disaster that was Impressions—the illegal dumping, the sexual assault claims—and I can barely meet her eyes. "I'm caught up in it, even though I didn't know about any of it. Even though I should have known."

"Damn." She nods her head, and I hate not knowing what she thinks of me right now. "That explains the No Google rule."

I don't need to tell her about the Tate job because that's not a definite thing. What is definite is I can't sit around and hope a teaching gig will do the trick.

"What I do next could define my career, and I think this could be it, Daze."

"It sounds incredible." She runs her finger along the edge of the coffee table where the polish has faded. "I can't, though. This is a whole new thing that sounds high risk. Right now, I'm in low-risk mode."

"But what I—"

"People come here to get away from it all. I can't have heaps of visitors driving here and interrupting them. Would they park on the side of the road? My lot can handle hotel guests, but not a museum, so I'd have tons of folks crossing the main street. It's an accident waiting to happen."

Within thirty seconds, she's poked holes in my genius plan.

"In some universe, this could be a really amazing idea," she says. "But a museum? That's a new thing to market. There'll be people to hire and infrastructure needed that I don't have."

"We'd figure it out." I swallow, my confidence on shaky ground. "If this is a tough season for you, then you shouldn't be going low risk."

"You would say that. You traveled around and set up these museums, and if something didn't pan out, it wasn't a big deal because you had this company, and they'd just contract you to do some other museum somewhere else. But me?" She puts a hand on her chest, the rings on her fingers glistening against the mood lighting. "I have one job, one place. It is my sole responsibility, and I can't risk losing it. I don't have anything 'next' after this. Nothing bigger and better to move on to."

All the hope and excitement drains out of me. I want to promise her that this would work, that it would be alright in the end, and that I would never, ever abandon her. But I can't make those promises because I don't know what I'm doing, and I already have one foot out the door.

We eat the rest of our Thai food in companionable silence. It doesn't taste as good as I remember.

Chapter Ten

Daisy, 14 Years Old

"This is..." Mom counted the guests in the lobby one by one, her pointer finger bouncing through the crowd. "Wow. It's everyone."

"Everyone?" I tempered my excitement, but the question came out more like a squeak. "I told you people'd be interested."

"Max is gonna be the belle of the ball," Dad said. "I'll get the car situated for our little caravan."

Mom and Dad kissed, and I had a good feeling about them this time. Dad had been home for months already, and they barely fought.

I toyed with the wildflowers I'd picked for Max—my tradition for any of his art events. He would receive an extra-large bunch this evening since it was his first high school showcase.

"This is a very sweet thing," my mom said, wrapping an arm around my shoulder and planting a kiss on my temple. "I'm glad you mentioned it."

I couldn't change his parents' minds, and neither could my mom. *Buncha damn fools*, she'd muttered after talking with them on the phone. I didn't understand why Max's mom and dad were so negative with him, especially when he was clearly not born to be a lawyer.

"Max is a good friend," Mom said.

"Yeah."

"Just a friend?"

"Mom."

I'd had crushes, but with Max, it was different. Max knew me better than anyone, and what we had was steadfast and reliable. Dating would turn all that reliability into dramatic fights and pain, like my parents. And even if what I felt for Max was a crush, I wouldn't complicate our friendship.

"Just checking," Mom said, hands lifted in resignation. "It wouldn't be the worst thing in the world, would it?"

"I'm with Will."

"Not Bradley?"

"That was like two weeks ago."

"Right. So, Will." My mom hip checked me. "What's he up to tonight?"

I faltered. Honestly, I hadn't asked Will about his plans. This night was for Max. Not that Max and Will couldn't hang out, but I liked keeping my romantic relationships and my friendship with Max separate. After all, boys would come and go. Max was my friend. He was forever.

Chapter Eleven

Daisy, Now

The door to the outhouse slams shut, and my dad's girlfriend, Oona, waves wildly at us, her fingers glistening with hand sanitizer. Despite her size, she possesses the stamina of a pack of huskies.

"Be nice, alright?" my dad mutters.

"I am."

"You know what I mean."

Guilt pricks me, because as they pulled into the dirt parking lot, I *was* disappointed she was joining our father-daughter sunrise hike. God, I could really use another one of those hugs from Max right now—burrowing into his arms yesterday was like wrapping up in my favorite blanket. His unflinching grip on me gave me the safety I craved, and his lips skating over my forehead...

The way he pressed his mouth to my skin was purely innocent, but the flashback makes my lower belly flare with heat.

"Ready?" Oona prances over, and honestly, no one should have this much energy this early. She slips binoculars over her neck and gives me a toothy smile. "Sorry to keep you waiting this morning. We wanted to squeeze in a meditation."

"Big meditation guy now, huh?" I ask my dad.

He makes a noncommittal *mmm* in reply and folds up a trail map. "I'm a bigger fan of the weekly massages we book. If you ever want a rec, Oona's got some good ones."

My mom and dad had been together since their school days, but Dad still found love effortlessly after she passed. My parents and Oona were part of a hiking club, and after Mom's car accident, Oona slipped into my dad's life in such a covert way that I didn't have the brain space to question it. One day she's bringing him a casserole, and the next we're out bowling and they're making lovey eyes at each other. I don't want him moping around forever, but seeing him with someone new pokes a bruise that won't go away.

We start down the trail, a fiery summer glow inching across the sky. I love the desert in these peaceful morning moments, the quiet ones before the world wakes up.

"Nice workout pants," Oona says, piercing the silence like a bubble popping. "Where'd you get them?"

"Thrift store." I examine them, searching for some kind of obvious logo. "I don't know which brand."

"They're very chic. How's the hotel?"

"Busy." As much as I find joy in keeping my mom's legacy alive, I'd enjoy some time not in work mode. My dad never involved himself with The Mirage, either, because it's the reason my mom dragged him out here, so I offer nothing more on the topic.

"How's...oh, who was that man you were dating? Alex?"

"We broke up. A while ago, actually."

Oona winces. "Sorry to hear that."

We fall into silence as Oona leads the way, and my dad thumps me from behind with his trekking pole. *Be nice.* I *am* nice to Oona; she just asks the wrong things.

"Um. I have a friend in town." I turn back to Dad. "Max."

"Who's Max?" Oona asks.

"Really?" His eyes light up with recognition. My dad and I never had deep conversations. No sex talk, no emotional stuff, nothing. My parents were living apart when I returned from Dublin, so there's a chance my mom never told him a thing. But that doesn't explain the flash of wariness that crosses my dad's face.

He turns to Oona. "Max was Daisy's best friend from when she was a kid."

"Oooh." Oona drags out the word and nods. "Are you two still close?"

"Kind of," I say. We reach the end of the trail and find a couple of boulders for a makeshift breakfast nook. Oona lays out blankets for padding while my dad sets out tea and fresh fruit. "We've hung out a few times, and there's this combo of knowing each other but also not, if that makes sense?"

Oona's head bobs up and down. I haven't had an honest conversation about Max's return to Harlow with anyone. Gwen has her own past with him, so discussing Max is as simple as a stroll through a minefield. Even my dad has his own preconceived notions. At least with Oona, she has an open mind.

"They were inseparable growing up," my dad says, reaching for the baguette on Oona's lap. "Always wondered why you two never went steady. You dated a bunch of stinkers back then."

"That's not kind, Richie," Oona says with a scowl.

"I'm sorry. But he obviously liked you, and at least in high school, he was a good kid."

"Just because he was a nice guy doesn't mean Daisy needed to date him."

"Thank you, Oona," I say, touched to see her stand up to my dad on my behalf.

"I thought you had a tiny crush on him."

Despite the morning chill, my body heats. I sometimes dared to consider something more with him—that moonlit dance, that transatlantic flight—but I always pulled myself together.

"We were, and are, just friends," I say. Friends do forehead kisses. Friends do lingering stares in barns.

"Hm," Oona says, buttering her bread. "Friendship is its own kind of love. And going from friends to lovers is difficult. All those feelings of kinship turn into something else. When your father said we should date, I needed to think about it. I wasn't sure if I was ready to lose him as a friend."

"Charmed you anyway." My dad smiles at her.

I divert my eyes from their locked hands and examine the sunrise instead. We finish breakfast and enjoy the sky transforming into a brilliant blue. Crisp and clear today. My dad whips out his map and inspects it.

"There's some abandoned mine carts off in that direction." He points. "Want to check them out?"

"I should get back. Not all of us can be retired like you two."

My dad clambers up and offers a hand to Oona. "Well, actually, we have something—"

"No, Pooks, let's wait," Oona says to him quietly. "Some other time."

"I'd rather tell Daisy now."

"Tell me what?" I ask.

My dad turns to his girlfriend, curling one arm around her shoulders as he beams at her. "Oona and I, we wanted to share some news with you."

The two of them look cheery, and a heavy pit forms in my stomach. The way she's looking at him. The way he's pulled her close. The nervous glances at each other and then at me. Hosting weddings at The Mirage means I know how freshly engaged couples act, and I can guess what he'll say before the words leave his mouth.

"Oona and I are getting married."

The announcement knocks the wind out of me. "Wow," I manage. I'm drowning on dry land, and I'm not faking anything very well because they've both crinkled their brows in concern.

Digging deep into my heart, I summon all the happiness I can and paint on a smile to try again. "Wow! That's...that's incredible."

"Really?" Oona's face stretches into a huge smile.

"Yes. Congratulations!" I throw my arms around her to buy me a few seconds. *Go away, tears. Go away.* She pulls back, but I hold on to her for a moment longer before embracing my dad. He seems so happy, and I wish his wonderful news didn't have a sharp edge to it.

The three of us hug once more, and I congratulate them again before hiking the path to my car. The tears I've been holding onto cascade down my cheeks once I reach the safety of my truck. I hate myself for crying over this. My dad deserves happiness, and Oona makes a good partner for him. But I miss my mom. A laugh bubbles up at the thought of calling her right now to tell her how everyone is moving on.

Everyone except me.

Gwen's pregnant. My dad's remarrying. Even Max, with our complicated friendship rekindling—he's had his life turned upside down, and he's in the process of righting it.

And me? If I keep doing the same thing I've been doing, the hotel will disappear. I won't have the casita—the place I grew up. No amount of missing her can save The Mirage. This may not be the career I envisioned for myself, but it's all I have. I'm the only one preserving her memory, and I can't lose something she loved so much without a fight.

I freshen up using the rearview mirror, swiping on lip gloss and redoing my ponytail. With the car in drive, the windows down to dry my eyes, and Sheryl Crow blasting through the speakers, I'm ready.

Big risks.

Driving past the hotel, I pull up to Max's parents' house and don't even turn off the truck once I park. I can't give myself a moment to reconsider.

After a few knocks, I wait. Nothing. I knock again, this time louder.

"Damn it," I mutter and spin on my heels. I pull out my phone to call him right as the front door opens. My eyes scan Max up and down, and my neck warms when I notice his bare chest. He's wearing plaid pajama bottoms and nothing else, with the long, lean lines of his arms and torso on full display. His hair is a twister of short curls. He leans to one side with an arm in the doorway as he towers over me.

"Hi," I say. "Hey."

"What's up?"

"Um." I rip my gaze from his taut stomach and the trail of hair that begins just below his belly button. "Did I wake you up?"

"At six in the morning? Absolutely."

"Sorry," I say, whipping around. "Text me, okay?"

A warm hand encircles my wrist, whirling me back almost directly into his half-naked body. I'm so close I could lick the curve of his biceps.

"Is it Freddie?" he asks, his brows furrowed.

"No, he's fine. I just...I wanted to tell you—let's do it." I give him one brisk nod. "The exhibit. The museum, I mean. At The Mirage."

"Really?" He crosses his arms—and does Max Weber have the most subtly defined pecs? For the briefest of moments, I picture myself nuzzled against his chest, running my hands up his smooth skin and around his neck.

I steer my thoughts back on track. Max said that this project would be a risk, but I sense the weight of a risk greater than that, too. We'll be working together, and I'll have to let him back into my life. I'll have to get used to him being here, and I'll have to be okay when he goes.

The museum won't just be for me, though. I'd be helping Max get back to what he should be doing, and that makes the leap worth it.

"What made you change your mind?"

I exhale and stand up straighter, taking in the zesty scent lingering on Max's skin. "I guess I needed some time to come around to it."

"When do you need those renovations done?"

"End of August?"

The whole summer. Just under three months for a lengthy list of repairs and a museum.

His gaze lingers on me, his expression unreadable, like he's not yet ready to agree. My stomach flip-flops because maybe he's changed his mind. Maybe the timeline is too rushed. But then the corners of his eyes crinkle, and that cheeky smile on his lips makes me feel like I swallowed a butterfly.

"Alright, Daze. I'm in."

Chapter Twelve

Max, Now

In the blinding afternoon sun, The Mirage is exactly like the image burned in my memory. Muted colors on the plain exterior, so it seems to grow out of the earth itself. Shaded patios with dangling hammock chairs. A haven in the desert heat.

Daisy watches with sad eyes as the site contractor's van bounces down the uneven driveway and out of sight. "He said we'd need to remove everything," she mutters, studying the paper rattling in her grip.

"That's a suggestion. We don't have to go full concrete for the parking area."

"We'd be removing a lot of plant life, regardless." Daisy gnaws on a thumbnail. Her nervous habit hasn't changed, and she's already chewed three others down to the quick. During the whole meeting, she dug in her heels on every single thing—where the lot entrance should start, how wide to make it, and how much space we need. At this rate, the pop-up will happen a decade from now.

"Look, we have to remove some plants, otherwise it'll be a game of cactus minesweeper out there. We don't want guests getting hurt." I grasp for a middle ground to move our plan forward, and to salvage Daisy's poor fingernails. "What did you think about leaving some brush in the center and using the large cacti as a natural curb stop?"

"He said we'd still have to clear from here to here." She shows the space with wide arms and shakes her head for the billionth time today. "That's too much disruption."

"What about replanting?" I ask, holding back a gritty exhale as we walk to the casita. "Businesses do that to keep operations eco-friendly."

"Maybe." Daisy examines the paper and holds it up to me. "Did you see this number?"

The funding has me on shaky legs too, though I wouldn't tell her that. I never had to be the one to make the financial part happen, so I've got long nights of research ahead of me.

"Focus on the vision right now," I say, "not the money."

"The money is the only thing I'm focusing on. We're barely forty-eight hours in and we're dealing with more than I spend on land maintenance in a year."

I stop Daisy, putting one hand on each of her shoulders to ground her, and the honey-toned flecks in her eyes catch the sunlight. "It's always like this at the start. With every museum I've ever worked on, the beginning is the toughest, the most stressful. All the expenses roll in, and you have this moment where you doubt yourself."

She inserts the corner of her ring finger between her teeth, and I pull on her wrist to stop her.

"You're going to run out of fingers."

"Maybe this isn't worth the trouble," she whispers, avoiding eye contact.

My body tenses with worry. This place owns a part of Daisy's heart, and she has every right to want to protect it. But if she backs out, then we're left with a nice idea, all of the same problems, and nothing more.

"Remember what we're working toward." I can figure out the budget, but the big picture will have more sway. "Reservations booked for weeks, even longer. We'll be in the news. You'll have a gorgeous, renovated barn for weddings. The Mirage might look a little different from when you were a kid, and it'll be different than when you took it over from your mom. But it'll be something that would make her proud." I meet her eyes again and lose my train of thought momentarily. "But it...it's gonna be worth it."

"You think?"

"Absolutely."

Daisy bites her lower lip. After a beat, she tucks the quote from the contractor into her back pocket and continues down the gravelly path. "What if we ditch the bathroom add-on?"

"We need bathrooms."

"When we've had weddings in the past, the couples rented porta-potties for the event. My mom found this company that has fancy ones."

"Fancy?"

"Yeah, they're nice. Wash stations and everything."

"The whole point of this is to get the barn in the best condition possible." Although we can't rule anything out, the suggestion primarily cuts corners. "And renting those will add up."

She *hmms* in agreement and pauses. "You can still back out, you know. I'd understand."

"No." I shake my head because I need this pop-up as much as she does. "I wouldn't do that."

"This isn't the ideal location you thought it would be."

"It is exactly what I want. You're being cautious, and there's nothing wrong with that."

"I can't envision this the way you can."

Looking at Daisy, I'm eighteen again and ready to leap at any opportunity to make her happy. I want to chase away the storm on her face and bring out the sunshine of her smile. All of our work could pay off with the pop-up, and I can picture the end goal—I just don't know how to help her see it, too.

She leads me into the casita, and the air conditioning welcomes me like an ice bath. I swipe the sweat collecting on my forehead, and Daisy places a cool glass of lemonade in my hands.

"You used to love hot days like this," she says, plopping down on a stool across the kitchen island.

"These temps are kicking my ass."

"It's only nine-thirty in the morning."

I chug half of my drink in one go, and the cooling effect on my insides prompts a satisfied groan. "Fuck, that's good."

Daisy's cheeks look red from the sun, and she busies herself with something on her laptop. "So how are we paying for these renos?"

"You said no porn, but…"

She keeps her eyes on the computer, the left side of her mouth twitching.

"Donors or investors were my first thought," I say with a chuckle, studying a bead of sweat sliding down her chest. "People who will put their money into the project simply for the love of it."

"Like folks from the community? Local businesses?"

Eyes up. "Exactly."

"Sal's?"

"That's a good start. The Rotary Club, coffee shops, maybe? Any amount helps."

She nods, wordless but clearly paying attention and willing—at least I hope—to follow my lead. We create a list of places and people in Harlow to contact, on top of resources from my network, like Eleanor.

"We could…" I hesitate, then throw out my next suggestion with a bitter scoff. "I could ask Judy and Bill."

"They could donate all that money they're saving on the storage unit," Daisy says, which causes a laugh to burst from me.

"I..." I run a hand through my hair. "We know they have the money."

"You're not actually considering them?"

"Maybe? I'd like to succeed without their help."

Her eyes go soft. "Of course."

"They'd never agree, anyway."

"Probably not for you," she says, flashing a winning smile. "But for me?"

"Wow." The best way to deal with my parents' attitudes is jokes and sarcasm, and Daisy knows this. "Nice."

She giggles, and the sound flickers inside me.

"You...you don't actually think they'd funnel money into some artistic endeavor of mine, do you?"

"If this ends up becoming as popular as you think, then maybe." She sinks lower into her seat and speaks her next words with care. "I completely understand wanting to do this without them. But if you really wanna show 'em, this could be a great way to do it, right?"

Daisy knows that my parents have never seen my dreams as equally valuable as passing the bar exam. Imagining them walking into the barn, their jaws slack in awe, fills me with a hunger I didn't even know I had. How would I feel proving them wrong? And if the pop-up's a total disaster, then could they be any more disappointed in me, anyway?

"I'll think about it." I stare at the list, wishing she were wrong. "Last resort, though. Who else have we got? What about Sunridge?"

"I thought we were keeping this local."

"The town's not even an hour away. Plenty of people will come up for the exhibit."

Sunridge is Harlow's fashionable older sibling. People venture to Harlow for nature, the park, and simple desert living; they head to Sunridge to spend cash. It's a small, quirky city for a flashy trip full of expensive restaurants and extravagant bars.

Daisy bends down and scratches at her calf, her cropped shirt rising to reveal ink I don't remember on her ribcage. I resist the urge to lift the fabric up and peek.

"So, art galleries?" she asks.

"Anything. Stores, restaurants. Obviously, having a personal connection to you helps. But whatever you've got, we can work with it."

"I'll reach out to some folks and see what they say."

"No, we're brainstorming." I tap my pen on the paper. "Give me names so I can research."

"Let me handle stuff in Sunridge." She pours herself more lemonade, even though her glass is almost full. She's not telling me something.

"Do you know any people down there?"

Daisy avoids eye contact and does a mix between a shrug and a shake of her head.

"If you have suggestions, you need to tell me, Daze. The more I can learn about them, the better I can tailor our proposal."

"Fine," she says after a moment. "I might know someone who could help us."

The chef. He can't be all that bad if she remained on good terms with him. While I'd love it if she didn't bound back into a relationship with him—we need to focus on the pop-up—it's not my business if she has lingering feelings.

I can still dislike him, though, for hurting Daisy. She didn't tell me explicitly what happened between them, but she's been fidgety all afternoon, and I'd guess it's because he broke her heart.

"I look okay?" Daisy finger-combs her hair. She wears a long, flowy dress that's strappy on the top, showing off her strong shoulders dotted with constellations of freckles. To someone passing by, we could be going on a date.

"You look more than okay." I clear my throat.

She checks herself out one more time in the restaurant window's reflection, and my gaze skims over the smooth curves of her cleavage. The cut of her dress goes so low I catch the start of a sternum tattoo, and I flick my eyes away before she catches me staring.

"This guy will regret things ever ended with you."

Her steps falter. "But not enough that he won't throw money at us?"

"Precisely."

The restaurant buzzes with trendy couples and affluent families. My vision adjusts to the dim, romantic lighting while relaxed electronic beats pump in the background. Despite the bustle, the atmosphere remains calm. With the ample space between tables and gold accents shimmering against gray concrete furniture, I immediately know Daisy's instincts were spot-on. This is the type of establishment any of my art acquaintances would love, so we're in the right place.

The host asks Daisy if we can meet Mr. Chef in the kitchen, since the night ended up unexpectedly busy. The request seems odd to me, but Daisy leads me to the back of the house like she knows the way by heart. I follow her, mesmerized by the moth tattoo on her back. Its wings flex with her every movement, and below it, the slinky material of the dress waterfalls down her backside.

Walking through the swinging doors pulls me out of my trance. A gust of warmth knocks into me as I take in the frantic scene. Pans sizzle, someone shouts a string of numbers, and plates clink against a stainless-steel work surface.

To prepare for tonight, I spent the day researching everything I could about Alex—every news piece, blog, and social media post. He's held positions in restaurants since he legally could, studied in France, and worked his way up from a line cook here in Southern California. The guy's talented—now with five restaurants in the region. A tinge of jealousy strikes when I consider my recent career setbacks. He seems to have it so much more together.

I recognize Alex from a photo. He uses tweezers to situate some greens on top of a scoop of ice cream with the precision of an open-heart surgeon. Once the wiry herb has found its rightful place, Alex's eyes shoot right to Daisy. "My Daisy Flower," he says, grinning as if it's the cleverest nickname in the world.

Alex marches toward Daisy and wraps her in a bear hug. "Missed you. Guess this was worth the drive, huh?"

Her mouth falls open in shock.

"Aw, I'm only teasing you." He play-pushes her shoulder. "Bad joke. And you," he says, turning to me. "You're Max."

"Nice to—" I hold out my hand, which he crushes with a tight embrace.

"Pleasure's mine, my man. Daisy told me all about you."

"Oh?" I manage, peering over at her. "Like what?"

"Everything. And can I say, it's an honor."

He releases his grip, and I would love to ask him what *everything* means—and why Daisy never told me *anything* about him.

"Chef," a young woman approaches, a bowl of soup in one hand, a small tasting spoon in the other. "I think I added too much salt."

Alex transforms into Gordon Ramsay in an instant. He dips the utensil into the yellow liquid, tries it, and smacks his lips. The woman observes him, her hands clenched as she awaits his response.

"A little," he says. "Vinegar, a fourth of a teaspoon at a time." He turns back to us. "Sorry about tonight. I got some outstanding produce at the farmers' market this morning, so I wanted to push out some new seasonal dishes."

"It's fine," Daisy says, smiling too big. "Did you, uh, read over our email?"

"Yeah, a museum. Great idea."

Daisy tips her chin at me. "It was all Max."

"Genius." He puts a hand on my shoulder and squeezes it like a lemon. I wish I could wriggle out of his grip. "Unfortunately, we can't do any more donations this quarter."

Daisy's shoulders sink, and I curb my disappointment. We came out this way, and Daisy's gotten all stressed, only for him to turn us down in two minutes flat.

"Chef." A different, equally frazzled member of the kitchen staff approaches Alex. "We're low on the special. Should we hold it in case the level three reservation at eight wants it?"

"Hold it," he says with a curt nod.

"Hold the peach and burrata," they announce to the room.

"We'll get out of your hair," I say, grabbing Daisy by the elbow.

"No, I love the idea." He grabs both our shoulders so we're huddled up like teammates. "We can't make a donation, but what about hosting a fundraiser?"

"That's..." Daisy pauses, and I half shrug, half nod, mostly because I'm an idiot for not having suggested that.

"We'd host," Alex says, "provide food, drinks. You could run a silent auction. We did that last week for the local library."

"Would that work?" Daisy looks at me, her gaze steady and trusting. My chest expands, knowing how much she values my input and experience, and I don't want to let her down.

And damn it, a fundraiser *is* a brilliant idea. I'd been so focused on donations that I hadn't thought of it.

"Sounds great," I say. "It'll be a big help."

"Chef," says yet another kitchen worker.

"Gimme a sec," Alex replies, his finger in the air. "So," he says to us, "our calendar's full until mid-August, but we have a few spots right before summer ends."

"It's close," I admit. "But we could work with that." For a free venue, food, and drinks, we'll have to.

He tells me to shoot him an email, shakes my hand, and draws Daisy in for another too-long hug. When we finally get in the car, I adjust the mirrors three times and pick some music for the ride back. The single-lane highway stretches into the night as the glow of the city behind us dims.

"Let me guess," Daisy says, slicing through the silence. "You didn't like him."

"I did." My pitch climbs half an octave, and even I hear the overcompensating. I don't know what to make of him, and I clocked how Daisy's entire demeanor changed around him. She's ordinarily confident and brazen, not shy.

"Everyone in the area knows him. There are very few people here who haven't been to one of his restaurants." She sighs and tucks a leg underneath her in the passenger seat. "And, unlike me, Alex is amazing at running a business."

"What are you talking about?" I refuse to let her fall into a pit of self-deprecation. "You're amazing at running a business."

"You're biased."

"But I'm right."

She shifts her weight. Despite the dark, I catch the sheen of her thighs where her dress has ridden up. I imagine running my palm along her leg and sinking my fingers into her skin with a gentle squeeze.

"My accountant would disagree." She lets out a breathy laugh.

"How The Mirage does financially isn't a measure of its worth, or yours. It's perfect." I swallow and lighten up on my steering-wheel death grip. Daisy doesn't give herself enough credit. "I'm not doubting his restaurateur genius. He's successful, and you were right to suggest him. It just...I honestly don't get how a guy like him would ever break up with you. I don't care how many restaurants he has or how much money he makes," I grumble, worked up over the evening. "He didn't even bother to sit down and have a proper chat with us."

"Well, so, you and I never—I didn't talk about relationship stuff on our calls, but Alex didn't break up with me. I broke up with him."

I assumed he had called things off because she'd been on edge all day, but my view of everything shifts. She wasn't begging some douchebag who'd dumped her because she was harboring feelings—she was swallowing her pride for the sake of my crazy idea.

"That...shit, that's awkward."

"We were both busy. Half the time we saw each other, one or the other of us was squeezing in work, just like tonight. And the distance...the drive's not that bad, but whenever we were together, I felt far away from him. I told him I didn't feel like it was worth continuing to drive forty minutes to see each other during the week."

"Brutal." I catch her eyes in one of the streetlights we pass.

"Yeah," she says, a laugh slipping out of her. "But better than you having to ask your parents, right?" She smiles as if she's happy with her choice, and guilt weighs heavily on my chest. She didn't go to Alex tonight for the pop-up—she went for me.

"I'll call them tomorrow. I don't think they'll care, but I could—"

"What?" Confusion flashes on her face. "No. Your mom and dad...your relationship with them is fucked up. I need you to at least stick around a few months and see this through, but they'd probably drive you crazy enough to want to leave."

"You're saying you want me to stay?" I grin, but my heart pounds against my ribcage—because where did that question come from?

And more than that: what if she says *yes*?

"I don't want you to hate it here," she replies, not exactly answering me. "You should enjoy your time back in Harlow."

We're doing this until the end of summer, and then that job at Tate might open up in the fall. Daisy is just being gracious and making the next couple of months more pleasant.

"Well, thank you," I say as I turn into the rutted driveway to the casita. "I'll make sure to thank Alex, too. He was cool."

She hums in agreement. "We met in a grief support group. I wasn't exactly the most fun person for a while, and even though he'd lost his best friend, he was there for me. He's a good guy."

My throat tightens. *I* wanted to be there for her. Daisy had mentioned her counseling and talked about her grief with me, but she said she couldn't handle me flying out for the funeral—probably with all the people and chaos. As much as that crushed me, at least we started talking again, even if it was only through recorded messages. They made me feel closer to her, but I'm stupid for thinking they were enough. She needed someone, and I should have come back sooner.

I park and stare at her over the center console, memorizing her in the moonlight. Daisy's pupils trace an invisible line from my cheeks to my nose and my lips—until a pair of headlights trails across the windshield, snapping us out of the moment. She exits the car, tossing a "Good night, Max," over her shoulder without looking back. I whisper my own good night to her, or maybe just to myself.

Chapter Thirteen

Daisy, Now

Current Coffee's patio has cream-colored metal tables and chairs, which look absolutely darling but lack comfort. Perfect. I'd like to keep this meeting with Dawn about the proposal as short as possible.

She waves me over to a table, holding her phone in her other hand. Dawn's filming her coffee-filled kraft paper cup with the café's logo on the side.

I lift my fingers in a wave.

"Oh, you can talk," Dawn says. "I'm not recording audio, just B-roll."

"Cool." I have no idea what that is. "Sorry I'm late," I say over the moody dream pop playing on the speakers.

"It's all good. Wasn't sure how you like your coffee."

She tilts her head toward a cup resting on the railing and out of the shot. Dawn won't win me over that easily, but I can't waste a perfectly good coffee.

"I drink it black," I say. "As black as possible."

"Oooh, my kinda gal."

I take a sip and can practically feel my body come to life, cell by cell. "That's good."

"This place opened less than a year ago, but it quickly became one of my faves."

I know this already because I have Dawn's blog bookmarked to hate-read her posts. She has a way of taking her audience along on the journey with her, and I secretly enjoy the armchair travel every week. She's maddeningly good at the influencer thing, even if she has impossible standards for hotels.

"Good coffee, good vibes, and good Wi-Fi," Dawn says. "I'd rather be in my home office, but...well, this is what I'm working with."

"They sell their beans here."

"Oh, no, I mean with the divorce and everything. Sorry, I sort of assume everyone knows."

"Shit, I—" I forgot about that update on her site, and sweat drips down my calves in the dry June heat. Dawn may not top my list of favorite people, but I wouldn't wish anything bad on her. "I'm sorry."

"Yeah, it's a nightmare. The fucker wants to move to LA with his new boyfriend, but he doesn't want *me* to have our house. So for now, neither of us gets it, and I'm couch surfing with a friend who owns an angular mid-century modern sofa made of bricks." Dawn grips her beverage with both hands and leans over the table toward me, like we're two close girlfriends catching up. "Word of advice?" Her voice deepens. "Whoever you date, whoever you marry, whoever you fuck, make sure they adore you."

My mind flashes, not to my ex-boyfriends, and not to Alex—who texted me only last night to say that he missed me. Instead, Max jumps to the forefront of my thoughts, like he always seems to lately. How he's willing to beg his parents for money for this project, or how he cupped my face when he found me crying about Freddie...I'm clearly still adjusting to him being a regular presence in my life again.

"Cherry on top," Dawn goes on, "I have to hire a new designer because my ex was the one behind my site. We were in the process of launching T-shirts and everything."

The sheer absurdity of her comment makes me laugh, and Dawn's face scrunches in confusion.

"Sorry, it's...your divorce seems hellish, but you're more worried about a clothing line."

"They were really nice shirts. I had hats planned, too." The corner of her mouth tilts up. "Anyway, what else am I supposed to do? Wallow over the fucker?"

This time, we both burst into laughter. I suppose Dawn is more fun than I gave her credit for. She could let her divorce destroy her, but she's here instead, joking with me and powering through her pain. Discovering that the world keeps spinning even when your own world stops—I know what that's like.

"Actually, I—" Overcome with compassion for her, I blurt out the words without thinking. "I have a guest room in my casita. Small, nothing fancy, pull-out couch situation."

"Oh." Dawn's eyebrows jump to her hairline.

"When my mom died, people were incredibly kind to me," I explain. Dawn and I aren't exactly on a stay-at-each-other's-places level of familiarity, but she could clearly use the help. "Kindness didn't change that life was shit, but I won't forget the generosity."

I remember very little from those first few days. It wasn't until someone ordered delivery for me, and my neighbors stopped by weekly with casseroles, that I realized I was barely eating. But I couldn't stay sad. There was too much to do, so rather than sit around and dwell on her death, I focused on what could keep her alive.

"Sorry about your mom. She sounded like quite a lady."

"She was." I nod with a tight smile.

"And I'll stay at my friend's place, but I do appreciate the offer. I'm surprised, though. You never seemed to like me."

"I-I like you perfectly fine," I reply, too brightly.

Her mouth falls into a thin line. Damn, this woman's good at reading people. She and Gwen can never team up. I would have no secrets.

"How close were you to begging Ms. Willow to remove me from this project?"

"I..." There's no point in making up excuses. Something happens when your personal life falls apart the way Dawn's did, and the way mine did two years ago—you gain X-ray vision to see through people's bullshit. "Okay, I *was* kind of hoping I might get paired with someone else."

Dawn snorts. "No, you were hoping no one else would volunteer so you could do this alone."

I open my mouth, at a loss for words. That *would* have been ideal.

"I'm a woman of color. I'm used to people shooting me looks and not giving me a chance. If we're working on this, I don't need you to like me, but you do need to respect me."

"I do," I say, shaken by her bold approach.

"So what's the deal?"

"You..." I lower my voice, somewhat aware of how childish I am to bring up a couple-years-old article. "You slandered my hotel in a review."

"The Mirage is cute." She looks genuinely confused. "What's there to slander?"

"*Slander* might be exaggerating. But you gave my hotel a three-star review."

"Three is good."

"Not great, and The Mirage *is* great." I grit my teeth, my anger over the whole situation returning. "You stayed with us when we were in transition. My mom had died, I was taking over, and—"

"Oh, fuck."

"For a small business, three stars hurts. The first thing that shows up in Google is that review."

"Seriously?" She whips out her cell phone and taps the screen with rapid-moving fingers. "Damn, he did a great job with my SEO."

"People see that before the link to my site."

Dawn's expression shrinks when she catches my eyes. "I'm really sorry, Daisy." She shakes her head and leans toward me. "I didn't realize...and honestly, I wrote that when I was starting out on my own. After years in journalism, I wanted everyone to take me seriously as I got the blog going. Guess I kind of took it out on The Mirage." She continues scrolling on her phone. "Geez. I called it 'standard'? This is nothing like how I review now."

"I know." I don't need to tell her I visit her site multiple times a week.

"Like, I'm honest with my readers. But The Mirage is adorable."

"Then why not include it in roundups or something?"

"Because I thought you hated me. Why would I promote your business?"

"Oh, my god." I can't help but laugh. "We've been disliking each other for years for basically no reason."

"Well, not no reason. That review sucks. I'll take it down. No, wait—I'll revise it. I'll book a room at The Mirage and update the page."

"You don't need to do that."

"I update posts all the time when I go to a place more than once. Aren't you doing some kind of event?"

My brain does a cartwheel at the prospect of a revised review. I clear my throat and give her the spiel, as best as I can.

"My friend, he's a curator, and we're making a museum together. Temporary, but with all kinds of popular artists. It's—Max explains it better than I do."

"Wait, is he that hottie with the dark curly hair who was following you around at the sustainability meeting?"

"He's…" I chuckle, taken aback by the *hottie* comment. In high school, I wouldn't have called him that, but we're not in high school anymore. I'd be lying if I said he wasn't good-looking.

"Sure, that's him," I say. "He's a friend."

"He's not my type, but damn, girl. If I had a friend with a penis who looked at me the way he looked at you, I'd be having a lot more fun post-separation."

I don't want to think about Max's penis right now. Or ever. Or just not now. Because that thought unearths more thoughts, like how big he might be. How it would feel to wrap my hand around his length. What he'd look like, erect and pressed on top of me. The sounds he makes when—

"Daisy?"

"Y-yeah?"

"I was saying, you deserve to have fun, too." She waggles her brows, which makes me smile.

"He's a friend," I say again, a reminder to both her and me. "Anyway, he knows artists all over the world, so it'll be a great lineup."

Dawn looks like she wants to push the topic further, but resigns herself with another sip of coffee. "And local artists, right?"

I scramble for a response. Max's spreadsheet with prospective artists listed everyone's locations, but I didn't notice Harlow on there.

"This is such an artsy city," Dawn says. "It'd be a shame to airdrop a bunch of outside work like stuff doesn't happen here, too."

Dawn's right—it would be cool to see a mix of local and international art. But Max seems so organized and in charge, I don't know if I want to question anything. He's done this hundreds of times before.

"And let me know what dates to book for my stay," Dawn says. "We gotta bump up that three-star review."

I could leap across the table and kiss her on both cheeks, but I stick to squeaking out a "Thank you."

"Of course. That's what community is for. Now let's get to work, shall we?"

Ava opens the door and tackles me with a hug, her hair blocking my vision as she squeezes me like a python.

"You're gonna crush Daze," Max calls from behind her.

Ava releases me, leading me by the hand to show me the new layout of her room. I almost stop in my tracks when I catch Max in the hallway, a towel slung low around his hips. He runs another towel through his hair, the cords of his muscles pulsing with each movement.

"Sorry," I say, not sure what I'm apologizing for. "Didn't think to text back."

"It's fine." He wears an easy smile. "Just give me a minute."

Max messaged during my meeting with Dawn that he had something important to show me, so I stopped by on my way back to The Mirage. I hadn't imagined I'd see Max wet and half-naked when I got here. He has two delicious lines on his abdomen that make a V formation, and a drop of water glides across his skin. Warmth inches down my torso along with something like longing.

I'm only noticing him like this because it's been a while since I've had sex. A little solo session at home with my vibrator, and I'll get over whatever attraction I think I have.

Max saunters to his room, and *Hello, gorgeous back muscles.* The view of his sculpted shoulder blades and the contours of his back leaves me speechless.

Once Ava's given me a full tour and I've gotten my mind off of Max's body in that towel, I knock on his bedroom door. "Decent?"

Max greets me and gestures for me to come in. "Make yourself comfortable, if you can."

Growing up, we hung out at Max's house more since his parents each earned way more than my mom, meaning a cooler home and better snacks. But his room looks completely different now. Rather than an unmade bed, cluttered desk, and clothes strewn on the floor, he has an indoor bike and treadmill. A twin-sized air mattress rests in the corner, and he must literally live out of that red suitcase by the weight rack. Despite all the workout gear, he keeps the space tidier than his teenage bedroom.

He closes the door, and that's new. His parents had a strict open-door policy, but we're not eighteen anymore.

"You don't have a nightstand in here or anything," I say, appalled that his mom and dad have barely made room for him.

"No nightstand needed. The gym rat vibes aren't really me, but I'm comfortable enough."

"You sure?"

"Absolutely." He gestures to the mattress, and when I sit down, I sink so deep that my butt touches the ground.

"I think this has a hole."

"It's not—" He waves his hand at the floor. "I haven't refilled it in a few days. Here." He sits next to me, boosting me off the ground, though not much. "See? It's actually really comfortable."

I press the mattress with an open palm, not fully convinced there's no leak.

"And I can go straight from sleeping to a StairMaster with minimal effort, which is all I've ever wanted." The corner of his mouth lifts, and that damn dimple sends a shock from my head to my toes. "No one can claim that Judy and Bill Weber are ones for sentimentality. Guess that's what I get for being gone so long."

Max scours the contents of his messenger bag, and for a split second, he is Max from when we were young—an adorable, art-obsessed kid who cared too much about what other people thought, even though he'd deny it. His years of joking that he's a disappointment to his parents have clearly worn on his self-esteem.

Max hands me one of those massive folders he used to carry around at school. Carefully, I pull out the thick pieces of paper painted with a gorgeous pastel color palette of light pink and dusty brown and sage green. It's a building—a hotel. *My* hotel.

I flip through the five paintings in speechless awe, my mouth gaping. The Mirage at sunset, people mingling with wine glasses in hand, and cars in the parking lot, with cacti throughout. Another shows the inside of the barn, busy with guests having imaginary conversations and pointing at the art. This version of The Mirage is one I would never have imagined.

"You seemed hesitant to go through with some suggestions from the contractor," Max says. "I thought I could paint you a picture instead. Literally."

I let out a wet laugh, my eyesight blurring.

"Daze, this is it." He leans closer, and the pressure from the air mattress pushes our knees together. "This is what we're working toward. This vision might feel far away, but it's possible, and it will be special."

I sniffle and cozy up to the warmth of Max. This is the sweetest, most thoughtful thing he could have done. I'm weepy over these gorgeous paintings of The Mirage, the fact that my mother will never see her hotel like this, and how incredibly talented the man next to me is. How he would spend his talents on *me* and something I love so much. And how, even after years apart, Max still understands exactly what I need.

"Freddie's in there." He points to the black-and-white cat in the lower left corner of one image, and I laugh.

"These are fantastic."

He sets his hand on the mattress behind me, and we feel impossibly close. "I just want you to see what I see."

Max once told me that art is noticing, and the way Max notices The Mirage makes my hotel seem like the most beautiful place on earth.

"Can we put these in the exhibit?"

"We can do whatever you want, Daisy."

When I look up and find our faces inches apart, all I want is to kiss him. Max has every right to be frustrated with me for resisting renovations, but rather than pointing out how I'm holding us back, he met me where I am. He's the Max I've always known—kind and devoted, creative and driven—but I can't ignore the stronger pull between us. Not again.

I don't give myself time to second-guess the desire, leaning forward and pressing my lips against his. Everything goes quiet, like the desert at dawn. His mouth is soft and safe, and although we've never kissed before, I feel like we've done this a billion times. Like we've lived a hundred lifetimes and always ended up here.

One of Max's hands trails up to my jaw, and I could weep all over again at how gentle he is. I press into him more, exploring the newfound closeness, and a jolt of electricity courses through me. With his arm supporting my side, I swing one leg across, and it bounces against the air bed. I straddle him, his hardness pressing against me, and we both groan. I can't recall the last time I made out with someone like this, and I don't remember it ever being so good. My fingers in his hair, his hand around my waist, and my hips slipping further into his lap as we push and pull against each other.

Max twirls me onto the mattress, which definitely has a hole because my entire back is on the ground. My foot hits the weight rack as Max latches onto my neck. The sensation is like the rev of a motorcycle in my veins, and it comes to an abrupt stop when his sister yells from downstairs.

"Hey Max, can you drive me to the library?" Her voice causes us both to freeze in place. "Maaaaax?"

He pauses, groans, then turns his head to the door. "Sure, just...hang on."

His mouth on my neck again knocks the breath out of me, and I have to laugh at the absurdity of the situation.

"What's so funny?" he mumbles.

"This is ridiculous."

Max pulls back and searches my face. "What?"

"Just like...this is crazy, right? We're in our twenties, and we're here." I gesture to the room around us—the bike and rower on either side, and the droopy mattress we're humping on. "Your little sister could walk in at any minute."

"So..." Max props up onto an elbow. His hardness digs into me, and I have to restrain myself from grinding into him. "Is it so crazy, kissing me?"

"No. I mean, a little, maybe."

"You know—*you* kissed *me*."

"You kissed me back."

"Because you kissed me first."

"I—" I scooch out from under him and sit up. "Was that not okay?"

"Daze, I..." His voice gets quieter, and he stands. "You have to have known how I felt about you in high school."

He levels me with a stare, and my heartbeat picks up. I'd suspected back then, and my own attraction simmered even deeper below the surface. But he never made a move. Never initiated. And that didn't bother me for the longest time because I thought I should keep our friendship free from the complications of romance.

"Sometimes," I admit quietly, "I thought maybe there was a crush."

"Yeah. A *crush*."

"Hey, you ready?" Ava calls from downstairs.

"Be down in a sec," Max replies, clipped, before he turns back to me. "There's history between us. You can't kiss me one second and then laugh about it the next. It's shitty."

"I didn't mean it like that," I say, regret prickling my cheeks. Max doesn't deserve to be treated that way. "I'm sorry."

"What did you mean, then?"

"I just—" I don't know how to explain that this was more than an impulse, but it didn't help that he was so close, and he smelled so good, and I've been dying to taste him and couldn't resist anymore. "I got carried away."

Max considers this and runs a hand through his curls. "With what happened at my last job, it's not the best idea to get involved with a business partner. Might look...not great."

I don't blame him for setting some boundaries. This is why I was right to leave romance out of our friendship before—even when the decision hurt. I stand up, straightening my clothes in utter humiliation. I wish I could rewind the last fifteen minutes. While fantasizing about him pushing me against the wall and outlining my every curve with his fingertips, I forgot what he's here to do and how his entire reputation relies on this. Neither of us can afford to lose sight of the end goal.

"Let's just keep things professional." He walks over to me, not toe-to-toe, but closer than business partners. Even closer than friends. "It's for the best."

"Right."

His eyes dart down to my mouth and back up. For a second, I swear he's going to lean in and say *to hell with what we just agreed*. But his hand juts out, waiting for me to grab it as if we've just met.

We shake hands, and his palm is hot. *Professional*. I can do that, no problem.

Chapter Fourteen

Max, Now

I scan the colorful bar littered with tiki paraphernalia. Wooden deity masks, fake palm fronds, license plates from Hawaii. I'd heard about Mai Tai Hideaway growing up but was never old enough to go inside, and I'm appreciating the years away from Harlow—the break lets me experience the town for the first time.

"Well, I think they're awful," the mousy young woman to my right says with disdain. She's an art theory instructor named Susan, and she and a few other people from the art department are discussing the new whiteboards. "They've got this thick layer on top, so it's impossible to write on them."

Nodding along, I half listen to her claims. I would go home, but after yet another fight this morning with my parents—this time for using the wrong setting on the dishwasher—I'm looking for any excuse not to sit around at their house.

Or think about Daisy. I wish I could forget yesterday. Kissing her, *feeling* her—my hands tense, longing for her hips. I wanted to taste more of that freckle below her lip, to lick the saltiness off her skin, to explore the peaks and valleys of her body. Then, like a complete moron, I took us from heavy petting to shaking hands like some suits at a work lunch.

But if I want the job at Tate that Eleanor mentioned, I shouldn't complicate our situation with kissing, or sex.

That thought sends a fever through me.

Tropical music swells, and the bartender comes around to check on us. I order another fruity concoction bursting with sweetness.

"Watch out." Frank, the middle-aged man who teaches ceramics, points to my almost empty glass. "Those're strong."

"They're delicious is what they are." I run my thumb over the cup's textured skulls and flowers. In Dublin, I'd gotten so used to drinking pints of beer that this goes down like water. "But, noted," I add, uncomfortable under his gaze. Frank is the only art teacher I had in high school who's still around. I did an intro to ceramics class one semester and made about twenty awful mugs before deciding that pottery wasn't my thing.

Eight years later, we're at happy hour together, bonding over tiki drinks.

"I'll order some new markers for the team, but in the meantime, try this one out." The head of the department, Regina, rummages through her bag. She produces a dry-erase marker and gifts it to Susan, who looks like she just won the lottery.

I sip the last of my saccharine-sweet drink, a mishmash of coconut, pineapple, and rum that punches its way through my system and leaves me wanting more. If I close my eyes, I picture other things I want more of, like Daisy straddling my lap and panting against my skin.

The bartender arrives with my next drink, pulling me back to the present.

"Do you know when we'll hear about the fall semester?" Susan leans over the table.

Regina chuckles. "I'm not at liberty to say."

"Ugh." Susan's face scrunches up. "I hate the waiting game."

"The trial's going well, though?" Frank asks.

"It is," Regina replies, and Susan squeals. "Come September, we may be looking at our very own school."

Regina hopes to get enough interest to launch an art school by the end of the year. Students would have their core classes at their high school and two days a week dedicated to arts coursework. Sort of like how some students go to trade schools alongside their high school curriculum, but for the visual arts.

"Congrats," I say, holding out my fourth—maybe fifth?—drink of the night.

After we clink our glasses together, Susan leans forward again. "But when will we *know*?"

"Sweetheart," Regina says, her voice smooth, "you'll know when I know. Once the district sends approval, I'm bringing you all with me to the next semester, and the next one, and the one after that."

"I'm not..." I grab my straw and stab at the clumps of ice in my drink. "Honestly, I don't know if teaching's for me."

"Your classes are a hit." Frank's mouth drops open into a small O shape. "Is it the pay?"

"No, just—"

"All the kids are raving about your classes," Regina says in an obvious attempt to reassure me. "They can be difficult, but trust me, they've really grown to like you."

"I mean, sure, I'm fine at it. Shaping young minds." All of their eyes are on me as they wait for me to explain myself. "I've got a kid sister, so relating to people younger than me comes naturally. But I..." I sip on my Painkiller to find the right words, the dregs of the drink gurgling up the straw. "I want a career in art."

"You're teaching art," Susan says.

"I mean *in* art. Not just teaching."

"You...you realize, we're all teachers here?" Frank asks, keeping his tone even.

Susan cocks her head to the side. "Teaching art is a career in art."

The three of them eye me, and I regret the last ten seconds.

"There's nothing wrong with teaching," I say in a hurry to backtrack. "I don't think it's for me."

"Oh. Okay." Regina rests her elbows on the table and quirks a brow at me. "Well, what is for you?"

"Curating. I'm a curator for museums around the world. That's what I do."

They all nod their heads to a chorus of *ohs*.

"So you mean like..." Susan holds her water glass, sticking one pinky out as she uses her other hand to stroke a fake mustache. "*Art.*" She draws out the word with a long A-sound and a half-decent British accent. Frank and Regina crack up at this. "The hoity-toity stuff. Gotcha."

"Like, let me tape a banana to the wall and call it a masterpiece?" Frank chuckles.

I laugh along with them because, at a certain level, art people *can* be pretentious. It doesn't make me love the job any less, even if people take themselves a little too seriously sometimes.

"Okay, fine," I interject. "But you all sort of seem to have a bias against what I do."

"We could say the same about you," Regina shoots back.

I gulp, aware I'm coming off like an asshole in front of my boss. "I mean, art on a global scale," I go on. "Extraordinary pieces that people travel to see. To be moved by. Doesn't that excite you?"

"But why is it extraordinary?" Susan asks. "Because some crusty white guy said so? Like, did I cry when I saw *The Execution of Lady Jane Grey* in London? Sure. But I think the most fired up I get, and some of the best stuff I've made, is because a revelation hits me in the middle of teaching. Then I stay up half the night painting."

"People have bought plates off my Etsy shop from as far away as Tuvalu," Frank says. "I didn't even know Tuvalu existed."

Their stories make me shrink in the booth.

"Art can, and should, be different for different people," Regina says diplomatically. "Creating. Curating. What works for one of you might not for the other, right? If Harlow's art scene isn't for you, then it's not."

She changes the subject immediately to summer vacations, and I excuse myself to the bathroom. My coworkers must think I'm a dick, putting their careers down like that. As I wash my hands and examine my reflection, I admit I have been hard on this place. Not just the school, but Harlow. Does everyone see me like Susan and Frank do—uptight and thinking I'm better than them?

Is this how Daisy sees me? I cringe. Daisy has always seen Harlow and found beauty in it, and isn't that the job of a curator? The last thing I want her to view me as is a stuck-up asshole who doesn't respect her. There's not a person I admire more, and the possibility that she could think otherwise settles heavy in my chest.

I reach for my phone to dial her up and tell her, because I should have told her this every day I've known her—told her how incredible and amazing and gorgeous she is. Or at least tell her I'm ready to give Harlow a real chance while I'm here, because she deserves that much from me. I don't get past the lock screen, and after a few failed attempts to unlock my cell, the display duplicates before my eyes, my vision splitting. Frank was right—these drinks *are* strong.

"Max?" Frank asks. He's materialized behind me.

"Hey, 'm I in your way?"

"No, you're good. But you just tried to make a call using the calculator app. You okay?"

I look back at my reflection. *No,* I think. *But hopefully, I will be.*

"How 'bout I give you a ride home?" Frank asks.

Looking down at my phone again, I see three screens instead of one. "Yeah. That's probably a smart idea."

"Sorry I'm late." I sigh and collapse onto Daisy's couch. With everything this morning—oversleeping, a brutal hangover, a shouting match with my parents—I forgot our planning session. "I feel like shit."

Daisy pops her head out of the kitchen. "Well, you look like an angel," she says, biting back her mirth.

"Not in the mood, Daze." My skull pulses. I have zero energy for jokes, especially at my expense.

"Sorry."

"I brought this upon myself with four to six tiki drinks."

"*Six?*"

"We've all done things we're not proud of."

Daisy laughs, and the sound resurrects me almost as much as the savory scent of sausage. She disappears into the kitchen again as my nausea transforms into a stomach-twisting pang of hunger. I close my eyes. Even Freddie pities me—he jumps onto the couch and curls into my side. The stove clicks off, the faucet runs for a second, and food gets scraped onto plates.

"Hope you're hungry," Daisy says, resting the cool edge of a ceramic plate by my arm. I could cry at the kindness.

Daze sits cross-legged on the floor, apron still on, and hair in a bundle on top of her head. I'd love to set my hand at the nape of her neck, pull her close, and kiss her again, but that's just the hangover talking. As much as I want to say a billion things and do a billion more, that's a bad idea. An *unprofessional* idea.

"Crazy night?" she asks, her eyes on her plate.

I grunt a response as I readjust some pillows, elevating myself enough to hold the food.

"Hanging out with friends?" She lifts one brow. "Hot date?"

"Teacher thing." I take an enormous bite packed with egg, sausage, and hash browns, shoveling it into my mouth with a groan. "That's—" I inhale my next forkful exactly half a second after swallowing the first. "Ohmygod, that's so good."

I release another food-induced moan, not caring that it sounds like breakfast is taking me to third base. Daisy's focus skates up and down my body, and color rises to her cheeks.

I continue to eat in a fugue state until I clean my plate. It's so Daisy to do this—to have a feast prepared for me and to take care of me when I need it.

"Wanna talk about it?" she asks. "You don't have to, but—"

"They kicked me out." I lay back on the couch, like a lion after a meal.

"What?"

"To be fair, I got their car towed."

I had hoped the Jeep would be secure there overnight, but the bar owner didn't recognize the car as any of the regulars', so they called to have it hauled away. Frank delivered me home safe, but I've paid for my responsible decision with parents who think I'm trying to turn their place into a party house. No more car, no more roof over my head. I see their actions for what they're worth—they want to say *told you so*. But even if I changed my mind today and enrolled in law school, I'd never satisfy them.

"They're your *parents*." Daisy sets her plate down with a clang. "Who cares about a tow?"

"I was suffocating over there, so I'm glad they told me to leave," I say, stabbing a yolk. I'm glad, too, to have a place like Daisy's where I can breathe again.

"I'm sorry, Max. They're so hard on you. I don't get it."

"They live in milestones." I shrug, my eyes catching on the jolt of blue from her bra strap. "Married by twenty-five. Partners at their respective law firms by thirty. Two kids, nice house. To them, I'm too old to be where I am in life right now."

"Where're you gonna go?"

I blow air out of my pursed lips. "I'll check Craigslist. Ask around. I'll find something."

"Stay here."

"I couldn't." While I appreciate the offer, I can't take up one of The Mirage's accommodations. "You need every room you've got for guests."

"I don't mean the hotel. I mean *here*." She points to the hall. "My old bedroom. No holes in that mattress."

The suggestion makes me hesitate. Daisy's always looked out for me, and the proximity to the work for the museum would make my life easier. I'd be around Daisy more, too—late nights and early mornings, and she'd be sleeping one room over. That's not necessarily a good thing.

Daisy wriggles around, reaching into her pocket and removing a key from her key ring.

"No."

"It's the hotel owner in me. I would have offered sooner, but I didn't realize how bad things were. The thought of someone I care about getting a terrible night's sleep pulls at my heartstrings."

"I..." *She cares about me.* I lean to one side so I'm facing her, propped up on my elbow while an alcohol-induced headache claws deeper into me. That spare room *would* be practical.

"You don't need to do this," I go on.

"I know."

I lock eyes with her, the rich brown of her irises like an antidote to my headache and nausea. "Can I—last night, I had sort of a come-to-Jesus moment."

"Six tiki drinks'll do that to a man."

"I really care about this project. You've got a lot riding on it—we both do—and I want to make it something incredible." I scratch the back of my neck. "I never meant for you to think that I'm looking down on you, though."

"Oh." Daisy rolls her lower lip between her teeth. "Well, if we're swapping confessions, I know I've been a pain in the ass about renovations."

"You're being smart. We're just learning how to work together. Be a team."

She nods. "A team." Her eyes linger on me for a couple of seconds, and I get the tingling urge to reach out and tuck some stray strands of hair behind her ears. She holds up the keys again before I do something stupid. "So does that mean you'll take me up on my offer?"

I smile. "I can look for something else."

"Why do you want to play life on hard mode right now? Take the damn keys."

She's not doing anything other than giving me a safe, comfortable place to sleep—but I can't pretend the last time we were together didn't happen.

"Will it be weird for you having me here?"

"Why would it be?"

"Because." I lift an eyebrow at her. She's going to force me to say it. "Because we made out. Because I told you about my crush in high school."

"I don't think so." A hint of a blush creeps up her cheekbones, like pigment added to water. "Do you?"

"Nope." I shrug. "People make out all the time."

"Mhmm."

"It could be weird if it was bad, you know. The kiss." I lean back, creating a pillow with my hands behind my head, and I try not to replay the other day. *Her arms wrapped around my neck. Her mouth on mine. Her hips rolling against my cock.* "I don't think it was, though."

"Same. Just unexpected." Another pause, and she swallows. "Well, good. You're right. Friends kiss sometimes. It's unbelievable we made it through high school without letting any horny teenage urges get the best of us."

We almost did, I want to say. But the hangover and food coma combined with Daisy saying the word *horny* all make me think I need some rest.

"And crushes are...they're no big deal," she goes on. "What matters is that we're friends."

"Friends," I say, doing my best not to wince.

She stands, taking both of our empty plates into the kitchen. We've put it all out in the open, and things don't have to be weird between us. We could even joke about it. *Remember the time we dry-humped on a dying air mattress? Good times.*

Ignoring the growing erection in my pants, I readjust and sink into the couch. "Hey, can we do a rain check for our meeting?" I ask with heavy eyelids. "I'm spent."

"Sure. There's a pull-out sofa in your room."

"Okay. I'll stay."

She slips the key into my hand, patting it before heading to the lobby for work.

Everything will be fine.

Chapter Fifteen

Max, 15 Years Old

I sensed Daisy's scowl over my shoulder. "I'm paying attention," I assured her, a small smile playing on my lips. She and Gwen flanked me on either side of the couch, both of them reclining on the arms, with their feet pointing inward. Daisy's toes rested inches from my knee, and I sat crisscross in the middle, a pillow and papers in my lap.

"Are you one of those people who thinks better when you're doodling?" Gwen asked. She and Daisy had lockers next to each other, and we'd started hanging out as a trio recently.

"Sometimes," I admitted.

"You might miss something good," Daisy said.

"I could recite this show." I'd watched *Gilmore Girls*, one of Daisy's favorites, countless times with her. She wanted a distraction and also thought Gwen would like it, so we planned an all-day marathon at Daisy's place.

No significant others, Daisy had clarified, although that wasn't necessary. Gwen barely knew anyone, and Daisy broke things off with that last guy a couple of weeks ago. I'd gone on a few dates with this girl from my homeroom, Lily, but we weren't serious. I liked not worrying about dividing my attention with someone else today. It meant that when I was with Daisy, I really got to be with her.

The front door opened, and Daisy's mom beamed with an over-the-top smile. "Pizza!"

"You just missed Lorelai finding out about the kiss," Daisy said.

"Oooh," her mom swooned, setting the pizza boxes on the coffee table.

I followed her into the kitchen to stick some more popcorn in the microwave while Daisy and Gwen sang along to the intro of the next episode. Daisy's mom had both palms on the counter, her eyelids shut, as she took in a deep inhale.

"You okay, Mrs. J?"

Her eyes flew open, and although her mouth turned up in a smile, her eyes were red-rimmed and glassy. Mr. Johnson had moved out again earlier in the week, and my heart sank to see Daisy's mom this way.

"I'm fine, my sweet boy," she said, forcing her smile further.

"Here." I enveloped her in a tight hug, and she melted into it. I liked Daisy's mom so much. My parents cast dark clouds over every decision I ever made, but Daisy's mom gave me sunshine.

"Thank you," she whispered.

"Anytime."

I offered Daisy's mom my spot on the couch, and Daisy scooted over so that I could sit on the floor next to her. She handed me a throw pillow for added comfort, and I settled in. Leaning back and chomping on pizza, we both relaxed enough that her legs rested against my left side. Skin-to-skin contact with her always made my breathing pick up, but I ignored it. If Daisy experienced the same zing whenever we touched, she never let on. We were friends. It didn't have to be that deep.

I never felt this way when Lily was around, though.

I tried to ignore that, too.

Chapter Sixteen

Daisy, Now

I flop face-first onto the sofa. "Nggg," I say, a blanket muffling my voice.

"Long day?" Max clicks pause on the television.

"You were there."

"We made good progress."

We confirmed the layout for a parking lot that removes the minimum amount of wildlife, nailed down plans with the plumber to get a water-efficient bathroom up and running in the barn, and prepped the space for the countless pieces of art we'll be receiving soon. This, on top of operating the hotel as normal, felt like managing a circus of cats today. A clogged toilet in Room Six. An emergency supply run for laundry detergent. Someone who canceled last minute, resulting in a phone call spent explaining our cancellation policy fifty times.

Whenever my mom had days like this, she seemed so calm and collected. I, however, may perish with exhaustion. These past few evenings, Max and I watched an episode or two of a cowboy show set in the early 1900s, or we just hung out and talked while I put my record collection to use. Tonight, I barely have the energy to move.

"Take a bath," Max says.

"I stink?" I squeeze my arms into my side, preventing the spread of any odor. There have been days when, after plenty of manual labor, I smell far less like a desert rose. I'd like to keep up the illusion for Max, only because my roommate shouldn't think I reek.

"No, I drew you a bath."

If guests ever want, they can call or text when they're leaving the park, and I make sure the water finishes filling the moment they pull into the lot. It's a luxury after a long hike or full day of sightseeing—a luxury I don't indulge in myself.

"Go and unwind 'til dinner gets here."

"You ordered food?" As if on cue, my stomach growls.

"We blew through lunchtime, and you've got to feed yourself. Hope tacos are okay."

I bite back a satisfied smile. "Tacos are always okay."

I want to get up and crawl right over to him for a hug. Or better yet, curl up on his lap, snuggle into that perfect spot below his jawline, and inhale his aftershave. If only I had the excuse to pull him into and onto me and to kiss him, hard.

No, not kiss. I let that thought slide like I did on Monday, when he hung up his bathroom towel and his shirt rode up, revealing that tempting trail of hair beyond the top of his jeans. Or yesterday, when our hands brushed as he grabbed some papers from me to sign. Or when he holds the door open like a goddamn gentleman wherever we go. We have less than two months left until the pop-up at the end of August, and I really need to get over this little attraction *now* so I can focus on The Mirage.

"That's nice of you," I say, peeking into the bathroom. A wave of lavender engulfs me. Heavenly.

He shrugs. "You're letting me stay here for free."

"There are zero strings attached to that offer."

"Would you like me to drain the bath?"

"No," I say with a laugh. "Can't waste all this perfectly bubbly water."

"Then get in there already, would you?"

Max unpauses the TV and I step into the bathroom, closing the door behind me. He has not only tidied up and wiped down every surface—I'm admittedly much better at keeping guest rooms in order than my own home—but he's also lit candles and prepared the water to the perfect temperature, like some kind of sorcerer.

Max had always been the type to gift me a book he saw at the thrift store—just because. When we went to house parties, he offered to stay sober and drive us home. If I needed a last-minute date to a school dance, he was there. I'd considered these nice things a friend would do, but as I remove my clothing, I reflect on them in a new way.

You have to have known how I felt about you.

God, I was stupid not to realize my own feelings until it was too late. Now, all of that pent-up yearning from our teenage years combined with Max making it pretty damn hard not to like him—and yeah, that I could use a good lay—has me thinking unprofessional, unroommate-like thoughts about him.

Roommate, I remind myself, and a temporary one at that. I ignore how my heart twists and instead slide into the steamy tub with a sigh, relishing how the water envelops me and the delicate bubbles suction to my skin.

When I lean my head back to give in to relaxation, a trilling alarm in the other room reminds me why I'm more of a quick-shower type of gal.

"Damn it," I mutter.

"I've got it."

"It's a daily reminder." I stand and reach for a towel, suds careening down my body as the tub water sloshes side to side from me standing so quickly. "For Freddie's meds."

"Daisy Johnson, sit your ass down and have a bubble bath for once in your life. I'll handle it."

The sternness in Max's voice sends a delicious vibration down my spine. I don't enjoy relaxing, and I definitely don't like being told what to do—but that bossy tone has me melting back into the tub, timid and obedient.

"He's squirrelly," I say. "And he prefers when you pop it into the left side of his mouth, not the right. And you'll need an oral syringe to wash it down with water so that—"

There's a soft knock on the bathroom door. "May we come in?"

"Um. Sure."

Max enters, and I can't stop adjusting the shower curtain and strategically arranging bubbles over my body.

"So." Max inspects some pill bottles as Freddie purrs in his arms. "One of these pink ones and half a white?"

I tilt my head. "How do you know that?"

"Been paying attention."

"To a cat's medicine schedule?"

Freddie mews, sending the corner of Max's mouth skyward, and my heartbeat trips.

Friend. Roommate. Business partner.

Max sinks next to the tub on the floor, close enough that I can feel his breath on the damp skin of my arm. I forget why he's in the bathroom in the first place, and I surrender to the possibility that he'll lean over, invade my space, and lick the lavender off of me. When he scoots closer, locked in intense eye contact with me, I'm certain that's what is about to happen, and it feels like falling.

"You've offended him," Max whispers with that gorgeous, boyish grin on his face. "Freddie's not just *a* cat. He is *the* cat of the house." Max scratches underneath the purring feline's chin, and I am officially experiencing jealousy toward my own cat. Freddie even looks at me with a smug, *Bet you'd like this right here, wouldn't you?* expression.

"These heart meds are a big deal, right Fred?" Max says to him. "Okay, left side. C'mere." In one deft movement, Max pops both pills into the cat's mouth. Freddie, oblivious, turns and rubs his face into Max's knee, purring like a generator with four legs. Max pets Freddie's head and scratches around his neck like it's his calling, and I swear, my uterus explodes. If there is one undeniably sexy thing a man can do, it's care for a poor, helpless animal.

"What?" Max shoots me a quizzical look, and I close my gaping mouth.

"Nothing," I say, my throat like sandpaper. "Freddie puts up a much bigger fight when I do meds."

"What can I say? Magic touch."

He rinses his hands in the sink, and they're good-looking hands. Elegant, confident. He has long fingers and a few prominent veins traveling from the knuckles. I shudder with a chill and plunge deeper into the warmth of the bath.

"You doing okay in here?" Max's gaze glides across the edge of the tub, and I'm hyperaware that I'm naked and shielded by a flimsy piece of plastic and suds. I wonder if he's hyperaware of that, too.

My response is incoherent, I'm sure, but I nod, so Max takes that as his cue to go, carrying Freddie with him. I can't relax, but not due to my usual workaholic tendencies. A tremor courses through my veins, and a pit of something forms low in my belly.

Not something. *Desire.*

All he did was give my cat medicine, but seeing the tenderness with which he treated Freddie—and the way he knocked a task off my to-do list like it was no big deal—has me wondering what else that magic touch can do.

I lean back and use my hand to trace a path down to my thigh, then up and over to the other one. Then up and over yet again. The next time, I let my palm rest in the center. The bubbles dance on top of the water, floating left and right a little less, and I remain still until they stop completely.

My memory flashes like heat lightning to last week in his childhood bedroom—his body melded with mine, his hands holding me closer, closer, and the hardness of his cock through his pants.

I know myself. This craving won't go away until I make it go away. I'm only going to keep thinking of Max in ways that no friend, no roommate, and no business partner should, and I can only ignore my needs so much...

Or I could handle them on my own terms.

The best orgasms of my life have been solo, and I consider myself skilled at getting myself off in record time. Most of the work happens in my head, so with a little fantasizing, I'm halfway there. And with Max practically everywhere these days, I have a lot of mental imagery to choose from.

My fingers move in slow, meticulous circles as I picture Max opening the door. My body hums. He strolls in confidently to the tub, no questions asked, and with those gorgeous hands, he rolls up his shirt sleeves. As he glides a palm down my torso, it's like he already knows the map of me. Max cups one breast as his thumb runs across my nipple. He's leaning into my neck, his lips against my skin, his fingers dragging lower and lower, until finally, *finally*, he's working my clit at a rhythmic pace.

I bite my lip to hold back a moan and savor this version of Max that I will never have. A Max who follows through on all the glances that seem to linger a second too long. A Max who wants me and won't let anything get in the way of having me. A Max who isn't bound for bigger and better things beyond this town.

With a breathy exhale, I inch closer to release—and the thought of him a mere ten feet away while I'm masturbating tips me into a series of shudders and near-silent sighs. An explosion of heavenly heat overtakes me, swelling at my center, and I only realize how quiet this bathroom is when I come down from the high of my orgasm.

There's an abrupt knock, followed by Max clearing his throat. "Dinner's here."

"Great," I croak, a swarm of stars still twinkling on the outer edges of my vision. "Be right out."

Chapter Seventeen

Max, Now

Becs, one of the artists I'd like to confirm for the exhibit, takes contemplative strides through the barn. She graduated a year before me, and we stayed in touch. At a pop-up in Dubai last spring, she did some outstanding work that played a lot with textures, and she'd be perfect for our show.

"Love the place," she says, inspecting the space. "Reminds me of this coffee shop I went to every day in Morocco during my residency. I'm tempted to stay the night."

"I could get a room ready for you, if you'd like."

So she can talk. That might be the first full sentence Daisy's said in days. Ever since tacos last week, she's limited her responses to three words or less. I would have asked her what was up, but between applying for permits, designing flyers, and making endless calls with managers, I've barely had the chance to breathe.

"I wish," Becs replies. "Early flight out of LAX for Art Basel. Have you been?"

"Uh." Daisy twirls a ring on her finger. "No."

"Why would you, though?" Becs gestures to the setting sun. "When you're surrounded by this? I'd never leave."

"It's incredible, isn't it?" Daisy's tone is wistful, and she looks at the landscape like she's seeing it for the first time, too. Her shirt has ridden up in the back, revealing some peach fuzz that glistens in the light, and I want to rub my palm on it.

"Max always talked shit about his hometown," Becs says to Daisy.

"No more than any kid talks shit about their hometown," I say.

"On our first date, you told me you were—"

"Okay, we don't have to get into that."

"Oh." Daisy looks between us. "Max didn't mention that you two dated."

She doesn't look jealous or annoyed, just curious—at attention. I wish the comment bothered her as much as it bothered me.

"God, it was nothing." Becs shakes her head. "In art school, everybody dates everybody. Very incestuous."

A few months into my freshman year, I started dating. There were women who I thought could be my type but really weren't, like Becs. There were a couple of longer-term partners—girlfriends who I liked a lot—but once things fizzled, we parted ways and stayed friends. Reflecting on it now, I don't know what I was looking for in those relationships. I guess I never found that invisible string connecting me and someone else.

"He told me," Becs goes on, "that he was from Bumfuck, California."

"That was a joke," I rush to explain.

"It wasn't always like this," Daisy says, more to Becs than to me. "For someone like Max, someone ambitious and so great at what he does, the town can have its limits."

My defensive mode thaws, and Daisy smiles in a way that doesn't quite meet her eyes.

"Not so limiting anymore," Becs says. "So, tell me all about this pop-up."

Daisy gives her a tour around the barn while I explain the vision. Anytime I speak, Daze looks distracted—like she's listening to me but her mind is elsewhere—and then she leaps back into business talk.

I can't match that dedication. Any time she gives her attention to Becs, my focus trails up her legs, all the way to the fraying, stringy ends of her shorts.

"Sunset here's something else," Daisy says. "We're able to catch the last bits of light splashing against the mountains over there, and then it's cotton candy skies 'til the stars come out."

"The setting is its own art piece. And then to have a museum here? Very meta."

"We've got advertising, a fundraiser, some blog features, and an upcoming interview." I glance at Daisy and give her an encouraging smile because I know she's nervous about being on camera. "We haven't sorted out specifics, but you'd likely have this corner here."

I rattle off a list of other artists I've been in talks with—some bigger names than others—and Becs nods and offers some additional suggestions.

"Also." Daisy clears her throat. "Also, I have some artists to recommend."

"Great." I worry she might overestimate my reach and propose someone unattainable, but I like that she's done research. "Who were you thinking?"

"They're locals."

I stall for a beat. Holding a spot for someone in the area had crossed my mind, but well-known artists remain my priority. People with a bigger following will mean more to Tate and set Daisy up for months of packed reservations. Besides, artists of Becs's caliber don't want to fight for placement with someone who makes air-dry clay toothpick holders in the shape of a sun.

"It's a great idea," I say, letting her down gently, "but I'm not sure that's the right direction for what we're creating."

"I like it," Becs says, nodding. "You could call the pop-up...*Here and There.*"

"Or *Near and Far*," Daisy says, and Becs gasps.

"Oh, that's good. Better watch out," she says to me, a thumb hooked toward Daisy. "She might take your job."

"We should try to save as much space as we can for artists on the list," I say. "Which is why we're all here in the first place."

This chat has gone completely off-track, and my eyes widen in Daisy's direction, as if I can communicate through unseen forces. *Trust me.* She responds with a subtle eye roll—she really shouldn't look that pretty when she's giving me attitude—and I invite Becs back into the conversation, showing her around before she departs.

The second the tires from Becs's rental car hit the road and a cloud of earthy debris kicks up in her wake, Daisy turns to me. "Becs thought it was a good idea."

"It is, but not for this."

"Why?"

"I've been thinking about who we'll have in this show since day one. The whole thing is a balancing act of who will draw in a big crowd, who's right for the pop-up, who's available…I have a list a mile long of dream artists, and they're the priority."

"What about my list?"

"I didn't know you had a list."

"Well, now you do." She shrugs again. "This is our project, and we can change it or add to it."

"Sure." Although Daisy threw me a curveball, we're in this together, and her ideas matter. "But if we open the floodgates for artists in Harlow to claim a spot, that looks more—"

"Bumfuck, California?"

"Hey." I step forward, wishing that comment had never come up—wishing that I'd never said it in the first place, all those years ago. "That was shitty of me." Her face falls to the ground, so I cup her chin and meet her gaze. "I was dumb and young and said whatever for a laugh." My attention darts to her mouth for a nanosecond. "I just want us to have the best chance at success here, and I know how artists think. If—"

Daisy doesn't stick around to hear what I have to say; instead, she breaks the connection, walks away, and I instinctively follow. The sunset has painted the sky a stunning combination of rose and lilac—a bouquet strewn across the sky. A sliver of the moon pokes out from behind a cloud, and a smattering of stars dot the multicolored blanket above.

"Artists don't want to compete to be in a museum like this," I continue, hoping to knock some sense into her stubborn ass with my years of experience. "There are egos involved. Politics. They want a prime spot, reserved for them. I'm not saying it's right, but we have to play the game if we want the audience we're aiming for."

"You'd be surprised at what people in this area can do." She falters at the door to the casita. "If you're so embarrassed by this place, then why bother with this project at all?"

"I'm not embarrassed. I only want the best artists we can get, and—"

"But what if—"

"And that doesn't mean people here aren't talented. But we want a big crowd, so we have to appeal to that."

She tips her chin up. "We'd spend less on shipping."

"That's...okay, good point. But I don't want shipping costs, which I budgeted for, to get in the way of an amazing exhibit."

"Maybe you're the one getting in the way. Wanting all these hotshots but turning your nose up at anyone from here. *You're* from here, in case you forgot."

"This is my job, Daze," I say through clenched teeth. "Curating. Making choices, eliminating options, and tailoring what this museum will be. You have to trust me."

"Trust goes both ways," she says, stepping close enough I can smell her shampoo.

Words escape me because she's right. Daisy has a lot on the line, and so far, she's followed my lead. She knows Harlow the way I can't after years away, so I should at least consider her suggestion, do more research, and decide if it's feasible.

"Okay," I concede. "Send me your list. I'll look into some things, and...I'll think about it."

"I knew you'd come around." The tiny victory makes her eyes gleam, and she presses her pointer finger into my chest. "People will show up."

"Don't poke me." I grab her hand and chuckle, guiding it away as she struggles against me.

"Don't laugh at me," she says, scowling as she tries to re-poke me. Her other hand flies into view, but I snatch that one. After a handful of more failed attempts from her, she wriggles as a giggle escapes her.

Once I've gotten a hand encircled around both her wrists, I hold her arms taut, pulling her close enough that there's no space between us. If I could freeze time, I'd stop right here and memorize every shade of chocolate and chestnut in her eyes.

She looks at me and swallows. In the dusk, her face and body glow a gorgeous golden hue. The nighttime chill must be setting in, because she shivers. "You're not making this easy, Max."

"I said I'd think about it. I meant that."

"Not about the artists." Daisy holds my gaze for a moment before looking away and gnawing on her plump bottom lip. She shakes her head. "We can't work like this. *I* can't work like this."

My heartbeat picks up. She doesn't mean the artists—she means *me*. She must want to send me packing to a motel and cancel the pop-up altogether.

"So this is what I think we should do." She straightens her back and lifts her face to meet mine, confident and so achingly perfect. "We should have sex."

"Say something." Daisy sits at the other end of the sofa, hugging her shins like a shield.

My mind is a hurricane of a million thoughts, so I steady myself by leaning my elbows onto my knees. She poured us two whiskeys, neat, but they remain untouched on the coffee table. I spin my glass, flirting with the idea of drinking like we're both flirting with the idea of *this*.

I'm not convinced I'm even awake right now.

"There's been...tension," Daisy says. "Ever since that day at your parents' house."

Desire stirs deep within me. Daisy had crawled onto my lap like she belonged there.

"And rather than tiptoe around each other," she goes on, "especially with a project that's important to both of us, let's just take care of it. You made it sound like maybe you wouldn't hate having sex with me, either."

The corner of my mouth quirks up. Sex with Daisy—what alternate universe have I landed in that this is not only a possibility, but something we're talking about as casually as grabbing a drink after work?

"Wouldn't be awful."

She thwacks me with a pillow before I have the chance to blink, and we both laugh—deep, genuine laughs, like the ones we shared over ice cream cones and late-night phone calls.

"So...just tonight?" I croak out, making sure I understand her correctly.

"Get it out of our system, then back to business as usual."

We've spent the last twenty minutes nursing our undrunk whiskey, discussing what "usual" would look like. Daisy's a pro at compartmentalization, so she laid out the terms. The museum would remain the priority. Also, we wouldn't have sex again, which would minimize further complications with me living here—all the more reason to make sure I don't mess this up.

Tonight only, and only tonight.

My chest aches knowing that this is the only way Daisy would ever want me: a single night, a memory as transient as my time in Harlow.

"You can tell me no," she says. "But if we're both feeling some attraction, and we're both curious, then we don't have to put the pressure of a relationship on ourselves, or anything beyond one night. But once we know what it's like being with the other person, we can stop imagining it."

"And..." I turn the idea over in my head, trying to understand where Daisy's coming from. "It wouldn't be this big unknown anymore."

"Exactly. Not a missed opportunity. Just...a reality of our friendship."

"What if you regret it?" I ask.

"Would you?"

"If I hurt you, I would."

I let Daisy down once in my life, and I never want to again. She has only ever been mine in the wild imaginings of my mind, so as much as I might want this, I don't want to douse our friendship in gasoline and throw a match over my shoulder. With reality knocking, all the reasons we shouldn't do this have me second-guessing.

"What about you?" I ask once more. "Would you regret this? Me?"

"No, but I don't want to hurt you, either."

Would one night with her be what I need? Maybe I've unknowingly placed Daisy on a pedestal all these years, and I could learn something from the way she packs her feelings away. With all the women I've dated, I knew in my heart that I held back from them. Breaking up and staying friends was easy because there was always a niggling part of my brain wondering, wishing...

If I close the door on that for good, then maybe I could move on.

"Okay." My heartbeat pounds like a drum in my ears. "But if it gets too intense, then we stop. No questions asked."

"Agreed." She nods. "And no matter what, we stay friends."

"No more six-year silences?"

A smile plays on her lips. "Deal."

The joy and terror of the unknown swallow me. We won't be able to go back to who we were before tonight. But I've always kept my emotions in check with past girlfriends and hookups, and I tell myself Daisy doesn't have to be any different.

"So should we...?" She looks at the couch we're on.

"Eager."

"Max," she says with a laugh, rolling her eyes.

"I get it. No time like the present."

She smacks my arm. "I just figured I'll call a food order in, we can do our thing, and we'll have a delicious pizza waiting for us once we're done."

"Already planning the post-sex meal? Thorough."

"Thank you."

"But what makes you think this will take the twenty minutes tops it takes for a pizza to get here?"

She stutters out a tense laugh. I'm not joking, though, and when I don't reply, she goes quiet. What guys has she been with if she expects to wrap things up, start to finish, in under half an hour?

If this is our only night together, then I'm going to make it one to remember.

"Let me be clear," I say, leaning back on the couch, my body angled in her direction. "We're doing this your way, your rules—and I agree to them. But it's still sex, and I don't do sex with a timer. It's not even about an end goal for me. It's about feeling good—about making you feel good." My cock is already hardening at the thought of what Daisy will look like and sound like when we're together. "If you and I are doing this...getting each other out of our systems, then I think another rule should be that we don't hold back."

"Okay." She licks her top lip, then nods. "Then pizza can wait."

"Good. The bedroom's better." I stand and offer her my hand. "In the common area we share, it might make things weird."

She leads the way, running her hand over Freddie, who's passed out on the back of the couch. Her room reminds me a lot of how she decorated as a teen, but more refined. A gallery wall of framed images and concert tickets has replaced magazine clippings and vision boards. Instead of a beanbag chair, she has a red vintage armchair and an ottoman. She's added a cute touch to every lamp, covering them with silk scarves to diffuse the lighting.

I pause between the doorway and her bed, and she turns to stare at me. We're standing on the edge of something, ready to fall together, but we have to jump first.

"Is this strange for you?" she asks, bathed in the golden light.

"It's more formulaic than I'm used to."

"Sorry. Alex and I were so busy most of the time that we had to schedule sex, so I talk about this like I'm making brunch plans."

"Don't apologize," I say. She has some strands of hair dangling in front of her eyes, so I brush them behind her ear. "But please don't mention Alex right now."

"Sure." She swallows, and her eyes dart down to my mouth for a millisecond. "Are you going to kiss me?"

"Maybe. Are you going to laugh at me again?"

"If I can find an air mattress on its last breath, then probably."

I grin. "Let me run a quick errand."

"Max, would you kiss me already and—"

In an abrupt swoop, I dip my head down so our lips meet. The connection is sweet and simple—the kissing equivalent of reading the room. Our mouths together feel like coming home after a long trip away, comforting and right. We both take tiny steps to close the space between our bodies, and my hands lift to cradle each side of her jaw. Daisy wraps an arm around me, her hand snaking under my shirt while her cool palm on my back makes me shudder. Our lips find each other again, this time parting so our tongues reach out, seeking and searching. She releases the softest moan against my mouth, and the sensation travels directly to my dick.

All the nagging worries—that this will change our friendship forever, that I won't be good enough for her, or that Tate is too far away from Harlow—escape my thoughts whenever I'm around her. They all shift to the background as we become two entangled bodies, heat and breath and need. She tastes minty and sweet, overpowering and gentle, and the flavor instantly becomes my favorite.

"We're really doing this," she murmurs, trailing her hands to my chest.

I grunt in response. All that talk before about not racing to the finish line, and I can't wait for what's next. I'm overwhelmed by her—her curves, her soft lips, her satiny hair, and the way my skin turns to fire under her touch. She coaxes me to the mattress and we fall onto it, enmeshed in each other.

I'm here with Daisy Johnson, my childhood fantasy. My adult fantasy, if I'm being honest. She's perfect, and I'm in bed with her.

"I can't believe I get to do this," I say between kissing the clusters of freckles and beauty marks on her neck. "In high school, I dreamed of this."

"You could have told me. I always liked hearing you talk about your dreams."

"Even if you hadn't been dating someone, I didn't stand a chance."

"Don't do that." She pulls back an inch so we're breathing each other in. "Don't make me some unattainable thing. I'm just Daisy."

The Daisy I rode bikes with and broke into neighbors' pools with. The Daisy I always looked for first at house parties. The Daisy who, whether I liked it or not, I compared every other woman I dated to.

"Just Daisy." My breath hitches, and she hooks one leg up and over my hip.

"Good." She fights a coy smile. "So when you fuck me, it's like fucking any other girl, okay?"

That will be impossible, but I gulp and nod anyway.

She presses into me for another kiss, and my chest explodes.

"Since we're sharing," she says, "remember when you ran me that bath earlier this week? I, um, I had a solo session thinking of you."

I immediately prop up on an elbow. "Seriously?"

Her *yes* sparks through me. Daisy was thinking of me while she was getting off. I'm pretty sure I can die happy now.

I look at the ceiling as I recall that night with new information. "Guess that explains the humming and splashing sounds."

"You *heard* me?" Her jaw goes slack in half amusement, half horror.

"I suppose so," I say, resting my hand on her hip. *I can't believe I get to put my hand here.*

"You let me walk around all week after you'd overheard me masturbating through the bathroom door?"

"In my defense, I didn't know you were masturbating. Or thinking about me."

She crushes me with another kiss, and she's laughing into me—melting into me. My hand slips underneath the hem of her tee, searching for her bra. I cup her left breast and my brain hits a snag because this is all too good. We're back to wrapped limbs and wet kisses, and I'm sucking on the crook of her neck while she's gripping my butt. In the organized mess, she lifts my shirt up and over my head. I've never been the guy who works out all the time, but Daisy scans my body while her strawberry-pink tongue darts out to wet her lower lip, like I'm all she craves.

I help her shimmy out of her T-shirt, revealing more tattoos—a rabbit perched atop one hip bone, a coyote howling above the other, and a hissing snake at her breastbone. My fingers skim each design as I commit them to memory. They're miniature pieces of art, just for me. Just for tonight.

She's draped in front of me in jeans and a semi-sheer bra, so see-through I could trace the outline of her pert nipples. I've seen her before in bikinis, and I stole glances that time we went skinny-dipping—images of her naked body are seared into my brain for life—but seeing her partially undressed has my cock pressed so tight against my pants I could come right now. Reminding myself to breathe, one of my hands works its way up Daisy's lean torso. I take one nipple in my mouth, bra and all, and she lets out a sharp breath.

Daisy writhes next to me, and in a fleeting moment, I tug the undergarment out from between us. Her skin is as smooth as still waters, and her nipples are rock hard. My tongue trails around one, but I barely get a taste before she pushes me into the mattress and perches atop my erection. The pressure is too much, too right. She scooches her hips back and fumbles with my fly to give me some room. Then, Daisy grinds against my crotch, and I let out a guttural groan.

"What do you like?" she asks, pinning me with a hand on each side of my head.

"Whatever you just did."

Her laugh is a hit of dopamine, and I'm already riding the high of every touch and burning gaze.

"What turns you on? We're not holding back. So, any certain positions? Kinks? Blindfolds?"

"No blindfolds." I don't want a single thing getting between my eyes and Daisy coming undone. "Any position." I free my hands so my fingers trace a path to her breast again, outlining her pillow-soft curves. "I guess...I like dirty talk, from time to time."

"Dirty talk?" Her pupils expand, and I can't tell if she's surprised or turned on. "Giving or receiving?"

"Both. But only if it feels right. Only if you'll let me."

"Mhmm." She nods, eager. "Yeah, I...that sounds nice."

"Okay." I smirk and settle my hands at the dip of her waist. "What about you?"

A wicked smile spreads across her mouth. "Coming."

"Yeah?" I pull her down to my level, mouth to mouth, and her breasts mold to me. She's a dream, and that's what tonight will always be: a dream. I can handle that—I can do just one night.

I'm going to savor every second, though.

She juts her hips forward, sending a jolt of pleasure from my cock to the rest of my body. Electric. Breaking our kiss, Daisy shifts to my left and gropes around near the nightstand, seeking, I presume, a condom. I follow the line of her arm into the drawer and notice an oblong, bright fuchsia object tilted on its side.

"What's that?"

"Just...it's my vibrator."

I lift an eyebrow and reach, needing to hold it myself. "Let me see."

"It's nothing," she says, shutting the drawer.

"C'mon."

She huffs. "Fine. Go for it." She shrugs and motions toward the nightstand.

Curiosity piqued, I pull out the toy and examine it. The outside has a velvet-soft touch, and it has a long shaft and bulbous tip. I press a raised button on one end, and the device hums to life.

"It's got different speeds. You can rotate through with—"

"I've used vibrators before." I situate another pillow behind my head as I familiarize myself with the intensity and vibration patterns. Daisy fidgets, obviously getting impatient.

"Can I use this with you?" I ask.

"You want to?"

I might lose my mind, but I'm willing to risk it.

"I'll only use it if you want."

"Sure. I just..." She bites at the wet, thick bottom part of her lip. "With any guys I've been with, they seemed kind of threatened by it. I don't use it with other people."

"Well then, I guess I'll be your first."

Chapter Eighteen

Daisy, Now

Coming. I can't believe *that's* what I told Max I like in bed. Orgasms haven't happened for me with every partner, every time, but I should hit the brakes on the horny-girl truth bombs if I want to look anything less than desperate.

"Any particular speed?" he asks while inspecting the bright pink toy in his hand.

"Lightest setting. To start, at least. She's a powerful one."

"She?"

"Obviously." I flash him a winning smile. "Pretty and gets the job done."

"Makes sense." He barks a laugh, and it disturbs the butterflies swarming in my stomach. "Well, now it's time for you to let someone else get the job done. Can you do that for me?"

I nod, my tongue too heavy in my mouth to speak. The thrill humming through me is more than physical desire—it's the years I wasted ignoring how I felt, the devastation of realizing my feelings too late. That anticipation sparks through my body as Max has one hand on the vibrator while the other rests on my shin. My back arches as he trails his fingertips up my thighs, lighting the fire. I would crawl on my knees down every jagged backroad in Harlow just to know how he feels inside me.

He undoes the fly of my jeans and slides the thick denim down my hips and off my legs. Max grabs a handful of my thigh, then my ass, and I squeal with the heady rush of familiarity. He fingers the edge of my underwear, tracing the lacy edges—and thank god I wore something semi-cute today.

"Your body's incredible."

"Thank y—" His warm mouth sucking on my nipple traps the words in my throat. He uses teeth and tongue, teeth and tongue in a rhythm that takes over my senses, like he's conducting every beat of my heart. Seeking release, I shift my hips to ride his thigh.

He captures my other breast, and I rub against him again. His lips work my body in a way that's inquisitive yet self-assured. He kisses a line to my waist, and he pauses.

"You still have it." He presses a finger against my rib cage.

Max inked that miniscule flower on my side junior year. What better way to put his artistic skills to use than on a tattoo I wasn't legally allowed to get yet? I sometimes forget about it because of the position, but it's my favorite.

I admire the California poppy on my skin. "Surprised you noticed."

"I notice everything about you."

He grinds his thigh against my center, sending a current through me. Then, with an electric *bzz*, our focus goes back to the pink vibrator in his hand. He brushes the toy over one nipple, and my body tenses with pleasure. Max wields it like a magic wand, and the buzzing coasts down and down until the silicone skates over my underwear. The touch is delicate but enough to make my skin prickle with need.

"You're still wearing too much. This." Max hooks a finger around my panties and gives a gentle tug. "Off. Now."

After I work the piece of fabric down my legs, Max hisses with a sharp inhale. His attentive gaze makes me squirm. As much as I want to embody a carefree sex goddess, my jittery nerves tell a different story. I don't just want to sleep with him—I want it to be good. I want *him* to think it's good.

"What, um, what do you want to do to me?" I embrace my inner sex kitten as best I can, dipping my toe into dirty talk. I worry he'll think I'm pathetic, but he looks at me with dark, dilated pupils.

"Everything." He runs his tongue along the length of the vibrator. "But I'll start with this."

He traces a path with the toy up one thigh and down the other, gliding over my labia so it teases me. Once more, he goes through the motions, narrowly missing my clit and sending a rough groan of frustration through me. Max pulls the sex toy away and chuckles from where he's kneeling, right between my legs.

"You were never very patient."

"Fuck you," I say through a smile.

"I will." He presses hungry kisses from one knee up past my hip until he's hovering over me. When he takes my nipple back in his mouth, I buck into the air—and finally, *finally*, he rests the vibrator where I want it.

"Shit." I've shut my eyes, but I'm seeing stars. Max holds the tip close, but not close enough, so I instinctively jut my hips forward for more connection. He scrapes his teeth against my skin, and I yelp in pleasure and pain.

At that, he pins me with a stare and presses the vibrator flush against my wet, hot need—not inside me, not yet—but it's enough to make me whimper with want.

"Did you use this and think of me?"

"Mhmm." If only he knew how many times I'd silently screamed into my pillow this week, thinking of him while getting myself off.

His gaze crackles, as if he has a glitch in his system. "And what did you imagine?"

"This," I gasp between waves of the vibrator.

"Just this? Or more?"

I moan against the pulses, unable to form full thoughts, much less sentences.

"Tell me, Daze. If it's just tonight, I wanna know. You told me you wouldn't hold back, so say it. What were you thinking about?"

"All of you." A nervous laugh bubbles out of me. "You touching me everywhere. What could have happened in your room. How much I want you inside of me."

The confession hangs between us, and I worry I've been too honest with him. He exhales and shifts back between my thighs.

"For now," he says, "this'll have to do."

When he bends down, the first touch of his mouth to my clit is ecstasy. Then he swipes his tongue, broad and firm, against me, and bursts of warmth compound low in my body. Max doesn't just know what's doing with a vibrator—he knows damn well what he's doing, period.

"You taste so good," he murmurs against me, his hot breath forcing me to shudder.

I'm about ready to beg when I feel the hum of the device poised at my entrance. The sex toy goes inside me, first a little, then more, then a lot—pressure building in me in the most satisfying way. With Max sucking hard on my clit, I throw my head back in response.

"My god," I hiss. "That's so good."

He keeps a steady rhythm going, lapping me up and up and up, and the vibrator sends subtle shock waves through me. The intensity builds until I'm dizzy, poised at a tipping point, and ready to surrender. My orgasm crashes into us both, sending me bucking wildly against him while he holds on for dear life. My vision blurs, and I cry out a string of curse words as Max hums against my most sensitive parts.

I ride the aftershocks, and once I've come down from the high, I open my eyes. My room. My bed. *My Max.* He's sitting back on his heels—his mouth and chin glistening, his pupils wide and wanting.

"That was the sexiest thing I've ever seen." He's looking at me like I'm a feast and he's a starved man, and although I just came on his face, *hard*, I'm aching for more of him. All of him.

"I need you," I whisper without realizing. "I need you so fucking bad."

My chest aches, because what if what comes next isn't enough? It has to be, though. We're not doing a full-blown relationship with all its complications. We're friends. Friends who have sex, but only for one night.

The glint in Max's eye makes me stupid again, and all I can think of is getting closer to him. If this really is only for tonight, no holding back—then I need all of him.

Ravenous, I tear the jeans off his legs and tug at the waistband of his boxer briefs. He's got a gorgeous, taut stomach and a dapple of dark brown hair below his belly button. He slips his underwear off, and his dick bounces, hard and thick and *Oh my god*. The things I want to do to him.

Still lying on the bed, I wrap my hand around his length, and his eyes roll to the back of his head. Has he been hiding this in his pants the entire time I've known him? In high school, I caught a glimpse of him when we stripped down and sneaked into his neighbor's pool—but I don't remember *this*.

He settles onto all fours over me, giving me easier access to stroke him and feel his hard-on as he grows with every touch.

"Good girl," he rasps out as his breath hitches. "God, you give me exactly what I want." The praise courses through me, and I'm salivating and desperate.

"I'll give you anything."

"Shit, Daisy." He holds my wrist so I can't move. "Give me too much, and I won't get to do what I really want to do."

"And what's that?" I ask coyly, a grin playing at the side of my mouth.

"The same thing you want." Max lowers his lips against my ear, and barely audible, he says, "To fuck you 'til you scream my name."

Impatient, I reach for a condom from my nightstand. I'm on birth control, but I always use a second form of protection for one-night stands. I suppose this qualifies, even if it is with Max.

He rolls the condom onto his dick, not letting his eyes leave mine. He hovers over me, his tip nudging my entrance. "I want you to look at me," he says—no, *demands*—and his tone causes my pulse to jump. "You look at me while I fill you up."

He pushes into me, inch by agonizing inch, and I whimper because it's not just his cock stretching me. I feel something bigger and brighter, something that almost makes me want to cry.

"Yeah? Is that what you wanted?" he asks against my lips.

"Yes. And more."

He backs out and slides into me, faster this time.

"Oh god. That. Again."

"How hard do you need me, Daisy?"

I bite back a moan at the sound of my name on his tongue. "Hard."

He grips my ass with one hand, thrusting into me again and sending raw, almost punishing pleasure up my spine.

"S'gonna take a lot more than that to make me scream."

"Never guessed you would like it so rough."

"Normally I don't." I lock eyes with him for another agonizing thrust, willing him to understand that I'm not simply saying what he wants to hear. "Guess it's something just for you."

He slows his pace and takes my chin between his thumb and forefinger, gentle yet commanding. "Tell me if it's too much, Daze."

"I want 'too much.'"

His devilish grin ignites a rush inside me. "You're such a good girl for me." He dips his head and nips at my breast. "Fuck, so good."

"Max." My voice is breathy, uncontrolled. He's sending me back over the edge, pumping at a steady pace—in and out—so that at the peak, my skull bumps the headboard. He leans on an elbow, his hand padding the impact.

"Such a gentleman," I say into his chest.

His lips hover by my ear. "Tell me that after I've made you come again."

The sheer determination in his voice lights me up from the inside, but with every thrust, my head crushes his hand against the metal bars of the bed. "Here. Let's switch."

We do a clumsy tango as I guide him to the pillows and shift my weight so I'm now on top. I stroke his dick and then settle onto him with a sigh.

"Better?" I ask on a breath.

"Perfect."

He rests a hand on one hip, gently guiding me forward and back. The friction makes me snap like a firecracker. He slips his other hand between us, resting his thumb on my clit, which sings with pleasure. Max filling me up and rubbing against me is more than anything I've ever felt. Having him inside me feels like the safest thing in the world, even though it's our first time together. And our only time.

It can only be this once.

As I rock on top of his body, his expression changes to something shy, reserved. Like he thinks I'm made of crystal, and he's afraid he might break me.

"Hey," I say, angling forward and gripping his face, forcing eye contact. "It's just me. Just Daisy."

"Just Daisy." He nods his head quickly. "Just my Daisy."

My heart lurches. As one hand slides to my ass, his other hand pulls me toward him so I'm flush against his chest. I close my eyes as he sends me, once again, into the thrill of something explosive and sublime. The release runs like a roller coaster—a massive burst followed by more and more ripples of euphoria that send my body shaking, gripping around him, and calling his name. When he comes, he groans into my mouth, and I relish in more orgasm aftershocks of my own.

I hold him close and breathe in the warm, zesty scent on his skin, trying to make "just tonight" last just a little longer.

The next day, I vow to spend as little time in Gwen's shop as possible. I'll drop off the monthly supply of Mirage postcards for the local businesses table and scram. Maybe I'll get lucky and she'll have a swarm of customers, offering me an easy out. With a calming breath, I open the door to a mostly empty store.

Damn it.

"Hey you, I was hoping you'd be by soon." Gwen bags whatever crystals and incense a sole customer has purchased at the checkout counter. "*Whoa.*" She looks at me with wide eyes. "You are practically levitating."

"Just dropping off postcards." I channel cool-girl energy. After all, last night was a onetime, no-big-deal arrangement. Never mind that I haven't had a single productive thought in my head longer than twenty seconds before flashbacks of Max all over me, *inside* me, render me useless. At the front desk today, I answered a phone call with, "Yes, please."

"Can't you sense it?" She taps the person at the counter and points at me. The customer's eyes dart back and forth, like he doesn't quite understand what she means.

"I should head out," I say, averting my gaze.

"Oh no you don't." Gwen clasps the man's hands in hers and smiles. "Thank you for coming in. I hope these bring you the peace you're looking for." She ushers him out of the store to block me from sneaking out. The dainty chime on the door is cheerfully ominous. "Good news for The Mirage?" she asks, a glimmer of optimism in her voice.

I shake my head, almost ashamed that my orgasm high made me forget about everything with the hotel.

"Freddie's tests came back negative?"

I busy myself with flyers to avoid eye contact, arranging a pink pyramid-shaped rock on top of the stack. "No, we don't have an appointment for another couple months."

"Then *what*?" she squeaks. "You float in here like a goddess, your aura all shiny and bright, and you're not gonna give me anything?"

If I share what happened, then the night seems more real, more serious—which it most definitely isn't. I love Gwen to the stars and back, but she doesn't need to know that Max Weber gave me multiple orgasms last night.

"I got a good night's sleep. You must be picking up on my restedness."

She says nothing and just lifts an eyebrow.

"Look, I should get going. Love you." In a swift movement, I hug her and give her a peck on the cheek as I hurry out, and I pray she'll let this go. I expect joking threats that I can't avoid her forever, but instead, she wails a cry that stops me in my tracks.

"Gwen." I scramble back to her side as her face contorts, tears spilling down her cheeks. "Ohmygod."

"Hormones," she blubbers. "The baby's making me super emotional lately. But we've..." She hiccups through a thick sob. "You and I have barely seen each other, and I can tell something is going on, and you won't share it with me, and there is so much about having a baby that Bob does *not* understand because of his stupid penis, and I know you're busy, but I'm busy too, and I've got a literal human in me that craves fettuccine alfredo all the time, even for breakfast, and I miss you."

"Aw, Gwen." My heart cracks, and I embrace her as she leaks snot and tears onto my shoulder. These past few weeks, I've been so preoccupied that we've barely texted. My best friend is going through an enormous life change, and I almost walked in and out of here without even asking how she's doing.

"I miss you too," I say, rubbing her back in circular motions. "I'm sorry I upset you."

She sniffles, pulls back, and grabs my hands. "You could make it up to me by telling me what's up."

"Are you legit using your pregnancy to blackmail me?"

"You're going to deny a crying pregnant lady's wishes?"

I might not believe in the mystical powers of gemstones and auras, but my best friend has a knack for knowing when the vibe is off. She's bound to find out at some point.

"Fine," I concede. "But Gwen, you...promise me you'll stay calm. And you can't talk about this with anyone."

"Yes and yes. Girl Scout's honor."

"And you know it's really weird how you're able to do that."

"What?"

"Whatever aura, vibey shit you do."

The familiar chime of the door sounds again, the delicate ring spreading a joyful grin across my friend's face.

"Welcome in."

"Hi. Oh, hi!" Dawn registers me and waves. "Got your message about speech prep. Happy to help. And I've been talking to local businesses all day for our project. Also, you are *glowing*."

"Thank you," Gwen replies, cradling her still-flat belly.

"Wait, you're pregnant?"

They both let out uneasy chuckles.

"Uh, yeah. I am."

"Well, you're both glowing, then."

My best friend examines me closer, and heat travels up my neck. "Your skin's all dewy," she says, "and you have this natural blush thing going on. Did you get a massage?"

"No," Dawn says, "that's the face of someone who got dicked down."

Gwen's head whips to me, and her eyes bulge. "You did not."

"Before we jump to any conclusions—" I say, but Gwen cuts me off.

"You had sex with *Max*?"

"Hello?" I gesture to Dawn, whose mouth forms a scandalized O shape. "What part about not talking about this with anyone did you forget?"

"Ugh, sorry." She covers her face as if she can hide from the mistake.

"An orgasm would explain the glow." Dawn nods in approval. "Good for you."

"No, not good," Gwen says to Dawn. "There is a lot of baggage with him."

"We don't need to discuss my baggage. Just because not all of us were lucky enough to find our life partner like you have, doesn't mean—"

"You're right, I'm sorry." She puts her hands in prayer position, resting her fingertips against her lips. "But Max? *Max.* The same Max you hopped on a—"

"Things have changed since eight years ago."

"Hang on." Dawn steps between us and holds up her hands like an MMA referee. "I don't want to get in the way, so I can leave. But if I'm going to stick around, I'm gonna need a drink."

And this is how I end up sitting at a table used for tarot readings in a dim back room of Gwen's store, with her on one side and Dawn on the other. Flickering candles with earthy, spicy scents make the space feel mysterious yet comfortable. The crystal shop has wine and sparkling grape juice for special events, so we've each got a glass as we perch on floor pillows.

After I fill them in on last night, Gwen holds her juice, mouth gaping. Dawn, on the other hand, giggles into her wine.

"Multiple orgasms and pepperoni pizza after?" Dawn sighs wistfully. "Some women really can have it all."

Maybe it's the buzziness of my second brimming glass of pinot—or that I just shared every detail of my sex life—but I am so glad she's here to balance out Gwen's protectiveness.

"He knew what he was doing then?" Dawn asks.

"Mhmm." I smile at Dawn, then at Gwen, who appears to be processing everything. "You're awfully quiet."

She sighs. "I never would have pinned Max Weber as a dirty-talking type."

"People can surprise us."

"I'm not surprised one bit," Dawn says. "He seemed *into* you. Buy a collar and teach that man to bark on command. Woof woof, baby."

"He was a complete simp for her in high school."

"You should fuck him again," Dawn says flatly, pouring us both more wine before filling Gwen's glass up with juice.

"Not happening," I say with bravado. "We're keeping things professional."

"He called you a good girl, and you came on his face." Dawn scoffs into her drink. "Good luck with that."

"We are," I reply, with a confidence that turns the beverage bitter in my mouth. "There's so much riding on this pop-up. The whole point was to get it out of our systems, and we did."

"Multiple times." Dawn hoots and kicks up one foot.

"Are you freaking out?" Gwen asks and rests a compassionate hand on my arm. I know what she's asking—*Are you freaking out because, in case you forgot, you had feelings for him too, once upon a time?*

"No." I look right at Gwen, putting her—and maybe some of my own—concerns at bay. "I think I've been in survival mode with The Mirage for a while, so honestly, it was nice to do something for me."

"I'm sure." She searches my face. "Well, it's not the self-care I would have planned for you, but orgasms can really nourish the second chakra. They're good for the soul."

"And so is getting to share all this with you. I promise to make more time with the baby on the way."

"I won't argue about that. So…you'll go back to normal with him? That's the plan?" Gwen cradles her head in her hands. I love that even when I decide on something she doesn't entirely agree with, she doesn't guilt me.

"You two are supposed to be working together," Dawn says.

"And living together," Gwen adds.

I shrug their worries away. "We'll go on like it never happened. Simple as that."

Last night was a lot of things. Some of the best sex of my life. Impulsive. Insanely hot. My masturbation material for the foreseeable future. But we agreed we'd move forward like adults, and I can do that. Max can too…other than a few gazes this morning that lasted milliseconds too long, and one of those painfully awkward trying-to-step-out-of-the-way-but-acciden-tally-running-into-each-other moments in the kitchen, we're good.

"You need to be more proactive." Gwen taps her finger against the table. "Otherwise, someone's feelings will get hurt. Meet in a public place and do something thoroughly unsexy so there's no temptation to hook up again. Set a new precedent. Reiterate your ground rules."

"Unsexy?" I ask.

"You know." Gwen waves her hand in the air, conjuring sug-gestions. "Assemble IKEA furniture. Watch a war documentary. Go to the DMV."

"That's insane."

"It's not a bad idea," Dawn says as she nods her head. "I'm Team Fuck Again, but I respect there's history there. And if anyone can attest—from personal experience—that mixing business and pleasure can go wrong, it's me. So if this guy has liked you as long as Gwen says, she's probably right. Make sure you're clear on things, you know?"

I hadn't considered that. If I'm feeling this conflicted over what we did, I can only guess what he's experiencing. I'd hate to toy with his emotions.

"I'm happy you got laid and that it was good," Gwen says, nudging my knee with hers. "But this is Max we're talking about. When the time comes to let him go, will you be able to?"

"Yes," I insist. "He is officially out of my system."

Just Daisy. Just my Daisy.

I try to chase the image out of my brain, but he's all I can think about the rest of the night.

Chapter Nineteen

Daisy, 17 Years Old

I tensed from the stabbing pain in my side. At least the pop music blared loud enough and there was plenty of alcohol at this party to distract everyone from me acting like a baby during my first tattoo.

"Stop moving," Max said, eyes trained on his work in deep concentration.

"Trying."

"Almost done. Elmo was a good choice."

"Not funny."

Max held the skin of my ribcage taut with his palm, and his fingers curled gently around my torso—something to take my mind off the sewing needle jabbing into me. The way I'd yanked my shirt up and settled onto my back, he could probably see some of the lower part of my breasts. Gentleman that he was, he kept his hand clear—for my sake, his girlfriend's, or both.

"You parents're gonna kill me," he muttered.

The basketball player throwing the party while his parents were away stumbled into the room, leading a blonde girl from my English class with him. They both halted at the sight of me sprawled on the bed and Max kneeling on the floor for the best angle.

"Shit," the guy slurred.

"Oh, hey, Daisy," the girl said with a smile, and I waved back.

"When'll you two be done in here?"

"Ten," Max said, pausing his work. "Maybe fifteen."

"Cool."

The couple tottered closer, and the stench of beer radiated from them.

"Damn, that looks *good*, Matt," the girl said.

"It's Max," I corrected her.

"Fuck yeah." This dude's eyes had definitely shifted from the flower tattoo up to the spillage of my underboob. "Real nice."

"You next?" Max asked with a smirk on his face, pulling their attention away from my body. "Couple's tats?"

They shook their heads, and the girl tugged on her boyfriend's hand to lead him out. "Let's find another room."

"I want my first one to be epic," he announced to nobody in particular. "Classic design, back piece. My cousin told me he could do it."

"Let me guess," Max said and eyed him. "Phoenix. Rising from the ashes."

His eyes glimmered in awe. "Dude, how'd you know?"

"No idea, Ash. But I can't wait to see it."

When the two of them left the room, we laughed.

"How did you get that from just his name?"

"I could hear him talking about it from up here." Max picked up his improvised pencil-and-needle mechanism for tattooing me. "C'mon. Just a little more." He continued poking the design into my skin, and I admired his dedicated focus. His eyes flicked up and met mine, sending the corner of his mouth up. "You're doing great."

"What's Lily up to tonight?" I blurted out, diverting my attention to the photos on the dresser. Max hadn't mentioned her at all this evening. True, we didn't discuss relationships much, and I usually kept time with boyfriends and time with Max separate. I liked having hangouts with Max and Gwen, or just

Max. Friends. But he'd been with Lily for a while, and I could tell he wanted us to be friends, too.

"Family reunion," Max said. "Why?"

"Just curious. She's gonna be next for your stick-and-poke service?"

"Doubtful. I don't think Lily's a fan of needles."

"Nobody's a fan of needles."

He chuckled under his breath. "She's squeamish. If we're watching a movie where there's blood, she has to cover her eyes."

I imagined them sitting together on the sofa, his arm around her as she squealed and squirmed closer to him. Lily was perfectly nice, but annoying. She always had to be by Max if we hung out in groups, she held his hand whenever we walked anywhere, and she kissed him all the time. Sometimes she'd plant one on him out of the blue, and all I could do was stare at them making out.

"I really like her," Max said, getting more ink. "I think I love her."

"Ow." The needle felt sharper. Max was in love? Was he certain? I'd liked some of my boyfriends a lot, but never loved them. "How do you know?"

"Know what?"

"That you love her." My gaze roamed to his jawline for a millisecond.

"I don't know for sure. It's not the first time. It's just the first time with someone who...you know, I think feels the same way." He paused and scratched the back of his neck. "Done. You should take a look."

I didn't care about the tattoo anymore, but I stood and admired the artwork in the full-length mirror anyway. The lines were crisp, the curves elegant, and he did larger dots to create the shaded sections. No one would believe I got this at a house party instead of a boutique tattoo shop with a year-long waitlist.

"A Max Weber original." I smiled at him. "I love it."

"Hey, you twooo." Gwen appeared in the doorway, her pupils the size of the moon. "Good goddess, you're both so beautiful."

"How much of that tea did you drink?" Max asked, holding back a laugh.

"I'm discovering colors I didn't know existed." She gasped at my tattoo. "Oooh, pretty."

"No touching." Max blocked Gwen's incoming palm, and she pouted.

"No fun."

"Just watching out for our Daze here." He rested a hand on my arm and inspected the artwork again. My body heated under his attention. "I have to grab the Aquaphor from downstairs. Be right back."

We watched him go, and Gwen grabbed both of my hands in hers.

"Daisy, can I ask you something?"

"Is it what I think you're going to ask? Because you've already asked it before. Multiple times."

"I sense the energy there." Gwen's brows soared. I enjoyed having her around, even though she was infuriatingly intuitive, sober or not. "You've thought about it. You and Max?"

"I—" With a glance down the hall, I made sure no one was coming. "You won't tell anyone?"

"Not a soul."

"So..." I sighed and halfway hoped Gwen was too far gone to remember what I'd say next. "Maybe there's been little crushes between us here and there, but nothing's ever happened."

Her shoulders slumped, deflated from my lack of salacious details, but my heart pounded with the confession. That was the closest I'd ever come to admitting I had a crush on Max. That's what those feelings were, though—crushes. And I'd have to be an idiot to think he didn't also have a crush now and then, too, but that was before Lily. She wasn't even his first love.

"Do you want something to happen?" Gwen's voice went soft.

Max returned, giving me an excuse not to reply. As he rubbed some healing lotion into the ink, my thoughts stumbled. Sometimes at night, I'd lie in bed after a date or making out with a guy in his car, and my mind would travel to Max. Throughout our friendship, we'd talked on the phone until the sun rose or sprawled out for movie marathons on his couch. He'd dropped me off hundreds of times at my house before, like a boyfriend, but we had never kissed. And I knew why.

Max had already started getting mail from colleges across the US, over a year out from graduation, and I struggled to keep my grades decent. He was bound for something amazing and artistic, and he deserved to get out from under his parents' scrutiny. I wouldn't stand in the way of him and Lily, someone he *loved*, and I wouldn't be the reason he stuck around, either.

Relationships meant sacrifice. Resentment. I could never bear to have him look at me the way my mom and dad looked at each other during their fights.

It was a crush, I reminded myself. A crush wasn't worth blowing up our whole friendship over. It would pass.

Chapter Twenty

Max, Now

Daisy grunts as one of the hairiest men I've ever seen helps her onto a chocolaty-brown horse. As she settles in, my attention slides to her ass, which looks perfect perched on a saddle. The visual transports me instantly to the other night—the warmth inside her, the mesmerizing rhythm of her gyrating on top of me, the satisfying rush of her coming against my mouth.

"Need an assist?" The ranch owner is a stout, mustachioed man with a juicy smoker's cough that's an insanely effective antidote to the semi growing in my pants.

I thank him but manage on my own. He's brought over a stunning black mare, and once I climb onto the saddle, I pat her on the side. "Good girl," I say, stroking her mane.

"Mr. Cowboy over there." Daisy lets out a breathy laugh, her cheeks the shade of a setting sun.

"Ride often?" the man asks. His bushy brows arch upward in surprise.

"Now and then. An ex-girlfriend of mine grew up outside Dublin on a farm. I spent some holidays there."

Daisy clears her throat and pivots her body away from me. "We'll go down Glimmering Canyon Loop."

"Helmet for either of you?"

Daisy used to work here and said he would ask, even though they're optional. I signed a waiver, and we're not planning anything strenuous, so we both decline.

He sticks a satellite phone in her saddlebag, and we set out on a trail wide enough for us to travel side by side. The ground has a sandy texture here, and the horses' hooves squish with each step. The land rises to hills on either side, so some splintered tree trunks and small boulders have collected in the center—something that happens after a rare, heavy rainfall.

She flicks her attention to me, my hands on the reins, and then back to the path, which is strewn with a few broken-off cacti and wiry twigs. "We should talk."

"That sounds ominous."

Her playful glare forces the corner of my mouth to twitch.

"Is there a reason we're talking on horseback?" I ask.

Her horse's pace slows, and he huffs, followed by letting out a thundering fart that seems to echo off the terrain.

"Neutral location," she says. "Somewhere we won't be distracted."

As if on cue, her horse halts completely for a bathroom break.

"Well, I don't know about you," I say, waving my hand against the earthy manure scent, "but I'm not distracted at all."

"Max." Daisy tilts her head and her face cracks into a reluctant smile. She clearly doesn't want literal horseshit to be the reason she devolves into giggles, but she does anyway. "Damn it. Gwen did not think this through."

"What about Gwen?"

She snaps her wrist and heels Derry gently on his side. "I stopped by her store last night."

So that's where she was. I'd lingered in the living room, thinking she might walk in the door anytime. Maybe hoping.

"I told her what happened. With us."

This causes me to pause. As much as I've wanted to scream from the mountaintops that we slept together, I haven't told a soul. Keeping it between us was never part of the agreement, but I didn't think we had to explicitly lay that out.

"What did you tell her?"

"Girl talk." She shrugs and tosses me a coy look. "Dawn was there too."

"Anyone else?" I ask, half joking. Telling other people makes it feel less special, less important. Daisy never even told *me* how she liked our night together. While heated images of her wrapped up in me will keep my mind and hand busy for years to come, what if the experience wasn't so stellar for her?

"Did you invite Sal?" I go on. "Or that nice lady at the gas station?"

"I wouldn't have spent the evening talking about you if I hadn't enjoyed it. I had fun." She catches my gaze and smiles in a way that makes me speechless. "It was good things, Max."

Our horses fall into a steady rhythm next to each other as I process what she's said. *Good things?* I can handle good things.

"So..." I fight the desire to hop off my horse and do a backflip. "Is horseback riding your way of telling me I'm a good lay?"

She laughs, and the sound is loud and unexpected, sending a jolt of satisfaction down my spine.

"Don't get cocky. And put that dimple away."

"I'll try." I shake my head and glance at her with a laugh, giving her one last look at it.

"Stop."

"Fine."

She waits a beat. "It's still there."

"I can't help it." I shrug. "Not used to seeing you all flustered. Not over me. I'm enjoying the moment."

She snorts a little laugh. "I'm sorry that I haven't held up my end of our deal."

Does she mean she's changed her mind? My heart soars, dreaming of what she might say next. *I want more than just one night. I want you, again. Need you.*

"I told you I wouldn't let it get weird between us," she goes on, "and I definitely did the past twenty-four hours."

"Ah. Yeah." I swat at a fly on the back of my neck. "You were pretty preoccupied with the laundry this morning. You ran about seventeen loads."

"Are we good?"

I look at Daisy and try not to think about how I've seen every side of her, every curve and edge and angle. How I've found the quiet places of her body that make her moan, and how I've come inside her. But more than that, I have a connection with her that I don't have with anyone else.

I don't want to ruin that or push her away. Part of me wants more, but Daisy made the terms clear—and I can't always be the guy who's yearning for more with Daisy Johnson. I hate to admit it, but the *only one night* plan was a smart one.

"We're good," I say. "Actually, I wanted to talk about something. You mentioned bringing on local artists for the exhibit."

She takes a long, deep breath. "Yeah."

"I think—" I say, as she bulldozes ahead with, "It might not—"

"No, let me go first," she says firmly. "I understand this wasn't your original vision, and you think local artists won't have as much of a draw for a wider audience. And maybe this isn't how you've done any kind of pop-up before, but this isn't like any other pop-up. People travel to discover places with character—with heart. This shouldn't be a museum that you could find anywhere in the world—it should be special, because Harlow is special.

"And," she says, closing her eyes as if gathering her strength to tell me this next part, "I can't budge on this. Setting up a place with a bunch of artwork from outsiders is the same thing to me as folks buying up land and building chic homes to rent out. We need locals."

"All right."

She pulls the reins so her horse comes to a stop with a snort. "What?"

"You want local artists, and we'll have them. I reached out to some people, and there's a lot of interest."

After some consideration, I understood what she wanted for the pop-up and agreed it made sense. Sure, I was coasting on an orgasm yesterday when I contacted some of Harlow's favorites in the creative scene, but I wouldn't have done so if I thought the idea was misguided. It would certainly be a unique mix of artists, but that would be exactly what Tate is looking for—and Daisy's onto something. It feels right.

"So who's in?" she asks.

I give her the names of people I've connected with, some of whom she knows, others who she's less familiar with, and we continue on to the bottom of the gully where rocks and branches have collected. This terrain requires even more attention—like walking a tightrope on horseback.

"I thought for sure I'd have to fight you on this," she says.

"I don't want you to fight me on anything. Besides, I may have the experience, but I'm not doing this alone. I'm doing it with you, and it's a good idea."

She smiles, her lips pressed together. "What made you change your mind?"

"You're passionate about Harlow." I direct my horse around a blackened tree trunk, likely charred from lightning. "Some of my preconceived notions from high school may not be so true anymore, and I can admit that. Places change. People change. And at the end of the day—at the end of everything, I trust you."

And the sunny smile that spreads across Daisy's face makes it worth it. I hate that I'm a sucker for that smile.

"So what you're saying," she says, her look turning mischievous, "is that my vagina convinced you."

I don't point out how she's using humor to deflect talking with me more honestly, and I don't ask if she washed the same load of laundry over and over to avoid running into me today, because my body has gone cold. All I can say is, "Daisy, stop."

"Jeez, it's a joke."

"No, *stop*." I reach over and yank on her reins, jerking her to a halt.

"What—" The unmistakable shake of a rattlesnake cuts her off. We've encountered a fat, coiled one sunning itself in the middle of the path.

"Back up," I whisper to her, patting her hands into action. I haven't seen a rattlesnake face-to-face in years, but I remember how to deal with snakes on the trail. Daisy and I move in slow motion, one step, then another, not losing sight of the snake. Then, behind us comes a crack—her horse's leg gives out, and he makes a high-pitched whinny. I reach for Daze, but it's too late—her horse rears, and she soars toward the gritty earth.

My heart flies out of my body at the sight of Daisy in a puddle on the ground. I dismount so fast I trip, which spooks the horses even more.

"Whoa," I say, holding up my hands to calm them.

I kneel next to Daisy and call her name to no response. Panic rises in my throat, but I swallow it. Now's not the time to lose it, and all those Boy Scout meetings my parents made me attend have officially come in handy.

When I scan for the snake, I catch its tail end slithering away. I fight every instinct in me and leave Daisy's side, fetching the reins for the horses to secure them to a large branch on the side of the trail, before grabbing the satphone. As I head over to Daisy, she's lifting her upper body, and her eyes quiver open.

"Hey." I rush to rest a firm hand on her shoulder, preventing her from moving around. "You fell, but you're safe. I'm gonna call 911."

"Holy shit."

"Stay calm."

"I just fell off a horse, Max, nothing about me is calm!"

"I know." I ditch the phone to grab her head in both my hands, steadying her skull and forcing her to focus solely on me. "But I need you to listen to me, okay?"

She blinks a few times in rapid succession, finally whispering an "Okay" in response.

An anxious pit forms in my stomach seeing her less stubborn than her usual self.

"Do you remember what happened?" I ask.

"I f-fell."

Her pupils look normal for the amount of sunlight right now. I give her my sunglasses anyway, since she's wincing from the sun overhead.

"You passed out," I say.

"How long?"

"Ten seconds, maybe." It may as well have been an eternity.

"That's not bad."

"It was ten seconds too long." I rest a palm on her cheek and stroke it with my thumb. The sooner I get her to a doctor, the better. "Do you know where you are?" I ask.

"The ranch. It's like," she says, waving her hand to our left, "literally right over there."

I'm about to make the phone call, but I look in the direction she pointed. We're close enough to the stables that a corner of a building appears down the path. If I want Daisy to be seen by a medical professional as soon as possible, I'm better off driving her myself, if she's okay to move. An ambulance might take a while, half an hour even, and I'd rather not have her cooking in the sunlight with a concussion when she could be getting help in the emergency room.

"How's your neck?"

"Fine, I think." She tilts her head from side to side in slow motion. "Yeah, fine."

"No pain, discomfort?"

She takes some time to consider my question. "My head hurts a little."

"But your neck and your back feel okay?"

"Yeah, I'm good."

Cautiously, I guide Daisy's arms over my shoulders and hoist her up, her back supported by one arm, her legs hooked over the other.

"I can walk," she says, half laughing.

"Not chancing it. Your balance is probably shit right now, anyway."

"Rude."

One horse snorts behind us, and I catch the concern in Daisy's furrowed brows.

"I'll let him know where they are, Daze."

I make the short trek back to the barn, powering through the muscle burn. It must be the adrenaline turning me into some kind of trail-accident triathlete. A screen door slams, and the owner zips out, worry in every corner of his face. Daisy's grip on me tightens, and her head bobs into my arm as I tell the rancher where his horses are and ask him to open the passenger side of my car.

When I set her in the seat, Daisy looks out of it—it's probably the shock setting in. I want to teleport to the hospital, because I need her lying down, with a doctor checking her vitals. When I buckle her in, I catch her wary eyes tracking me.

"You okay?" I ask, checking in.

"Mhmm."

It takes ages to get to the ER, even going at least fifteen over the speed limit. Daisy shakes her head when we pull into the lot, muttering, "I can't go in."

"You need a doctor, Daze."

"No, please. I hate it in there."

This is different from her usual defiance, and my heart sinks when I realize why. The hesitation in her body, the fear on her face...I don't know what it was like when her mom died. Daisy told me about the wreck—her mom swerved to avoid a coyote, lost control, and collided with another car—but she didn't tell me about the immediate aftermath. How long did Daisy pace those cold hospital halls? Did she arrive and get the bad news instantly, or did Amy hang in there for a few hours before the end?

My gaze locks on Daisy, regretting what she went through and that she went through it alone. Not alone—but without me.

Grabbing one of her hands, I say, "I'm with you. We're together, okay?"

Her eyes are glassy as she looks between me and the doors. Eventually, she nods, her arms encircling my neck as I carry her inside.

We get checked into a room right away, much to the dismay of a few people in the waiting area. Other than a form I fill out with Daisy, the nurse gets most of the information verbally and enters it into the system. The doctor orders a few tests, and when they escort Daze to get a cautionary CT scan, I take my first breath since that horse reared and she tumbled off the saddle. My adrenaline has sucked up my last drop of energy, but I'm too wired to relax. I lean against the wall and stare at the ceiling, taking deep breaths as I avoid thinking about how much worse this could have been.

"I got here as quick as I could." Gwen rushes into the room, the fabric of her oversized dress waving behind her. Daisy asked me to reach out to her when we arrived, and ten seconds later, Gwen responded. Something clicks into place, seeing an old friend who's as frazzled and worried as I am.

Gwen stares at the empty bed, and her expression falls. "Oh, no."

"She's okay," I say, taking a step forward and folding her into a hug without a second thought. "Getting a CT scan, and she'll be back here soon."

"Okay. Okay." She exhales, gripping me tight. "What happened?"

I rehash the events as she nods with every piece of information. When I tell Gwen how Daisy slumped to the ground, I swallow the thick dread of reliving that moment.

"I'm glad you were there." Gwen lets out a measured exhale. "I'll also need to have a few choice words with that snake."

"I can make that happen."

"Did you call her dad?"

"He's on his way." My skin prickles as I recall the heartbreaking sob from Richard's end of the line.

Gwen slumps in the chair next to the hospital bed and twirls one of her rings. "She told me about your arrangement."

"I know."

"Please, just...don't be stupid, okay?"

"I'm trying."

"Do more than try," she says, crossing her arms. "Consider it your life's purpose. You're both adults, so have fun, but I really don't want anyone's heart destroyed here. Especially Daisy's."

"What are you—"

Daisy's laughter prompts both our heads to whip toward the door. A nurse wheels her in, and although Daisy looks exhausted, she is the same warm, wonderful woman as always. Gwen bursts into tears and dotes on Daisy while I replay what she said. I only ever did what Daisy asked. To claim I have the power to destroy her heart seems extreme, especially when she's the one who destroyed mine first.

The doctor comes in to let us know the CT scan showed a minor concussion, and a nurse will arrive soon to discuss aftercare. Gwen gets a salty-and-sweet craving, so she pops out to visit the vending machine, leaving me and Daisy alone.

"Relax." Daisy fiddles with her ID bracelet. "You look like a wreck."

"Yeah, well…" I can't attempt to express how grateful I am that nothing truly terrible or irreversible happened. "I was worried."

"Thank you."

"Daze, you fucking *fell*. What'd you think I would do? Leave you on the trail to fend for yourself?"

"No, for being here. I don't…I don't love hospitals."

She looks so small, so helpless, hooked up to all the wires and machines. I long to curl up with her, without getting tangled up or hurting her, just to give her a place to feel safe.

"Of course, Daisy."

"But also, thank you for the research you did," she says, her tone shifting. "With the local artists." Her smile is soft.

"You're in the hospital. You have a concussion." I shake my head in disbelief. "And still, work is the top thing on your mind."

"The hotel is my life, Max." She shrugs. "My life is the hotel. I can't separate the two."

When Daisy is in, she's in completely. It's why life with her feels so full—almost too much—she gives all of herself to what she really wants. That truth sucker-punches my gut, because she's holding back with me and keeping a careful distance. I won't push her, because she has every right to feel that way, but I can't lie to her, either.

"I understand that, Daze," I say, sitting in the guest chair by her bed. "I mean, I think I do. You act like an emotional cruise director with certain things in your life, but I know how much The Mirage means to you. But when you fell, I stopped breathing." I scoot closer and reach for her forearm, overwhelmed that she's real and here. "I hated every moment out there, and I had all these thoughts and concerns going through my head. But nothing—none of it—had to do with the museum or with work. Because I wouldn't care about anything else if something happened to you."

She blinks a couple times, her gaze falling to her hands in her lap. My chest echoes with emptiness, seeing her so visibly uncomfortable with my vulnerability.

Gwen storms back in, shocking us both out of the moment. "Okay, no caffeine, obviously, but I asked the nurses, and they said dark chocolate has magnesium, which is good after a concussion. Want some?"

Daisy pauses, looking at me again for a split second before turning to her friend. "Yeah." Her voice cracks. "I'd love some."

Chapter Twenty-One

Daisy, Now

"Missy." Stacey threatens me by waving a spatula in my direction. She has stepped up from her usual Mirage duties to help Max care for me, and it's a responsibility she takes seriously. "Plant your tush back on the couch or else."

"I can walk around my own house."

"Nuh-uh. Rest and relaxation. Doctor's orders. Besides, we need you camera-ready in a couple days."

I avoid dwelling on the interview—because I *really* don't want to think about that—and I give Stacey a dismissive hand wave. "That doctor's overly cautious."

"Ma'am." Stacey gives me an icy, mean stare. "Sit."

"Okay," I grumble. Everyone is acting as if I've caught the bubonic plague. I hate being useless, and I don't like leaving The Mirage in the hands of other people, even if those people are as trustworthy as Stacey and Max.

I hobble back to the couch, using the armrest for support. My ankle still hurts, and I'm sure I'll have a headache within the hour, but I can work. I *want* to work—not sit on the sofa all day. Because right now, it's that, or recall the fear in Max's voice. The concern written on his face as I got my bearings in the dirt. His confession in the hospital.

I wouldn't care about anything else if something happened to you.

Maybe a soap opera would do me some good. I nestle into the couch with the extra pillows Max brought out from his room. They smell like him.

"Tonight's guests show up?" I ask Stacey as I flip through channels.

"They were pulling in as I came over here to help you out. Max is giving them a warm welcome. He's a natural, you know."

"That's Max." I can imagine how every guest has fallen in love with him.

"You should hire him."

"Max is the whole reason the pop-up exists."

"I mean for the hotel." She wipes the counters down, despite having done so right before loading the dishes. "Extra help wouldn't hurt, 'specially someone like him."

A stabbing pain in my leg prompts me to resituate myself on the couch. "He's an art curator, not a hotel manager. Besides, he doesn't have plans to stay in Harlow." My throat feels sandy.

"With good enough reason, he might."

I give her a flat look to smother whatever her imagination has convinced her is going on. "Stop it with the matchmaker stuff."

"Who said anything about matchmaking?" She peers out my window as if she can see him in the lobby, working away. "Although he did grow up to be a handsome young man. Easy on the eyes." She practically swoons as she folds the towel and places it in a drawer. "Got that whole sensitive thing going for him. He's such a *man*."

"I can pass along your number, if you'd like." I laugh, and she playfully flips me off. "Didn't realize you liked the soft boys so much."

"Oh, yeah. Give me an emotional guy any day of the week."

"Is Paul in touch with his emotions?" Her husband always seems so stoic and reserved.

"My Paul? Cries more than me. Can't take that cutie to the cinema without a full box of tissues in my purse."

"What movies are you seeing with him?"

"All kinds. Don't matter if it's an animated one or one of those action ones with all the cars. He's a blubbering fool, but I'm pretty sure the sun shines out his asshole."

I laugh again as Max himself opens the door, ushering in some refreshing night air. He looks me up and down on the couch, lingering on my legs. They're exposed, save for the barely-there pajama shorts I'm wearing.

"You look good."

He simply means that I look well, that I'm recovering—that's it!—so I ignore the heat inching up my neck. "Thanks."

"The Winstons are checked in—they love the room. I told them about Monday karaoke at Sal's, so they'll book an extra night."

I snort, equally impressed and irritated. "How are you better at my job than I am?"

"I'm not. Am I more persuasive? Maybe. Do I have the Max Weber Charm? Of course. But—"

"Okay, that's enough," I say, flinging a pillow in his direction, which he snatches midair.

"You are the one who runs this place. Along with Stacey, who has her own lovely charm." Max nods toward her, and she titters a laugh. "I'm simply filling in until you're better."

"Which I am."

"Not for two days, you're not," Stacey says, one hand perched on her hip.

"Stace, when you had your fall, I had to practically get a restraining order for you to stay home. You enjoy me being bedridden way too much."

"Damn right I do." Stacey dries her hands on her thighs and smiles. "Alright, you kids need anything else before I head out?"

We send Stacey on her way, and Max relaxes onto the sofa next to me. I pull my knees into my chest to give him some more room, and my left side pulses with an aching discomfort.

"Easy," Max says.

"How was today?"

"Not bad. Stacey did a great job of doling out tasks. Kind of hard without a solid list, though. You should have the daily routines documented for events like this."

"Events like this are incredibly rare."

"But not impossible, obviously."

"I know," I say, connecting the dots of the beauty marks on my thigh. A guide to running The Mirage would have been helpful two years ago, and I couldn't believe that my mom never wrote one. I scoured through her files—a chaotic mix of invoices and personal reminders—but never found anything comprehensive. I've had that task on my list ever since, but something else always takes precedence.

"It's usually just me and Stacey, and we know what we're doing."

"I never understood how much work goes into running this place. Making sure the rooms are totally cleaned, refilling used-up items, laundry, answering phone calls—all of it. A few of those things on their own, no big deal. But all together? And then there's, you know, *you*."

"What's that mean?"

"You, I don't know...you welcome people here in a special way. Make them feel like they're staying with their cool cousin or something, not just paying for a few nights at a hotel."

His pride is unmistakable, and it makes me fidget with the hem of my shorts. He's so supportive, even when half the time I'm not doing this job right, and the other half it drains me completely.

"Sorry you got roped into being a hotelier," I say.

"I don't mind. Here." He taps the armrest to his left and motions for me to stretch out my legs. I do, strapping him in like a seatbelt with my shins. He lifts the foot I didn't injure and starts massaging the arch, thumbs rubbing relaxation right into my soles.

"Oh my god." My head tilts back. "That's so nice."

A satisfied smile creeps onto his face. "Has it been miserable sitting inside all day while everybody does your bidding?"

"I fucking hate it."

Max lets out a loud laugh. "Most people would consider it a vacation."

"I hate vacations."

"Only you, Daisy."

"I do!" I switch feet for him. "Gentle on this one, please."

His hands glide over my foot in a way that feels too good for a soothing foot rub between friends. But I can't get used to this—not in a friendly way, or in a more-than-friendly way. Max won't stay here forever.

"You okay?" he asks.

"Yeah. It's, um, it's just difficult to sit here while my hotel is out there, waiting for me."

"It's not going anywhere."

My usual end-of-day tasks nag at me. "Did you remember to dust the lobby?"

"Yes."

"And rearrange the pebbles on the path? So they're not all kicked around?"

"Yes, my *god*." Max rests my foot on his lap, right between his thighs. The warmth is cozy and inviting. "Stace and I have it covered."

"I know, it's just..." I shift my attention to a loose thread on the couch. "I like doing it myself."

"You like being in charge."

Except in bed with you, the voice inside my head says. *Then you can do whatever you want.*

Max rests a hand on my knee, and I have the feral urge to spread my thighs a few inches and see where this could go.

His thumb rubs once, then twice, but he pulls away like a spell has been broken. "What should we do for dinner?" He taps my calf so I lift up my legs, and the absence of his body makes the couch its own vast desert landscape.

I must be imagining that our time together edges on something deliciously dangerous. Clearly, Max is managing just fine with me in the house.

He stalks to the kitchen and starts opening and closing cabinets. "Pasta? We've got tofu in the fridge. Or should we order a pizza?"

"Indian."

"Okay. You call the order in, and I can do pickup."

"I'll go."

"You're cute, thinking that's even in the realm of possibility." He walks back to me with a glass of water in one hand and two pills in the other. "Here."

"Thanks," I say as I sit up halfway. "I forgot."

"Busy worrying about everyone and everything else, and not taking care of yourself. Stay here and relax." Max stands beside me, looking down while I tilt my head back and dry-swallow the medication. "Drink. All of it."

I'm acutely aware of how close I am to the fly of his pants and how a single zipper is all that separates us from another evening of *just tonight* promises. My heart can't handle anything more than what he and I are right now, in this moment—but that won't stop my imagination from running wild with reminders of that night.

I empty the glass gulp by gulp, never losing eye contact with him. Max tracks my every move. His Adam's apple bobs, and he wipes some of the water from the corner of my mouth with his thumb.

"Good girl." His words send a current of longing straight to my core, and too soon, too quickly, he pulls his hand away. As he heads toward the door, I'm left yearning for all the things I shouldn't want.

When Max said we landed some television press, I expected something small. A camera person and a host, maybe. This is a full-on production, complete with lighting people—*people*, as in multiple—a makeup artist to dab our faces, someone holding the mic, numerous other tech people, and another person walking around looking highly professional with a clipboard.

"We need more light from the left side." The cargo-pants-clad woman behind the camera points to her screen. "Can someone pop a reflector over there to fill the shadow?"

"This is a lot for the news," I say to Max as a lighting lady zips past us.

"It's a special segment, so they go all out. Sure you want me on there?"

I nod. The series highlights women business owners, but he's part of this team, too. This museum wouldn't be happening if it weren't for him.

I'm so glad Max is here.

Also, I might throw up if I have to do this alone. We've gotten publicity for The Mirage before, but that happened via email or phone call. Nothing on camera.

The host, Ysabelle, strides over from the other side of the barn in her sky-high heels. She looks effortlessly glam—far more suited to go get drinks and dance the night away than chat in a two-minute segment with us.

"Sixty seconds," the camera operator calls, prompting Ysabelle to jump to her mark.

"Remember what Dawn told you," Max says, rubbing my lower back. It causes my insides to growl. "Be natural. Keep it short and sweet. It comes off more confident."

I steal a glance at him. He's probably done this a billion times before. I've even seen some of those interviews over the years, thanks to my internet sleuthing, and he has a way of reeling a viewer in and answering questions that's patient and kind. I must look like a child in an elementary school talent show in comparison.

"Ten, nine, eight..."

A horse is galloping in my chest.

"You've got this," Max says with a wink, and for a split second, I'm free-falling. He's doing this museum thing for him, I know that—but he's been such a wonderful presence on the property and in my own place. He made me believe that maybe there's a light at the end of this tunnel.

"Daisy?"

Ysabelle and Max have their eyes on me. I glance around the room to the cameraman, the lighting person, the makcup guy—they're all staring.

"Um, what?"

"I would be speechless too, in a gorgeous space like this." Ysabelle giggles, lightening the mood. God, she's good at her job. "Tell us why you've decided to host a pop-up museum at The Mirage hotel."

"Well." What did we rehearse earlier? "My mom liked art—the community and all. Max came to me. He's a curator and he worked at—" *Shit.* I'm not supposed to mention his old company. "As a curator. He worked as a curator. So it made sense."

Max picks up my slack. "It wouldn't have been possible in just any space, though. Daisy has always been very involved in

Harlow, like her mother, and she thought this was something the community would love."

"Yeah."

"And what do you hope visitors will get from the museum?"

I really wish Max would step in here, but it's a stupid women-in-business segment after all, so he's looking at me to take the lead. "Um, there'll be lots of art. From all over." The lights are scorching, making me feel like I'm out hiking in the height of summer. My stomach gurgles, and it was probably loud enough to hear based on the jump from one of the audio folks.

"Okaaay." Ysabelle refers to her note cards and pauses. "So..."

"It's an incredible space, as you can see," Max says. "And the outdoors." He whistles, as if catcalling the very land we stand on. "Breathtaking. This is a place where the beauty of the desert and the arts merge—and, of course, guests at The Mirage have it right at their fingertips. Anyone staying here will have exclusive pieces displayed in their rooms."

I nod halfheartedly as a faintness comes over me. This morning's coffee—twice as big of a cup as my usual—has turned in my stomach, and I'm ready to finish this interview, stat.

"And Daisy—as a successful female hotel owner, what advice do you have for other women looking to innovate with their business?"

A light laugh plays off my lips because *successful* isn't the word I'd use. I'm about to respond when an unmistakable sensation crawls its way up my throat, and my stomach morphs into lead.

"'Scuse me," I say through a burp.

I panic and race to the bathroom, shutting the door behind me and finding the toilet in time to vomit all the coffee from this morning into it. I'm sweating all over, and my heart and head are pounding.

Max says some final words to the newscaster, and I hear someone call out, "That's a wrap, I guess?" Our best publicity yet, flushed down the drain like my morning caffeine.

After splashing my face with water and rinsing out my mouth, I crawl back out, expecting everyone to look my way. But only two people from the crew remain—Official Clipboard Holder and Ysabelle, who's enthralled in a conversation with Max.

"You doing okay, hon?" Ysabelle asks.

"Mhmm." I don't have it in me to make eye contact with Max yet. "Hey, Ysabelle, think we could maybe reshoot that last bit?"

"Oh." Her face falls. "Oh no, *chica*, I'm sorry. We film live."

Live. How did I miss that?

"Don't you worry, they didn't pan to you running, and they adjusted the audio levels so there were minimal gurgly sounds from your tummy. You did *so* good." She pats my shoulder, but I know it's a pity pat. "And he was so clever with that last question."

"What'd you say?"

Max shrugs. "Just that you're a big believer in community, and to not be afraid to lean on that community."

"He knows what he's doing." Ysabelle air-kisses us both and says goodbye, wishing us luck and telling us she plans to stop by for the opening.

Once the barn clears, Max turns to me. "Good thing we got the contractor to finish the bathroom, huh?" His attempt to bolster my mood does nothing. I shoot him a pointed look.

"I almost puked on live TV."

"It's fine. Maybe you'll get made into a couple of memes."

I groan at this, and he laughs.

"Some pregnancy rumors, perhaps? But you know what they say. There's no such thing as bad press."

Max wouldn't remind me that bad press is something he'd especially like to avoid, considering what happened with his last job and all the negative coverage they got. That has to be at the forefront of his mind.

"I let you down," I mumble. No wonder Max got out of Harlow—he's nailing every part of this, carrying the whole project on his shoulders, and I can't even keep my morning coffee down.

"You didn't." He steps into my space, and for a moment I don't know if he'll lean down to kiss me or just let me exist in his orbit for a while. He goes with the latter, and I tell myself I'm not disappointed. I inhale him, the scent settling my stomach. "We'll find other opportunities. We'll get on other websites, we'll do other features."

"We still have the fundraiser," I say, grasping at straws.

"Exactly. With a bit more public-speaking practice with Dawn, you'll be set."

"Okay," I manage to say, wishing his suggestion made me feel better. I can't admit the truth out loud. The success or failure of the pop-up may very well affect whether The Mirage survives, but it affects more than me. He won't admit that I've let people down, but I did—not just myself and my mom and the hotel, but him.

Chapter Twenty-Two

Daisy, 18 Years Old

"Mom, I said I'm fine." I told her twenty times already, maybe more. All I wanted was to be left alone to watch Netflix in bed under Freddie's judgmental gaze. He normally followed my mom around, but cats are intuitive, and he spent the evening lying with me instead.

"You have a visitor, sweetie," Mom said, opening the door.

Anger thundered inside me. Why would I want to see him after he decided to take some other girl?

"Tell him he can—oh." I saw the curls on Max's head before I saw him, and as much as the comfort of him made my throat tight, I shoved the emotions down. My mom disappeared into the background, and I waved at him. "Hi."

"Surprise," he said, holding a bouquet. He'd put on a tux—a nicely fitted one so he looked quite grown-up. "Got you a corsage, too."

"But..." I softened at his thoughtfulness, and the corner of my mouth tilted up. "You hate prom."

"I've technically never been to prom."

"You said it was for all the popular kids who peaked senior year."

"You agreed."

"Sure, but...you hate dancing."

I could list the other reasons he gave me for why he was skipping out. He hoped to get a shift that night at the thrift store to save up for college. He and Lily had ended things in January, and he didn't have a date. He was here, though, flowers in hand, tux pressed, and ready to take me to one of our last-ever high school events.

"If you don't wanna go, we won't," Max said, sitting on the edge of my bed. "But if you've got a dress, then it's a shame for you not to wear it tonight. Let's just have a good night together."

I felt foolish for making such a big deal about prom—I didn't even like my ex-date that much. But with school ending, and everyone seeming so certain about their career paths and their futures, I found myself getting oddly sentimental. If I could just have one more night before people started college or a business or a family...or left Harlow. Nostalgia gripped me because whatever came next scared me senseless.

But the boy—the young man—sitting next to me pulled my head out of all the concerns over the future. All he wanted was a nice night with me.

I was so glad he was here.

Chapter Twenty-Three

Max, Now

I park the car, and Daisy suggests for the hundredth time that I drop her off and spend my evening doing anything else.

"You really don't want me in there," I joke.

"Things have been off with my dad."

"I can handle uncomfortable family dynamics. Trust me."

I never got to know Daisy's dad the way I knew her mom. Her mom welcomed me over all the time, came to events at school that even my parents didn't attend, and more than anything, she believed in me. When I saw Daisy's parents together, her mom was always the more talkative one—the one who laughed louder, the one wanting to connect. Plus, half the time, Mr. Johnson wasn't in the picture.

Daisy hasn't reached for her seatbelt. She had such a steadfast relationship with her mom, and it can't be easy to see her dad remarry.

"How can I help tonight?" I rest a hand on her thigh. Her eyes dart directly to the point of contact. Her skin is buttery soft.

"Just be yourself. We'll eat, we'll chat, and hopefully we'll be back in this car before Stacey's even left The Mirage for the night."

Daisy's dad greets us at the door, and he's exactly as I remember him—stout, jolly, and on the quiet side. Going in for a handshake with him sends a pang of missing Daisy's mom straight into my heart.

He introduces Oona to me, a petite woman who is the human equivalent of a hummingbird. She cranes her neck to smile up at me before wrapping me in a bony hug.

"Come in, come in," she urges, waving us into the house. The place appears modest from the outside, but they definitely splurged on furniture. They have a sitting room filled with ornate art, a small library of travel books, maps, and an entire shelf of birding gear—and the dining area has an impressive mid-century modern table that looks like real teak. A hallway storage desk has photos resting on top, many of Oona and Daisy's dad, but one of Daisy and some other family members.

"When Daisy said she was bringing someone tonight, I couldn't believe it." Oona turns to Daisy and pats her on the shoulder. Daisy doesn't pull away, but she doesn't soften with affection either. "You never bring guests. Does she, Pooks?"

He barely has a moment to nod before Oona continues.

"Well, I made plenty. Lots to eat. Are you allergic to anything?"

I shake my head. "I'm an adventurous eater."

"Oh, I love that." Oona beams with a smile, but it falters when she sees Daisy gripping the handrail up the two steps from the foyer. "You poor thing. Need help?"

"Just taking it one step at a time."

"Here," I say, swooping my arms under her to do a fireman's carry into the living room. Oona gasps with joy. I wink at Daisy, and she snorts out a laugh, which she then pretends is a coughing fit.

Sitting on the sofa, Oona asks me a billion questions. I'm happy to keep the attention off of Daisy. I get what Daze was talking about—Oona's a lot. She doesn't seem malicious, though, just enthusiastic. She conducts a mild interrogation until a timer dings in the other room.

"It needs to cool, and I have to set the table," she says, standing. "Dearie, can you show Max the rest of the house? Pick up some wine from the garage while you're at it. Give me and Daisy some girl time. Or—" She rubs her hands together. "If you'd rather go with your dad, that's fine."

Daisy smiles and says she doesn't mind. It's the same smile I saw her use with Mr. Hollis—polite and warm, but restrained. Definitely not the kind when she's laughing at a joke I told her or when we catch eyes from across the room.

Her dad leads me on a tour through their home. Compared to Oona's mile-a-minute talking pace, Richard seems like the most laid-back dude in California. He shuffles through the house, pointing out an interesting art print or the unique aspects of the architecture as he goes.

"How are your folks?" he asks as we head into the garage.

"I've had a lot going on since returning to Harlow, so we haven't spent a ton of time together, but, uh, good."

"I barely see Daisy sometimes, what with all the hotel stuff. What about your sister? Ava's her name?"

"Yeah. She's killing it at school. Setting out to become a lawyer."

"Bet your parents are pretty pleased 'bout that."

"How'd you guess?" I say with a wry smile.

"They were always tough on you, weren't they?"

I definitely underestimated Daisy's dad and his memory of me.

"Here, whaddaya like to drink?" he asks. "White, sparkling?" We walk to one corner of the garage where he's constructed some bottle storage and made space for a wine fridge. "We've got a bit of everything. Daisy usually goes with something like a Sauv blanc."

"No alcohol for her tonight. Cautionary measure with the fall."

"That's right." Richard's eyes light up. "Thank you, by the way, for watching out for her. I...I worry."

"She's done as good of a job resting this week as someone like Daisy can."

"Figures." A distant expression passes over his face. "Carbon copy of her mom." He clears his throat, then taps a few fingers atop the wine fridge. "I don't, well, I don't want to be that stereotypical dad. I never have been. And I made mistakes with Daisy's mom, choices that..." He rubs his brow. "Choices that pushed Daisy away. But I love her, very much."

I'm rooted in place, unsure where he's going with this.

"You're both adults now," he says, tapping a bottle. "But, uh...just know that when you left, she really, really missed you."

Daisy had advocated for me to leave Harlow—she always said I was bound for greatness that even I couldn't understand. She told me she would miss me, and by the way she tried to stay in touch that summer leading up to freshman year, I knew she did.

Until she didn't. Like missing me was a liability—more trouble than it was worth.

I think it's better if we take some space for a while. I have to figure some things out on my own...

What a shitty text. As if I hadn't spent the entire summer figuring out how much I hated not having her around and wanted to work out a way to stay her friend, even from afar.

"I missed her too," I confess.

Her dad pauses, assessing me from behind his glasses. "I don't know what happened between you two. She never told me, and her mother only gave me vague details. But whatever it was, I really hope she's not in store for a repeat."

I scratch the back of my neck. Her dad's talking like I'm the one who pulled the trigger on ending our relationship. "It was her idea to cut things off."

"Doesn't matter to me who instigated what. Tread carefully, that's all."

Some days, I think of what Daisy always used to tell me: that I would leave Harlow to achieve incredible things in the world. That was my choice. But choices are violent, and there have been days—a lot more, recently—where I wonder what that decision destroyed for us, what was sacrificed. To go from two souls intertwined to months without talking or texting. Then years. And then, what do I say to a friend who's slipped out of my life like quicksand?

Because she let me go, but I let her go too.

"Anywhoo." Richard's demeanor changes from somber to chipper as he pastes on a smile and elbows my side. He grabs a white wine with one hand and a red with the other. "I'll let Oona pick. Let's eat, shall we?"

Chapter Twenty-Four

Daisy, Now

"What's new at the hotel?" Oona asks.

"Um, well…" I chew on some sautéed green beans, holding up a finger. She loves to question me right when I've put food in my mouth. "Not much. The pop-up is the focus at the moment."

"She's being modest," Max says. "Reservations are up, and word is getting out about the exhibit. She was on HSNC, too."

"We saw," Oona says. "You seemed nervous."

I nod and take another bite, because I'd rather not rehash that experience.

"Oh! Almost forgot." Oona gets up and rummages through her purse on the entryway table. She returns, offering a piece of paper to me. "This is for you. I talked to Stacey at the front desk. She said you sometimes have a mobile massage therapist come to The Mirage for clients. I heard good things through my network as well. Thought you could treat yourself for once."

"This is…this is so nice." I look at my dad, moved by the gesture. "I can't remember the last time I got a massage."

"The idea was all Oona's," Dad says.

"It's just because. I figured after your accident, it might ease some tension. And with the museum in a couple weeks, this gives you a chance to relax."

"Thank you." I fold the gift certificate, touched that Oona went through the trouble of researching and buying something like this for me. She used to run a massage studio, so the gift has a personal touch to it. I guess we're at the point where we buy *just-because* presents for each other.

My dad pats her hand, and she shoots him a megawatt smile. If my dad were going to find love again, I guess he could have found it with someone worse than Oona.

Over dinner, she barrages Max with questions. She asks him about the pop-up, about Ireland, about his favorite artists, and he happily goes down any rabbit hole her probing inquiries take him. I can already tell Oona's obsessed with him.

The meal wraps up, and I breathe a sigh of relief. Usually, when I hang out with my dad and Oona, I get annoyed or say something unintentionally bratty, and I feel like a jerk afterwards. Maybe it's because Max is here to act as a buffer, or maybe I'm starting to like Oona.

She stands by my dad, wrapping an arm around him, and they kiss. Seeing them affectionate with each other still throws me—I don't remember my dad being this lovey-dovey with my mom all the time. But he's happy, and that's what's important.

"Should I do it, or you?" Oona asks him in a volume I almost can't hear over the smooth jazz from the speakers. My dad nods, urging her on. "As you know, we've been planning the wedding, and your father and I wanted to ask you something."

My stomach turns. I hoped I would get out of tonight easy, but now she's going to ask me to be their officiant, or maybe a bridesmaid. The thought had crossed my mind that they'd want me involved in the big day, but with everything at work, I haven't had the time to reflect on how I really feel about that.

"We've talked a lot about the day and what we're envisioning. Something small, intimate. Close friends and family only. And Harlow is where we met, so it feels like the right place to have the wedding."

"I've got some contacts, you know," I say. "Caterers, coordinators. Officiants."

Oona looks at my dad, then back at me. "Oh, that would be marvelous."

Damn. She's gunning for maid of honor duties.

"But before any of that, we have to decide where to have the ceremony and reception. And we both agree there is one place that makes sense. If you're okay with it." Oona seems like she's holding her breath, and I've never seen her so nervous. The affectionate arm she has wrapped around my dad might be more for her to stay steady on her feet.

"We were thinking," she goes on, "The Mirage would be perfect."

"Oh," I squeak out like a deflating tire. The request blindsides me like walking full-speed into a closed door, but I add, "Wow."

"Yes, wow. It's..." Oona nods, then laughs. "You can say no. But—"

"It was my idea," my dad butts in, rubbing salt in my wound. "Thought it might be a nice way to have her there in spirit."

Forget salt. This is a bottle of bleach.

"And the place is...well, it's yours now," he says. "I'm proud of what you've done with it."

Under the table, Max cups my thigh and squeezes. His eyes have homed in on me. I don't know if he's just checking in, ready to go to war for me, or both. His face becomes blurry, but I refuse to let myself lose it here.

"Of course," I say, fighting back tears with a plastered-on smile.

"Really?" Oona chirps.

"Yes. I'll have to check the dates, but...absolutely. Family discount," I manage, struggling to breathe. "I'm happy for you."

Oona comes over and wraps me in a hug, and my dad joins. They're both overjoyed—so grateful, beyond excited—and so deeply in love.

I'm hollow as we say goodbye. Max offers to drive, and it's not until we pull into the driveway of The Mirage that I notice the tears streaming down my face. I go inside the casita and crawl into bed, and Max shows up thirty seconds later, glass of water in hand. He pats the comforter to entice Freddie to curl up with me, and he kneels by the side of the mattress, his palm firm on my arm, his thumb rubbing in circles.

"Do you wanna talk?" Max asks.

"No." To myself more than to Max, I say, "I miss her, that's all."

"What do you miss most about her?"

I sniffle. "Everything."

Max watches me, his eyes sad. "There was this one fight with my parents in high school. College talk, I think. I came over here because, well, I wanted to vent to you, but you were sleeping over at Gwen's." He brushes some hair off my face, and I ignore the urge to kiss the pads of his fingertips. "Your mom ordered Hidden Moon, we sat on the couch, and she listened to me complain. She always treated me like I was someone worth listening to."

I attempt a smile, because Max has given me the gift of knowing my mother a little better, even now. "She never told me about that."

"Probably didn't want you to worry."

"It felt good to be loved by her, didn't it?" Freddie rolls onto his belly, and I stroke his fur, which instantly makes him purr. "Whenever she saw me, no matter when we last saw each other, whatever we talked about before, or if we'd had a fight...she looked like the happiest woman in the world, just to see me.

That sounds kind of selfish, I suppose—that what I miss most is how I felt because of her."

"That's the whole point. That's what people remember. How you make them feel. And she made people feel really good."

I nuzzle my cheek into the pillow, attempting to dry my face.

"Your dad and Oona, they..." Max blows some air out through his lips. "They don't understand what they're asking. But you focused on them and their happiness."

"I *am* happy for them," I whisper, continuing to pet Freddie as a distraction. "But I'm confused. He can continue on without her and get a new wife, but I can't go out and get a new mom. I wouldn't want to even if I could."

"Oh, Daze." Max leans towards me, and for a moment, I think he's going to kiss me. He does, but not on the lips—on my forehead. And if I could, I would cry all over again at the sweetness of his simple gesture.

"My parents really hung on for all those years, you know? On and off, but always married. It's crazy that he's ready to replace her and try harder with the whole marriage thing."

"I guarantee you that's not it. Hey." Max's hand slinks under the covers, his warm palm cupping my waist, as he rocks me until I look at him. "There's no way. No matter who he loves, she'll always be there. You Johnson women are unforgettable. Trust me."

I know he's talking about my mom, but my chest somersaults.

"We're stubborn, too," I say, meeting his eyes as a smile pulls at the corner of my mouth. "And hard to work with."

"It's part of your charm."

I laugh, play-shoving his shoulder. As I examine the lines of his jaw, a sobering thought hits me.

"Do you think…" My heart's pounding in my ears. "Maybe my parents were just two people who made their relationship more complicated than it needed to be."

"What do you mean?"

"They met in college. They knew each other for years before they dated. What if they were better off as friends? Did they make a mess of things?"

He swallows, and I hold my breath, waiting for his response. He has to know the real question I'm asking. *Did* we *make a mess of things?*

"No." He shakes his head, his eyes trained on mine. Max tugs me closer, mere inches from his face, and he plants another one of those forehead kisses on me.

"Would you sleep here tonight?" I close my eyelids, not wanting to see a rejection reflected at me. "Not for…it's just, it's nice, having you here."

"Of course."

Max lifts the covers and slides under them next to me, big spoon to my little one. He's a heater, and I want to collapse into the comfort of him. His arm drapes over me, tugging me closer so my back rests against the plane of his chest, my head tucked under his chin. I burrow closer, and he kisses the top of my head once more as I fall into a heavy sleep.

Chapter Twenty-Five

Max, Now

I take a break from setting up the exhibit to answer a call outside. The sun has hit the highest point in the sky, and aside from a steady breeze and the distant sound of cars on the main road, Harlow has entered an afternoon calm. Inside the barn is the opposite—chaos, at least to the untrained eye. There are canvases, hanging wires galore, and tools everywhere. We're on track, though.

We were, that is, until a minute ago.

"She would never do this," the artist manager says, "but given the circumstances, you must understand."

The niece of the most well-known artist in our show is one of the victims of my former boss. She hadn't realized this when she signed on, but in an act of solidarity, she intends to back out.

We're two weeks until opening.

"I'm putting this pop-up together independently. No ties to Impressions. You've explained that to her?"

The manager scoffs, as if I dare tell him how to do his job. No amount of reminding him how her name appears on the press releases or the pamphlets sways him. He doesn't care that she had offered a personalized set of art supplies for the silent auction, either. According to the cancellation clause in her con-tract, all they legally have to do is ship her pieces back on their dime.

We hang up, and I tell my gallery assistants to take ten. I'll need more than that to come up with a miracle, though. I will always be myself, and I will always have worked at that place.

And now that's Daisy's problem, too.

"I brought coffee and tea over from the main house." She enters the barn, bumping the door open with her butt in a cute way that I'm too stressed to appreciate. Her body lurches to a stop as she surveys the space. "Is it supposed to look like this?"

"Surprisingly, yes." I scout out a spot in the center of the hanging-supplies hurricane to sit down, utterly defeated.

"Where is everyone?"

"We've got a problem."

Daisy doesn't ask questions. Instead, she marches straight to the floor across from me, cradling a mug in one hand while offering me the other. Her support makes this hurt even more, because she'll be suffering because of me. I describe the phone call, and she nods along.

"Dropping out?" she asks coolly. Either she doesn't compre-hend what this means, or she's doing her best to keep it together for my sake. "She can do that?"

"It's rare but not unheard of."

"Well..." Daisy pauses, her eyes roaming over me like she's calibrating her response to mine. "That's shitty. Like, really, really shitty of her."

I nod, then bury my head in my hands and let the self-pitying thoughts win.

"We'll get someone else," Daisy says in a chipper tone. "Someone better."

"I can't get someone else."

"We will."

"It's not possible," I say, lying down and ready to forget this whole stupid idea. A pop-up. In Harlow. What was I thinking, dragging Daisy into this? Because this affects me, but it affects her, too.

"I've already booked the artists who expressed interest," I go on. "We can't replace someone of her caliber on such short notice. It would be an insult to reach out this late in the game."

"Maybe that one girl, Becs—she's an artist. She might have a suggestion."

"That's not the point. This is more than how many people show up, how many tickets we sell, and how far out your reservations get booked." At a loss, I sit up and rest my elbows on my knees, enjoying whatever floral body spray follows Daisy around. "This is about a reputation that I can't separate myself from. That anyone who works with me will get tied to, too."

She chews on the cuticle of her thumb, and I don't have the heart to stop her.

"I can tell myself I'm not to blame, but there's this feeling that I *should* have known, *should* have done something." That regret gnaws at me endlessly. "And understandably, people aren't exactly excited to attach their name to anyone who has ties to that place. I want to run away from it, too. I just...more than anything, I don't want that to affect The Mirage. The exhibit. You."

If Daisy somehow gets dragged through the mud for working with me, I couldn't live with myself.

"C'mon." Daisy startles me by smacking me on the thigh. "You got this. There's gotta be something."

"I...I guess I could ask Becs if she knows someone," I say, my voice straining under the stress. I should never have talked Daisy into this.

"That's good."

"But next weekend? Who would go for that? And what if other people drop out? All because of my stupid fucking last job."

"Don't do this." Daisy sounds desperate, and I look up to meet her worried eyes. "You cannot give up on me right now." Her words come out shaky, like she can't trust her own voice. "You're scaring me. If you really think people are going to always associate you with the shit your skeezy ex-boss did, don't let them. Let everyone know you aren't your former workplace or your former boss. Everything they stood for—that's not you."

Daisy's unwavering support and belief in me are exactly why I can't give up. I got her tangled up in this mess, and I won't abandon her now. And if I were to make a comeback, I'd want it to be with someone like Daisy. Someone who makes me feel like I could make the sun rise and dictate the phases of the moon if I tried hard enough.

"Make this museum incredible, like only you can," she says, her gaze searing into me as she slides close enough that our knees touch. My mind travels to last night, holding her so tightly our bodies molded together. What would Daisy have done if I hadn't been there? She would have managed—she did for eight years without me around. But getting to support her, protect her, and cradle her into sleep in the safety of my arms is a heartbreaking privilege I don't take lightly.

"I've seen the list of artists you've talked to," Daisy goes on. "There's got to be someone on there that can keep us moving in the right direction, so we won't have a blank wall where her stuff was supposed to go." She hands me the printed-off spreadsheet and points to it. "So who's it gonna be?"

This is the Daisy I know—headstrong, take-charge, no-nonsense. I glance down at the paper. "Someone who is guaranteed to bring folks in on opening night is ideal."

"Okay. We could have more than one person, right?"

"I guess."

Anyone in Los Angeles who wanted to join us already has, and anyone famous enough to attract lots of people would be a long shot. Plus, no one likes to be the next choice in line—people will take reaching out so last minute as an insult.

"Damn." Daisy peers at the list in my hand. "You never had problems getting people to show up to art shows in high school. How is this so much harder?"

And that's when I know what we need to do.

Regina's classroom has a quirky familiarity about it. The boldly colored bookshelves brim with sculptures, and massive art reference books occupy half of her desk. She has a circular clock on the wall covered in disco ball tiles, and instead of the time, the face simply reads *NOW*.

"Thank you for meeting with us." I wipe my sweaty palms against my pants.

"Of course," Regina says with a hesitant smile.

"I have a project I'm working on. A pop-up, here in Harlow. My..." *Fuck buddy, but just for one night? Woman I've had a crush on for ages?* "My good friend here, Daisy, runs The Mirage hotel. She and I are partnering together on an exhibit on the property."

"Oh." Regina's body relaxes into her chair. "That sounds incredible. You're more than welcome to flyer in the appropriate spots here on campus."

"We wanted to inquire about something else." I reach for my bag, but Daisy's already holding the notes and photos I need out to me. At the top is the painting I made for her: the one of The Mirage in all its glory. The one that put her lips on mine.

Daisy looks like she's about to burst with excitement. "We want to get the students involved," she says in a rush. "Have them in the show."

She was right about the showcases I had in high school. Teachers, siblings, parents—well, most parents—and anyone and everyone related to students would show up. Students bring a crowd, and that could bolster our opening-week sales, although that's not what Regina will care about.

"In addition to the portfolio for their end-of-semester project," I say, "this will give them a real-world scenario to showcase their work alongside accomplished artists. Professionals."

Regina's eyebrows raise, and she nods her head slowly as if she's processing the proposal. "It's certainly an incredible opportunity." She taps her lips in thought. "It'll depend on the principal and superintendent. Do you have a theme for the evening? Since they're teens, it can't be anything risqué."

"We'll keep things PG," I say. "By involving the school and younger artists, I'd revise our concept. Something that will suit everything we've already accepted into the show, but also makes room for the student work to fit."

I catch Daisy's face on me, her mouth turned up.

"Do you have a list of artists?" Regina asks.

She slides a pair of red acetate glasses onto her nose and skims the printed Excel spreadsheet of names, artwork, and thumbnail-sized photos of what the artists are providing. After a moment, she removes her frames and sets them down on her desk. "Ms. Johnson, Max may have mentioned that I'm aiming to expand the art program here. Something like this is..." Her eyes turn glossy with dammed-up emotion. "On its own, this will mean so much for these students. But considering what it could mean for launching a visual arts school, this could be immense. In so many ways. Thank you."

My throat tightens, overwhelmed by her reaction. When I was a weird little teenager sketching in classroom corners, this chance could have changed my life. Even in college, I would have loved participating in a show like this. And now, I get to pass this chance on. I can't predict the butterfly effect this could have on the art scene in Harlow.

We shake hands with Regina as she fights back tears. The second Daisy and I step into the hall, she loops an arm through mine. "I'm excited."

"I couldn't tell."

"Will we have enough room?"

"That's the beauty of a pop-up. We can change the lineup, rotate through student work more frequently, and keep things fresh. We might—what?"

Daisy stops and stares up at me. "You never would have gone for this when we started planning."

"You don't like my idea?"

"I *love* your idea. It's brilliant."

"Yeah," I say almost to myself, the excitement bubbling inside me like a pot on low heat. "It's pretty cool."

"It's more than that."

In one smooth movement, Daisy rises onto her toes and wraps a hand around my neck, pressing her mouth against mine. She gives me the simplest kiss, but it completely warps my mind—I forget where I am, what I'm doing, why I'm here.

She lowers her heels but keeps her body angled toward me.

"What was that for?" I ask, her breath mingling with mine.

"I just really wanted to kiss you again."

"Oh, good, you're still here." Regina's footsteps grow louder behind us. We turn, but there's no rush apart from each other. I'm too stunned by kissing Daisy in the hallway of our old high school to process what's going on.

"I...I'm sorry," Regina goes on as she approaches, "but with all of your news, I completely forgot." She holds out an envelope. "Do you have one more minute to chat?"

Daisy squeezes my biceps. "I'll pull the truck around." She walks away, and all I want to do is chase after her forever—to never leave her side. To kiss her again, but this time to be ready for it, to enjoy it even more.

"I can't believe I forgot this," Regina says, tapping the envelope against my arm. "When you emailed, I thought you were going to tell me you were quitting. The past ten minutes have been an emotional roller coaster."

"What's this?"

"It's a request for you, for next semester."

I take the sealed letter and turn it over in my hand. "What kind of request?"

"A contract. The students love you, we have a waitlist a mile long in case of any dropouts, and we have parents asking if you're on the schedule next semester—next year even."

When I think back to my schooling, my teachers were the people who got me passionate about art and encouraged me to be creative. I never envisioned myself in their shoes, not beyond this summer semester.

But I never envisioned myself back in Harlow, either.

If someone had asked me when I first arrived, I would have said I'd be itching to leave by now, and I'd be following up with my mentor daily about that job at Tate. But when I reflect on the past couple months, I'm not antsy, and I don't really know what to do with that. If I go, it's a momentous choice. But if I stay, that's just as massive. Whatever I'm facing, I have no middle ground to play with.

"I sort of hoped your feelings about teaching may have changed since our tiki drink night. Or that the better pay might sway you," Regina says with a tentative smile. "More hours, too. Everything's negotiable, and when we do get the art school all set up, you're one of the first people I'll bring on board."

"I..." I stare at the envelope, and reality comes down hard on me. Another kiss with Daisy doesn't mean I should rethink my future—it just means I'm the guy always carrying a torch for her. The man who's ready to rearrange his plans at the slightest show of intimacy. She packs up her emotions in boxes so tightly, a simple kiss doesn't mean she wants me to stay. I don't even know what I would say if she asked, and I can't imagine her reaction if I told her that's what I wanted.

The shiny opportunity at Tate twinkles off on the horizon in my mind. It appears less lustrous at the moment, but it's still there.

"I can't make any promises past this summer."

Regina shrinks slightly but keeps a smile on her face. "I'm sorry to hear that."

"I've got some other things going on."

Hopefully she doesn't ask me about what *other things* I'm referring to. My upcoming plans are built on hope and delusion. The only thing I know for sure is the pop-up takes precedence. There's no next step until I pull that off.

"I'm sorry," I say, genuinely feeling bad for getting her hopes up.

"Don't be. We'll just have to enjoy having you here for the time you can give us."

Chapter Twenty-Six

Max, 18 Years Old

"This is way better than prom." Daisy had her bare feet propped on my car's dash, a trail of In-N-Out special sauce dribbling down her chin. I drove us to the lot for one of the local trails. The parking area overlooked Harlow and the lower desert, all glowing with twinkly street lights and the steady flow of head-lights.

"Agreed. Definitely better."

"Sure you wouldn't rather be in a room with the senior class, sweating to the latest top forty hits?" she asked.

"It's all part of the high school experience."

She rolled her eyes. "I can't believe I said that."

At the last minute, Daisy's date dumped her and took some-one else. The jerk. Who would do something like that, and to Daisy Johnson?

Mrs. Johnson had called to say Daisy wouldn't be joining in the stretch limo our friend group had rented. I had no idea what she was talking about—I hadn't planned on going to prom.

"That's weird, I thought she mentioned that," Daisy's mom said over the phone, her tone especially upbeat.

So one guy's idiocy became a chance to show up for Daze. But more than that...I didn't want our upcoming summer to fly by without being honest with her. I was in love with my best friend. I had been for a long time, and the feelings never went away. The deadline of college starting in the fall made me bold enough to want to say something, because otherwise, I'd run out of chances to tell her the truth.

Daisy's cheeks sparkled in the moonlight. She had her hair done in a half-up, half-down style, shimmery makeup flashing on her eyelids, and a pretty dress that was cut lower than the worn-in band T-shirts she usually wore. Knowing that she got all done up for a night with me made it extra special, like an actual date.

"You look beautiful," I said.

"Thanks. You, uh, you clean up real nice too. You should consider tuxes more often."

"Yeah?" I inspected my tuxedo—the only one that came close to fitting, and it was still two inches too short. "I'll admit, I'm feeling very James Bond...who hasn't found a reliable tailor yet."

"No, you look good. There's something about seeing a guy in a tux that's..." She trailed off, concentrating on the line of ketchup she was drawing on a french fry. "Really hot."

Our eyes snagged over the center console, but I couldn't tell if she was blushing or not. Did she mean hot in general or that *I* looked hot?

"So." Daisy said, crumpling the wrapper from her burger. "Michelin-star meal."

"Check."

"Some damn fine views."

"Check."

"No dancing, though." She tucked some strands of hair behind her ear. "There should be dancing."

"I think Dua Lipa will have a different vibe out here."

She laughed, and the sound was a sparkler in my chest. "I mean slow dancing."

Right. I fumbled with my phone to find something to play. My reception was terrible, so I'd have to select a song from my library. After a few seconds of scrolling, I found something perfect.

"Oh, I love this one," Daisy said, as if I didn't already know.

The otherworldly vocals for Mazzy Star's "Fade Into You" came in. I exited the car and hustled to the passenger door, holding out my hand with a flourish. "Daisy Johnson, would you like to dance with me?"

"I thought you'd never ask," she said, giggling and linking her fingers with mine.

This was my chance. After swaying stiffly a couple of times, I found more confidence and relaxed my arms around her, bringing her closer. This was better than I had ever dreamed. Daisy closed in, letting my fingertips meet on her lower back. She smelled incredible.

"Los Angeles is far," she whispered.

"We'll see each other all the time." We would; I would make sure of it. I pulled back and searched her eyes. "I'll be in Harlow on weekends and holidays. You can visit me anytime."

"Mhmm." She started playing with some errant strands of my hair, something she'd never done before. The newness of the gesture had me floating.

"What's it like being so good at something?" she asked. We'd had this conversation a lot recently.

"You're good at all sorts of things. You're passionate, you're friendly, you're a great listener."

"I can't get a career with that." She sighed, leaning into my shoulder, and I ran my thumb across the bare skin of her back. "I'm not like you with art. I don't know what to do next."

Daisy liked nature and animals, but she hadn't found her calling. Her grades didn't win her a scholarship anywhere, so she enrolled part-time at the community college to give her a couple of semesters to figure things out. It bothered her endlessly, but to me, she was exactly who she needed to be. She was just Daisy, and that was more than enough. That was everything.

She wouldn't stop comparing her path to my arts program in LA with a partial scholarship, though. I actually hadn't sent in my deposit yet. There was a long shot of an opportunity in Dublin, but my hopes dwindled each day. The chances were so low, I didn't tell Daisy I applied. She'd always told me to dream big—that my talent would take me far...but I didn't know what she'd think about a Europe kind of far.

"I'm glad you're here, Max," she whispered. "I'm glad I'm here with you."

My body became lighter from her words. "Daze, I..."

She looked up, and her gaze settled on my lips. She leaned in impossibly close, and our back-and-forth swaying stalled. We shared a few shallow breaths, and I nudged my nose with hers, nervous and elated out of my mind.

This wasn't in my head. This wasn't one-sided.

A set of car headlights blinded us, squashing the moment. We both recoiled and shielded our eyes as a Jeep pulled up, the window rolled down.

"Park's closed," the ranger said, oblivious to what she interrupted. "I'm gonna have to ask you two to leave."

Something switched in Daisy, and she pulled back, refusing to meet my eyes. My insides sank. Daisy was pulling away in real time, and I knew that if I pushed her, she'd only retreat more. I'd gotten close to her—closer than ever before. Maybe with a little patience, we could get there. This could be our best summer ever, if I only found the right moment.

Chapter Twenty-Seven

Daisy, Now

A server walks by with a forced smile, probably because she knows I could be the person to tip her at the end of the night. Catering to a room of privileged clients doesn't sound like fun to me, either. I'm the odd one out, catching some air amidst stifling conversations about vacation homes in Tuscany and private planes.

The people inside the restaurant's event space are exactly who we need, though—folks with influence, money, or both. I remind myself of Dawn's encouraging words. *Steady breaths, go slower than you think, and talk to one person.*

"Hey." Max's voice interrupts my mindful breathing, and I clench a fist around my note cards. "You okay?"

"Mhmm. Heading back in a sec."

"Alex really went all out with the menu for us. Have you tried those bacon-wrapped figs?"

"Not yet." I eye his champagne flute. "You mind?"

He barely has the chance to nod before I snatch the glass and pound it back, the cool, fizzing liquid releasing the tension in my shoulders.

"Easy, tiger." Max rests a hand on my upper arm, and I halfway hope he'll pull me into his chest. I could use the comfort. When I saw a speech—from *me*—on the fundraiser's schedule, I almost cried. But Max said he could stand up there and talk about art all he wanted, and that wouldn't make a difference. My story would get them to care on a deeper level.

And, more importantly, it would encourage them to bid in the silent auction and donate.

The past couple of weeks involved a lot of listening to podcasts on public speaking while I cleaned The Mirage. Dawn came over almost every afternoon to offer private coaching, although I've hardly absorbed a fraction of the stage presence she has. Gwen endured enough speech run-throughs that she could probably recite this thing for me. I wish she would. No amount of preparation could stop the damp, slick sweat of my armpits or my stomach tying itself into knots.

"Most of the work's already finished, Daze. Everyone in there is already a couple drinks in and ready to throw down some cash. And you look great in that dress. Your hair's all done up in that..." Max waves his hand around his head, mimicking the half-up, half-down style.

He's trying to calm me down, but satisfaction simmers under the surface knowing he noticed how I look tonight. Max is effortlessly handsome in a black suit, button-down, and tie, and I wish I could trace the line of his jaw or douse myself in his musky aftershave. If it weren't for the billion thoughts in my head, I might kiss him again...although that would only intensify the yearning between my legs.

Max glances at his wristwatch, and I already know.

"It's time, isn't it?" I ask him.

"Do you need longer?"

"No, I'm ready," I lie, the weight of not only the pop-up but also The Mirage and Max's reputation weighing on me.

We return without another word to the private room in Alex's restaurant, and the air gets sucked out of my lungs. I can't count the number of people here. Cocktail tables host throngs of guests, all of them dressed in sparkly ball gowns or elegant suits. The banquet hall is basked in a lavender-blue glow, save for the elevated platform and microphone.

Max must sense my trepidation, because he turns to me and rests a palm against the small of my back. His touch burns like an ember.

"Once I'm done, I can stay on stage with you," he whispers into my ear, his breath irresistibly warm.

"I've got it." I think. "Maybe stand off to the side with a bucket?"

His face splits into a grin, lighting up the whole damn room. The event coordinator gives Max a curt nod as a cue to walk toward the mic.

"Remember to breathe," he says. "Go slowly. And you're talking to a bunch of people, but just talk to the one person who matters, okay?"

Max strolls up to the microphone like he belongs there. "Hello everyone, and thank you for coming out tonight." Max's speaking-to-a-roomful-of-fancy-strangers voice is far more con-trolled than mine. It's deep and inviting, like this is his house, and he's invited us over for a grand party.

He introduces himself and thanks our sponsors. My heart-beat must be banging loud enough the folks next to me can hear, and I'm not even up there yet.

"The desert has a special magic," he says to the room. "Hav-ing grown up not far from here, I didn't always appreciate my hometown. But after spending some time in Harlow as an adult, I can see why people love it. Life is meaningful in every small moment there. You're surrounded by nature and wildlife that's as beautiful as it is life-threatening. Harlow's a mixture of awe and danger, of bliss and risk. I didn't get it as a kid, but I think I do now."

Max didn't rehearse this with me. He only asked for a few talking points that I thought would be important to hit. I put a hand to my chest, touched to hear him speak about his hometown in a way that sounds so...loving. I couldn't have explained that connection better myself—it's like he lifted the thoughts from my mind.

"I wanted to explore that dichotomy with a pop-up in Harlow—big and small, young and old, near and far—and how one ecosystem can encompass all of that, all at the same time. This is how *Desert Daze* came to be."

I smile when he announces the name. We'd been sitting around with the gallery assistants when Max said my nickname, and their eyes went wide like it was the most brilliant idea. At first, I thought they were all joking, but the name stuck.

"Before I talk about the artists you'll see just over a week from now, I want to say how nice it is to work with people like Daisy, who many of you have already met." He gestures to me, and I lift my hand in a timid wave. The countdown until I'm up on that stage is ticking lower and lower, and my breathing has already gone shallow.

"I spent years as the curator for pop-up museums with Impressions." Max does an expert job of scanning the room as he speaks, making eye contact with every single person. Everyone pauses from eating their canapés and drinking champagne, intent on him. "While I'm proud of the work I did during that time, I'm not proud of who I worked with. So you can imagine what a relief and joy it's been to be on Daisy's team for this."

As he introduces *Desert Daze* and some of the star artists he's lined up, pride rises in my chest like a wave in the ocean. I had told him, rather than avoid talking about his previous workplace, to face it head-on. Talk about it before anyone else, and let them know *Desert Daze* is his. Ours.

"While she's never worked with artists directly like this before, she has curated memorable experiences at The Mirage, a boutique hotel in the heart of Harlow's rugged landscape. With our project, Daisy has created opportunities locally and taken care of each artist we have, whether they're flying in from Paris or they have a pottery shop down the road. Honestly, I should watch out. She's as good as me at my job, maybe even better."

He pauses for the light laughs, locking eyes with me for a breath. Then he smiles.

"You're up next," the coordinator says, tapping me on the shoulder. My stomach drops.

Max introduces me, and I clamber onstage. The lights blind me, which means I can't see anyone in the audience—excellent—but I also can't see anything on my index cards—terrible. As my eyes adjust, familiar faces like Gwen, Bob, and Dawn come into view. Their presence does virtually nothing to relax me, but I'm glad they came tonight.

Then my sights land on Max, who has carved out a spot on the left-hand side of the crowd. Knowing where he is calms my nerves. He has an almost imperceptible grin on his face, and he's leaning casually against a cocktail table.

Just think about one person who matters.

"Hello everyone." My words get thrown back to me in a loud screech of microphone feedback. I cover my ears and wince. The sound technician at the far end of the room looks at the electronics in front of them, tweaks some knobs, then flashes me a big thumbs up.

"Sorry 'bout that," I chuckle. "Um. Hello. Hi. I'm Daisy, the owner and manager of The Mirage, the site of *Desert Daze.*"

Everyone is waiting for me to say something brilliant. Something funny or worthwhile. I rehearsed this speech endlessly, but every word has escaped me. Without letting my head dip too low, I catch the notes written on the damp index cards creasing in my death grip.

"I've been at The Mirage for decades. Some of my happiest memories are on that property, growing up there with my parents. My mom ran the place, and The Mirage was her baby. It was sort of a weird sibling relationship, but I managed."

This gets some chuckles from the audience. Dawn added that joke to get some laughs, and the sound puts me more at ease.

"So..." I glance at my note cards again. Dawn and Max probably wanted to keep my speech easy and predictable for me, so we lifted a lot of the wording from the hotel's website. But now that I think about it, the audience could just as well get this information by scrolling on their phones. Max gave an amazing speech, and I want to do the same.

When I look up, the lights assault my vision again, and I've lost the spot where Max stood. He's the person who matters. *He's the person who matters.*

I lick my lips, which have become dry as dust, and I imagine him in the general direction I saw him before. With a deep breath, I continue.

"For a really long time, since my mother passed, I tried to keep everything the same. You know, really honor her. And I haven't done a whole redesign and turned all the rooms into that boring shit you'll find in all the chains." Dawn had advised me to avoid cursing, but the delighted murmurs amongst the audience make me think they don't mind. "The Mirage is what it always has been: this perfect, tucked-away oasis where you can exist in this world, just you and what matters. A place where you can feel insignificant. And I know that's probably not anything you'll ever see on a travel brochure, but it is quite special."

I haven't taken my eyes off the dark, blurry area where Max is. He's the only person who matters, and the realization makes me want to run and hide. But I can't anymore.

"*Desert Daze* is a wild child of an idea. So different from anything I've done before. But somehow, it fits—as if it was supposed to have been here all along, and I just needed to be ready for it. Now I am." I refer to the note cards out of habit and realize I might as well just toss them because I've veered away from my original speech. "What I'm trying to say is, what you'll find at The Mirage is always gonna be there. It's my whole heart. And I hope you can love it, and love this museum, as much as I do."

Applause takes over the room, the sound tech brings back the music, and conversation fills the air again. My legs want to march me straight to the bar for the strongest drink possible, but I scan the crowd instead, looking for Max.

I spot him, smiling and handsome and perfect. But he's not scouring the room for me in return—a gorgeous woman almost as tall as he is has glued herself to his side.

And all his attention is on her.

"Thank you for all your help." I hug Dawn as other attendees trickle out of the restaurant, slipping on coats for the chilly evening. Gwen and Bob left after my speech—the pregnancy has tapped Gwen's energy—but Dawn wandered the floor with me, talking me up to elegant strangers and drumming up more interest in the silent auction.

"I did nothing," Dawn says. "That speech was all you. The student has officially become the master. You should be proud of yourself."

Dawn helped make tonight a success, and I force a smile for her. I should be walking on air. I got through the speech—but more importantly, we exceeded our fundraising goal. None of that money guarantees the museum will do well, but the funds cover most of the upfront pop-up expenses and allow us to pay off the loan for the renos.

Max and that tall, stylish woman haven't stopped talking for most of the night. She's even more gorgeous now that the lights are up.

Shrugging my bag over my shoulder, I say goodbye to Dawn and head outside. I parked my truck on the top level of a multi-story garage, underneath the golden gleam of a light post. Max catches up to me on the sixth floor right as I step out of the elevator, hustling to match my pace but not breathless from the flights of stairs he must have climbed. There are only three other vehicles up here, and the evening breeze has accelerated to a steady gust.

"Great turnout tonight, huh?" he asks, an obvious pep in his step.

"Mmm."

"I had some interesting conversations."

"Looked like it."

"You crushed your speech."

"Surprised you noticed." I search my bag for my keys, avoiding eye contact. The entire night was full of big moments—some that I surely missed, too. But my moment was more than the hotel or *Desert Daze*, and the only person I really wanted to share it with spent most of the evening chatting up a leggy blonde.

"Of course I noticed," Max says.

"You and that woman were in deep conversation all night."

"She was relentless." He at least has the decency to sound irritated by her. "Couldn't shake her. But she's kind of the whole point of an event like this?"

"What, for you to get a pretty woman's number?" I joke, glancing at Max to gauge his reaction.

"No." He tilts his head in amused confusion. "She likes art and design, she's got cash, and she wasn't afraid to bid on items."

As we approach my truck at the far end of the garage, Max follows me to the driver's side, tugging on my arm to whip me toward him.

"What's up?" he asks.

"Nothing."

"We received more money than we can count for the pop-up, and you seem...I don't know. Did I say something that upset you?"

I look into Max's eyes, and I can't hide. When he was living in Europe, it was easier to make a clean break and tell him what he needed to hear. But right now, with him in front of me, I can't pretend that everything's okay.

"Tonight was important—for The Mirage and for me and for our project—and you spent half the time flirting with someone."

"Seriously?" He scoffs and shakes his head. "I'm not sure what to tell you, Daze." He pauses, his dark eyes grazing over me. "If you thought I was flirting with her, then you haven't been paying attention at all this summer."

My skin tingles. The lights of the city around us glow and fade into the midnight blue above, sprinkled with sparkling stars.

"What's going on? Be honest, Daze."

"You..." I push down the lump forming in my throat. "You abandoned me tonight. I did exactly what you told me to do and talked to the one person who matters." I pause, giving him the chance to put the pieces together. "Then the lights came up, and I looked for you, and I...I was alone."

He doesn't move, and I feel silly for caring so much.

"I'm..." He scratches the back of his neck. "I'm sorry. For what it's worth, I watched you every second you were on stage. You were incredible." Then, more quietly, he adds, "I didn't realize you felt that way."

"I kissed you. Yesterday, at the school."

"Because you said you wanted to. Kiss, bam, that was it. You've otherwise been very clear about what you do and don't want from me, so what am I supposed to think? And even if...even if I feel the same, what could I have done, knowing you're just gonna push me away?"

Humiliation makes me want to call a rideshare for him so we don't have to be in the same vehicle for the ride home. I should have told him that seeing him embrace Harlow and bring in students for the pop-up felt almost like a love letter addressed to me. I should have told him everything.

"Why did you shut me out after high school?" he asks, and the question is a dagger to my chest. Things have been good between us since he got back, but I was naive to think this wouldn't come up.

"We needed to focus." I recall the text message I sent him, the reasoning I gave. "I had classes and an internship. You had college, your friends—your life. I didn't want to give you any reason to feel you shouldn't have listened to your calling."

"Don't act like you did that for me. You were a part of my life. You always have been."

"The last thing either of us needed was to be coordinating FaceTime calls with someone in another country."

"What I needed was *you*."

I did too, I think. But I knew I couldn't have him and also encourage him to chase his dreams thousands of miles away.

"It was shitty," he goes on. "There are always imbalances in relationships—a person who cares more. But it sucks to know for certain you've been this secondary character in someone else's life. When you realize they don't think about you as much as you think about them."

I shake my head because he couldn't be more wrong. "I thought about you a lot." My voice breaks, my vision blurs, and I blink up at the sky to prevent frustrated, hot tears from falling. He's always been the one that matters the most, and that terrifies me.

"Not the way I thought about you," he says. "I don't believe in the friend zone or dumb shit like that, but how I felt about you and going from...from what we had to not even getting a text back, it was awful. I was barely myself freshman year."

"I'm sorry. I really didn't know what to do with all the things I felt for you. When I got that first voicemail from you, I didn't realize how much I needed to hear your voice until I actually heard it."

"But you didn't really want to talk? You never called when I was awake." The anguish in his tone grips me. "And I'd call on Mondays or Tuesdays when you'd be less busy. I tested different times of day. You never picked up."

"I don't know, they just...the voicemails felt safe." Like I could keep my feelings buried and not impede on Max's life, but we could still talk in our own way. "Hearing you, like really hearing you on the phone would only make me wish you were here. And you going to Dublin was always the right thing, but being apart was...I never stopped thinking about you." I sniffle, then wipe my nose with the back of my hand. "Did you stop thinking about me? Wait, that's stupid," I say, backpedaling from my question. "You had your life and friends and everything there."

"Daisy, I thought about you an annoying amount. For someone who made it clear they didn't want to hear from me for months—then years—you were always around. When your favorite sunset colors splashed across the Dublin sky. Burnt orange and pastel pink. Whenever someone said they wanted coffee, black. Anytime I ate Thai food." He stands at the passenger door, his hair windswept and wild. "I thought about you all the time."

"And now?"

He shifts his weight and slips his hands into his pockets. "Why does it matter?"

"It just does."

"What makes you think anything's changed?"

I'm tired of pretending we can ignore how we feel about each other, because we can't. At least I can't. I don't want to.

So I reach out, grab his jacket, and pull his mouth to mine.

Chapter Twenty-Eight

Max, Now

Daisy's lips land on mine, fervent and needy. Every luscious curve of her presses against me, but I want us closer. *Need* us closer.

That's not what we agreed to, though.

"What are you—" I'm cut off by her mouth, and I have to press a hand to her stomach to give us both space. If I were a smart man, I'd shut up. But we promised each other this wouldn't happen again, and I have to understand where her head's at. "What happened to 'professional'?"

"Fuck professional."

She crashes her lips into mine once more, and the desire in my brain eclipses my ability to reason. I don't want to say no. I don't want to stop her. I don't want to talk this out and ruin the moment and miss this chance. But I also can't do this without knowing what my heart's up against.

"Just once more?" I ask as I trail kisses across her jaw. "Is that what this is?"

"No."

"Then what is it?"

"I need you."

"You said that before." Forcing us both to slow down, I cup her head in both hands, my thumbs stroking either side of her face. If we do this again, I'll be welcoming heaps of complication into both of our lives. "I don't want this if all you plan to do is push me aside after. I've been fighting my feelings for you since the moment I even *knew* I was coming back to Harlow. We'd have a good time," I say, running the pad of my thumb across her plump bottom lip, "but help me out here. You got a little jealous tonight, is that it?"

"Not jealous." She has me pinned between her body and the car, so I feel every slight movement as she shakes her head. "I mean, I sort of was. I am." Her admission sends a flare straight to my heart. "But what if we find a middle ground? Like..." Her eyes search mine. "We have to be honest with each other. And if it reaches a point when one of us doesn't want to do this anymore, then we stop, no hard feelings."

"Friends with benefits?" I ask, wanting to understand.

"I think it's more than that."

My gaze darts down to her lips, and it's near impossible to stand here and talk our situation out rather than kiss her again. But she's right. Whatever I'm feeling is light-years beyond casual. I nod.

"You said it would be a good time. So let's have that. Let's have as much good time together as we can before you go."

The way she says that crushes me, so I pull her closer, wrapped up in that sweet scent of hers. "Daze."

"People in workplaces date."

"True."

"We don't have HR to report to. *We're* HR."

"We should tell the assistants setting up the gallery." My hands skate up and down the arms of her jacket, rubbing to give her added warmth. "Because of my last job, I don't want them to think something's going on that's not supposed to. Is that okay with you?"

"Of course. And they'll understand. You and I aren't just coworkers. We know each other."

Daisy draws me into a long, slow kiss. She coaxes my mouth open, her tongue darting in to play with mine. My hands travel down her coat, skimming her too-perfect ass at the bottom. She moans into me, and my dick jumps.

"Just, when you leave," she says, panting in between kisses, "make sure you say goodbye."

Pushing her back by her shoulders, I level her with a stare. "Do you think I wouldn't do that?"

"Promise me. When you leave, you'll say goodbye."

"I promise. Of course, I promise."

I used to believe that Daisy flipped switches on her emotions, but I'm beyond wrong. She doesn't refuse to feel things—she feels *everything*, maybe too much. She protects herself the same way I do. We're both putting our hearts on the line here, and we recognize that at the end of this, we won't be the same.

Our breathing syncs as we melt into each other. Then, she's grinding into me, I'm gripping onto her with every ounce of strength I have, and we're wearing too much clothing to be making out like this. If she keeps rubbing against my hard-on, I'll be driving home with a mess in my pants. I rake my hands under her coat to slide it off, chucking the garment into the cab of the truck.

"Get in," I order her. "Now."

She shoots me a puzzled look, her eyebrows high. "Here?"

"You don't get to kiss me like that and then expect me to wait forty minutes to feel all of you."

She gulps and scrambles into the passenger seat. Once I close the door behind us, I draw her onto me so she straddles my lap. The hem of her dress rides up her thighs, and the lean muscles there are more beautiful than any piece of art in any museum. Transfixed by her body, I run one hand up her leg. When I lift my gaze, I get a face full of Daisy's chest, which makes my pants impossibly tight. She rests in front of me, breasts rising and falling with each inhale and exhale. I trace the neckline of her outfit with my hands, and she shivers underneath my touch.

"Cold?"

"No," she says, breathy. "The opposite."

"I like this dress on you." I look into her eyes. Her head is only slightly higher than mine. "I want to fuck you in it."

She doesn't give a response so much as whimper one. I rest my thumb against her lips, bee-stung and glossy. I was an idiot to think I could get her out of my system. When she rolls her hips forward, angling her crotch against me, I groan.

My lips make a map of all the places I adore. I kiss every freckle, every tattoo, every curve. I worship her neck, traveling from one shoulder to the next, while I slip under her dress to finger around the edge of her panties. She's already soaked through the fabric.

"I haven't even felt you come on my hand yet."

"Hurry up, then."

"Daisy." I push her underwear to one side and find her clit, applying gentle pressure that makes her writhe. "You like to think you're in charge here." Her body is slick and soft, and my middle finger follows her wetness until I'm inside her and beckoning her closer. She bows her head against mine, gasping out an *oh* while rocking her hips to dig harder against my hand. "That's not how this is going to go. Understand?"

"Mhmm."

"Do you understand?"

"I understand."

"Good girl. You say you want me? You need me? Then you don't come unless you ask for permission. Got it?"

She nods, grinding with my fingers inside her.

"I love watching you get off." I match the pace of her swaying, relishing every sharp intake of breath and every whine that comes out of her mouth. "Riding my hand. Losing control."

With my thumb firmly pressed against her, I slide another finger in. I've seen her come before, so I know the tells, and she's close—her eyes flutter closed and her head tilts back. Before she tips over the edge, I pool all the power in me to retract my hand.

She cries out in exasperation. "Please."

"Ask."

"Pleasecanicome, Max?" My name on her lips makes me grunt.

"Since you asked nicely."

"Damn you."

I kiss the sass off her mouth, simultaneously returning my hand to the place it belongs forever. She moans, rocking back and forth with more fire every time. I love the warmth of her, this deep part of Daisy that I'm only getting to know. I curl my fingers more, putting pressure in just the right spot. She closes her eyes again, her chin lifts, and the whole of her tightens, a pulsing that we relish together as she cries out.

Once Daisy comes down from her orgasm and I slide my hand out of her, I fumble with my belt. "Condoms?"

"Glove box," she pants, reaching behind her and retrieving a strip.

I grab myself with the hand that got Daisy off, still warm and wet with her. While stroking myself, I stare her down. "Open one."

She obeys, tearing the foil and rolling the rubber down my length. Her fingers encircle me, and I stiffen more in her grip.

Pulling her closer with my hand on her hip, I search underneath the bunched-up fabric of her dress. I tug her panties to the side and guide her onto my length. We moan in unison, both of us enjoying this again—what was intended to be a onetime thing.

But it couldn't have been. Not with her.

A rock of her hips sends me on a ride of pleasure. I lick the hand she came on, sucking off the sweet-tart flavor. And although I now have all of her, right here on top of me, I want more. I slip the skinny straps of the dress down, revealing two dark, pebbled nipples at the tips of her breasts. I take one in my mouth and the other in my hand, and then our bodies move in a synchronous rhythm of push and pull, filling the car with the murmurs of *deeper* and *more* and *yes*.

"Don't stop," I say, nibbling a path down her arm, past her biceps, and to the inside of her wrist with one last playful bite.

"Never."

When I settle both hands on her hips, I push her further onto my cock after every backward rock she takes. Daisy growls and grips my shoulder, pushing her torso backward. She knocks her head on the ceiling, hard, and collapses into my chest.

"Ow, shit."

I wrap both arms around her, cupping the back of her skull. "You okay?"

"Yeah." She looks at me with a giggle. "I have a perfectly fine bed at home, and we're acting like a couple of teenagers."

"Don't worry, we'll get to the bed. And the kitchen counter. And the shower. But I like having you here."

"I like having you here, too," she says, barely audible.

I toy with her left nipple, rolling it between my thumb and forefinger. "Anytime you sit in this truck, I want you to remember tonight. To remember me inside of you." As I bury my face in her breasts, we begin the give and take again—the blissful sensation of us rocking into an orgasm.

"I'm close. Please..."

"Yes?"

She moans. "Please. Let me come on your cock."

"Only," I pant on a thrust, "if you stay here with me. No closing your eyes or escaping somewhere else. Look at me while you come." I rest one hand on her collarbone, creating more pressure as her body envelops me.

"I don't know..." She pants and presses a gentle kiss to my wrist. "I don't know if I can control that."

"Try. Will you try for me?"

I hold her gaze, all heat and thrill. I *know* Daisy. I've looked into her amber eyes since I was a kid. But we have something new between us now.

She nods her head. "For you."

Daisy wraps her arms around my neck, and we're studying the minute indications of pleasure in the other person. Her mouth falls open with shallow, quick breaths, and her pupils are wide, endless drops.

"Max."

"I'm right here. It's just you and me, Daze."

She tightens around me, pulsing with pleasure, and that chokehold makes me come undone. My entire body pulses with the sheer satisfaction of the release, but my eyes remain locked on her. Daisy lingers in bliss with me, crying out, and she's more raw and more gorgeous than I've ever seen her before. As we both settle into the aftershocks, she sinks closer to me.

"Coming with you is..." I search for the right description.

"Fucking amazing?"

I laugh. She lifts one strap back onto her shoulder and I manage the other, enjoying how her contented, unhurried movements give me more time to take in her softness.

"Here." She reaches into the back abyss of the truck, producing a plastic bag for me to drop the condom in. I swear she watches my every move as I tug my pants on.

"We should go."

I glance around at the sparse number of cars. "When's the garage close?"

"It's twenty-four hours. But you mentioned my bed. And kitchen counter. And shower."

I reel her in for a kiss. Against her lips, I ask, "How quick can you get us there?"

The next few days pass in a haze of sex with Daisy, sleep, waking up beside her, work, and then repeating the cycle. When I go to meet my sister for thrift shopping on the weekend, I'm in a blissfully exhausted state.

"You should call Mom and Dad sometime." Ava throws on an enormous cowboy hat and examines herself in one of the store's mirrors. After a beat, she shakes her head and trades it for a beret. "They keep asking about you. It's annoying."

"Work's kept me busy." So has Daisy, I don't add. I clear my throat. "They, of all people, should understand."

"They're not as bad as they used to be. Like with schedules and stuff."

I scour the clothing racks of sunglasses and *hm* in acknowledgement. My parents never embraced a healthy work-life balance, but once Ava was old enough to make memories, they backed off at the firm. No use in regaling her about the days the nanny would wake me up for school and end with her tucking me in. They're better now because I was never their priority the way Ava is. I don't know what switched, but I blame them, not Ava.

"Oooh what about this?" She grabs a floral top off the rack, holding the fabric against her body. "I love this."

"Them's 'gainst the rules," I say with a forced drawl.

"Fine." She frowns and examines the shirt in her hands. "I still want to buy it, though."

During high school, I got my first part-time job at this exact shop. The place sells all kinds of strange finds and has been appropriately designed like an alien spaceship. My parents appreciated me becoming a responsible and productive member of society—their words, not mine—but they didn't view a retail job in a saucer-shaped thrift store as respectable.

I loved it, though, because I got to sift through the wacky treasures people tossed, which were art in themselves. The manager gave me first dibs on donated painting and drawing materials, too. Combined with the modest income, that meant less grumbling from my parents while checking out at the art supply store. My discount also let me come up with this silly after-school activity with Ava—blindly choosing ridiculous outfits and then grabbing something to eat at the diner down the block. A decent portion of my paycheck ended up right back here, but I didn't mind.

Ava strolls to the end of the pants section and smiles wide, one hand on the hangers and eyes squeezed shut as she walks. Once she reaches the middle, somewhere around a cluster of especially heinous prints, I tell her to stop. Her hand lifts the hanger from the rack, and she peers at it, pulling a face.

"This is awful."

"Neon green and yellow leopard will look great on you."

"Your turn," she chirps.

On the opposite side of the aisle, I walk slowly forward while my hand trails along the uneven row of hangers.

"Aaaand stop."

"Very stylish. I always wanted camo overalls. Water-resistant, too."

We continue like this throughout the store, grabbing tops, picking up accessories, and cackling. Once we pay and get sufficiently decked out in our new wardrobe, we leave the shop looking like we really are from another planet.

As we walk the block to the diner, I admire how Harlow's changed. The vibe is funkier than I recall—more lively. As a small desert town, there's always been a level of quirkiness. Lots of shops have popped up, though, making it a bit more of a destination and less a mere thoroughfare.

Ava bounces down the sidewalk, and it's one of the best things in the world listening to her talk about her life. She's cooler than I was at her age—more mature and self-aware. She tells me about her favorite classes, her least favorite teachers, the colleges she's thinking of, her debate team, and all the drama of who's dating who.

"What about you?" I ask, half joking. "How's the love life?"

She makes a fart sound with her mouth.

"You're sixteen. It'll get better."

"It didn't for you."

"Wow."

"Kidding. There is a girl at school, but she's like…" Ava shrugs. "Everyone wants to date her. She broke up with her last girlfriend like a week ago, and people are already asking her out and stuff."

"And you?"

"Don't want to pressure her. It's been one week."

Ava, my precocious baby sister, is sixteen going on thirty-six. And she's much more like me than I ever would have guessed.

"What's this girl's name?"

"Zinnia," she says in a hushed tone, scanning the sidewalk like this girl might pop out from behind a bush.

"'Ava and Zinnia' has a nice ring to it."

"Ugh." She rolls her eyes. "You're embarrassing."

I follow Ava into the diner—a neighborhood staple that's stuck in the '80s. The chairs and countertops have faded to a muted orange, and sepia-toned photographs of people from another era cover the walls. An acne-riddled teenager ushers us to a spacious booth next to the floor-to-ceiling windows.

"C'mon," I say, kicking her foot under the table. "Tell me about this girl."

"Not much to tell." Ava scooches onto her seat and grabs a pink packet of fake sugar to fidget with. "She's pretty, funny, smart, basically everything amazing rolled into one. And she has no idea I exist."

"You're pretty, funny, smart, and amazing."

"You're obligated to say that."

"Sure. But I mean it."

A smile spreads on her face like warm butter on toast. I'll forever be glad I kept up enough of a relationship with Ava while I was away that she's comfortable sharing these kinds of things with me.

"Ask her out," I say.

"She's barely been single a week."

"Fine. Wait. Watch her date one person after the other, always passing you up."

She waggles a finger in my direction. "You're projecting."

As I open my mouth to protest, the server comes by to fill our mugs and take our order, calling us "honey" and "sweetie." Only once do her eyes catch on the absurd clothing we wear. When she shuffles to the kitchen, Ava rests her elbows on the table.

"So when did you and Daisy start sleeping together?"

Mid-sip, I choke on my drink. "Ava."

"You're obsessed with her. Always were."

"I'm...you're really nosy, you know that?"

"Are you two gonna get married?"

"No, I—we..." I lean back in my seat with an exhale. "Whatever's going on, marriage is definitely not something we've discussed."

"Ohmygod, wait." Her eyes sparkle with glee. "I was joking. You *have* slept together?"

"Let's talk about something else."

I don't want to share these details with my baby sister. She may almost be an adult, but she also has her own relationship with Daisy.

"Tell me *everything*." Ava scoots to the edge of her seat, bobbing up and down with excitement. "Are you two dating? Are you sharing a bedroom? Did you propose yet?"

"Ava."

"Are you?"

"No."

"To which question?"

"All of them."

She sinks back into the seat with a glower. She adores Daisy, so the prospect of her brother and the most incredible girl in town getting together has her mind moving straight to wedding bells and babies.

"Well, why not?" she asks, that teenager attitude in full force.

"There's a lot about my relationship with Daisy that you wouldn't understand."

"Did you ever tell Daisy how you felt?"

"Things between me and her aren't so simple."

"You like her; she likes you."

Warmth fills my veins at the sound of that.

"If it's so easy for me to ask you-know-who out," Ava says, looking around the diner, "then you should take your own advice."

"That's not how it works in adult relationships, Ava."

"Stop it." She points her fork at me, and the server shows up with our greasy eggs and pancakes. "Don't talk to me like you're Mom or Dad."

"Sorry." I pick at the yolk, smearing gooey yellow across the plate. There's something about talking to a teenager with the purest outlook on life that simplifies things. "You're right. I care about Daisy. A lot."

"Duh." Ava stuffs a forkful of hash browns into her mouth. "Daisy deserves so much better than friends with benefits, and you know it."

"I agree. But Daisy's capable of making her own decisions."

"She is way too important to you, and you're way too important to her." Ava takes another bite of food. "Daisy's my friend, too, you know. And she should have someone who is here, one hundred percent."

I'd love to be that person for Daisy—I would in a heart-beat—but that means a commitment from me to stay and a commitment from her to let me in. Eleanor hasn't whispered a word about that job with Tate, if they're even still planning to hire someone. I could make a home here, but would that just spook Daisy into establishing more rules for our relationship?

"Why don't you wanna stick around?" Ava asks, and she looks so small, like the eight-year-old who waved goodbye to me at the airport before I left for college.

"Hey. I'm...I'm sorry I wasn't here for you."

She shrugs. "It's no biggie."

"I don't want you to feel like my leaving is ever, or has ever been, me abandoning you."

"I know." Her eyes flash to mine, and she grins. "You can't get rid of me that easy. But I can hold a grudge like nobody's business, so figure out what you really want, okay?"

I smile, despite the unease gnawing at my insides. "Noted."

Chapter Twenty-Nine

Daisy, 18 Years Old

Max's acceptance letter shook in my hands. Los Angeles was far, but this was another world.

"Crazy, right?" Max sat next to me on the bench outside of the casita, a huge grin on his face.

"Not crazy," I said, nudging him with a halfhearted smile. "Of course they want you."

I thought he was coming over today to…what? Talk about last night? I dreaded the conversation as much as I yearned for it. I'd wanted to kiss him so badly, but I knew it was a bad idea. Wasn't it?

But, no. Max ran over to my house breathless for another reason.

I scanned the paper again. World-class professors. Opportunities he could never find in Harlow, not even in California. And most importantly, a full scholarship. He wouldn't be indebted to his parents—and he'd probably like the distance from them.

My heart pinched, but I smiled through it.

"What about…" I looked for the paragraph. "The summer institute. That starts—" I swallowed. "It's like two weeks away."

"It sounds interesting." He shrugged, taking the paper back. "I'd meet people in the program, get some extra training. The visiting instructors sound cool, too."

His eyes lit up the more he talked about the pre-college program offered only to selected rising freshmen. An opportunity of a lifetime that he would only have this summer. He needed to decide, and soon.

"I don't know, though." He scratched the back of his head, his attention flicking to me. "It's not a requirement."

"You're not actually considering not doing this, are you?"

"I got in last minute. They won't hold it against me for wanting to keep my summer plans."

"What plans?" As far as I knew, he wanted to get as many shifts at the thrift store as he could to save up for school.

Max shrugged again, his cheeks turning red. "I kinda thought it would give me more time here. We could hang out and stuff."

Oh.

He'd pass up this incredible opportunity for a few months with me, but that wasn't fair to him, or to me. At the end of August, what would he do? He'd still go to Dublin, and that departure would hurt even more after a perfect summer together. Or maybe he'd change his mind. That turned my stomach. When someone gives something up in a relationship, bitterness bubbles up—Mom and Dad were living proof.

I couldn't do that with Max—be the person who dims his life and goals. I shouldn't have ever let prom night go as far as it did.

"What d'you think?" he asked, his knee bumping into mine.

With tears burning, I smiled. "I think you'd be a fool not to go."

Chapter Thirty

Daisy, Now

"I didn't get any, Mr. Dub."

No matter how many times Max corrects his students, they insist on calling him this nickname. It's adorable. The flyers in my hand become a shield to hide my smile.

"Take some of these," he says. "You've all got your designated sections to flyer. Buddy system, look both ways, yadda yadda. Grab the old ones and replace them with these. And when you talk to people, let them know you'll be in the show."

At this, a few students grin.

"My mom was wondering if you're rescheduling 'cause of the weather," one girl asks.

"No plans to," Max says. "We have our eyes on the forecast, though."

Reports of a freak storm rolling through has everyone nervous, and I've tried to keep a level head. If we have bad luck, the heaviest rains would arrive shortly before opening night—three days away—and scare people into staying at home. But these systems go around us 99 percent of the time.

For good measure, I had Stacey do a run-through of the rooms, and I checked the gutters this afternoon.

A young man who introduced himself as Xander narrows his eyes at me. "You look real familiar, Ms. Johnson."

"I thought so too," someone else says.

"Oh." I don't think I've seen his face before. "We may have crossed paths sometime."

"No, I have *seen* you."

"Wait," gushes a short, spunky girl who told me her name is Zoë. "That portrait. Remember? The one Mr. Dub did."

The group of six teens murmurs amongst themselves in recognition.

"Portrait?" I ask, but Max talks over me.

"We should get started." He brings his hands together in an abrupt clap. "See you back here—hopefully with no flyers—in thirty. Got it? Great. This is your extra credit, so you better hop to it. Perfect. Bye."

The students break off into duos, talking amongst each other as they head down the block. "Just a friend," I hear one of them mutter, but I don't catch the rest.

"Should I be concerned with what you're sharing with your students?"

"It's—" He waves a hand. "They wanted to see what I could do. So I drew a quick portrait."

"Of me?"

He nods and starts our journey down the street.

"When?"

"First day of class. Trial by fire sort of thing."

I pick up my pace to walk next to him, mentally flipping through a calendar. That would have been months ago, back in early June. Of all the people's faces fresh in his mind that he could have drawn, he chose mine. I suppress a smile.

"Why didn't you show me?" I ask, feigning indignance. "As the subject, that only feels right."

"Not my best work. I had two minutes, and I drew from memory."

"Does this make me your muse?" I lift my shoulder, playing coy.

His arm wraps around my waist, pulling me to him, and his lips effortlessly find mine. The kiss is a tantalizing vertigo—I don't know which way is up, and I don't know who's watching, but I really don't care.

"If you only knew," Max mutters against my skin before grabbing my hand and leading me down the sidewalk.

That zip of a new relationship, or a new *something*, shoots through me. I want to dip into an alleyway and get even better acquainted with his mouth and every other part of him, but we're here with flyers in our hands for a reason. I'll just have to enjoy this delicious in-between—exciting, unknown—and not think about the end.

We start down the dusty sidewalk, heading for the gas station. We're on the cusp of golden hour, so the day's heat lingers, although the temperature at dusk will drop by the minute.

"The kids like you," I say, holding a sheet of paper in place against a light pole for Max to staple-gun.

"They like extra credit."

"Only the best teachers get nicknames."

"They talk too much. And they ask too many personal questions."

"But they like you." It's not a question—I can tell they worship him, even if he won't admit it himself. "And you like them."

"They're not bad." He shrugs, clearly trying to play cool. "I enjoy seeing them excited. They're not jaded or full of themselves—they just have this passion for creating. And I like helping them."

"They're lucky to have you. They looked stoked about getting their artwork featured, too."

"I have you to thank for that."

My brows furrow. "You made that happen."

"The town is a big part of *Desert Daze* because you stood by what you believed in. And I'm glad for it." He sticks both hands in his pockets and clears his throat. "If this had happened when I was in high school, it would have been the coolest thing."

I think of young Max participating in an exhibit like ours, and how he wouldn't have been able to contain his excitement. How would that have changed Harlow for him if he didn't have to travel halfway around the world to pursue the career he deserved? It's an opportunity that's years too late.

We make the rounds on the far side of town. Shonda's at the gas station, and she shows me photos from her recent vacation to Aruba. Dr. Feines greets us at the vet and asks how Freddie is doing. María at the taco stand doesn't let us leave without a couple specials of the day. I like the chance to catch up with everyone, and I loop Max into all the conversations.

With ten minutes left before we need to meet with the students, we turn around and walk shoulder to shoulder on the sidewalk toward our last stop.

"Harlow's one big Daisy Johnson fan club," Max says.

"Please."

"People light up when they see you."

I shrug. "Sometimes I get so preoccupied with the hotel that I don't feel like a great neighbor."

"You show up for the community. You have conversations that go deeper than surface-level small talk. That's its own form of support."

My insides fizz. "Well, it's how we all thrive."

When we reach Gwen's gem store, I stall the last few steps to the door. Max's hand hovers over the handle, but he pulls back once he notices my hesitation.

"I texted her about the other night," I admit.

"And all the other nights? And this morning?"

"Max." Thank goodness for his humor, but also, thoughts of his head between my legs before my morning coffee send a fire to my cheeks. I peer inside to see if Gwen's working the counter, but a shelf of chunky, jewel-toned rocks blocks my view.

"What'd she say?"

"A bunch of emojis." A long string of them that could be good or bad—I couldn't tell and didn't ask her to clarify. But if she's upset with me, I shouldn't let that fester.

"Do you want to go in alone first?"

"No. She's just acting like the big sister I never had. It's fine."

"I was actually asking because I'm scared of her."

A laugh rips out of me, and his smile sends goosebumps up my arms.

"C'mon," he says, opening the front door.

I love Gwen, and I know she loves me no matter what choices I make. She's been there for the bad haircuts, the bad boyfriends, and the bad hires at The Mirage that didn't work out. But the last Gwen heard, Max and I were a one-night stand with no intention of more. Now we're...

Well, I don't have an answer for that. And I might never, and that's fine, because we both agreed: a good time together, for as long as we can. But I feel like I've let my best friend down by not being able to resist Max.

Behind the cash register, she's perched on a chair while she scribbles notes down. Her left hand rests on her belly. She's not showing yet, but she should any day soon.

"My favorite person!" She wriggles her butt off the stool and wraps me up in her arms.

"You don't have to get up for me." I breathe a sigh of relief at her warm reception.

"You sound like Bob. He's infuriating."

"Is everything okay?"

"Oh, yeah. He just won't let me do anything around the house. Like, if he could bring the toilet to me, he would. I have to remind him I'm pregnant, not incapacitated. He doesn't have to do *everything* for me."

"Sounds awful."

"I know." She squeezes my hand, and her eyes skate to Max. She straightens and looks him up and down. "Sooo."

"So?"

"You and Daze, huh?"

"Me and Daze."

"I had a feeling about you two."

"A good one?" Max's head cocks to the side.

"A complicated one." The corner of her mouth twists into a smile. "You can leave a stack of flyers at that register. And feel free to pin one on the bulletin board."

While Max finds a spot on the cork board, Gwen turns to me and mouths, *OH MY GOD.*

I KNOW, I mouth back. *YOU MAD?*

A look of shock crosses her face. *NO.* She points to herself, outlines a heart in the air, and then stabs a finger in my direction, causing us both to smile at each other. She then gives me a thumbs up, and she juts her pointer finger into the O shape of her other hand in a lewd gesture. *GOOD SEX?*

I bite my lower lip. Amazing sex. Transcendental sex. Still-sore-in-a-good-way sex. I don't know how to communicate that, so I just nod, and Gwen appears to understand.

YOU, she mouths with her finger directed at me, *GOOD?* Again with the thumbs up.

I nod once more.

"You two done talking about me?"

Gwen spins to Max with a syrupy sweet smile on her face. "For now. Daze, call me sometime soon so we can discuss..." She waves her hand in Max's general direction. "I want all the details. And you," she says, turning her attention to him. "It should go without saying, but if you hurt my friend, I will hurt you."

"Ohmygod, Gwen."

"I'm leveling with him. Gotta look out for my Daisy."

"Love you, Gwen." I usher Max to the exit.

"Love you, too. And you—just because you've got the sensitive Pisces thing going for you doesn't mean you're not trouble. I've got my eye on you!"

We exit and I close the door behind us, muting Gwen's loving threats. With a couple minutes to spare, we get back to Max's students where we started, right on time.

"Mr. Dub!" Xander yells from across the crosswalk. "We need some more flyers for the salon."

The rambunctious crowd of students inches toward us, and Max hands some of his papers over. "That's all I've got. So how'd it go?"

The students share who they talked to, who said they would show up, and who's going to bring friends and family. All of them want Max to notice them, enjoying their moment in the spotlight when he looks at them.

I feel like one of those students, soaking up as much of his attention as I can. Basking in the sun that is Max, until inevitably, that big star in the sky dips below the horizon to where it belongs. But I can't ignore the shred of me that's hoping I'm wrong—that's wondering if Max might ever change his mind.

Chapter Thirty-One

Max, Now

I set a heavy box behind the check-in counter, hoping all this effort will be for nothing. We didn't take forces of nature into account for opening night. Daisy slipped out this morning, waving around a news update on her phone that showed the bad weather was, indeed, likely to hit us, and about twelve hours earlier than expected—meaning tonight.

Maybe I'm overreacting, she had messaged, *but better safe than sorry.*

Every hour today will shed more light on what we're up against. In the meantime, Stacey and I handle some of the preventative measures on site, like double-checking window closures and taking in decor like the wind chimes.

"Patio furniture's next," Stacey says as she crosses an item off her list.

"On it."

"Oh, please. I can do that."

"Daisy said to leave the heavy stuff to me. Show me where it should go."

Stacey curses under her breath, but when we reach the first room, she respects Daisy's wishes and directs me to a cleared spot in the lobby—right in front of an old painting of mine, actually. Despite the stress of the day, I smile. Daisy's mom put that there, and Daisy didn't replace it.

By the time we're done, I have slick sweat trailing down my temple.

"Catch." Stacey tosses me a small canteen of water from the fridge. As much as I want to down the cool liquid in one go, I first hold the bottle to my cheek. The chill is glorious.

"You've been quite a helper around here, Mr. Weber," Stacey says, eyeing me. "Not just today, either."

"My pleasure."

"You enjoy workin' here?"

"Sure, it's great. I wouldn't say that running a hotel is my calling, but I'm happy to help Daze."

"Bet if you asked, she could set you up with something more long-term."

I take a gulp, and the refreshment of the near-freezing water causes me to let out an *ahhh* like in a '60s soda commercial.

"You'd get to see Daisy every day," Stacey goes on. "Be here, support her. You like that."

First, the stern warnings from my sister and Gwen, and now I have Stacey attempting to nail down my five-year plan. Everything about Harlow has surprised me, but staying? What would that look like?

"Family and friends get a pretty sweet discount." Stacey continues, listing off her health benefits and paid time off.

"Why are you trying to sell me on this?"

"This place sells itself, don't ya think?"

I frown at her.

"Fine." She huffs. "Not a word of this to Daze, though, y'hear." She closes her eyes, and worry swirls in my stomach. Is something going on financially that Daisy doesn't know about? Or maybe this is more personal, like something medical-related. If that were to happen to Stacey, how would Daisy handle that loss?

"I wanna retire."

"Well, that's..." Relief rushes in, and I laugh. "Congratulations! That's exciting."

"More exciting if I could tell my boss."

"Daisy doesn't expect you to work here forever."

Stacey's brow quirks. "The girl is go, go, go and accepts help from no one. You know that. When I had my fall, she took on my hours instead of hiring a temp. When I asked her why she didn't, she said the thought hadn't crossed her mind. She's so consumed by The Mirage sometimes that she forgets to give herself a break." Stacey opens her tote bag for me to see a small collection of papers. "I got some resumes here from folks looking for jobs. But I can't very well have interviews for my replacement without telling Daisy first, can I? I don't want to stress her out, but I...it's time for a new chapter in my life. I'm just..." Her voice catches and her eyes glisten. She reaches into her bag and pulls out a tissue to dab her tears. "Shoot, there I go."

The sight of her face creasing as she cries makes my big-brother instincts kick in, so I open my arms to hug her.

"Hey, Daisy will understand. She'll be sad to lose you, but only because she cares about you."

"She's the daughter I never had. The thought of how she'll look when I tell her I'm moving on...oh, it breaks my heart. If you were here, I'd feel like at least..." Stacey sniffles, backing away from our embrace. "Sorry. That's not fair of me to ask."

"It's okay. You care about her."

She nods, her expression still watery. "I get why she likes you so much. You two're good together. I like seeing her so happy."

My mouth opens to object, because I'm not the only reason. It's the pop-up and the success of The Mirage that have her in high spirits.

"I know her," Stacey says, tucking her tissue away as she eyes me up and down. "She *likes* you."

"If you're about to give me one of those 'break her heart, then I'll break you' speeches, then you're too late."

"Please. Daisy knows what she's getting into. She'll do fine. She always does. Was doing just fine when you left before, and she'll do just fine again. But be careful for *you*." Stacey rests a hand on my shoulder. "I watched you grow up alongside her, and I might not know for sure what's going on in that handsome little head of yours, but I have a hunch. And whatever happens between you two, well...I don't want you to have a reason to stay away."

My entire childhood, I wanted to get out of Harlow. I probably convinced the very girl I pined after since forever that I didn't want to be here. Then, for eight years, I avoided returning to my hometown. The cost of flights, my disapproving parents—those were excuses. I didn't hate the thought of coming back to Harlow, but the reality of seeing Daisy petrified me. I knew that once I saw her, I'd question why I really ever left.

"You wanna sit down?" Stacey examines me, flipping the back of her palm against my forehead. "You look...not well."

"What if Daisy's not the reason to stay away?"

"What d'you mean, hon?"

"What if...what if she's the opposite?"

I have to see this through. Us. If the job at Tate comes up, I'll handle that when it happens. But right now, everything except for Daisy fades to the background.

A slow smile creeps onto Stacey's face, and she gives me a hearty slap on the back. "Well that's pretty damn romantic, if I do say so myself. Don't wait around on that."

And I definitely don't intend to.

Chapter Thirty-Two

Daisy, Now

"Last name?" I check off the sporty couple listed on the clipboard, hoping they don't see my hands shaking. "Welcome, you two. Stacey will take you to your room, and if you need anything, let me know. We want to make you as comfortable as possible."

Reservations have become a nightmare today as guests called to delay their arrivals, but I've opened up The Mirage to campers so they have a safe place for the night. Flash floods are no joke around here. With so little moisture in the ground—when *was* the last rainfall?—an abrupt, heavy downpour can wreak havoc. We've experienced it before with power outages, fence damage, and mud seeping under doorways.

Max returns in my truck, and thank god he spent all those years in Europe and learned how to drive stick. He's been running all over town to gather supplies while I oversee operations here. Although I always have a stash of emergency provisions, those ominous clouds are the color of a nasty bruise and moving in fast. We're less than forty-eight hours from opening, and Mother Nature has decided she wants to play.

"When the guy at the store found out they were for The Mirage, he threw in some extra sandbags," Max says, slamming the truck door shut. He looks rugged, with a sheen of sweat on his brow and his shirt wrinkled, and I wish I could melt into him and forget everything else.

I survey the trunk, disappointed by the small haul of sand-filled sacks. We cleared the lot mere weeks ago, and all of that hard work and money will wash out to town.

Max's warm hand links around my upper arm and sucks me out of the negativity. "Combined with what we already have, we'll have plenty of ground covered. We've got this."

"You can't promise that," I say under my breath. I need to stay calm for the sake of our guests, and for the sake of Stacey and the gallery assistants who are all working their asses off. If anyone sees me losing my serenity, warmth, and wonder, that would only add to the turmoil.

But we have so much on the line.

"The guests are safe, they're getting settled in, they have food and flashlights, and their rooms are secure." He moves to stand in front of me, both hands on my shoulders. The gesture grounds me. "The people are the most important, and you've got that covered. Maybe they'll have some minor leaks, but it's nothing we can't handle."

Then, as if doing so is the most natural thing in the world, he rests a hand on my hip and pulls me in for a kiss. His lips on mine set everything right, if only for a moment. We have guests exploring the property and another couple sitting in the lobby revising their vacation plans, but all I know is him, here. We're at that point—still not labeling "us," but not worried about what other people think either. Not hiding.

A distant crack of lightning reminds us what we're up against. We're plowing into the first big storm since the renovations, so I don't know what points of failure exist.

Which also means every piece of art is in danger, too.

"I'll use as many painter's tarps as I can find." He scratches his head, like some other brilliant idea might be hiding in there. "Not ideal, but workable."

"We can turn my living room into storage." Poor blind Freddie won't understand a thing, but I can keep him in my bedroom, and at least we know everything will stay dry.

"Or..." Max pinches the bridge of his nose. He hesitates, pulls out his phone, and stares at it before pulling up a familiar contact's name.

"No."

"What other choice do we have?"

"You said you wanted to do this without their help." My shoulders sink with the realization that Max couldn't count on me, or on The Mirage.

"They have the room. With the extra travelers staying in the guest room and on the couch, wouldn't it be better to put everything where no one will run into it or knock it over accidentally?"

I hate the idea as much as he does, but we're past desperation.

"Are you sure?" I interlock my hands with his. Despite what we're dealing with, I love this—being able to touch him like this without caring what anyone thinks.

"We can't afford not to. Everything will be safe there, and it's just down the road."

Five seconds later, he has his cell on speakerphone.

"I'm about to head into a meeting," his dad answers. "Three minutes."

"Hi to you, too."

I tap Max's foot with my own to keep him on track. He looks at me and whispers, "What?"

"Hello, Mr. Weber." I adopt a honeyed customer service voice. "It's Daisy."

Mr. Weber's tone brightens, and he asks how I'm doing. I answer honestly: we're busy and stressed. I wait, giving Max the opportunity to step into the discussion, but he doesn't bite.

"Um, actually," I say, "we have a favor to ask of you. With the storm, we have a lot of items from the pop—"

"Can we stop by the house and store some stuff?" Max asks. "To keep things from The Mirage safe tonight, with the weather and all."

His dad pauses. "How long will it be there?"

"Tonight, and that's it. In and out in less than twenty-four hours."

"Be right in," Max's dad says to someone else. "Well, sure. Anything you need, Daisy."

I catch how he's offering support to me, not to Max, and if we weren't in the middle of an emergency, I'd like to have a nice, long talk with Max's dad.

"Thank you, Mr. Weber."

"Great," Max says. "Thanks."

"Your mother and I are gone this week. Working in Beverly Hills. But Ava's home."

We hang up, but Max's mood remains as stormy as the clouds rolling in the distance.

"You didn't tell them about the museum, did you?" I ask.

"They wouldn't have cared." He turns toward the barn. "Need help with the truck cap?"

"Ava's probably already told them," I call after him, but he keeps walking.

"If they want to come, they'll come. But they won't, and I don't care."

By the way he's hunched over, his body in a defensive position, I know he cares very much. My heart aches, and I wonder if it's too late for them to make up for all the shows they missed, all the offhanded comments, and all the times they let him down.

"Let's just..." He shrugs, then rakes his hand through his hair again, mussing it up in a way that makes me want to run my own fingers through it. "Let's pack the truck before I change my mind."

"I'm sorry."

"Don't be." He gives me a sad smile before turning to get back to business.

We take a couple of trips to transport the pieces there, with Stacey's help. Max asks if it's okay for Ava to stay with us—he'd rather have an eye on her, and she's excited by the prospect of a sleepover. Of course I say yes, although I also yearn to have a moment alone with him, to talk one-on-one and really understand what's going through his brain. He's looked at me all day like we're a missed opportunity in the making, but all we can do now is settle into the casita with mugs of hot drinks in our hands, staring out the window into the darkness as heavy raindrops fall.

When the rain stops at three in the morning, I want desperately to sneak out and survey the damage, but I can't. Never mind the danger of walking on the property after the rainfall has tracked brush and debris—and who knows what else—onto the land. But I am literally trapped between Ava on one side of my king-size bed and Max on the other, with his arm snug around my waist. "No funny business," his sister had joked as she dozed off last night. Max waited until she was passed out and snoring gently to nuzzle close. His fingertips traced the soft parts of me—my hips, my stomach, my thighs—until he fell asleep too.

I don't rest, though. Under the dim glow of my computer charger, I examine Max's dozing profile. Even with so much at stake and so much going on, life feels right with him here, resting next to me. I can't remember what I was doing for the last eight years. It's as if the time without Max never happened, and he's been here all along.

These dangerous thoughts lull me to sleep, and the next thing I register is sunshine stabbing through the blinds and assaulting my eyes. Freddie has found a home between my legs, stretched out on his back like he's a hot dog in a bun. Max and Ava are gone, the sheets cold. I check my phone. 8:49 a.m.

"Shit." I slink out of bed, careful not to disturb the cat, and toss on my boots. When I emerge from the house, my property looks like the inside of a shaken-up snow globe, except instead of snow, we've got dust and dirt. I suck a breath down and walk toward the turmoil, and I trip over a sandbag.

"Watch out," Max calls from the barn. He waves, his mouth curved in a gentle smile, and I head in his direction.

"I wanted to wake up hours ago." I don't mean to snap at him, but I can't believe he let me lie in bed so late. "I should have been up with the sun."

"Freddie's a pretty cozy blanket."

"You should've woken me up."

"Daze," Max says, resting his hands on my upper arms. "You needed rest."

"No, I needed to know what the damage is. Is everyone okay?"

"Everyone's safe." He squeezes my shoulders and turns so I can look at the property in its entirety. "Stacey and I have already checked in with all the guests."

My body relaxes with the good news, but with the landscape in disarray, I know not to get too comfortable. "The barn?"

"One major leak, focused in a single area. That little alcove. We can close that off tomorrow. Move some pieces around."

"You spent days setting everything up."

"The gallery assistants are already on it." He tilts his head beyond the barn, the corners of his mouth turned downward. "The lot is our big focus. Needs serious clearing."

I needed this pop-up to go off without a hitch, and the universe couldn't cut me a break. One storm made this an impossible task. Max held up his end of the bargain: get the art, organize, promote. He sucked down his pride and asked his parents for help, whereas I let him down. Maybe it's the bad night's sleep, or maybe it's because I haven't had my morning caffeine, but hot, thick tears blur my vision and my face crumples.

"Hey, whoa," he says, rubbing my arms. "It's okay."

"No, it's not. How will we open tomorrow night? All those reservations will probably cancel." I wipe my eyes with the back of my hand. "What other museum has given you this many problems? At any other pop-up, I bet you didn't have to worry about some natural disaster sweeping through and ruining it. You needed a solid, reliable place, and I couldn't even give you that. I can't fix this," I say through a quiet sob, frustrated with myself for getting so emotional over the one thing Harlow's always had: harsh weather. "I know how to fix a lot of things on my own, but I can't fix this."

He cups my face with both of his hands, a bemused look on his face. "Daze."

"Don't laugh!" A storm of emotions surges inside me as my raised voice only makes him chuckle more. Has he lost his mind? "We can't do all of this."

"We don't have to."

I follow his line of sight to the cars parked near the lobby. Some of them are Max's students, since the school district issued an inclement weather day, and their parents chauffeured them here. The kids bounce out of their vehicles, practically shouting with excitement about the storm, bragging back and forth about the frightening sounds they heard and how much debris landed in their yard. Then there's Dawn, Gwen, Bob, my dad, and Oona—but also Shonda from the gas station, the barber, the thrift store manager, and the line cook at Sal's.

"I made some calls," Max said. "Everyone knows we're in crunch time."

Every single one of them has arrived with tools and buckets of supplies and smiles on their faces, ready to save me.

"That community you're always talking about? The people you're always helping?" Max checks me with his shoulder. "They wanna help you, too."

"Max." It's the only word I can manage, and at barely a whisper. He could guess that I would have spent all day and night attempting to do this myself, not wanting to suck people's energy and resources dry. I hate that he knows me so well. Rather than pick a fight, he's guided me to a better place.

I turn into him, wrapping my arms around his body and letting his quiet strength envelop me. "Thank you."

As we tackle the property, I catch Max looking at me more than once with a contented smile, and I beam back at him. People showed up. The *community* showed up. I could cry. On two occasions, I run to the bathroom to do just that.

We start by removing the standing water from the alcove, and we situate borrowed fans to dry the floor. Max fetches the art from his parents' house and directs his assistants and students as they rebuild the pop-up. We spend hours shoveling and rearranging piles of dirt, and by the day's end, the parking area looks rough-and-ready, but usable, and with the same number of spots. We manage it all without a single room cancellation coming through, and the members of the media we've invited for the event are still thrilled to attend the next day.

The sun jumps out from behind a cloud in time for a muted golden hour, so we get literal sunshine and rainbows after the storm.

"Food and drinks on me," I announce to the small group who remains. The students and parents have all gone home, but we have a crowd of other folks from around town. "See you at Sal's in twenty."

Max, Ava, and I walk into the casita to change. A rinse-off might do me good, but I go for a healthy dose of body spray instead. If I hop into a hot, steamy shower, I'll crash.

Gwen and Bob will take me to Sal's while Max drops Ava off at a friend's using my truck. His sister hugs me goodbye and bounces out the front door.

Max looks at me, his expression conflicted.

"Everything okay?" I ask.

"Yeah, it's fine. Just—I've been wanting to talk to you about something."

My stomach sinks, and he moves in to hold my hand.

"Not something bad," he says, and the reply soothes me. "But something important."

"Right now?"

"No." He glances outside to where Ava sits in the car. "Later tonight? I want some time alone with you."

I blush. His words imply something sexual, but his tone has an earnest gravity to it. "Okay, well, tonight," I say. "After Sal's."

He rests his other hand on my jaw and kisses me like I'm the only person who matters in the world.

Chapter Thirty-Three

Daisy, Now

Everyone in a thirty-mile radius must have had the same idea, because I've never seen Sal's so busy. After a night of wild weather, the entire town has shown up to let off some steam. There are out-of-towners galore, some of them in head-to-toe hiking gear and others clad in black leather jackets. With luck and good timing, we snag spots at the far end of the room. Sal brings us pitchers of beer and takes our orders, and we all toast to our efforts.

I want to grab my drink and go to the cocktail table Max and my dad have claimed. For the beast of a day we conquered, their conversation seems less celebratory and more serious—no smiles, but plenty of terse nods. Before I can slip out and interrupt them, Gwen slots into the booth beside me.

"Mmm, I forgot how criminally good this lemonade is." She slurps some up through her straw. "Want some?"

I shake my head.

"Positive? Because I'm picking up some very melancholy energy from your little booth over here."

"Contemplative energy, that's all. Today was a lot."

"Yeah." She nudges me with her shoulder. "You pulled through, though. I'm proud of you."

"Thank you for being here." I lean against her, overwhelmed and grateful for all her support. "You and Bob."

"Always and forever, babes. I know I'm no Dawn or anything, but I'll help however I can."

I pick my head straight up and gawk at her. "What are you talking about?"

"She's...she's a really good person, and a good friend to you."

"Sure, but what does that—"

"She helped you with that speech. She didn't act like an annoying big sister when you talked about sleeping with Max. She's not pregnant, so she could do more than just refill people's water today. I see why you like her."

"I like when you act like my big sister. And I like you pregnant." I can't believe I even have to say this. "I like you *so* much. More than like. I love you, you idiot."

"I love you, too." Her bottom lip pops out, and her eyes turn glassy. "I don't want you to not be in my life when the baby is born."

"Did Stacey give you some of her stash or something?"

"Babies change things."

"Sure," I say, my heart hurting that my best friend has been holding onto this fear. "You're gonna have mommy friends, and me and Dawn will become closer, but nothing could ever get in the way of you and me. I promise."

She smiles and loops her hand into mine. "Me too."

Everything around us buzzes with energy, and I admire how many people came out to help. My heart might explode. If I could, I'd buy them all a hundred pitchers of beer and a hundred pizzas. More, even. But guilt clouds my vision.

"I can't wrap my head around all these folks giving up their day for me," I say, hoping my friend doesn't think less of me for putting the needs of The Mirage first. "Everybody here, you included, has businesses and homes, too."

"I ask for your help all the time." She lets out a rueful laugh and lists out all the times I've stepped in at her shop or helped with special events. I didn't complete these tasks with an expectation of something in return, and I certainly never looked down on Gwen for asking. If she needed something, I would make it happen.

"We love you," she goes on. "The whole town loves you. If you need help, we're there. Me, especially. At least somebody gets it."

She nods to Max, who's now sitting at a nearby table talking to Bob and Dawn. One of them must have made an incredible joke, because he's laughing, his wide smile like the sunrise on a clear day. It's my favorite smile.

"I thought you were anti-Max," I say.

"Not anti-Max—just pro-you. And him being back seems good for you. You've been happy, and that's all I ever wanted for you. You deserve it. Or, who knows, maybe you're just in a good-mood sex bubble because of getting laid regularly."

I shoot lighthearted daggers at her with my eyes.

She hooks her elbow on the backrest, positioning her body toward mine so no one can overhear our conversation. "If you had asked me what kind of partner I wanted when I was single, I would have told you to give me some chakra-aligned, vegan-eating, yoga-loving California blond boy. And then I met Bob. He can't touch his toes, his favorite food is mozzarella sticks from Sonic, and he has a buzz cut. He's allergic to nature, and he has a spreadsheet for everything. Seriously, *everything*."

"Even—"

"Yes, even that. And when we started dating, you could have pointed to all of those things and told me he's not a good match. Half the time, *I* was telling myself that."

I think back to their early days together. When I pictured my best friend with someone, it wasn't someone like Bob. "But," I say, cutting off my own thoughts, "he makes you happy."

"The happiest. And I can't fully comprehend how he's the one, but you have never, ever questioned my sanity. You trusted me. Supported me. So I wanna do the same." Her eyes shimmer with tears, so she looks to the ceiling and fans them. "Hormones." She composes herself and clasps my hands in hers. "Seeing you in shambles after Dublin destroyed me, but I will always help you pick up the pieces when something—anything—goes wrong. So I can either give you a hard time or accept that you know what you want. Just be careful," she says, part request, part warning. "Did you tell him you were there?"

My attention flits to Max, who's attracted a mixed audience of folks from our cleanup crew, campers, and motorcycle-club members, all of them with expectant faces as he tells a story. He's a chameleon, and the crowd of people hangs on his every word.

"Not yet." My stomach tightens.

"He'll understand."

"You think?"

"He might be upset that you weren't honest, but he deserves to know."

When I returned from Dublin, Gwen begged me to let her message Max and say anything to convince him to come back, even for a weekend. *He would ditch Dublin and get back here so fast*, she'd said. And that was the problem with Max transferring to somewhere in Los Angeles, or maybe even closer. Proximity to his parents, missing out on opportunities in big cities with big artists, and his resentment growing day by day. The two of us fighting, and Max wondering if it was worth sacrificing what he wanted, just for me.

But she's right—I can't keep holding back on him.

After everyone eats, people depart in large groups. The desire to get horizontal and stay that way as long as humanly possible yanks at my eyelids. I hug the last person in our group goodbye as Sal brings the check. As we wait for him to return with my card, Max plops down on the seat to my left.

"Crazy day, huh?" He drapes an arm over my shoulder, like he used to when we were young. The gesture holds much more weight now.

"Tomorrow'll be crazier. All those people. The big event."

Sal drops off the credit card, giving me a wink on his way back to the bar.

"Hey, so, I wanted to tell you something," Max murmurs in my ear, his breath deliciously hot against my skin.

"Oh?" I snuggle closer, and he presses his lips to jawline. My pulse races with the anxiety of what I need to say next. "Me, too."

"Then let's talk." He kisses me again, and he's too damn sweet, it breaks my heart.

A rumbling voice by the billiards table shouts, "Enough already, asshole!" Then comes the sound of a fist clashing with a face, and a large, leather-clad, bearded man flies horizontally into the seats across from us.

The room explodes into chaos—yelling, broken pint glasses, and the scuffing of feet and chairs and tables. I cower in the booth in fear as a trio of men tussle closer. Max hops over the backrests into the next booth, deftly grabbing my hands and guiding me through the heart of the pandemonium. Weaving through the screaming and punching patrons is the last thing I want to do, but with Max leading me, I would go anywhere—even as the bodies bump against us, the angry sounds grow louder, and I swear someone soars overhead. Max stumbles at one point, but we reach the exit by coasting along the edge of the mob.

We make it outside, where other skittish patrons have gathered as the drama unfolds in the bar. Sal's voice booms over everyone, and the commotion lessens—as a teddy bear with bite, Sal has that effect on people.

"You okay?" Max asks.

"Yeah." When I turn to him, the breath gets sucked out of me. "Holy shit. You're bleeding."

A gruesome ruby red oozes in between his teeth and dribbles out one side of his mouth. "I'm fine."

"Who was it?"

"Gonna defend my honor?" He grabs my wrist, preventing me from marching into the bar to find the guilty party. "An elbow to the jaw, that's all."

I step inches away from his face for a better look. When I put my hand against his cheek, he sucks in a sharp breath. He needs ice, or he'll swell up to the size of a grapefruit.

I break only five speed limits on my way home, adrenaline surging through me. When we get back, he rinses out his mouth, and at least the bleeding has stopped. Whoever knocked him hit Max hard enough that his teeth scraped against the inside of his cheek, but the cuts didn't go deep.

"Have any painkillers?" he asks. "Advil or ibuprofen?"

"I've got something even better," I say, rummaging through a drawer. "Stacey gifted me some joints to help me sleep." I don't mention that ever since Max and I have been sharing a bed, my sleeping problems have disappeared. I hold it out to him. "A couple hits'll take the edge off."

"God, she's cool." Max takes a few hits for some immediate relief and pops an ibuprofen. Wrapping a bag of frozen peas in a tea towel, I steady my shaking hands and lean close to Max's face.

"Ready?" I ask.

He nods, then hisses again when the peas touch his swelling cheek. After a pause, he leans further into the coolness, clearly finding some relief. Max peers at me, his eyes heavy. "You can fawn over me all you want."

I laugh.

"I like that I can make you laugh even when I'm disfigured."

"Must be that Max Weber Charm." My thumb strays from the bag of peas and presses into the corner of his mouth. I kiss him there, and he groans.

"I wish I could kiss you more," he says.

I place my lips at his temple, then his jaw and his neck. "Be right back."

I call Sal's from the lobby to make sure he and everyone else are okay, and then speed through my evening errands—dishwasher loaded, blinds closed, lights off. When I return to the casita, Max is sprawled out on the bed, staring wistfully at the shrunken joint in his hand.

"That's enough for now, I think." I pluck the tiny white nub from his grip and stub it out on my ashtray.

"I haven't weed smoked in forever."

"Here. One more pillow so we elevate your head."

"Did I say weed smoked?"

"Yeah," I say with a chuckle.

"Your laugh. Ugh, it's perfect." He looks at me, his eyelids at half-mast. "Daisy, can I tell you? I was so scared at Sal's. Scared for you."

"You're stoned."

"Stoned cold sober."

"Shut up."

I laugh anyway, which causes him to laugh back. Once our giggles die down, I realize we're holding hands. His is warm, firm, and safe.

"Will you kiss me again?" he asks, pleading.

"Only because you're pathetic." As carefully as I can, I kiss him on the lips.

"I love that. Your kisses." He's so out of it. If he weren't in pain, I'd find his nonsense kind of cute. "What did you wanna talk about, Daisy Daze? Because what I wanna talk about is you. And how I love you."

My stomach flips hearing the L-word. He might not even realize what he's saying, though, he's so high. But if he does, then what will change when I tell him about Dublin?

"You should sleep, Max."

"I mean it." He props himself up on both elbows. "As a friend, but also like *that*."

"I'm turning off the light."

"You don't have to say it back. But I'd have to be dead to stop loving you, and even then, I could probably figure something out."

"Max." I search his eyes, so earnest and innocent under the guise of a few too many tokes. My heartbeat skips as I ask myself the question, *Do I love him?*

I always have, in my own way. Always as friends. But when I arrived in Dublin, prepared to bare my heart to him—even that didn't compare to now. This is a hundred times bigger. I want to chase the feeling as much as I want to run away from it.

But with him half asleep, now is not the time for this conversation.

"Let's talk about this later. If you even remember."

"I'll remember," he says, resting his head back on the pillow. "It's only been nineteen years, so I won't forget. Tomorrow."

I pause and collect myself. Nineteen years—how long I've been in Harlow. He passes out before I even tuck him in properly, but my pulse thrums in my ears. I don't know what scares me more—that he'll wake up tomorrow and forget this conversation ever happened, or that he'll wake up tomorrow and tell me he meant every word.

Chapter Thirty-Four

Max, 18 Years Old

A girl from my floor walked by in her towel, and I nodded in a polite greeting.

"You coming out, Maximus?" she purred, pulling my attention from the FaceTime call with Daisy.

"Not tonight."

She pouted in disappointment, but I didn't care. "Sorry," I said, turning back to my screen, "what were you saying?"

"Maximus?" Daisy's brow lifted.

"Yeah, it's—" I chuckled at the memory. "Kinda funny. For movie night, someone put on *Gladiator*, and—"

"You're frozen."

"Shoot. Hold on, let me..." I raised the phone, as if that would help. "The Wi-Fi's not usually so bad. That better?"

After a pause, Daisy said, "Mmm, I think so."

I didn't want to waste time talking about a stupid film night in the dorm, so I changed the subject. "How's your mom?"

"Good. She's repainting all the rooms since it's slow season. She says hi."

I didn't miss my parents, but marching to Daisy's house right now, curling up on the couch, and eating pizza with the two of them sounded better than anything. A Friday-night phone call—late-morning in California—would have to suffice.

"She wants to see more Dublin photos from you," Daisy said.

"Sorry, it's been crazy, I just—"

"It's fine, I get it." There was resignation in her tone. I needed to get better at making time for Daisy, but the summer schedule was intense. With the time difference, my class load, and everything going on in the city, this felt like my first free night all summer.

"She misses you a lot," Daisy said, her voice weaker. "Harlow's really different without you here."

"That your mam?" A guy from the floor below sneaked up behind me, hooking an arm around my neck. "Shite. You're not Max's mam."

"I am not." Daisy laughed, igniting an immediate flicker of jealousy inside me. I wanted to be the one to make her laugh, not a gymbro finance major she just met on a video call.

"This your sister?" he asked me.

"This is Daisy."

"Oooh." The guy nodded his head cautiously, and although I mentioned Daisy to my new friends any chance I got, he couldn't have made it look more like the opposite. "Well, good to meet you, Daisy." He released his grip and walked backwards, a finger pointing at me. "Pub night. Wanna join?"

"Maybe later." I slunk around the corner, slipping onto a couch in the common room. "Sorry."

"You should find some karaoke, like at Sal's."

"Sal's karaoke can't be beat. I'm not even gonna try."

"You're frozen again," Daisy said.

If we hadn't already rescheduled our chat three times, I'd suggest we do some other night. I had figured a Friday evening when most people were out would give us the best shot, but apparently not.

"Here," I offered, "I'm gonna head to my room. I might lose you, but I'll call you back."

She didn't reply, or perhaps her connection was so poor that her response didn't come through. Halfway down the hall, her still image breathed to life again, and I smiled. She smiled back, and my chest throbbed from the agony of missing her. Maybe that's why I'd been avoiding talking to her this whole summer—because I was still hopelessly into Daisy, and because I only ever felt homesick for Harlow when I thought about her.

Chapter Thirty-Five

Max, Now

When I wake up in Daisy's bedroom, I may as well be emerging from a coma. Every movement pairs with cracking joints and throbbing muscles. A quick glance in the mirror, and I at least don't have any visible bruising—mostly a tender, swollen cheek.

I round the corner from the living room into the kitchen, and the wall clock reads 9:54 a.m. Daisy's standing over the stove with a mug in her hand.

"Let me guess," I say, "that's your third cup of coffee already."

She whirls around, abandoning her cooking to investigate me up close. "Looks like those frozen peas did their job."

"Going into bed-and-breakfast territory?" I tease, nodding toward whatever's sizzling in the pan.

"Just for you. You took an elbow to the face for me."

"Just for you."

Daisy rests a gentle hand on my jaw. I could tell her not to make such a fuss over me, but I don't mind being showered with attention if it means having her this close. I love having her this close. I love *her*.

I didn't forget last night.

When she moves back toward the stove, I stalk forward and grab her wrists, wrapping my fingers around them gently so she sets the spatula on the counter. The morning light streams through the dining-room window, illuminating the house with an earthy glow.

"I don't care about breakfast," I say, interrupting her with a kiss. The pressure causes a brief throb of pain I gladly tolerate. "I love you, Daze. I've loved you a really long time, and I want you to know that."

"Max."

"You don't have to say anything. But I have been dying to get you alone."

"No." Her head flicks back and forth. "We can't—I-I have to tell you something."

My stomach free-falls, because her denial sounds like she's already slipping away from me.

"We should sit," she says, gesturing to the dining area.

"Just tell me." I don't mean for my response to be so clipped, but if this is the admission that she doesn't see us as anything more than friends, ever, that our arrangement was a mistake from the start, and that I'll never be the guy she's looking for—then I want to get it over with.

"I—" She clicks the stovetop off and takes a deep breath, not once meeting my eyes. "Do you remember a few months into your first semester at school, you had an exhibit on campus?"

The question catches me off guard. I had countless showcases in college, so they blur together. That fall of freshman year, I would have only had one, and it was the first in my life Daisy didn't go to.

"Sure, I remember."

"Well, I..." She gnaws at the corner of her bottom lip. "I was there."

A chuckle escapes me. I took a punch yesterday, but did she hit her head, too? She's getting timelines confused. "That was in Dublin," I say.

"I know."

I eye her. "When?"

"Opening night. The dates aligned with my college's Thanksgiving break, and I'd saved up some money."

She's doing a spectacular job of not breaking, so I play along with her joke.

"Right," I say. "We got ice cream after, went to a comedy show, and robbed a bank. It was a great night."

"I'm serious, Max."

I let out a laugh, expecting her to break down into giggles at any moment.

"It was in O'Connor Hall, third floor," she goes on. "*Time Travel* was the title, or the theme, or whatever you call it. You were wearing a new suit coat. Navy with this sort of darker trim."

I feel like I've stepped into oncoming traffic. "Y-you were there."

She nods. "I was there."

"And you never—why didn't you ever tell me?" My confusion morphs into something harsher. "Or, I don't know, you could've walked over and said hello."

"You had a massive group of friends. And they were all standing around you, and you looked so...I'd never seen you that happy and thriving. You had this big, new life, and you didn't need someone from your hometown inserting themselves into an evening like that."

"You're not just someone from my hometown."

"I shouldn't have gone."

Although I have a lot of information to process, she left a gaping hole in this story.

"Why did you come in the first place?" I ask.

"I missed you." She looks at her feet for a moment as a pinkish tint travels up her neck. "Everything with college and your summer program happened so fast, and I kept thinking about prom night with you, and I kind of realized that my feelings for you were more than a friend thing. So I thought maybe I'd go to Dublin and tell you."

I pinch the bridge of my nose, not sure how to feel. Thrilled that she ever felt that way and baffled that she bothered with a transatlantic flight only to never approach me.

And even more confused, because I know what she did next.

"That text." I look her square in the eyes. "Why would you send that?"

"I would have been a distraction."

"All you've ever done is distract me, Daisy. I don't mind."

"I would have, though, with your life starting in Dublin. You worked too hard, and you're too great to—"

"Don't pull the martyr card here." I can't buy her story—it doesn't add up. "What were you thinking?"

"I hated not telling you. Not being brave enough." She shakes her head, unshed tears glistening in her eyes. "But if I had, what would you have done?"

"I'm not sure. Anything. Everything."

"Exactly. You belonged in Dublin, giving your all to your classes and your friends and your life there. Not dividing your attention even more."

If Daisy had walked up to me that night and told me how she felt, who knows how I would have reacted. I wouldn't have dropped out of school, but would I have neglected schoolwork and social outings in favor of phone calls with her? Sure. And how would that have affected all other parts of my life?

I shake my head free of the millions of paths our lives could have taken. "You didn't have the right to make that choice for me."

She looks up, abashed, like a dog whose tail knocked over a vase. "Still love me now?"

She asks not like it's a dare, but like she already knows the answer and just wants me to let her down gently. But loving Daisy isn't something I can turn off. As long as I'm alive and breathing, there's a built-in shrine in my heart for her and whatever pieces of her she'll give me.

I rest my forehead against hers. "I was going to tell you I'm staying, if that's any way to answer your question."

Daisy blinks. Her jaw slackens and her lips part, but she says nothing.

"I've thought a lot about it. Regina wants to take me on for the next semester at the school. LA isn't far, so I could land some short-term work out there. And if the pop-up's a hit, we could consider making it a regular thing." Where before I only saw limitations, now I imagine all the possibilities here. Daisy's about to say something, but I cut her off. "And you don't get to tell me I can't, because we've seen what happens when you decide for the two of us." This is my decision, not hers.

I watch as her eyes fill with tears. Maybe it's having grown up watching all the pain her mom went through, married to her dad, but I can tell something's holding her back. Enclosing Daisy's wrists in my hands, I trace infinity symbols over the veins and tendons with my thumbs.

"But what if you hate it here?" she asks.

"I couldn't. You're here."

Daisy smiles, and I will do anything for that smile. "I've been busy preparing myself for heartbreak with you," she says. "To have you leave and only get little scraps of you. Watch from afar as you go out with some gorgeous, worldly supermodel artist."

"You vastly overestimate the other people I date." I pull her to me. "Even if I had a supermodel begging to be with me, I'd still choose you. Daze, we could be really good together. Give us that chance."

With a teary nod, she leans in, pressing her lips against mine, and I might be dreaming. Everything has led me back here, back to her. Everything I could ever want or need is right in my arms. I hold her tight, like our bodies could become one if I bring her close enough.

"Max." She traces a line of urgent kisses against my jawline as she toys with the waistband on my sleep shorts. "I'm yours. I'm your girl."

Those words send an explosion of heat throughout my body. "Say that again," I whisper against her skin.

"I'm yours."

I give her a playful smack on the ass, and she squeals.

"You like that?" she asks, laughing.

I run my hands up her hips and under her shirt, where two hard nipples greet me, hidden behind lace. She's perfect. With a pinch, Daisy bucks against me and groans.

"I'd like it better if you were on your knees," I say.

She doesn't take her eyes off me as she gets down on the floor, slipping off my pajamas in one swoop. One of her hands wraps around me, and she caresses my cock like she wants to worship it. I might collapse with how much I crave her.

"Slow," I tell her. I don't trust myself to last long, and I want to savor this.

She lowers her lips onto me an inch at a time. Daisy's mouth is warm and tight as she sucks me off, her head bobbing a couple times before she leans back on her heels and lets me slip out.

"I'm your girl." She takes all of me again, my tip nudging against the back of her throat until she releases me.

All I can manage are raw, raspy sounds while she goes down on me. The heat, the pressure, the buildup—they're too much. I grip the counter for support while my other hand toys with her hair. Guiding her off of me, my dick bounces freely, and she looks up at me, lips glistening and pure lust reflected in her eyes.

"Up," I order her. "Now."

She stands, and I cup her butt in both hands to lift her onto the counter, where she leverages her legs to loop around my waist. I'm lined up perfectly with her, and we grind into each other like a couple of high schoolers. After a bit of maneuvering, I tear her jeans and panties off, helping her rock onto one hip, then the other, until she's bare-assed on the counter.

She takes my hand and guides it to her pussy. She's velvet. I follow her rhythm, and our fingers twine together as they slide up, down, and around her clit.

"I want you," she whimpers.

"Want me to what?"

She nips my shoulder through a laugh. "To fuck me."

"Right here?"

"Yes." Her voice comes out hoarse. "Need."

Her eyes drift closed as I edge her to an orgasm. Just as she grinds against my hand with even more enthusiasm, I pull back. I interrupt her groan of sexual frustration with a kiss.

"Condoms in the nightstand?" I plan to bolt into the bedroom and back at lightning speed. Daisy hooks me with her leg before I can move.

"I'm on the pill." Her eyes flit to my mouth and then up again. "I'm clean, and if...well, if we're doing this, then I'm in."

Doing this doesn't mean sex—she means us. I've never agreed to something faster in my life.

She pulls my lips to hers again, my heart remembers how to beat, and we become a frenetic rush of heat and limbs as I position myself at her entrance. I slip into her like I've never belonged anywhere else, and we curse in unison. She's so comfortable, so right. I snake one arm behind her and cup her head so she won't hit the cupboard, and I begin, with painstaking pleasure, sliding in and out. I work my hand between us, feeling for her clit and rubbing against the slickness in a rhythm that causes her to let out a string of more profanities.

"That," she says, though it sounds more like a growl. "That right there is perfect."

"I plan to do this in every place in your house."

"Good." The side of her mouth tips up. "Make up for lost time." Against one of my thrusts, she clenches.

I swear, this woman was made for me.

She locks eyes with me, and though I'm already on the brink of falling apart, the sight of her close sends a hot need through me. "You say it to me," she whispers. "Tell me I'm yours."

Running my fingers through her hair again, I hold her firm while I hammer in and out of her. "You're my girl."

"Yes," she says as she comes, her face breaking into pure euphoria.

Her panting my name as she climaxes pushes me over a wave of release. She bites my shoulder, and I thrust into her three more blissful times, finding a home inside her.

We take a minute to come back to our bodies and minds. She's just Daisy, my Daisy, and this is how it should always be. I'm left slick with sweat and breathing into her neck. She smells like the desert after rain, like afternoons spent laughing, like everything I never knew I was missing. And for the first time in a long time, maybe in forever, I'm where I'm supposed to be and with the person I'm supposed to be with.

Thirty minutes after the first visitors walk in, I find a moment to breathe. Opening night receptions have a chaotic energy that I live for. The excitement of the evening fizzes like the sparkling drinks from the bar.

The barn, which I've gotten used to seeing in its work-in-progress state, has people crammed inside and a line of patient arrivals snaking out the door. If cars continue to arrive, we might have to turn attendees away.

Daisy does a last-minute makeup check in the mirror by the bathrooms, and the tension in my shoulders releases. We needed eight years—longer, really—but we're here, we're together, and we're each other's. I think she's why I've amassed a long string of *we're better off friends* girlfriends. No one can compare.

Two familiar faces emerge from the crowd, and I have to do a double take.

"You're kidding me," I say, racing over to embrace my good friend, Aidan. We haven't seen each other in almost a year. Although we keep up with regular texts these days, I can't believe he's here. "A short flight, huh?"

"Couldn't miss this." He slaps me on the back. "Hey, you remember June?"

"Of course." I hug her, recalling when the two of them stayed at my apartment in Dublin. The first time I saw him with her—before they were even dating and she was just a tourist replacing a lost passport—he was totally gone for her.

"You didn't fly out just for this?" I ask, piecing together how Aidan and June—who, last I knew, were somewhere in Southeast Asia—made it to this tiny town in the California desert.

"Couldn't miss it," June says, nudging my arm.

"We were already in Vegas for work," Aidan says, his face serious, "but if we weren't, we would have flown from anywhere for this."

My mouth turns up. "Finally followed your bliss and joined *Thunder from Down Under*?"

"They want Aussies, not Irishmen."

"Ah, then Cirque du Soleil?"

"He's not nearly flexible enough for that," June says, her eyes twinkling with mischief.

"A man can dream." Aidan pulls June toward him, his arm resting easily on her shoulder. "We have a project with the tourism board."

"Aidan's the one who booked the job," June says. "They saw his Instagram and reached out, and he's documenting everything."

"It was both of us," he says, the tips of his ears turning pink. "June's doing the copy. They want to highlight the surrounding nature and conservation areas, so we're focusing on that."

"You should meet Daisy." I look back at the mirrors, but she's gone. "Daze is all about sustainability and the natural beauty of a place."

"*The* Daisy?" Aidan asks.

I ignore his inquisitive, raised eyebrow. Years ago, when we were roommates during his postgrad studies, I made the mistake of drinking too many beers and divulged too much about this one girl I could never get out of my head. He let it go, but he obviously never forgot.

"Hey Mr. Dub." One of my students walks up. He's combed his hair back and put some gel in it, and behind him is a man with the same round face and bushy brows, checking something on his cell.

"Hi, Xander." I look between him and my friends, tugged in opposite directions.

"We'll leave you to it," Aidan says as he links his hand in June's.

"Catch me before you go." I turn to Xander, and he looks more dressed up than normal. "Congrats on the show." I tip my chin toward the person behind him. The guy's typing away on his phone, head down, and invested in his screen. "Who'd you bring?"

"Dad, this is—"

"Busy," the man says, holding up one finger. "Hold on."

Xander stares at his feet. At school, he's always joking and laughing with friends, asking me a billion questions. Tonight, though, he's folding in on himself and taking up as little space as possible. These students come into class and act so adult sometimes, but they're still kids—kids who want validation on one of the biggest nights they've ever had.

It's a movie I've seen before.

"Now, what'd you want?" His dad looks to his son, then to me, eyeing me top to bottom. "You the teacher?"

"I am. Xander is an extremely talented artist."

"He's something, alright. I'll let his mom know. She insists on keeping him in these classes, since he likes the doodles and stuff." Xander's dad gives the kid a noogie, ruffling his hair. "I've got a call I have to take, kiddo. Meet you in the car. We need to be on the road in ten."

He strides away, ignorant of the damage he's doing.

"You good?"

Xander shrugs. "My dad's kind of an asshole."

He is, but I don't think I can admit that to a student. "I'm glad you're here. And I meant what I said—you're very talented. Don't let what he says, or anyone else says, matter."

"So what you say doesn't matter?"

"You're a smart-ass, you know that?" I smirk at him, something like fondness crawling up my chest. "Not everyone will understand, and that's okay. The right people will."

Xander shrugs and stares down at his shoes again.

"You know, I'm sure someone could drive you home. If your dad's cool with you carpooling with a classmate, you could volunteer as a greeter."

"Spots were filled when I looked."

I peer around the room. "I just opened up another one."

"Really?" His face brightens with his smile.

"Sure. Check with your dad first, though, okay?"

"Yes, Mr. Dub," he says, racing off and almost bowling over three people. "Thank you, Mr. Dub!"

"That's not my name," I mutter, though a smile pulls at the corner of my mouth.

"Hey, you." Daisy curls one hand around my biceps, nestling into my side. The stress of the evening vanishes, and I lean as much into her as I can without looking obscene.

"You meet June and Aidan?" I ask. "They've got this cool project I think you'd like."

"I did. They were more interested in talking about you and how great you are and how any woman would be lucky to have you. Ultimate wingmen."

"I paid them to say that."

She snorts a laugh, and I want to grab her face in my hands and kiss her, but I shouldn't because I won't be able to stop. When I look at Daisy, her eyes are on my mouth momentarily before flitting up to meet my gaze.

"So," she says, tilting her chin in the direction of the door. "What was that about?"

"You remember Xander? His dad's with him, but he's kind of like my folks. Not so interested in art."

"I wouldn't say that."

Daisy bites back a huge smile and nods toward the entrance on the far side of the room. Ava steps in and brightens like a light bulb when she sees us. My mom stops behind her, her eyes widening as she scans the barn, and my dad follows. Ava plows into me with a hug before I can process that they're here.

"This is *so* cool. Daze, isn't this so cool?"

She laughs, a sound that gets better and richer and more beautiful every time I hear it.

"It's the coolest," she says.

"Everyone at school was talking about tonight. I'm kinda popular now since I know you both. Also." Her voice drops, and she leans toward me with a conspiratorial look on her face. She juts her chin at one of the attendees. "That's Z."

"Oh." My brows shoot up when I see the girl in question. She has a wild mane and a big smile, and she's looking right at my sister.

"Stop staring," Ava urges me, keeping her lips as still as possible so it sounds more like "Stah stahing."

"Why are you talking like a ventriloquist?"

"In hase she can hread liss."

Daisy loops her arm through Ava's. "C'mon. I wanna meet this Z person." They walk off, glued to each other's side, as my mom approaches. Ava had every right to tell them, but I didn't expect either of my parents to show up. My entire body tenses, preparing for a fight. I've never worked so hard or been so proud of a pop-up before. If they've got anything nasty to say, even anything mediocre, I don't want to hear it.

"You're here," I say, readying myself for the disheartened looks and disinterested conversation.

"I managed the time off," my mom says stiffly. "So you...you organized all this?"

I clear my throat, taken aback that she wants to know anything about what I do. I learned pretty quickly that not inviting my mom and dad to my shows meant avoiding disappointment altogether.

"Me and Daisy," I say. "We were in charge of everything."

Everything. Even with the pop-ups I did at Impressions, I was never as hands-on as I was with *Desert Daze*. A few months back, I didn't know I could pull this off.

"Well, it's impressive," my mom hums. "Very."

I wait for the *but...* When I realize that's not coming, I say a quiet, "Thanks."

My dad scans the room.

"No Van Gogh," I say, half joking. "Sorry."

"No, I was—" He cranes his head toward the entryway. "Is there a docent?"

"A docent?"

"Yes, someone who's like a tour guide but for—"

"I know what a docent is." I exhale. Of all the things they'd judge me on tonight, their respect for my career hinges on our having a docent. "There isn't, sorry. Maybe..." A student could give them a brief tour, but they're also teenagers high on nerves and hormones. I don't trust that combination. "I'll show you around."

Rather than divide the floor up into student work and professional work, everything blends together. The variety creates a sense of adventure. Every new piece and every turn brings an unexpected experience. My dad remains quiet, but my mom nods along and asks questions that prove she has a genuine interest in tonight. I think this is her making an effort.

Ava returns, and I'm about to scour the room for Daze when my sister lets out a dramatic gasp. She points to a drawing on the wall.

"Who did *this*? Has she seen it?"

"That's mine," I say, scratching the back of my head. "No, not yet."

"Oooooh." Ava waggles her brows, and I shoot her a glare.

"You drew this?" my mom asks, her brows raised.

I nod at my portrait of Daisy, the one from the first day of class. During the past couple of months, whenever I had some spare time and Daisy's face was fresh in my mind—which was always—I returned to it. Perfected the shadows. Added in the freckles I've now memorized. Deepened her gaze. Being back in the desert has gotten me back in touch with my artistic roots, and that funneled into my perspective for *Desert Daze*. Or maybe that was just Daisy.

"That's quite impressive," my mom says, repeating her favorite word of the night.

"How has she not seen this?" Ava asks.

"I added it last minute, and today's been crazy. I hoped..." I look around, but I don't spot her. "Where is she?"

Daisy handled so many logistical items today that I didn't get the chance to give her a tour through the space before we had a line of eager guests outside. I'd envisioned showing her this drawing myself—I'd like to be there when she sees it.

"She's over there talking to some people," Ava says and points, although I don't see Daze. "Do you want a picture of you kissing her in front of it?"

"Security?" I hold my finger to an invisible earpiece. "Yeah, you need to remove a young woman, sixteen, green jumpsuit and bows in her hair."

"Okay, you two. C'mon." My mom wraps her arm around Ava. "Let's continue our tour. We'll find Daisy after."

I intend to wrap up this tour as quickly as possible, because I can hardly wait to have Daisy by my side again.

Chapter Thirty-Six

Daisy, 18 Years Old

I weaved through friends and family and students, scanning for the only face that mattered. It only took an entire summer of holding onto any shred of Max that I could to realize how I really felt. Mom and Gwen lured the confession out of me as I cried on the couch, and they both encouraged me to do the big, romantic gesture. Book a trip to visit him. Tell him in person. They knew that the time difference, missed FaceTime calls, and sporadic texts had worn me down.

In moments, I would see Max again. I'd hug him and laugh with him and hold his hand and explain how I'd been miserable without him. Miserable without him knowing how I felt.

I spotted him at the end of the room, and the jet lag, the long flight, and all the worrying were worth it. I could breathe again. He looked so familiar but somehow different. Max wore a confidence that made him stand taller. Someone must have finally convinced him to put some product in his curly hair, and it appeared styled and freshly cut. He stood in a circle of people the same age as us, commanding their attention, and they all looked nicely dressed like him.

I shifted on my feet, wondering if my jeans, tee, and blazer look was too casual. No one else there was wearing cowboy boots, either.

I wanted to soar to him and wrap him up in a hug, but the group erupted into laughter. Before, it was a given that I'd go to his showcases. We'd spend the entire night walking around, and he'd tell me about each painting or sculpture—not just his, but every single one. I hadn't considered that he'd be here with lots of people. Maybe he had plans with friends tonight. Plans that didn't have room for me.

Even with such a large group, he seemed like the obvious center of attention. He had so many friends who came out tonight to support him. I spotted at least two young women who looked at him like he was all they cared about. I knew, because I was probably looking at him the same way as longing surged through me with each heartbeat.

A couple more people joined the cluster, handing him a massive bouquet. He'd never had this many folks show up for him back in Harlow. I eyed the pathetic bundle of daisies in my hand. They were the closest thing that the train-station florist had to the wildflowers I would always pick for his showcases.

Someone bumped into me, and I muttered a *sorry* as I pretended to scan the handout they gave me at the door.

Stupid. This was stupid, stupid, stupid.

Max had a hard time keeping in touch this summer because other things were more important. He had heaps of friends, more than the trio of me and him and Gwen. He had a life with these people. And what did I think would happen, exactly? That I would show up and we'd confess our undying love for each other? That we'd find magically perfect times to FaceTime? It's not like I would suddenly get a scholarship to go to school here, either.

I blinked back tears. I'd always said I wouldn't taint our friendship with romance, and now that I was about to do that, it was obviously the dumbest idea in the world.

This was Max's life, and he deserved all of it. The friends, the girls who wanted to be more than friends and knew it from the start, tons of people who showed up for his art show, the big city, everything.

I was only there to embarrass myself.

Swallowing the lump in my throat, I turned around, tossed the flowers in the trash, and slipped out the door into the night.

Chapter Thirty-Seven

Daisy, Now

After my phone call with Max's parents this morning, I thought I had ruined any chance of getting them here. Maybe I should have called them a couple of stubborn asses sooner, or maybe deep down, they knew how much they'd hurt him throughout the years. Either way, I could weep with relief that they both showed up.

"Daisy Johnson." A lady with a chic asymmetrical haircut and vivid pink lipstick approaches me. She says my name like we're familiar friends, but I rack my brain to remember who she is. She has a distinct style that only a confident, creative fifty-year-old woman can have, but I don't think I've ever seen her before.

"Eleanor Winsome, Deputy Creative Director at LACMA."

I almost spit out my wine. Max would moonwalk around the building if he knew someone from LACMA was here.

"Nice to meet you," I say, dumbstruck.

"And this," she says, gesturing to the short man to her left with a handlebar mustache, "is Antoine Archambault. He works at Tate Modern."

"Oh." I jut out a hand to shake his. "That's in Britain, right?"

"London. Lovely to make your acquaintance," Antoine says in a buttery French accent.

I almost squeal. If we have people coming in from Los Angeles and London, we *really* got the word out. "It's an honor to have you both here." I do a quick scan of the crowd for Max because he's surely the one they're here to see, but he's nowhere.

Eleanor leans forward, resting her bony hand on my shoulder. "This space is lovely. Rustic but in such an authentic, earnest way. The place isn't a bunch of faux-spiritual California clichés, and it's so much better than all those boring home-shares. Christ, they're all the same."

I chuckle. "I know exactly what you mean. Actually, I'm working on a proposal for council members. The policy would limit folks from snatching up property and damaging the surrounding area."

"Which they always do," Eleanor says. "Those practices are cheaper, so of course they do."

This Eleanor woman has quickly become one of my new favorite people.

"When Max told me about this barn, I almost didn't believe him."

"Oh, you know Max?" I ask, putting more of the puzzle pieces of Eleanor and Antoine together.

"Yes, I mentored him in Dublin." She stares around the space, nodding in approval. "He explained how much work needed to go into this building, and in such a short amount of time. You two did well."

"Thank you," I say, pleased with the compliment, like a teacher just gave me a gold star.

"When you mentioned the renovations," Antoine says to her, "I will admit, I had many doubts."

"Oh, I didn't," Eleanor says, lifting her hand off of me to swat the very thought of doubting Max away. "I am not the least bit surprised he'd put something extraordinary together. He is a force. Daisy, tell me, how on earth did Max get connected with you and such an amazing locale?"

"Me?"

Of course she means me, but I have to swallow some surprise. Max has evidently informed Eleanor about this project every step of the way, but it sounds like he never found our history important enough to mention to her. That makes sense, I guess. He probably kept their conversations focused on work and the pop-up, not on our personal history.

"We grew up here," I reply. "I'm his girlfriend."

The word slips out of me, but I like the taste. *I'm Max We-ber's girlfriend.* The realization sends an effervescence through me, like I'm a shaken-up soda can.

Eleanor and Antoine smile, and they share a knowing *oh.*

"Well," Antoine says, "I can already tell you have created something that is truly special together." He turns to Eleanor and adds, "If he really wanted to impress me, he has more than done it. If I could, I would secure his visa and fly him out tomorrow."

"I told you, he's got an eye."

The two of them are talking like I'm not here, and I have a billion and one other people to meet and greet—but my ears snag on what Antoine said.

"Sorry, wh-where's he going?"

"Oh, I only am kidding," he says. "We won't fly him out *tomorrow.* You will have him a bit longer. But just a bit!" At this, he and Eleanor laugh in unison while I'm left out of the joke.

All the voices in the room turn into white noise. Antoine must catch a hint of my confusion, and his tone gets serious.

"I'll discuss the options for you to join him, of course," he says. "You have six months for visiting, or if you have plans to..." He waits for me to fill in a blank I don't know the answer to. "There are spouse visas as well. It's not my department, but my team, they will talk with him."

"Right," I say, forcing my mouth to form words. "The visa. For the…"

"The job." Eleanor says this like she and I have talked about this job countless times before. "I told Max he'd have to pull off something spectacular. Of the many people I've had the privilege to mentor, I knew he could do it."

"The role is unique," Antoine adds, talking to me. "And it pulls on his skills but gives him room to grow within one of the most prestigious museums in the world. I am, of course, biased, but it is a dream job for any art curator."

"That sounds amazing," I say, trying not to choke on my reply. The tips of my ears burn with the embarrassment of having introduced myself as Max's girlfriend, while also having no idea that this plan was in the works.

"He'll be thrilled," I say with as much enthusiasm as I can. "Um, if you'll just excuse me…" I wave to them both, muttering some lame excuse that I need to check on the parking manager. I let the crowd swallow me.

Max wanted the pop-up to get back to work and clean the dark stain his last employer left on his resume. I didn't know he had a job already lined up.

A dream job.

One that plays to all his strengths and will grow with him. One like his past job but with infinitely better pay, I'm sure, and at a renowned museum. This job doesn't compete with occasional pop-ups here at The Mirage and teaching at his old high school—it obliterates them.

"There you are!" Ava rushes up to me, gripping my arm to drag me somewhere to the other side of the barn. "You have to see this."

I gulp down the lump in my throat and paste on a smile as I wave at the folks we pass. The crowd parts, and there's Max, standing tall and so heartbreakingly handsome, and he can't look away from me. If he's talked with Eleanor and Antoine, I don't find that written on his face; no, he looks as incandescently happy as this morning. He still thinks this, right here—what we have together and what he has in Harlow—is all he could ever want.

He steps to the side and then I'm staring at...me. Hanging on the smooth timber of the walls is a sketch of my face, unguarded and gentle, and so unlike how I present myself to the world. It's me on a Monday morning when all our reservations have checked out, and Stacey's left for the day, and I can chill on the couch with Freddie. It's the me that Max sees, which is probably more me than I've ever been. Ignoring the aching emptiness in my chest, I move closer to read the title: *Just Daisy*.

Chapter Thirty-Eight

Max, Now

Ava snaps photos of Daisy and me, and Eleanor appears before I can ask Daisy what she thinks of the drawing. Eleanor guides someone toward me, but not just anyone—Antoine Archambault of Tate Modern. The man who collaborated with luxury cruise lines to bring art to the seas, who spent over a decade managing the Frieze Art Fair, and who's worked with greats like Yayoi Kusama and Marina Abramović.

"Antoine," I say, starstruck as he shakes my hand. "What a pleasure to meet you. Eleanor, hi."

The two of them rave about everything—the vibe, the vision, every big-name artist. I reach to weave Daisy into our circle, but she's gone already. We've seen each other a grand total of thirty seconds tonight, but since she knows everyone here, that's expected.

I never mentioned the potential job at Tate to her, so it's probably best she's off somewhere else. Still, I wish she could stand by me as I resist the urge to morph into a complete fanboy.

"What you've done is unbelievable," Antoine says, and I need someone to pinch me. "This is not simply a museum, but an experience."

"I'm pleased to hear you say that," I say, or at least I think I say. "I—honestly, it's an honor, coming from you."

"When Eleanor told me you'd be a top candidate for the curator position with Tate, I trusted her, of course. But seeing your efforts personally only emphasizes what an outstanding addition you would make to our team." He holds out a business card, which I stare at, until Eleanor intervenes and nudges my arm to Antoine's. "I'd love to get you out there for a few days to show you our own vision and talk about the role."

I gape at the card for who knows how long, processing the possibilities. "Sorry," I mutter after a while. "This is...wow."

"We'd originally planned to hire later in the year," Antoine says, "but I got the finances cleared for this quarter."

Eleanor's face glows, and I wish I had talked to her sooner about my new plans. I don't want to embarrass her in front of Antoine, or make him feel like his trip was a total waste.

"I was talking with Antoine about it," Eleanor says and turns to him, "and what was it that you said?"

"That it would change the world with art. Not just in London, but everywhere."

Eleanor nods. "And I knew. I just knew this was the job for you."

"That's..." It's definitely a chance of a lifetime. Antoine gives me a brief overview, and I warm to the idea. With the pay from a respected museum, I could better support Daisy here. Between busy days abroad, I could travel back to Harlow for long weekends and holidays with her. I don't know what the job entails yet, so I could negotiate more time off, and maybe even a decent enough salary that I could fly her out there regularly. Success at Tate would boost *Desert Daze*. I can do the London thing, she can keep The Mirage...

We could make this work.

I thank them and seek out Daisy. My search leads me outside, past the long line of guests waiting for entry. The illuminated lobby appears empty, and the casita's motion-activated lights haven't turned on. Although there isn't an official footpath behind the building, I take a careful step over the brush and peer around the back of the barn to find a familiar silhouette.

"There you are." I keep my voice hushed even though no one would be able to hear us with everything going on. "Needed a breather?"

"Yeah," she says, crossing her arms and using her hands to rub her prickling goose skin.

"Here," I say, sweeping my suit jacket over her shoulders. I use the move as an excuse to hold her close and give us a moment of calm amidst the madness tonight. "Hey, so, you won't believe what just happened."

"I know." Daisy looks up at me, a sweet sadness in her eyes. "Antoine mentioned the job."

I furrow my brow. I've barely had time to process the opportunity with Tate, and I wanted to tell Daisy myself.

Daisy wriggles out of my embrace, her arms still crossed. "I wish you had told me."

"I've known all of five minutes."

"You didn't know about this until tonight?"

"I—" This must be what it feels like to be under a microscope. "My understanding of the position was all very abstract."

Daisy leans against the building, her eyes trained on me. "You said the pop-up was to refresh your resume."

"Eleanor mentioned a potential opening, and it was on my mind, but nothing was set in stone. I didn't even know they'd officially started looking to hire, and I definitely didn't expect that the person hiring would be here tonight. It's not how I would have wanted to find out about it, and not you, either."

These past few weeks, I forgot about the job. But *Desert Daze* gave me more than this chance—it brought me Daisy again. She sighs and tilts her head upward, and I don't care about the constellations, or the Milky Way, or how rich of a royal blue the sky is against the haphazard outline of the distant mountains. All I care about is her.

"I'm sorry." Eliminating the space between us, I take her hands in mine and press my lips to each knuckle. "I should have mentioned the position sooner."

"It's okay. I'm proud of you."

"Thanks." I kiss her forehead in gratitude. That's not a phrase I grew up hearing much, and it means a lot coming from her. "Look, you are the most important, but we could give this a try. There are direct flights from LA and Vegas. The UK gets more built-in vacation time, so I could swing back here all the time. I can fly you over, too, whenever you want."

Her head perks up, as if she's surprised I've thought this through already. "You want to do long distance?"

With an uncomfortable laugh, I shift on my feet. Why else would I be suggesting transatlantic flights for the weekend?

Daisy's head shakes from side to side. "You can't say that you'll stay one moment and then take the next great gig that comes along."

"I wouldn't call Tate Modern a gig."

"Whatever. We aren't doing long distance."

I scan her face, from the stubbornness in the set of her jaw to the determination glinting in her gaze. She's right—taking the Tate job would require a lot from both of us. We're just at the start of our relationship, so if it's not the right time, then I have my answer.

"Alright," I say. "I'll message Antoine and let him know I'm not interested."

"Max." Daisy slinks her arms around my torso, and I ease into her touch. "You're gonna take the job."

"So you wanna give it a try?"

"No." Her face falls, and she gives a small shake of her head. "You'll go, and I'll stay."

"What're you talking about? Just this morning—"

"This morning, you didn't have an unbelievable job offer dangling in front of you."

It takes a moment, but her words punch me square in the jaw. She was all in, ready to take the leap with me, but this offer from Tate has scared her off.

"No," I say. "No, no, no."

"Yes, you want this—"

"Don't tell me what I want."

"You do, though." Her eyes shimmer with unshed tears. "Otherwise, you wouldn't be doing mental gymnastics to figure out how to have it."

I hesitate. While I don't understand why I have to choose one or the other, I definitely don't want the job if it means losing Daze.

"You can't demand that I take this job."

"Max, there is no job like this in the world. This is bigger than a college scholarship or a summer program. You're passing up a once-in-a-lifetime opportunity."

"Happily."

"Well, I don't want you to."

She may as well have shoved me. "There are compromises in every relationship, and I'm—"

"I don't want you to compromise."

"I'm willing to do this. To put in the work. But you don't even want to try?"

"Try what? Try for phone call dates we can't even promise to keep? For quick weekend trips where one of us is too jet-lagged to do anything and then has to turn back around two days later? For a social life and a career while dating someone thousands of miles away?" Tears spill down her cheeks, and she smears them with an angry swipe. "I can't step away from The Mirage whenever the mood strikes, so you'd be the one doing most of the travel."

"I'd love that."

"I'd be holding you back from your life, Max. You know it."

"You are my life." Frustration surges through me, because she's doing this again—making a choice for me rather than *with* me. "I'm staying."

She looks at me like I told her I can walk through walls. "You can't do that."

"I can. Please, just—forget Tate. I want to stay."

"Why?"

"Because—" I almost say, *because I love you*, but Daisy's not one for cliché declarations. I run my thumb across her cheek. "Because we're each other's." We said so. "And because I want to be with you."

Her hand slips out of mine, and I lose my balance at the loss. "You're always going to wonder what that life would have been like, and you'll hate me for taking that away from you."

"I don't want that life."

"Three months ago you did."

"And a lot has changed in three months, Daze. A lot has changed since I was younger, too. I always thought I wanted to leave Harlow, leave my parents, and follow my passion. But my passion *is* here. It's you."

Daisy's chin quivers, and she shakes her head. The walls I spent this entire summer tearing down have gone back up.

"Don't do this." I point to the barn. "This pop-up is the most incredible thing I've ever done. I poured myself into this project."

"Exactly." Daisy holds my head in her hands, forcing eye contact. "You are amazing. So much so that some hotshot from fucking London flew here to offer you a job. Your passion is not just for Harlow, but it's for art all around the world. Mine anchors me here, but yours can take you anywhere. And it should."

Nausea roils in my stomach. I press my forehead to hers, wishing with all my might that if I hold her a little closer, if I plead with her a little more, she'll change her stubborn mind.

"What're you saying?" I croak.

"I think you'd be a fool not to go."

My blood runs cold. I release her, backing up a few steps and rubbing my eyes to clear my vision. "How am I never good enough for you?"

"You're too good, Max. Too good for this town, and too good for me."

That's the last thing I want to hear—that she'll sacrifice what we could be for me. I turn the corner, and her pleas get eaten in the breeze.

Chapter Thirty-Nine

Max, 18 Years Old

Heyyy, I know you've been busy with school and all, and I just wanted to say I totally get it. I got this internship at a stable on the park border, and between that and classes, I've been really overwhelmed. I think it's better if we take some space for a while. I have to figure some things out on my own, and the whole long-distance friend thing is distracting. Probably even more for you with everything you have going on. It's for the best.

I stared at Daisy's message for what felt like hours before sending a reply. And another. Then I called multiple times. Desperate, I texted Gwen instead.

I need to talk to Daze.

Three little dots appeared, and I held my breath for her response.

It sucks, I know, but I have to respect her wishes. You do, too.

Is she mad at me or something? I typed the reply in a panic.

I think it's just hard for her, you know?

Why was Gwen being so cryptic?

It's hard being friends? I texted.

She needs space.

We had thousands of miles of space. I replayed the stilted phone calls, interrupted FaceTimes, and missed texts. Sure, we hadn't nailed friendship from afar, but I still wanted her in my life. I would never not want her in my life.

Daisy's trying to figure stuff out right now, and as her friends, we can't pressure her, Gwen went on. *You know how she is. She has to do things on her own time.*

All the years I wasted flashed through my mind. The missed moments. I should have kissed her at prom. I shouldn't have done the summer program. I should have gone to school in LA like my original plan.

I lay back on my bed, my eyes stinging. During orientation, one counselor talked about adjusting to college life and how homesickness might hit. But I didn't miss home. I missed her.

This summer, I'd been a terrible friend, and every decision I made dragged me further from Daze. I was angry at her for pushing me away, too, but I was angrier with myself—especially because Gwen was right. The more I tried to patch up the damage I'd done, the more Daisy would withdraw.

Can you at least tell her I'm thinking of her? It was probably overstepping bounds, but I didn't care. She could ask me to stop reaching out, but she couldn't control if I thought of her. And I would, all the time, until I could find a way back into her life.

Chapter Forty

Max, Now

"Did Daze kick you out?" Ava asks.

"No." A hot spritz of grease hits my wrist, as if it's punishing me for paying more attention to my phone than cooking. There's no point in checking the device constantly. I only called late last night, and this morning was probably busy for her. I bet she hasn't even seen the notification yet.

"Then why are you here?"

"You hadn't mentioned you two were dating," my mom says, not lifting her gaze from the paper's politics section.

"You broke up with her?" Ava asks.

"No." I'm not in the mood to talk—even less so with my parents sitting at the dining table.

"So you're together?" Ava rests her elbows on the kitchen island to assess me.

Daisy didn't tell me to leave, but I would have rather collapsed into quicksand than sleep in the casita's guest bedroom again. We avoided each other the rest of opening night, and after an awful, fitful slumber on the sofa bed, I packed up my stuff from her house and headed here, which was an added blow. I wanted to go to Daisy, comfort her, and figure us out, but she made herself clear.

"Daisy and I..." What's the best way to explain this to my teenage sister? "We're taking a break."

"Forever?"

My parents don't chime in with more questions, but they both lower their papers and make eyes at each other.

"Can I cook breakfast without an interrogation?" I have a few hours before I'll be on the plane, so I should try to get some food in my stomach. I add the egg mixture to the other side of the pan, opposite the burned sausage. Daisy's so much better at cooking than I am. "I don't feel like having my love life analyzed at the moment."

"Ah." My sister nods her head. "So she broke up with you."

"Ava, hon," my mom says in a honey-sweet voice reserved only for her daughter. "I think Max doesn't want to discuss that right now."

I flip the food onto my plate and turn off the burner. I might just make it down the hall before another line of questioning.

"Max," my mom calls. I sink, wishing I could catch a break. "Yeah?"

My parents whisper about something, so I set my plate down on the counter and prepare for complaints and nitpicking. Maybe they'll admonish me for using the wrong detergent or leaving the bathroom light on overnight.

"I'm heading into the office," my dad mutters, grabbing his leather briefcase and exiting through the garage.

"I, uh..." My mom clears her throat, unable to meet my eyes. "We—I owe you an apology. I was so impressed with your show," my mom says. She really loves that word. "We—well, I didn't quite know what to expect, but you did such a good job."

"Oh." I don't know how to accept praise from her. I send a quick look to Ava since I suspect she put them up to this, but she shrugs. "Okay. Thanks, I guess."

"Your father and I have been hard on you. The life of an artist, it's...difficult. Money doesn't come easily."

I stab at the tasteless scrambled eggs on my plate. "Good thing life doesn't revolve around money," I say, bitter. "People can do things because they enjoy them. Art brings me joy. It always has."

"I understand that," my mother says.

"Do you?" I turn to the fridge for the creamer and am reminded that Daisy takes her coffee black, so I slam the door shut. "You two've treated art like an obnoxious hobby. I got a job right out of school, but you never cared. You were just...disappointed."

"It might not have been our first choice of career for you."

"I could tell."

She shifts her weight in her seat, and I've never seen her so restless. Then again, I've never pushed back. But I need to understand why they treated me the way they did for so long.

"You didn't attend a single showcase when I was a kid, and you never traveled out to see anything I ever did. Why the sudden change of heart?"

"It's hard to watch your own child choose a career path that has such a meager success rate," my mom starts slowly, "but we figured you needed to get it out of your system. That you would do art in high school but you'd select something more practical for college. But you didn't. You traveled around doing little museums, and then—"

"They weren't 'little museums.'" I should have expected this apology to be a double-edged sword. "Those pop-ups were my job. Legitimate work with people who've won awards."

"Then you moved back here, and we thought *this* time you'd go a more practical route. Then you didn't, and I saw...I realized that even on your own, you are very good at what you do. Passionate."

"It's more than the other night." I shake my head, not ready to accept her apologies—not after a lifetime of wanting to please them and always failing. "You two've never really been there for me. Ever."

"We had an idea in our heads, I think, of what we could accomplish as parents and what we dreamed of for our children." My mother wears a pained expression and sets her elbows on the table. "Especially as a woman in law, I felt this immense pressure to be great at everything—to have the high-powered job and the perfect family. And no matter what sports teams or clubs we put you in, all you wanted to do was run off and do your own thing, nose in a sketch pad. I kept..." She exhales, deep and heavy. "I kept getting it wrong with you. And then Ava came along, and she—" She appears to search for a word. "She was needier."

"Hey." Ava pouts.

"Well, you were, honey. And by the time she was headed to kindergarten, you were a teenager."

"So, because I was independent and had different interests than you expected, you stayed hands-off?"

"I didn't mean for it to happen, and I'm not saying we were right." My mom struggles to keep her chin high. "But once we realized it, the damage had been done. I'm sorry."

As much as I want to hear these words from her, I can't bring myself to celebrate. I'd love to know what Daisy would think of all of this. I wish I could walk over to the casita and tell her.

Taking my time with a bite of breakfast, I consider whether I could eventually forgive them. Or at least one of them.

"What about him?" I ask, my chin tilting to the door my dad left through.

She sighs. "He's not there yet. Our mode of tough love turned out too tough, I guess, and somehow he became his own father. He hates himself for it, but...he needs time."

I never understood my parents, and it turns out they never understood me, either. How they raised me affected my life, my everything—including the way I felt in this very town. If things with Daze hadn't imploded on Thursday, maybe I could handle this, but now I can only rub my eyes in frustration.

"I need to...I've gotta sit with this for a bit. And—" I glance at my phone. No missed calls. "I should get ready."

"Okay." My mom grabs and refolds her newspaper. "Just know that I'm glad I came out. What you made with *Desert Daze* was all your own. Well, you and Daisy."

Her name sends a piercing pain through my chest.

"So..." Ava trails off. "You're just gonna leave her with it?"

"I've got assistants on duty this weekend," I say through big forkfuls of bland food.

The turnaround time with Tate was faster than expected. Antoine reached out on his journey home, and he looped in his assistant. Within twenty-four hours, they'd secured me a flight for this afternoon to London. I'll spend a few days getting familiar with the role and fly back with barely a chance to beat the jet lag. A whirlwind tour, all to entice me to join their team.

Daisy insists I take it, but right now, I wish I'd never heard about this fucking job.

"Tate Modern, then?" my mom asks. "Well, clearly you've proven you can make *Desert Daze* work. So, if this was simply a stepping stone for something you care about more, then so be it."

That's precisely how I'd viewed *Desert Daze* when I conceived the idea, but now I don't care about anything other than Daisy.

My phone buzzes, but it's false hope—just a message from the driver Antoine's team arranged. I text them a reminder to avoid Camino del Alma at all costs while I think about how, only months ago, that was where I laid eyes on Daisy for the first time in eight years.

My mom trails me to the front porch, wishing me well. She looks uncomfortable, like she wants to say more, but what she said this morning gives me plenty to process. It's no "I'm proud" or "Good job," and it doesn't undo the hurt, but I get some peace thinking that she isn't simply saying something I want to hear.

Ava walks out with me to the black town car in the driveway. I wrap one arm around her, tucking her into my armpit. "Stop." She giggles, and I let her get some playful punches into my ribs. "Your shirt's on inside out."

The stitching on the hem of my basic tee faces outward. I put on clothes like a zombie this morning.

"I'll fix it in the car." I squeeze her. "So was that you? You talk to them or something?"

She shakes her head, and I narrow my eyes at her.

"I'm serious. Maybe someone talked to them, but it wasn't me."

Daisy. She's the only person who could have convinced them. Only Daisy understood how much it would mean to have them there.

"Progress though, huh?" Ava says, slapping my shoulders. "Exciting."

"Are you excited for me?"

"Sure."

"Convincing."

"I mean, whatever." She escapes my grasp, giving a timid smile to the driver as the woman plucks my suitcase from my hands. "It'll suck not having you around again. But it's no big deal. I can handle it. I'm an adult."

"Oh, really?"

"I practically am."

Something shifts inside me as I see this odd similarity between her and Daisy. Both fiercely independent, both willing to sacrifice closeness with me for what they know—or think—is best for me.

But what if I don't know anymore?

"You should call her," my sister says, tapping my foot with hers.

"I..." The comment is a paper cut to my already bruised and battered heart, because I *have* called. I barely lasted twenty-four hours before calling her up last night and leaving a voicemail asking to talk. Begging. "I'm not so sure Daisy wants to talk."

"Maybe not yet. But you spent years being obsessed with her, so it seems lame you'd call it quits like this."

"Obsessed?"

She looks at me and emphasizes the word with a single nod. "*Obsessed*. Don't give up if you really don't wanna give up."

If I do what Daisy wants, I'll be halfway around the world. If I go against her wishes, she may never let me back into her life. My throat constricts at the thought of never hearing her or seeing her again.

"C'mere." I squish my too-wise sister into a hug. "Text me."

"Obviously. Have fun in Londontown."

I make it ten minutes down the road before I pull out my phone and stare at her number, wondering if she'll pick up this time.

Chapter Forty-One

Daisy, 22 Years Old

"And how's Max?"

My mom and I didn't talk about Max anymore, but his parents would have found it odd for her not to ask. The mention of his name picked at the scab over what I let happen between us.

"Graduated in June," his mom said with a forced smile. She slid her grocery cart to the side of the aisle.

"He was doing an internship with some museum over there," his dad added. "He's full-time, so we'll see."

I smiled, proud of what he'd accomplished. His dad downplayed it, but Max was doing something with a museum start-up. Not his own work, but curating, which he would be amazing at. I didn't quite understand the job, but it seemed to keep him busy.

Sometimes I wondered if I made the right decision, but whenever I heard about his achievements, I had zero doubt. It had been a while since I'd gone on an internet excavation—aka social media stalking session—to find out what Max was up to. I checked in on him occasionally. Curiosity and all.

"And how're your classes going?" Max's dad asked me.

"I have a couple semesters left," I said sheepishly. Mom had assured me that retaking classes was sometimes part of the college experience. And by the time I figured out which degree

I wanted and which courses I needed, I'd earned super-senior status. But in a year or so, I'd have an Environmental Science bachelor's, and hopefully I could figure out what to do from there. Maybe a ranger position would open up by then. My destiny hadn't been as clear as Max's, but with a degree, I'd have options.

Mom and I said goodbye to the Webers and went through the checkout line. We packed the bags into the trunk, and I pulled out some chips to comfort me on the way home.

"You could always call him up." Mom eyed me as she closed the trunk. "You know he'd answer."

I wasn't so sure, and I didn't want to risk rejection. Max had achieved so much barely out of college, and what had I done? I got secondhand embarrassment just thinking about calling him and giving him a brief and boring life update.

He'd moved on, and that was for the best. It was what I said I wanted.

Chapter Forty-Two

Daisy, Now

When I lug myself back to the check-in area, Stacey has claimed a chair behind the desk. She's reclined, eyes closed as she fans her armpits. If she's sweltering in our open-air lobby, I can only imagine how the guests are doing in their rooms. I had to run out this morning to buy extra fans for everyone.

"What'd the technician say, hon?" she asks, aware of my presence without seeing me.

My soul sinks. I wish I could blame this catastrophe on anyone else—Max, the repairman, even my mom—but this is on me.

"You should get out of here." I lift my sticky, unbrushed hair off my shoulders and twist it into a rat's nest of a bun. "You're already past your usual time."

"This week's been a busy one, that's for sure."

"You're an angel."

"Tell my husband that."

"Put him on the phone right now."

"You really oughta consider hiring some additional help around here." She turns to me, her brows furrowed. "You look tired."

"Thanks." I resort to dry sarcasm, but she's not wrong. Yesterday, Gwen and Dawn forced me to relax with a girls' spa night—part celebration of the pop-up, part scheme to take my mind off of things with Max. Infused water and a sheet mask can't work miracles, though. When I caught myself in the mirror this morning, the bags under my eyes and my pale complexion aged me ten years.

"I didn't mean it like that," Stacey says. "We could all use the help. It'd be a good time, what with that museum kicking off."

Even thinking about *Desert Daze* feels as if I'm wringing my insides like a soaked towel. The pop-up's doing exactly what Max planned—exactly what we wanted when we made it together—but I can barely stand to look at it because it just reminds me of him. And yet, despite that, I *still* wish he were here to help. He did a lot this summer, not only for *Desert Daze*, but for The Mirage, too.

"HVAC comes first," I say, trading one god-awful topic for another. "Did you know my mom repaired the heat pump?"

"Oh, yeah."

"Stace," I whine. "Why did you let her do that?"

I inherited my mom's DIY attitude, but no matter how capable I fancy myself to be, I wouldn't dream of touching the geothermal heat pump. One mistake and I'd face a multithousand-dollar bill, exactly like the one I have now.

"You think anything I coulda said would have changed your mama's mind?" Stacey pulls her legs to the side so I can squeeze into the other desk chair. "Didn't matter if repairs took her ten times longer than hiring a pro, or if it ended up shitty as a back-alley spray tan. She liked doin' it her own way."

"But you knew about her repairing the heating system?"

Her shoulder lifts in a guilty *yes*.

Our HVAC system crapped out this morning, with multiple valves and connection points looking like they lived through at least one world war. The maintenance guy came out for his quarterly inspection two weeks after my mom died, and I was a shell of a human then. He's been gracious in tweaking and holding the place together without requiring significant repairs, and I *knew* he told me the parts couldn't hold out much longer. With everything going on this summer, though, this impending disaster slipped under my radar.

"She probably didn't wanna worry you," Stacey says.

"But what she did made it worse."

"Good thing for *Desert Daze* then, right?"

I have to catch my breath. The barn has become a living memorial to what Max and I had for the briefest blip in time. As much as I love seeing the place alive again and filled with people, the success rings hollow.

"Hon, you gotta book a few weddings, and you'll be set," Stacey says. "We can hold ourselves over until some of those deposits roll in, don't you think?"

I rub my temples to chase away a growing headache and nod. While I hate operating paycheck to paycheck, a few happy couples could make up for this loss. It would be great if they could email me in the next five minutes, though. Months sometimes pass between a couple viewing the property and actually booking. *Desert Daze* has gotten us some recognition, but we need brides and grooms to use that renovated space, stat.

Because I can't bear to talk about the barn anymore, I change the subject. "So, I heard you wanna retire."

Stacey opens her mouth to say something, but I cut her off.

"Max let it slip."

"The bastard."

"He didn't mean to." Even now, I want to defend him. "It's what you want, right?"

She deserves to retire at her age after many years of unwavering dedication. When Max mentioned it the other night, I was only shocked that the topic hadn't come up sooner. She's ready to sit back and relax, not work at a struggling little hotel in the desert.

"I shouldn't have made you work here as long as you have, and—"

"Nobody *made* me work here," she corrects me. "Working alongside your mama, and with you, has been one of the greatest joys."

"Stace." I can't handle any more goodbyes. The lump in my throat swells, and my vision goes blurry. "I'm so, so excited for this next chapter of your amazing life."

"I know." She sniffles, and the phone rings. "Oh, let it go to voicemail."

"'Kay." I battle the urge to pick up the receiver. "The best thing my mom ever did was hire you. I would have been truly lost these last two years without you here."

I didn't have years with Mom showing me the ropes. Even when I filled in from time to time at the front desk, I didn't comprehend everything that went into running this place. Stacey stood by me, patient and helpful and always letting me lead. She had to have known that taking over made me feel closer to my mom. I wanted The Mirage to live on—Mom couldn't, but at least her life's work could.

My gratitude and love for the woman next to me explodes, and I grip her in a tight hug as a few tears squeeze out.

"Aw, hon, you've done such a good job here. The best job."

"I'm not so sure about that." Releasing her, I let out a watery laugh and wipe my eyes. "I'm always behind, always chasing something with this place. I have no clue what I'm doing most of the time, even after a few years. I kind of hoped I'd...I don't know, grow into it here. Mom always seemed so on top of it."

"She clearly wasn't."

"That's what I mean," I say, looking at her. "What if I don't want to live the next twenty-five years of my life chasing a perfection that my mom didn't even achieve, and for a dream that isn't really mine?" My voice goes quiet, because I hate to admit this out loud. "But if I do something else...I can't stand losing this place. It's like losing her again. Losing that connection."

Stacey grabs my hand, squeezing my limp fingers. "You've made The Mirage what it is, hon. Look around." She gestures to the lobby, a space I designed and decorated to feel like a second living room for guests—one where the desert meets their doorstep. It's filled with trinkets and gems, harsh shadows from the afternoon sun, and the dull echo of brass wind chimes. "This is you, and it always will be, no matter what. What you've done with The Mirage...I know she'd love it because it came from you."

"Even my busted heat pump?"

"Busted heat pump and all." She slaps my thigh. "You've done your best here, and it was damn good. Your mama lives on in this place because she lives on in you. You take her anywhere you go, and nothin's gonna change that."

"I don't know what I would do if I gave up The Mirage."

"You don't need to yet. But...it's as good a time as ever." She smiles at me, something like pride in her eyes. "In the past few months alone, you and Max've turned this place around."

My shoulders sink at the mention of him, and Stacey is too wise and eagle-eyed to let that slip.

"No good there?"

I shake my head.

"The *bastard*." She tuts. "I wondered when I didn't see his pretty little face around. What happened?"

Instead of answering, I blow air out of my lips. I don't know why I panicked. I couldn't bear the thought of Max making himself small for me—of the bitterness that would bring. Ava told me he flew to London, and he's probably signing the contract right now. He's left a few messages, but I haven't had the heart to listen to them. He must want to figure out when he can empty the storage room in the barn where his belongings are, and then he'll be gone for good, again.

"I'll spare you the details," I say, "but he's—Max is out of the picture."

"I'm so sorry, Daisygirl. He's an idiot."

"I'm fine."

Stacey hushes me, then wraps me up in a massive hug. I repeat the words that have gotten me through tear-filled nights, long years, and all the lows. *I'm fine.* They're just not enough this time.

Chapter Forty-Three

Max, Now

Since landing two days ago, I've met every employee at Tate Modern, from the conservators to the gift shop cashiers. I could walk around the museum blindfolded at this point. My visit included discussing the job and how they hope to expand their traveling exhibits, and during any spare moment, the recruiting team packed in activities throughout the city for me to get to know London better. Through the travel exhaustion, the time difference, and the nonstop meetings, I've been moving on autopilot.

I think you'd be a fool not to go. My chest constricts as I picture Daisy saying those words—urging me to grab this opportunity—when all I want is for her to let me love her.

Antoine coughs, bringing me back to the trendy wine bar. He stares at me.

"Sorry, I—what did you say?"

"That we will pay for the hotel in New York and the priority visa, so you should receive the required documents in a matter of a few days. In the meantime, my assistant will integrate you into our technical side of operations."

"Perfect." I don't have the energy for more than one word.

"Is everything alright?"

"Yeah. Jet lag."

Antoine swirls his glass of wine and eyes me. My flight leaves London in a few hours, and after a frenzy of a trip, he suggested a drink before departure, one-on-one. He selected an upscale place that has too-dark lighting for the time of day, atmospheric jazz playing a fraction too loud, and chic but uncomfortable bistro chairs. I almost laugh at how opposite this bar is from Sal's.

"Did you enjoy your brief stay in London?"

"What's not to enjoy?" The response comes out canned, and Antoine's eyes narrow at me like he's inspecting a canvas in one of the impressive halls at Tate.

What am I doing? I've signed the contract. I shouldn't give my employer any reason to believe he made a mistake in hiring me, especially since I'm only just crawling out of the proverbial hole that Impressions dug for me. Eleanor also has her reputation on the line because she recommended me so highly. Even if I changed my mind, Daisy won't pick up the phone.

I've had my heart torn out of my body, and I have to act like this is all still exactly what I want.

"The city will take some getting used to," I say, making an excuse for my blasé attitude. "London's massive."

"Yes, Dublin has a considerable size difference."

I meant compared to Harlow, but I don't correct him. These couple of days have reminded me about the city life I left behind—the nonstop bustle of people, the endless choice of restaurants or museums or bars, and the never-ending list of activities that make every day different.

But no Daisy. London can be as big and exciting as it wants, but it will still be the loneliest, emptiest city in the world. Every city I'll visit for this job will be.

If this had been any other position or any other museum, maybe Daisy wouldn't have pushed so much. This is the career that me at the start of the summer would have tripped over, and she knows it. I wish I could tear my contract to shreds because I lose both ways. Either I spend my life never completely happy, or I stay in Harlow where Daisy would never forgive herself for thinking she's holding me back.

"I'll admit," Antoine says, shaking his head, "I was worried about this."

I shoot him a quizzical look.

"You don't want to leave Harlow. I can see why it would be hard. Even in the short time I was there, the town charmed me. There is something extraordinary about it, and to be frank, that was what I enjoyed most about *Desert Daze*."

"The location?"

"That, yes. The juxtaposition of nature and man-made pieces, and the reminder of what we all come from and what we're all capable of. But I mean the passion you have for where you grew up. The whole exhibit was a devotion not only to art, to childhood, to what we were and what we become, but also to the town itself. I sense how much you care for that place."

Harlow *is* Daisy to me. She's ingrained in my hometown, in every corner and crevice, and I can't separate the two. Everyone there benefits because of her—life is better, more interesting. More everything. Even the things that annoyed me about Harlow growing up, I liked because of her. I saw why Daisy loves being there.

I *should* do what she wants—get out, get away, move on, and probably stop calling, too. But I don't know if that can ever truly happen.

"You love it, don't you?" Antoine asks, interrupting my thoughts. "You love Harlow?"

I twirl my wine and watch the last of the ruby liquid swirl. "Always have." I press my thumb into the bulb of the glass, observing the ghost of a fingerprint left behind. Memories of the past few months flash in my mind. Longing looks over foamy beers at Sal's. The way Daisy's laugh causes me to instantly relax. How somehow desert heat has a smell, and that smell is Daisy's skin.

"A small town, though." Antoine nods, his eyebrows remaining furrowed. "Similar to where I grew up myself. Comfortable, but perhaps limiting?" His eyes search mine like he wants to know if he's struck a chord.

I chew on that sentiment. "As a kid, Harlow suffocated me, but being there this summer convinced me I could do almost anything." Maybe that was Daisy. "In places like that, you find the people who are the heartbeat of the town, and they open up the world there to you."

If I want to convince Antoine that I will drop everything and move to London, I should stop waxing poetic about my hometown. Do I actually think I'll take back my signed agreement with Tate, head to Harlow, and run *Desert Daze* the rest of my life? And that Daisy would welcome me back?

Antoine regards me silently for a few beats. "And your girlfriend? She is looking forward to this too? Spending time here in London with you, maybe she would relocate here...it must be quite exciting for her."

Antoine doesn't need all the details of my love life—what he expects is an easy *yes, she's thrilled*. He wants a prospective employee who gives him no doubts, not someone who's mid-breakup, or mid-end-of-whatever-we-were. But instead of smiling and nodding, I tell him the truth.

"So, the wistfulness for your hometown is heartbreak," he says.

"I've woken up every morning feeling like my organs are shutting down." I ruffle my hair, searching for the right words. "I signed the work agreement, and it's what she told me to do. And I want this job, but...I want her more."

Antoine pauses and pulls out his phone and starts scrolling, probably to call up Eleanor to talk some sense into me. Instead, he holds up a recent photograph of himself, smartly dressed in a burgundy suit, staring lovingly into the eyes of a woman in a white ball gown.

"This is my wife," he says, crow's feet crinkling at the corners of his face. "We'll be married two years this December."

"Congrats." It comes out more like a question because this information is coming out of the blue.

"We've known each other since we were fifteen. Her father did not approve of me. He envisioned a surgeon or doctor for his only daughter." He blows air out of his lips and shakes his head at the memory. "We ended things. She and I only reconnected a few years ago." He regards me with a serious look in his eyes. "Her father tried to convince her she wanted something else."

"So she tried to convince you that *you* deserved better?"

"No, actually. She believed in us wholeheartedly, always. It was I he had convinced. So, I empathize with your Daisy. Nothing would have made me reconsider. I wouldn't have been able to live with myself if we'd married young, and I couldn't have given her everything I knew she deserved."

"But you lost so much time." I imagine waiting years, maybe decades, for Daisy to be ready for us, and the thought makes me want to sink into the floor with despair.

"Not lost. I became who I needed to be for her." Antoine rests a palm on my shoulder. "Sylvie had her arm outstretched to grab my hand and walk with me back then. But I was not prepared to take a single step, and I wouldn't let her drag me along the path on her own."

Just like with me and Daisy. I'm poised to go on this journey, but she's not ready, not yet. If I want to find my way back into her life, I need to make the path clear for her to find her way back into mine and on her own terms.

I release an exasperated sigh and rub the pressure points on my eyebrows. "If your wife hasn't told you already, that's a pretty pain-in-the-ass move to pull."

Antoine chuckles. "She's informed me on many occasions."

"How...how long do you think she would have waited for you?" I ask, but deep down, I know the answer.

Forever.

Chapter Forty-Four

Daisy, Now

I sit next to the tree like we're two old friends taking in the view. My mom loved this spot—it's not the highest vista of the desert, but it encompasses everything, and I think that's why she enjoyed stopping here. The sepia-toned mountains, the flatlands, and the cluster of buildings spread out like a starburst.

"Hey, Mom," I say, relishing the slight breeze coming from the north. Two years and almost four months ago, I scattered my mother's ashes underneath this very tree on her favorite trail. The event was private, just for family and close friends. My dad came, and Stacey, of course, along with Gwen and Bob for emotional support.

Another gust blows, and the canopy rustles. This species looks stunning in the wind, with branches that sway in slow motion. Of all the trees my mom could have adored, the one she loved most was called a Desert Museum tree.

"Maybe someday I'll find that funny," I mutter. "I'm sorry it's been a while. My schedule was more than I could handle, and I..."

Excuses, that's all I've got about my absence. I promised myself I would not go months or years without visiting. The last time I visited was the morning of the two-year anniversary of her death, and that feels so long ago.

We're in for an extensive update today. I talk about Freddie's upcoming doctor's appointment. About the RV Stacey and her husband want to buy. I leave out how I'm scared to say goodbye to a living creature Mom loved so much, or how angry I am that I'll never get to see her be a retired lady. Not that I believe my mom can hear me or my thoughts anyway, because if she could, then she's witnessing the shitshow of my life and doesn't need a verbal report. But sitting here is the closest thing I have to talking to her, even if all I'm doing is letting my voice drift into the atmosphere.

I tell her about *Desert Daze*.

"Max suggested it. Yes, *that* Max." I can picture her face beaming with joy at his reappearance in my life. "We're friends again. Or, we were. Then we were more than friends. Now...I fucked everything up. Like before."

I worry my lower lip between my teeth, wishing with every cell of my being that she was here to comfort me over Max once more. She would hold me while I cried and feed me and binge-watch Netflix shows with me. Mom had the most understanding kind of love—she let me make my own choices then, and she would now, too. Although I wonder what she'd think about the messages I've been ignoring.

"I'm so scared of what we could have together," I say, my voice getting quiet. "If I asked him to stay, he would. I just..." With my eyes trained on the horizon, I inhale deeply to temper my emotions. "I want Max to have all the good things, not change his dreams because of me. He deserves everything because..."

Well, because I love him. I love Max—yes, romantically, but also as a friend, as a person, as a mentor to those students, and as a creative. I love every version of him, and I hate the thought of him closing himself off to some other marvelous part of himself only to get bored with me. I can only ever be Daisy for him.

Just Daisy.

"I'm mad." The dam breaks, and hot tears spill down my cheeks and onto my lap. "Not just at me, but at you, too." Mom wasn't perfect, but she was perfect to me. In my head, she ran The Mirage like the most knowledgeable, skilled business owner around. The HVAC mistake is more than a scratch in her shining reputation; it's a foundational crack that makes me wonder how else she cut corners and what other ill-advised decisions she made.

"I've always looked up to you," I go on. "But fixing that heat pump, I mean...what were you thinking? And the repairman told me about it, but I...this is a mistake that I have to deal with now, and I don't know if I can fix it."

The future I've been avoiding is officially knocking on the door. Possibly letting go of The Mirage makes me sick to my stomach, but the other choice is spending my life doing a job I'm not even that good at. Either I lose her all over again, or I lose myself.

"This spot free?"

The familiar voice rattles me, and I turn to see my dad. Hoping he hasn't been standing there for too long, I swipe my hands under my eyes.

"What're you doing here?"

"Me and Oona hike this one every once in a while."

"Where is she?"

He nods his head down the trail. "She wanted to give us some space."

"Oh, that's..." I like that she's given us breathing room. "That's nice. I didn't know you came here."

"Sometimes." His knees crack as he sits down, and he groans. "I update her on things. Here, you should drink." He hands me his water bottle. "What?"

"Nothing." I school my surprise and take a hearty chug of the ice-cold water. How did I walk out the door and go down this trail without the essentials? "Just, I didn't think you...um—"

"Cared?"

Hearing the phrase out loud, I know it's wrong. Of course, he cared about my mom. It's naive of me to assume that just because they didn't live a fairytale marriage, he doesn't care.

"Sorry." I hug my knees to my chest, sheepish.

"I owe you an apology, too. We shouldn't have asked to have the wedding at The Mirage. That place means the world to you, and we got carried away with the idea of a wedding there. It really sounded like a good idea at the time, but your boyfriend gave me a stern talking-to the other night, and he's right. I should never have put you in that position."

So that's what their private conversation at Sal's must have been. I set the water bottle between us and fake a cough to cover for my eyes burning. "Max isn't my boyfriend."

"Oh. I'm sorry to hear that." My dad fidgets, tucking a leg under his other knee. "Oona's not trying to erase the past. She wants to celebrate it."

"I know. I like her. I do. She's a good match for you, and I want you to be happy, so I'm glad she's that for you." The confession spills out. "But...I get frustrated thinking about how you can magically become this incredible partner to someone new. That's not Oona's fault. Maybe it seems like I've been taking that out on her, but really, I want to take it out on you." Admitting all this feels like popping a festering blister, and I keep going for the relief every word grants me. "The whole time you and Mom were married, you resented her for bringing you out here. And now that you're marrying Oona, you wanna live here and be some doting husband, and I don't understand why you couldn't be that for Mom."

"I didn't resent your mother," he says, a mix of genuine hurt and shock on his face.

"You—" I stammer over my words, because I'm doubting my memories. "You fought all the time once we moved here."

"We fought all the time before we moved here, too. You were just too young to remember."

"Then why stay married?"

He sighs and leans back onto his hands, staring up at the leaves of the tree. "We loved each other. And we wanted to be the parents you wanted—the people who you saw when things were good. We wanted that for you, and we did try. We were good friends, but maybe not the best lovers. It had nothing to do with being here, though."

I process this revelation, drawing eerie parallels to my relationship with Max. "Do you think…" My eyes flash to my dad. "Is there any way it could have worked out between you two? Or was it always doomed from the start?"

He chuckles, the corners of his eyes crinkling. "Doomed's pretty dramatic."

"You know what I mean."

"We were stubborn. Honestly, after my contract ended, I thought she and I might come out here and retire early. We had the money stashed away for it, but she had other plans. I wanted to relax, enjoy. She wanted to work, have her own thing. Neither of us would budge on our vision. Looking back now, I—" His voice catches, and his eyes shimmer against the golden rays of sun. "I wouldn't have been so proud. I would have given up more. It's so good to have someone worth giving it all up for." He pats me on the knee. "And The Mirage—I know you love it, but it occupied her time like crazy. Twenty-five hours a day. I hate to see that happening to you."

"It's not bad." I look out again at the horizon as the stillness of dusk covers the land. "I mean, yeah, it's a lot sometimes."

"If you need a hand, I'm here. You should feel like anything's possible, not like you're locked in to do this forever. I'd do anything to help you, if you'd let me. Your mom always wanted to do it on her own, to have it be her thing."

I make a *hm* sound at the irony. "Sounds familiar."

"Think about it, okay? And she might not be your favorite person, but Oona's very organized. She's a good one."

"I know." I give him a small smile and a hug in thanks. What would it be like to lean on him with The Mirage? I've spent the past two years micromanaging every aspect of the place in hopes Mom wouldn't be forgotten, but it's not only me who has memories there. It belongs to Harlow just as much as it does to me.

Dad sighs again, this time deeper, and his cheeks are wet. I look up at the sky where stars have appeared against the watercolor backdrop. We sit there until the sun sets completely, letting the breeze dry our faces.

Chapter Forty-Five

Max, 24 Years Old

I found the quietest corner of the airport lounge and pulled out my cell. Over the past six years, my hand floated over Daisy's contact a million times. She may have to do things on her own time, but I had to call her now. My teeth chattered with nerves as the phone rang. The voicemail service kicked in, and I groaned in frustration.

"Hey, it's Daisy. You know what to do."

Hearing her talk, even from a recording, stole my breath. I missed her voice.

"Um, hey, Daze. It's me, Max. We haven't talked in a while, and I hope you don't mind me calling. I heard about what happened to your mom, and...I'm so, so sorry."

My eyesight blurred. So many of my childhood memories included Amy Johnson—smiling, laughing, hugging me tight. She made me believe in myself. I knew life would move on while I was away from Harlow, but I didn't prepare myself for this.

"She was incredible, huh? I, uh, I don't know if you remember, but there was that showcase I had in ninth grade. My parents missed it, of course, but you and your mom showed up. And she brought all the guests staying at The Mirage, as if this dorky, stupid high school art show were some kind of big tourist attraction." I chuckled at the memory and swiped under my eyes. "That night meant a lot to me. Do you remember? Your mom actually asked for one piece I did for that show and hung it in the lobby."

I glanced at the departures board and saw my flight near the top. Boarding would start soon, so I needed to head to the gate.

"Ava told me about the service and the memorial and all. I'd love to be there for you. I'm about to be in Dubai for this new client project, but...uh, my coworker already said they can fly out and cover for me."

That was a lie, but I wouldn't give her any excuse to say no. My boss wasn't happy about me backing out last minute, but I would quit before I'd let him tell me no.

"I'm sure you're overwhelmed with everything." I swung my backpack over my shoulder and gripped the handle of my suitcase. "Just call me, okay? Or a text is fine. Carrier pigeon, even. If you want me there, I'm there. In a heartbeat."

I wanted to say so many more things, but this wasn't the time. "Alright, well...let me know. I'm thinking of you. Bye."

Chapter Forty-Six

Daisy, 24 Years Old

Dubai was eleven hours ahead of Harlow, so 4:00 p.m. in California seemed like a safe time to call. The previous two days, I thought I had cried all the tears I could cry, but then I heard his message. My entire body ached to have him back with me, and I doubled over on the floor of the casita while Freddie wandered the hallway and yowled for her.

My chest pounded as I rang him up and quietly prayed for it to go to voicemail. I let out a breath once his recorded voice kicked in. I wanted to play the greeting on repeat to fall asleep to. At the beep, I considered hanging up—but he'd know I had called. I sucked down my second guesses and talked.

"Max. Hey. Thank you for the message. It was really sweet." I tucked Freddie closer to me, my hand running over his back. "I got the flowers too. Did you…"

Someone else probably sent the food. A delivery driver from Hidden Moon showed up the night before with all of my favorites. I barely ate any of it, but Gwen packed it away in the fridge, and I had leftovers for a few days at least. It's something he would do, but the driver didn't know who placed the order.

"I remember that night you mentioned." I sniffled, recalling how happy my mom was to go see Max and his shows. Bringing the hotel guests was my idea, and it became a tradition. "She always loved you, you know. She was so proud of you."

I took a deep breath to stop myself from losing it. "About you coming out here...I don't think I could handle that right now." I kept my reasoning vague, because I knew that if I told Max how I was doing, he'd hop on the first flight out here. Even after years of not talking, I heard the determination in his voice. And as much as I wanted him here, I couldn't bear him comforting me only to leave again. My world was already falling apart—I didn't want it to fall apart further.

But funerals are for the living, and I couldn't deny him the chance to share his memories of her.

"Could you just...I don't know. I'd love it if you talked about Mom more. Maybe you could call and tell me more stories. And I wanna hear how you're doing, too. I'm—you know, I'm hanging in there. Anyway, I need to go. Thanks again. Bye, Max."

Maybe I suggested too much. But my emotions were too raw, and even though I shouldn't have, I wanted to hear his voice again. I needed that small comfort.

Chapter Forty-Seven

Daisy, Now—95 Days Later

I point to the computer screen where the familiar green button says *Guest Check-In.*

"Then you hit that to confirm," I say. "Easy."

The woman's face relaxes like I've defused a bomb for her. "Oh, brilliant. You've been a massive help."

"It's nothing."

"I swear, I'll get the hang of it one of these days."

"You will," I assure her. It wasn't all that long ago that staring at the booking software for The Mirage would send my mind spinning with how complicated it was. Combined with the past few weeks of training new hires, I could probably navigate it in my sleep. "Need anything else?"

"I should ask you that." She slides the room key across the counter with a welcoming smile. "*You're* the guest."

I run my thumb over the gold embossing on the key card sleeve. Checking in here feels like cheating on The Mirage—which is absurd. I'm not even on the same continent.

"Um..." I glance at my phone. My group chat with Gwen and Dawn is exploding with emojis and good-luck wishes, but it's the voicemail notification that makes my heart jump. "I could use a taxi. I'll pop into my room for a quick shower first."

"Absolutely, Ms. Johnson. I'll have one ready for you. Where will you be heading?"

I tell the woman at the front desk, and she remains unfazed—the complete antithesis of my emotions. Once I enter my room, my body turns to ice at the thought of showing up there tonight. I've played out this scenario, at least this far, in my head a billion times before.

Fly to London. Freshen up. Find Max.

I don't dwell beyond that, though. Since he left, I've felt as empty as the storage space in the barn after his parents cleaned it out. On the cab ride over, I focus instead on the cheery holiday lights decorating the buildings we pass and the bundled-up passersby, because I can't guess what Max will say when he sees me. He's been here for three months already, and tonight kicks off the first leg of the tour. The traveling exhibit premieres at Tate and then goes on the road until the end of spring.

I know this because he told me. Since Max moved out of the casita, he's called me every day and left a voicemail. It took me a week after his departure before I caved, listening to them all in succession, with tears pouring down my face at the mere sound of his voice. These messages are like before, but different. He still tells me about his life, his work, his day—but he also tells me he misses me, that he loves me, and that he'll never stop loving me.

I'm doing what you told me to do, but I want to come home to you. Please, Daze. I'm ready when you are.

I haven't called him back because I wanted to get The Mirage in order first, and if I spoke to him, it would have ruined the plan I hatched when I finally sat down to listen to his messages. Max needs to know I will change and that I'll work for us. As much as my heart beams with pride over his career and accomplishments, I don't want what my parents had—a love that was tainted because neither of them would compromise.

It's so good to have someone worth giving it all up for.

I would give up everything for a chance with Max in every lifetime, and it would always be worth it.

I'm shaking when the cab drops me off at the entrance to Tate Modern, and I follow the stream of people into the industrial-looking building. The man holding a silver platter of champagne flutes catches my attention. Against my better judgment, I snag one, if only to have something to do with my hands.

Everyone here looks dressed up—swanky, gorgeous, some even in floor-length gowns and tuxes. I chose a flowy dress with ruffles and a leg slit, hoping that would be fancy enough, and I am officially the only person here in cowboy boots. Just as I'm about to turn around and rethink this entire trip, I spot him standing there like the only star in the night sky. He has a group of people surrounding him, because of course he would. Everyone loves Max.

The crowd laughs at something he said, probably something brilliant, and I suck down my nerves as I step forward. Out of nowhere, my body jerks to the left as I slam into another person, and my glass falls to the ground with an elegant shatter.

"Shit, sorry," I say a little too loudly, considering the entire room has hushed to see what's going on.

The gentleman, about my father's age, lets his mouth fall into an irritated line, but he asks if I'm okay. Someone all in black comes over and begins picking up the shards of glass. Another person appears with a mop, and I wish I could disappear.

"Daisy?" Max's voice pulls me out of the chaos, and I know that wherever that voice is, wherever he is, that's where I belong.

"Hi." I smooth my hair and stand up straighter, hoping I don't look like a total disaster.

"You're here." He steps closer, his brows stitched together in confusion. "Is everything alright?"

I nod and take him in. He's gotten a fresh haircut, but it's curly and wild how I like it. He must have had his suit tailored because it perfectly outlines all the planes and angles of him. There's a weariness on his face—his cheeks more hollow, the lines around his eyes more pronounced. Exhaustion from the job, maybe? Still, he's so handsome it hurts. I have to stop myself from leaping into his arms and making more of a scene than I already have.

"I got your voicemail," I say with a shaky voice.

"Which one?"

"All ninety-four of them. Well, ninety-five. I haven't listened to the one from tonight."

"Why didn't you call?"

"I, um...I wanted to tell you face-to-face."

"Tell me what?"

I will burst if I have to hold this in for a second longer. "That I love you."

His expression glitches, and I can't fight the breathy laugh that escapes because of how adorable he looks. And also because I'm nervous as hell.

"Sorry, but I didn't come thousands of miles to make small talk with you." The words fly out like sparks off a campfire. "I've missed you every single day, and I've been missing you my whole life. It's awful. Even Freddie's miserable. I'm sorry I pushed you away, and I'm sorry I didn't call. I wanted to take care of The Mirage before coming out here for a romantic grand gesture, and there was also a big part of me that was being a huge chicken. I've been stubborn and scared and stupid with you, and I'm so sorry." I run my fingers under my eyes and pray my makeup hasn't melted. "It's just, when I look at you, I want you to have everything, and for the longest time, I knew I couldn't give that to you. But you know what?"

"What, Daze?"

"I still can't. I'll never be able to give you everything you deserve." I reach for one of his hands, his skin warm and familiar. "But I really, really would like to try."

"Ms. Johnson." Antoine's smooth French accent interrupts my grand confession. "How wonderful of you to be here." He turns to Max and puts a hand on his shoulder, leaning into his ear. "Perhaps this is a conversation for your office?"

My cheeks heat with the realization that several people are watching us. I fear that I've upset Antoine, and maybe even gotten Max in trouble on the job, but I swear Antoine winks at him before we turn to go.

Max uses his fob so we can travel up the elevator to the fourth floor. "I don't like you talking like that," he says, turning to me with a resolute look in his eyes. "What you said downstairs. Who cares what anyone thinks I deserve? What matters is what I *want*."

"And what do you want, Max Weber?"

"What I've always wanted. It's what I've been telling you on all those ninety-five voicemails that I want. What I'm going to want until the day I die."

There are a million things I need to tell him, but the pull to be closer to Max overwhelms me. Like he can read my mind, he steps forward and we curve into each other like we've always belonged there—my arms twist around his torso, his hand strokes my lower back, and our foreheads touch. The elevator dings and the doors open, but rather than lead me to his office, he cups my face and kisses me so sweetly my insides nearly explode. My past, present, and future click into place, and I moan in relief.

"You're right, this is better than a phone call," he says, tracing a path with his lips along my jaw. "I love you, Daze. I love you, I love you, I love you. What took you so long to get here?"

"Traffic was pretty bad. I landed like three hours ago."

He nips at my neck. "Smart-ass."

I giggle and pull him closer, only mildly aware that the elevator started moving again. "I had to figure out Mirage stuff."

"Please tell me you didn't leave poor Stacey alone."

With a playful smack on his arm, I meet his eyes. "No. Oona's experience running a massage studio came in handy. She and my dad are actually watching the place for a bit until I sort things out."

"Sort out what, exactly?"

Life. Dad and Oona offered to handle The Mirage for six months to give me the chance to pursue whatever I wanted. Max, a new career, anything. My dad didn't want me to feel stuck.

After a successful town hall a few weeks ago, I've seen a steady uptick in reservations. Fuller weekends and fewer cancellations are on the horizon. The updated zoning laws Dawn and I fought for go into effect January 1, and some of the money-hungry homeshares are already going dark—so I wasn't leaving my dad and Oona with a ticking time bomb. And with some wedding deposits thanks to Dawn's revised review and my more regular social media posting, I can take a moment to really consider what I want.

When I handed them the keys, I wept for a full twenty-four hours straight. I wasn't sad. I just couldn't remember having so much room to breathe. For the first time in two years, I could prioritize my desires, my needs.

And top of that list was Max.

"I need to sort out whether you'll take me back," I say. "I can't move here, but I can stay with you for a few months at a time. Maybe when you're traveling, I could join up. I..." I search his eyes, urging him to understand. "I spent too long thinking that Harlow tore my parents apart. That when someone gives something up in a relationship, it only leads to resentment, and I didn't want that for us. When you talked about staying in Harlow, I saw it as this immense sacrifice."

"It was never that for me. Growing up, I might have given you reasons to believe that all I wanted was to leave my hometown, but now? I don't care what I give up for you. To be with you, I would do anything."

"I get that. Holding you back paralyzed me, but I think I was holding myself back, too—doing what I believed I needed to do and not what was in my heart."

"So what do *you* want, Daisy Johnson?" He smirks, tossing my question back at me.

"I want to give us a chance. I don't know what that'll look like, but I want to work with you and figure it out together." I let out a wet laugh as he wipes my cheeks with the pad of his thumb. "I have to find out who I am when I'm not running the hotel and I'm chasing my own dreams instead. Oh, and I have to get back for Gwen's birth. But otherwise, I just want to spend my days loving you."

He shuts me up with a kiss, and the elevator chimes again. Someone clears their throat, and Max and I turn to see a blushing man with a walker and his wife. Max straightens up and takes a half step away, leaving his hand on my hip.

"What floor?" he asks them, holding his fob at the ready.

The old woman smiles, her eyes mischievous like a cat's. "We'll catch the next one, dear."

The doors close, and I use Max's tie like a leash, pulling him toward me so that I'm sandwiched between his body and the wall.

"Let's try this again, for real this time," Max mutters against my lips, and the elevator goes up.

Max, Now—1.5 Years Later

Daisy and I relish weekend lie-ins when we can get them, although usually we don't use the time for sleeping. Today, though, I let my girl rest, and I watch her chest rise and fall in the morning quiet.

Well, mostly quiet. Freddie snores with every tiny breath he takes, but he's cute enough, so I allow it.

"Are you watching me sleep?" Daisy asks, opening one eye to peer at me. "Creep." She scoots her pillow toward mine and locks our legs together like roots from two trees planted side by side.

"We should go soon," I say as a gentle reminder.

"I know."

"How are you doing?"

She breathes in deeply and burrows close to me. Today's a complicated day for her, and I want to make sure she has the space to feel whatever she needs to feel.

"Sad, but also..." Her fingers toy with some hairs at the nape of my neck. "It will be nice to have everyone together. I'm kind of looking forward to it."

I kiss her on the forehead, and we rest for a few more minutes until we really can't stay any longer. We perform some professional-level acrobatics to escape the bed without disturbing Freddie, and once I'm dressed, I wait for Daisy to get ready. I knock on the bathroom door once to check on her—she sounds sniffly, but when she comes out, she gives me the biggest hug. All I can do is be there for her today, no matter what she's experiencing.

We drive to the trailhead in Daisy's truck, and everyone's already there. We park, and Daisy gets out and walks straight to her favorite one-year-old.

"My baby Bob!" she cries out, reaching for the child in Gwen's arms. He lights up when he sees her.

"Sorry for making you third wheel to a tiny human with only eight teeth," Gwen says to me with a hug.

"I don't mind."

Gwen gave birth to Bob Jr. precisely on his due date, and aside from his lack of mustache, he's basically Bob in miniature form. Daisy's obsessed with the kid.

It's a mercifully cool morning, and our group starts down the trail with Richard and Oona leading the way.

"How's the museum?" my mom asks.

"We're ready for next week," I reply. "Our best collection yet."

In part, it's thanks to my parents, which I never would have imagined. Although my dad needed some time to come around to the idea, he and my mom have been one of the biggest financial supporters for our latest installment of *Desert Daze*.

Daisy traveled with me for most of the tour with Tate, but the only reason any of those places felt like home was because she was there. She enjoyed the adventure, but I could tell she longed to plant her feet back in Harlow. So, after we wrapped, I respectfully resigned. Daisy freaked out about my decision no less than a million times, but a dream job means nothing without my dream girl. So returning to Harlow made sense. I accepted an adjunct teacher position at the school, Regina's arts program officially launched, and we turned *Desert Daze* into a recurring event. When I'm not working locally, I'm traveling around the western US to help other organizations set up their own pop-up museums. It's no tour with Tate, but it's what I want, and it's mine. The legacy I always wanted to leave finally feels real.

We reach the tree, now speckled with bright yellow blooms, and we spread out blankets in its shade. Richard passes around Tupperware with fruits and veggies while Oona hands out scraps of paper and pens so people can write their favorite memories of Daisy's mom.

"I brought some extra camp cups, if anyone needs one," Dawn says, making her way through the group and filling up everyone's mugs with sparkling wine—and grape juice for Ava and Zinnia.

Daisy stands, cupping her drink in her hands. Despite the glisten in her eyes, a genuine smile stretches across her face. She stares at the circle of friends and family, taking it in for a moment, before she talks.

"Thank you, everyone, for being here. Today's a hard day, but it's special to get to share it with all of you. Max suggested we start this tradition last year, and I'm glad we did." She looks at me, and our surroundings fall away—for a second, it's just Daisy and me. She doesn't need to say it, because I know.

I love you.

"This past year has been a lot of change for me, and you all know how well I handle that. Um...handing off The Mirage was something I could never have imagined doing. It's been a process, but I'm confident the hotel's in good hands."

Daisy needed extra support to feel ready to sell The Mirage, but because of the success of *Desert Daze*, she could be choosy with what the transition looked like. The place went to a member of her mom's old hiking club—a person Oona and Richard recommended—and I think Daisy likes that it's someone who knew her mom and also loves the land. Daze retains a share of ownership, so she can remain in the casita, and now that she's not managing every little detail, she can focus on other things. Taking care of Freddie. Horseback riding whenever she wants. Her new job.

"It means so much to be surrounded by folks who loved my mom, especially today," Daisy says, holding up her mug and staring right at me. "I'm so happy you're here."

The Desert Museum tree sways in the breeze as people share their stories of the inimitable Amy Johnson. I wish she could be here to see Daisy now. After some much-needed time off and eye-opening travel, Daisy started consulting with hotels around the globe to make their operations more eco-friendly. She does most of her work virtually, but she joins me on my travels sometimes to meet with US-based clients in person. Dawn has extensive contacts since she works in tourism, and she's helped Daisy get her business going. Daisy guides properties with things like land maintenance and the best equipment to invest in that keeps water usage low. I've never seen her happier, using her skills and passions in this way.

Ava taps my shoulder, leans in close, and whispers, "Does Daze know?"

I give a subtle shake of my head, and my sister breaks into a toothy smile.

"Be cool," I tell her.

"Trying." She looks like every fiber of her being is vibrating. "Tomorrow at ten?"

"What's tomorrow at ten?" Daisy asks, wrapping her arms around me from behind.

"Meeting with Regina at the school," I say, my heartbeat racing. "Talking about the next round of student work."

My thoughts wander to the future, of days with Daisy, making a life with her, and growing old with her.

"That's exciting." Daisy seems oblivious, but my sister wears a dopey smile, and she's absolutely going to give this away.

"Here." I hand her Daisy's cup. "Can you top Daze off?"

"Just grape juice," Daze says in a rush. "Since I'm driving."

"Sure thing!" Ava dashes over to Dawn for more drinks before I can stop her.

"Have mine," I say, turning around and holding my drink to Daze. "I'll drive home."

"I, uh, really, really just want grape juice."

My breath stops. She went off the pill months ago, and we said we'd give it a year and see what happens.

"Just..." I whisper, pulling her aside. "Just grape juice?"

Her eyes twinkle in the sunlight in response, stealing my breath.

"Are you sure?"

"I'm late. And I took five pregnancy tests this morning, just in case."

"Oh my god." I might pass out, so I cup her smiling face with both hands to ground myself. "Seriously?"

"Yeah." She nods, but her expression twists into an agonized frown as tears threaten to spill over.

"Hey, hey. This—it's a good thing, right?"

"Very good," she says, letting me wipe the wetness from her cheeks. "I just...I wish I could share the news with her, too."

"Yeah." I press my lips to her forehead and pull her even closer, longing to give her that moment—at least as much as I'm able. "It's not the same, but you still could, here. In your own way."

She pauses, looking around at our family and friends on the picnic blankets, and gnaws on her lower lip. "Now?"

"Only if you want. I can't think of a more perfect place, though."

The corners of her eyes—still wet—crinkle from her smile, and she entwines her fingers with mine. We walk back to our friends and family, Ava hands Daisy a reusable cup, and I grab a spork for us to tap on the glass and do a proper trailside toast.

"Everyone," I say, euphoric and breathless. "We have an announcement to make."

Daisy gives my hand a squeeze before her confession comes out. "I'm pregnant."

Our group erupts with excitement. Ava bounces around like she might combust, Daisy's dad races up to congratulate us both, and Gwen shouts, "I knew your vibes were on!" My parents, Dawn, Oona—everyone hugs us, filling the day with even more tears and more laughter.

Daisy and I claim a spot on a blanket, and she nudges me with her elbow. "Just think. This time next year…"

My heart swells at the thought of us becoming a family of three—at the future Daisy's thinking of. I blink away the blurriness and turn to her, kissing her shoulder, her cheek, and her lips. "I love you."

"I love you back," she says, her entire being sparkling. My girl.

I don't have any meetings tomorrow. I'm picking up Ava and we're going to drive to an antique shop that's halfway to LA. Ever since I moved back, I've been searching for the perfect ring for Daze, and this store sent me a photo of one they'd gotten in stock that was exactly what I wanted—an ornate sage green sapphire with fine metalwork and diamonds. It's as unique as Daisy.

Then, I imagine my sister will want to sit down in a diner and plan out an elaborate proposal. I'll indulge her, but I honestly don't intend to wait another day—to overthink anything into oblivion or wait until I find the right time. Because every time, every second, is the right time with Daisy.

Thank you for reading *In a Desert Daze*. If you enjoyed this book, please consider leaving a review. Indie authors thrive with reviews from readers like you, so scan the QR code below to leave a review on Goodreads.

Newsletter

Want more spicy destination romance in your life? Sign up for Theresa's bi-weekly newsletter and receive her free novella, *Match Made in the Maldives*. Visit her website at theresach ristine.com/subscribe or scan the QR code below to join the journey.

About *Match Made in the Maldives*:
Luna Moore holds herself to the highest standards, but no one knows how imperfect her life is right now. Her priority is ensuring her family has an amazing time on their vacation to the Maldives, though—not burdening them with news of her struggling graphic design business or her cheating ex-boyfriend. She'll put up a façade this week in paradise, and then she can go home to fix her mess of a life.

Finley Robertson needs to figure out what's next after selling his business, and a vacation is the perfect reset button. As the long-time best friend of Luna's older brother, Finn's practically a Moore and they've treated him better than his own family. Although the way he feels about Luna is anything but familial, especially after that kiss three years ago...not that she remembers that.

The more time Luna spends with Finley, the more she lets her walls down. But getting involved with Lou means Finn could risk losing the only genuine family he's ever known. When their chemistry becomes impossible to ignore, will they take a chance on love—or will the waves of reality crash down upon them?

Acknowledgements

This story started with a cat.

When I sat down to write my second full-length novel, I was grieving the loss of my soul cat. I have no eloquent way to put it other than I was really, really sad and had zero desire to sit down and write about anything other than being really, really sad. Romantic, I know. Loss is always hard, but you experience that loss again and again with every realization that the world still turns and people move on. I wanted Daisy to be in that tricky spot with her grief—not reeling from the recent loss but clinging to it like a lifeline.

Despite the heaviness in my heart as I sat down to write this book, I adored this story and these characters from the very first draft. That is no doubt due to the wonderful people who helped me along the way.

Danielle, Jess, and Stephanie—you saw this book in its rawest, messiest form, and you helped me shape this story into something I'm incredibly proud of. I love how you always challenge me to go with the hardest choices. Thank you for pushing me and making me a better writer.

I'm deeply grateful to all of my beta readers. Josie, Rebekah, Annie, and Zoe, thank you for your honest feedback and unbridled enthusiasm for Max and Daisy. Lina, you are an absolute star. Your love of books and support of my work is an indie author's dream come true.

Thank you to the TC Hype Team for making this release a joy-filled one. Publishing a book involves countless Very Important Tasks, and it's nice to just have some fun with the process. I loved getting to share things with you and fangirl over this book with you!

A huge thank you to my editor, Stephanie Fung, and my proofreader, Angela Garcia at Romance the Page LLC. This book is infinitely better because of your feedback and notes, and I appreciate the care you gave this manuscript. Thank you for letting my voice shine, for not shying away from em dashes, and for answering my many (many!) follow-up questions.

Morgane Flodrops was my cover illustrator and designer—and Morgane, you should know that if I could wallpaper my living room with this cover, I would. Thank you for portraying Max, Daisy, and all of Harlow in such a beautiful way.

Matt, I am so lucky that the kind of life-changing love I write about is the one I get to have in real life. Thank you for being a swoon-worthy MMC IRL. Lub u bb.

Of course, to the cat who started it all, Little Bit. We still talk about you.

And to Cosmo and Celeste, thank you for sitting nearby while I wrote and edited this book, and for showing me how to open up my heart again.

About the Author

Theresa Christine writes contemporary romances where wanderlust meets heartfelt heat. Drawing on her years as a travel journalist, she sets her stories in unforgettable places around the world. She is the author of the vacation novella *Match Made in the Maldives* and the small-town Ireland romance *The Half of It*. She currently lives in Hamburg, Germany, with her husband and their two energetic cats.

www.theresachristine.com
@theresachristinewrites on TikTok
@theresachristinewrites on Instagram